To Rg'
with co              wish

# TRADER'S
# ROAD

MICHAEL BURRANS SYKES

Copyright @ Michael Burrans Sykes
All rights reserved. No part of this publication
may be reproduced, stored in a retrieval system
or transmitted in any form or by any means,
electronically or mechanically, including photocopying
or recording, without the written permission
from the author or Appaloosa Publishing

First published in the UK in 2018
**by Appaloosa Publishing**
jomoss.author@gmail.com

**This book is a work of fiction.**
Names, characters, businesses,
organisations, places and events are
the product of the author's imagination
or are used fictitiously.

ISBN  978-1-5272-3315-7
Printed and bound in Great Britain
by Book Printing UK, Peterborough

*I wish to thank Jo Moss, for firstly encouraging
me to publish this story and then for whipping
my original text into some sort of shape.
I would also add that any mistakes that remain
are my fault and that most of the characters are
figments of my imagination although, in one
or two cases, are heavily disguised real
people I have had the fortune to know!*

*Thank you also to Dr. Ruth Callahan of
Arizona U.S.A. who insisted that I should
write something other than articles
for trade journals.*
*MS*

# CHAPTER 1

I suppose that at one time or another we have all had daydreams about 'getting away from it all'. The success of the programme, 'Desert Island Discs' must be based on such a universal longing, in some part at least. No matter how much we love our families, enjoy our jobs, or live for a particular passion, I suspect that we all have secret thoughts of privacy, space and solitude.

I also suspect that were we to achieve such an ambition, we might very well hate it. However, we still crave an opportunity to find out for ourselves. Having spent the last twenty odd years living in Singapore - and you don't get much more forced intimate contact with your fellow human beings than from the populous in Singapore, I certainly needed space and solitude now.

The right circumstances came along, happily at the right time, for me to get out. With a sum of money in my pocket and a pension which meant that, should I wish it, I would never have to work again. I took both the money and the opportunity. I have spent the eleven months since then looking for the ideal place to be alone. I have found to my surprise that once you have left your normal stamping ground and if, like me, you are unaccompanied, you can be very alone almost anywhere. It isn't the right sort of solitude though. I had been thinking that solitude and being on one's own was one and the same thing. This was my first big mistake.

All this is a somewhat roundabout way of explaining why I was sitting in my car, outside a small village hotel on the banks of the river Lot in central France. I had spent the day prospecting for this 'Shangri La' that I had fixed in my mind's eye.

In the intervening months since I retired I had looked at Australia; not very scenic, too few native Australians and it seems to be beset by monster flies built by Boeing or Airbus.

New Zealand; possible - but a hell of a long way from anywhere else and small enough for everyone to know everyone else's business.

Several parts of the United States; again possible but for the Americans themselves. They were so relentlessly hospitable that solitude was virtually impossible.

I was currently doing Europe. More particularly France. Again, very attractive but mind-bogglingly bureaucratic. Despite the advent of the Common Union, it seemed that the French still have a labyrinthine set of their own rules which make life for the would-be settler difficult, to say the least.

I sat in my car, listening to the clicks and burbles of a cooling engine and marking up my map so that I would remember where I had been and plan my next day's excursion. Le Patron, seeing me, hurried across to the car. After some difficulty and a deal of hand waving, I got the message that a bureau in London had telephoned three times and would I telephone back. The matter was "Très, très pressant."

Not another problem.

I had had a bad day. Having nearly been run off a mountain road, by what could have only been a drunken driver in the morning and then nearly having had my head blown off by a careless hunter in the afternoon. It wasn't encouraging in the search for a 'haven'.

I had been inspecting a deserted derelict farm which was on the market. I was standing looking at the house, trying to reckon up how much it would cost to do up, when out of the blue there was a sound that I had heard several times before, in very different circumstances in Malaya.

The whiplash 'crack' of a high-velocity rifle as a bullet whistled past my head, taking a fair sized chunk out of the wall alongside the front door. I let out a healthy yell; using the only two French swear words I knew. There was no answer and no one came to see if they had hit anything.

I folded my map and followed the proprietor inside to his cubby-hole of an office behind the reception desk. As I went, the thought crossed my mind that success in this quest for this ideal retreat might prove to be the ultimate disappointment.

Curious, I sat down to try my luck with the French telephone system. After a bit of bother with the dialling codes, I was eventually connected. I think the message had lost a bit in the translation somewhere because I found out that the number was that of a firm of London solicitors. The one I vaguely remembered looked after the affairs of my paternal grandfather. After explaining that I was returning an urgent call but didn't know the name of the person calling I was connected to a Mr Harper, Mr Charles Harper.

The voice was nasal and thin, very 'home counties'.

"Thank you for calling back Mr Forest, we have been trying to contact you for some days." The rebuke was barely concealed.

I parried with, "I understood it was urgent."

"So it was, however, I am afraid the matter is no longer quite as pressing."

I explained that I had been visiting some of the more remote areas of France.

"Quite so." He said it with a hint of weariness, as if most of his clients were more thoughtful.

I kept silent.

"Some distressing news I'm afraid. I am sorry to have to inform you that your Grandfather, Mr Augustus Forest, passed away last Thursday evening." He seemed to sound as if he were playing a trump card.

I expressed sorrow at the news and explained that we hadn't been close for many years. Was there a particular reason why I had been contacted?

Harper 'hummed' for a moment and then said, "I thought, under the circumstances, that you would have wished to attend the funeral."

I asked him when it was and what the particular circumstances were.

"Yesterday, I'm afraid and since you are, under Mr Forest's will, the principal legatee, I would have thought that you might have wished to be there." The tone of censure was now quite clear.

"Where was the funeral?"

"In Oxford, I thought you might have known, he had been in a nursing home there for some years."

I explained that I hadn't known and that I was surprised that I featured in his will at all.

He 'hummed' again and then asked, "Will you be in London soon?"

I thought for a moment, "I have nothing planned that can't wait, do you need to see me urgently?"

"I wouldn't say urgently but it would be better if you could come in person…. so much better than trying to sort things out by letter or over the telephone."

Before I could reply he went on, "Especially since you do not seem to have a settled address."

I sighed; I had had enough of the man's rudeness.

"Look, I will drop what I'm doing and start for London in the morning. If I'm lucky with the ferry, I will be in town by the afternoon of the day after tomorrow - will that suit?"

Harper seemed happy at that and we arranged a time and I made a note of the address of their offices in Holborn. I rang off. I sat for a few moments, thinking what all this might entail. I pulled out my diary, looked up the telephone number of my own solicitors, 'Lewis,

Lewis, Lewis and Farr' and tried the French telephone system again.

Whilst I waited Le Patron slid round the door of his office and saying something about bad news, placed a glass of Champagne on the desk at my elbow. I smiled my thanks and he withdrew. A girl answered the call and I asked if Commander Black was in the office.

"Not today I'm afraid Sir, can I take a message?"

"Will he be in the day after tomorrow?"

She thought for a moment, "Oh, that's Wednesday - he's almost certain to be in on a Wednesday Sir."

I took that to be a 'yes'. "Can you get a message to him tonight or tomorrow?"

She said that she would leave a message for him that evening. I dictated the message, asked her to read it back to make sure she understood and thanked her for her kindness. "No trouble Sir."

I rang off. I spoke with Le Patron and made my arrangements for leaving at the crack of dawn. Before I went for my bath I took the car to the village garage and got them to fill the tank and check the oil and the tyres.

# CHAPTER 2

It was still dark when the girl tapped on my door and said that breakfast would be ready as soon as I was. I made a quick toilet and had finished, paid my bill and had my bags stowed in the car before it was fully light. It was going to be a perfect day for long-distance motoring. I won't go into the details of the journey but I did revel in every kilometre of it. I had a fast and biddable car and I pushed it near its limit when I could. I stopped twice for fuel and once to eat the excellent small picnic the hotel chef had made up.

I arrived at the hotel in Montreuil - within easy striking distance of Calais- to find that the reception was expecting me. The girl had also got the ferry timetable and had made a provisional booking for the next morning. I thanked her for her efficiency and asked her to confirm the booking that evening.

I had a long soak in the bath. Thank the Lord for those few French hotels which have really decent baths. A cracking dinner, with a half bottle of Barsac to start and finish with and a half bottle of Chateau Mouton '82 in the middle.

I went to bed a tired and contented man.

*** 

The ferry sailed on time and I went up to the top deck so as not to miss the first sight of the Dover cliffs as they showed up through the morning mist. I reflected that this was the third time I had come back to Britain at a point in my life where I was faced by the unknown.

I will, at this stage, attempt to explain the relationship I had, or perhaps not had might be more correct, with Grandfather Forest. I was born in Malaya, or Malaysia as we are now supposed to call it. My Father was a rubber planter and we lived on his plantation to the northeast of Kuala Lumpur.

Father had been a soldier in the First World War and against all the odds had survived. He had been destined to join his Father in the family solicitors practice and was up at Oxford, reading law when the war started. Much to his father's annoyance, he left to join the army before he took his degree. By the time the carnage was over he had become very much his own man and didn't fancy working in the family firm. He had had more than enough of an older, if not wiser generation, telling him what he must and mustn't do.

He went to Malaya to learn about the rubber industry which was then thriving. The war, like most wars, had brought about a technical revolution. The aeroplane, in its infancy before the conflict, had developed almost out of recognition. The motor car and the lorry likewise had become an everyday sight. The world had found thousands of uses for rubber. Father, farsighted as he proved to be on several occasions, was set on the rubber business.

After he had been there for just over a year his grandfather died and left him enough money for him to buy a small plantation and a good parcel of adjoining land which he set about developing. He worked hard by all accounts, learnt the language-which gave him an edge over those planters who didn't bother- and adopted the latest scientific methods and the best machinery. He made money. Father was well enough set up by the early thirties to take leave to come back to England.

About two days after his arrival he met the girl who was destined to become my Mother. Two months later they married against some stiff opposition from both sets of parents. Grandmother Forest thought her,' Not good enough'- her parents thought the match,' Entirely unsuitable'. Hardly a cracking start.

Mother's family was in trade, according to Grandmother Forest, and that was enough to dam them so far as she was concerned. The fact that the Davis family ran a large and well-established string of hardware shops in and around Birmingham in no way modified her opinion. Seemingly she thought that Charles Davis and his wife Emily spent their time serving behind a counter. Nothing could have been further from the truth.

As far as I can tell, at the time we are talking about, Charles Davis had about fifteen shops stretching from

Wolverhampton and Coventry to Worcester and down as far as Bristol. There was a factory in Cradley Heath which made much of the merchandise which was sold in the various shops. By all accounts, it was a well run and profitable little empire.

Judging by the house they lived in, on the hill to the north of Bromsgrove, they must have been financially on a par with the Forests but trade was trade in the Forests' eyes and thus their son John, was marrying beneath himself.

The fact that John Forest wanted to marry Hannah Davis and then whisk her off to some far-flung part of the world, in turn, appalled her parents.

My mother, Hanna, was, however, then just twenty-one and despite threats to 'Cut her off 'with the proverbial shilling, they were not deterred... They were married in the Lickey church near Bromsgrove and departed on their honeymoon, on a P and O boat two days later.

It was, in fact, an excellent match. My father, whilst being a taciturn man and not much given to socializing, loved her deeply. Mother gave balance, with an outgoing personality which some people mistook for frivolity but which was in fact backed by a steely determination to make life as comfortable as possible for Father.

She transformed the Estate house, which had been little more than sleeping quarters for a bachelor into a comfortable home. She took on a Chinese cook and created a vegetable garden so that everyone got a proper and varied diet. She quickly learnt the language and started a small school for the tappers children. Most of Father's fellow planters thought that he had done remarkably well in his foray back home.

In the fullness of time, I appeared on the scene. Much in the fashion of the time, I was largely brought up by a Malay nurse and since I proved to be an only child I was thrown very much on my own resources. Not that I was in any way neglected by my parents but with no siblings and few other children of my own race, I suppose I got to be quite introspective.

Of course, I played with the Malay children and what with that and my nurse I think I was fluent in Malay well before I was as fluent in English. My schooling was entirely in the hands of Mother. My Father treated me as a small adult and made little concessions to my childhood.

I became something of a loner. That's my excuse anyhow!

Father, the wise man that he was, decided in 1939 that a global war was inevitable and that in any coming conflict the natural alliance between America and Britain would mean that since Japan would not side with America, whom they saw as a Pacific imperial power, they would be against Britain and the Empire. My Mother told me that whilst his friends thought him totally wrong, he reasoned that if Japan did join in the coming war them Malaya would be one of their prime targets.

His belief that a nation couldn't fight a modern war without adequate supplies of rubber was born out of his experience of the Great War. The upshot of all this is that Mother and I were dispatched back to England in the late summer of 1939, me to a boarding preparatory school and Mother to set up another home in a modest, rented cottage in Hertfordshire. I didn't like boarding school any more than Mother liked Hertfordshire but it had been Fathers decision and she was determined to make it work.

The story developed inevitably. Japan invaded Malaya and took it much faster than anyone thought possible. Father joined the local defence forces and was killed in the brief fighting.

The details of his death remained a mystery until I myself unearthed them many years later.

I stayed on at boarding school and Mother, determined to do something to hit back, joined the Women's Auxiliary Air Force. I variously spent school holidays with Mother in Hertfordshire, when it was possible, or with the families of other boys if that could be arranged. On one occasion when nobody could be found to take me, I spent a Christmas with my Housemaster and his wife. Very boring.

The following Easter holiday I went to Mother's parents near Bromsgrove.

Grandfather Davis, what little I saw of him, was rather indifferent to me. But he also treated me as an adult. He took it for granted that I read the newspapers every day and would fire questions at meal times. "What did you think of Churchill's speech yesterday?" or "What do you think of this Stalin fellow?" I found it all pretty perplexing.

Grandmother was, however, a very different pill to swallow. "If it hadn't been for your father, you and your mother wouldn't be in this mess," "I don't know what will become of you."

The logic of her argument not only escaped me, but it also made me very unhappy.

Stories of the beastly behaviour of the Japanese were going the rounds. Even the comics we read at school showed lurid pictures of 'Nips' bayoneting their prisoners. To be told that my father's death was his own fault and that in some way he had deserted Mother and I, only made it worse.

It was in the following autumn term that the axe fell again. My House master called me into his study one Sunday morning after Church. I think I already knew what was coming.

"Forest, I am afraid that I have some very bad news about your mother".

He went on as if he were reading from one of those dreaded telegrams that everyone feared to get in those days.

"It is with very deep regret that I have to tell you that your mother was killed in an air raid last evening."

I stood there for a few moments trying to persuade myself that he was wrong but at the same time knowing it was what I had expected.

My housemaster was, I think, as shocked as I was. He had fought in the Great War like my father and was well used to grim news but then it had been more or less confined to the fighting services but now, while the total casualties were fewer, a far higher proportion was amongst women and children at home. It seemed barbaric by any standards.

I found out later that there had been an air raid on the RAF airfield where my mother had been stationed. A direct hit on a shelter had either killed outright or buried alive twelve girls and six men. There had been no survivors.

The rest of the boys didn't know what to say so they avoided me. I was more alone than ever. A few of those about my own age mumbled something about 'being sorry' and 'rotten luck' but the majority avoided me as if I was some sort of leper. Matron and my House master's wife were kind. The school Chaplain talked a great deal of nonsense about "A caring God".

I had loved my Mother deeply. The more so in that we had both shared in the grief of my Father's death. I overheard people saying things like, 'Of course he's too young to really understands' or, 'He won't have taken it all in at his age,' They were very, very wrong.

And I certainly couldn't see what was so wonderful about a God who allowed both my parents to be killed. I simply wanted them to be in this world, not the next! The Chaplain didn't seem to have much of an answer to that. I think the fact that I had doubted what he said made him reluctant to try any sort of explanation which might have helped.

The question of my further education and of what should become of me became acute. For my part, I was totally ignorant of the arrangements which were made. I don't suppose that the fact that school fees had to be paid ever crossed my mind. At eight I seemed to be adrift.

I only learnt the details of what did happen much later.

Both sets of my Grandparents were in fact, remarkably similar. They were essentially Victorians, at least in their outlook. They were both well-off, upper middle-class couples and in both cases whilst the husbands were, in business, masters of their world, at home, in matters of the family; they were both subservient to their wives.

The two Grandmothers were formidable ladies, implacable in their dislike of each other; although to the best of my belief they had never met, but they were united in their attitude to me. They wanted nothing to do with me.

Grandmother Forest held my Mother to blame for marrying Father and then leaving him to his fate in Malaya and also having the temerity to leave me behind for someone else to look after. Grandmother Davis held my father to blame for dragging their daughter halfway around the world, sending her home with a young child and then getting himself killed. The fact that whatever money he might have had seemed to be lost beyond recall only added to the insult.

I was definitely a loose end to be tidied up as soon and as quietly as possible. An unfortunate episode which befalls even the most respectable families from time to time.

They issued orders to their respective husbands that, 'Arrangements should be made'. Both Grandfathers were practical men who faced facts. I was a fact and provision had to be made.

The outcome was if not overgenerous, about adequate. A capital sum, each side providing half, was placed in a trust fund. The Trustees of the fund were to be the Davis's solicitors. The object was that the interest should pay for my education and upkeep - even to the detail that I should have 'half a crown per week as pocket money'. The residual capital sum was to be mine when I reached the age of twenty-one, 'Provided that the Trustees thought that I was worthy of receiving it!' Quite how they were to decide if I met that provision was unclear.

I still have the file of papers concerning the setting up and the running of that trust and pretty miserable reading it makes. There is about as much humanity in it as you might expect were they administering a right of way. Perhaps less.

I confess to 'coasting' through the rest of my time at Prep school, doing just about enough to stay out of trouble. At eleven I moved to a minor public school where I was still a loner and looking back, I suppose I must have seemed a pretty odd fish to my fellows. I was left alone by most but attracted the attention of the inevitable few that were inclined to bullying.

One thing in my favour was that I was quite large for my age and if it came to a rough house I was well capable of looking after myself, if sufficiently roused.

My popularity did, if not blossom, then reach respectable levels when I did eventually get fed up with the worst of the bullies, a thug called Bolton. I gave him not only a well-blacked eye but a magnificently broken nose. Luckily Bolton's pride made him tell Matron that he had fallen down the stone staircase. She was a wise woman who had been a school Matron for a long time and the matter went no further.

In Grandfather's arrangements, provision had even been made for the school holidays. An allowance was to be available so that my Housemaster of the time, whoever that might be should seek out someone who, for a weekly fee, would take responsibility for me.

That sort of arrangement would cause present-day social workers to have a fit but then, it seemed, if not ideal, a simple solution. On the whole, it worked quite well.

The selection usually fell on a youngish married schoolmaster who was probably struggling to make ends meet and to whom the prospect of a 'paying guest' for a few weeks was not unattractive. With one notable exception, their wives were kind and I could have fared very much worse.

One master taught me to sail a dingy another to shoot and a third to fly fish. I fell madly in love, as adolescent schoolboys do, with the fourteen-year-old daughter of a fourth who swiftly passed me onto a fifth who had two sons several years older than myself. They taught me to smoke. After I had been in my new school for a year or so, my Housemaster retired for the second time.

It seems strange now but during the war, most of the young Masters had left for the forces and recently retired men came back to take their places. As those younger men came back they retired, thankfully in most cases, for a second time, to make way for them.

His replacement was one Commander John Longland. He had gone straight from Oxford to join the R.N.V.R. at the outbreak of war and had had what people refer to as 'a good war'. That meant that apart from surviving to the end, he had done nothing outstandingly stupid.

Longland had finished by commanding a frigate based on the East coast and had taken part in the D Day operations, winning a DSO. He had recently married a super girl who had been in the Wrens. Most of the whole of the senior school; fell for her like a ton of bricks. The pair of them came as a breath of fresh air to the school in general and to me in particular.

At once, Longland made a point of learning everyone's name. Our old Housemaster, 'Boozy Bob', had called everyone, "You boy." If he did ever attempt a name, it was usually that of someone who must have left school many years since.

Longland also made a point of acquainting himself with everyone's background and their strengths and weaknesses. In my case, the latter heavily outweighed the former. I will never cease to be amazed at the difference a 'real' teacher can make to a pupil. You are fortunate in life if you come into contact with one. I came across two at the same time.

John Longland taught physics. Not, to most, the most riveting of subjects but he made it so. Introduced by example and then studied in theoretical detail it can be an absorbing and exciting discipline.

We would fire a shotgun out on the playing fields and then he would explain about action and reaction. A boat on the river, measuring rates of flow and the forces required to hold the boat to an anchorage was the road into skin and form drag.

A trip in his large and very noisy sports car, the internal combustion engine and thermodynamics. Kites, model aeroplanes, magnets, telescopes - the list was long but all part of his armoury for teaching a subject which in the hands of a lesser mentor would have been a bore.

The other brilliant teacher I came up with at that time was a German Jew, who had escaped to this country before the war and taught chemistry. Hans Herman, or in the way of schoolboys 'Herman the German'.

He taught along the same lines as Longhand. Explosions of varying magnitude featured heavily in his repertoire as did the making of soap, paint, fireworks, alcohol, photographs and a vast range of other practical examples which made study a joy. Whilst in other chemistry classes they were studying 'Atomic Number Tables' we were making gunpowder. We got onto the dreary part once the bug had bitten and we could see the reasons why you should know about 'the reasons why'.

I enjoyed physics and chemistry and that, in turn, meant that I needed to know more about maths. I applied myself to that as well. Shakespeare and Chaucer (except for the rude bits) left me stone cold, as did history and geography but then they were taught by people with whom I found it very difficult to communicate.

Longland could be scathing. "You're still coasting along Robin. You could do a whole lot better if only you were prepared to work at it."

He was right of course but in some way, I just didn't see the point.

"You enjoy physics and chemistry and are doing well at those; your maths is improving but that's only because you need it for the subjects you are good at".

"For the rest, well.... hopeless". He had a mannerism of spreading his arms wide as he made a point.

He did it a lot with me.

"You shirk responsibility, you hate games and you just don't join in the real life of either the house or the school." His arms flailed about.

He was right in every respect of course. I much preferred tennis to any team game - I could make my own decisions without being beholden to anyone else. Most of my fellows tolerated me but thought me a pretty odd sort of cove and they, by and large, left me alone. That suited me fine.

Longland kept hammering away.

"I can understand your thinking". He had me in his study one evening after prayers.

"You see it as if all the important people in your life have deserted you-- let you down".

I nodded in agreement.

"You have suffered a rotten string of events, there's no denying that but it's still a poor reason for avoiding any sort of relationship with others."

I mumbled some sort of agreement and prayed that he would shut up and let me and escape this all too accurate assessment of my thinking.

"One of these days, my boy, you will have to get along with other people and you will be totally unprepared for it".

That evening was by no means the first such lecture nor was it the last.

In the fullness of time, I took my exams and whilst physics, chemistry and maths were no problem I surprised everyone, not excluding myself, by doing just well enough in the other required subject to pass.

John Longland and his wife gave me a gold watch. I have still got it after nearly forty years.

My university was more concrete than even red brick but there was an advantage in its newness. I was one of the very first intakes and everyone had been so busy getting the place up and running that they hadn't, by then, formulated the rules for the students. Thus, I was able to get away with doing more or less as I pleased. It pleased me to work quite hard at my chosen subjects and ignore virtually everything else.

I got a creditable degree and, at the time, I was satisfied with my achievement but, in retrospect, I had missed out on the most important benefit. Had I joined in the social life I might just have overcome some of the failings which Longland had nagged me for so long.

*****

Gradually the ferry nosed its way into Dover harbour and everyone prepared to disembark. I stared up at the Castle which dominates the scene with the barracks, rather grim and forbidding slightly inland. It reminded me of the next phase of my life that I had to face, what? Nearly forty years ago.

The move was out of my hands. Conscription for National Service. I had had my call up deferred because I had been at university but the Government now wanted their pound of flesh. I chose the Army, mainly because Father had been in it. Because of the nature of my degree, I was posted to a Royal Engineer Training Regiment at Farnborough. The days of 'coasting along' were definitely over.

The first few weeks were hard but I had an advantage over the bulk of the other recruits. The one thing I hadn't been able to escape from at school was the 'Corps'. The Officer Training Corps to give it its old name. It had been obligatory.

That meant that however unwilling I might have been, I had had to learn to look after and wear a uniform. Do normal parade drill and to clean my equipment. All this to a high standard under the all-seeing eye of an ex Coldstream Warrant Officer who, it was popularly thought, was timeless enough to have trained with Attila the Hun

Compared with my fellow recruits I was halfway there before I started. Most of them had never been away from home before and they found the whole process something akin to hell. I could not be the first person to think that the best preparation for life in prison or the armed forces was to have been educated in an English public school.

I spent a good part of my time helping those who couldn't cope and writing letters for the surprising number who couldn't read or write. I think that was the first time when I started to appreciate that I wasn't quite at the bottom of the heap myself.

Near the end of fourteen weeks of basic training, I was summoned for an interview with my Squadron Commander. The splendid and aptly named Major Hector Blood.

He was a stout, ruddy-faced man with a chest full of medal ribbons gained in both world wars and a well known short-fused temper. He glowered at me for several moments from underneath shaggy eyebrows and then studied my file.

"Fairish degree". He glowered again, inspecting me from head to toe.

"Smart... well smartish" I stared at the gleaming cap badge on his own cap. Not risking moving my gaze.

"A bit bolshie according to your Platoon Commander". A loud sniff.

"And it says here that you speak Malay". I didn't think a reply was called for.

He slapped the file with a podgy hand.

"You will go for Officer training next week". He sat back in his chair which creaked loudly under the load.

I tried to explain that I didn't want to be an officer. Major Blood looked taken aback and his face assumed an even more alarmingly florid hue.

"See here, you miserable specimen, what you want or don't want doesn't come into it. Firstly, you are not here to spend your time doing what suits you. The Government, in its wisdom, is spending a great deal of money on your training."

I somehow doubted that statement but thought it wiser to keep my reservations to myself.

"Secondly, if that's how it is decided you'll spend your time, well that's what you will do. Thirdly, and most importantly, if I order you to go to Officer Training - go you will. Fourthly, you worthless worm, you will pass. If you should fail you will be posted back here and I will make your life such a complete misery that you will curse the fact that you didn't try harder. Do I make myself quite clear?"

I agreed that he had made himself crystal clear. I awaited permission to dismiss. But the old boy wasn't finished yet. With something which I thought might just have been a smile, he went on.

"If one day I see you in an Officers Mess I will stand you a pint. If ever I see you again and you are not an Officer I will make you sweat a gallon. You can pass easily if you put your mind to it. Don't be an idiot. Go and do it".

He relaxed another tiny notch. "I've read your papers and I am pretty sure I met your Mother and Father in Kuala Lumpur between the wars. If nothing else you owe it to them to try."

I wanted to ask him about them but he put me off. "Pass that course and I will tell you all I know."

I saluted and marched out. Much to my surprise, I enjoyed the course.

Even more to my surprise, I passed.

***

When I passed out I was asked where I preferred to serve. I opted for Germany.

In accordance with the convoluted thinking of the Army, I was posted to Malaya on the strength that I had owned up to having been able to speak the language. One half of me was appalled at the thought of going back. The other half was curious. In addition, I had virtually forgotten the language.

That I found odd, in that the pictures of the countryside and the people were as vivid as ever in my mind's eye and I could remember above all the smells. I just hoped that the language would come back as readily.

The journey out was a bit of a holiday really, in that apart from being responsible for a mess deck of soldiers, we had little to do. Like all troopships, it was hardly in the luxury class and the passage down through the Suez

Canal and the Red Sea, at the height of the hot season was a trial for everyone.

There were language classes on the ship and it did come back quite easily so that a few weeks after landing I was more or less fluent again. This, in turn, meant that since there weren't very many British Army people who could speak Malay those of us who did were much in demand, conducting contracts and the like with the native population.

Being a Royal Engineer also meant that I spent a lot of time travelling, both by road and on the single line railway going north from Singapore.

The communist terrorists would target the railway on a regular basis. The usual thing was to remove a few rails and then ambush the train when it either stopped or was derailed. I spent most of my time getting the thing put back in working order only to have the whole process happen again another few miles up the line as soon as our backs were turned.

The terrorists also targeted the civilian labourers whom we had used to repair the line. This was to discourage others from helping next time. So I also spent a lot of time trying to persuade village headmen to provide even more labour, usually against their better judgment.

My squadron commander was a fairly easy going sort of chap who, if you did your job well, didn't trouble you much. He was also not too strict about our use of the transport.

One weekend he let me borrow a jeep and drive to the plantation where we had lived before the war.

It was all much as I had remembered it. It had been looked after well, even during the war. After all the rubber crop was one of the main reasons for the invasion and it was in the Japs' interest to see that it produced as much as possible. Unlike the Germans, they had no synthetic rubber and they were dependant on the natural product for their war effort.

The house itself though was virtually new. The old one had been almost totally burnt down and only a small part of it had been incorporated into the new one.

The new owners, an English couple called Scott had built the new bungalow and it was surrounded with a tough chain-link fence for protection against the terrorists. The Scotts were proud of the two light machine guns they had, one in the bathroom trained to cover the garden the other in the hall commanding the road up to the property. A grim way to live but common enough in those turbulent times.

They were hospitable people and showed me around the part of the Estate near the house. They told me that they had bought the Estate some eighteen months before from the Government agency that looked after such things. They made no secret of the price they had paid.

I thought about that and decided I would try and see if there was any sort of claim I might make over the sale when I got back to Singapore. I asked about Shak Ling, the Chinese Malay who had been my Father's head tapper or foreman and they told me that he was now retired but still living in the village.

After the Scotts had shown me around and given me tea, I drove the short distance to the kampong and sought out the old man. He remembered me after I had introduced myself and seemed glad that I had taken the time to find him. His wife brought us a cool drink and we sat in the shade and he talked of the days before the war.

After a little prompting, he told me about the invasion. No one had thought that the Japanese would come so quickly. The British military mind had never envisaged that an invader might come by bicycle, which is what most of them did. The defenders were thinking of the tactics of a European Army, with their dependence on roads and railways but as Shak Ling put it the Japanese "Flowed across the country like the flooding of a rice paddy".

The defences were overwhelmed almost before they knew the enemy had arrived. It seemed that my Father, with many others, had been captured after a brief, fierce struggle. In the end, all the whites had been lined up and shot. Their bodies had been thrown into the river.

In a way, Shak Ling's account of Father's death was a relief. Not the 'comic book' stories of torture or of having been worked, beaten and starved to death, as were so many but a relatively 'clean' death in a place he had known and I think, loved.

It was another of my ghosts laid to rest.

Shak Ling walked with me to the spot where he said my Father had died and then without a word seemed to vanish into the surrounding trees. I stayed there for a while; thinking about my parents and my own life.

I must have stayed longer than I had thought.

The rising moon's reflection on the water was like a giant, bright silver coin. In the fading light, I walked the two or three hundred yards back to the village, bade Shak Ling and his wife 'Goodbye', made my little offering at the village shrine and started back the way I had come.

# CHAPTER 3

My remaining time passed quickly and almost before I had got used to Malaya again I was back on a troopship, bound for England, demobilization and a totally uncertain future.

Looking back now, I enjoyed the Army; somewhat against my expectations. I had found a substitute family which I felt I had been lacking. Perhaps it's an unfashionable thought now but in those days there was a very real sense of 'family' in the Army.

At the lowest level, or perhaps it's really the highest level, I'm not sure which, you were responsible for one another. If you didn't look out for each other, especially in the jungle, someone was going to get killed. At the other end of the scale, removing leeches from your pal's backside wasn't the most desirable task but he had to have faith in your ability with a lighted cigarette. Besides which, tomorrow he might have to do it for you.

I had met and rubbed shoulders with many first-class men. Men whom you had to trust if you were to achieve anything at all. I had also come across a few whom you wouldn't trust at any price.

It was a steep learning curve, sorting the bad eggs out before they could wreck whatever you were meant to be doing or, even cost you or those under you their lives. It was a valuable lesson learnt at very high speed.

I wasn't set to lose from my new found family straight away, however. In those days you were required to serve, "Two years with the Colours and three with the Reserve".

In other words, after two years full-time service I was obliged to serve a further three years, part-time, with the Territorial Army Reserve.

I can barely remember the first time I came to England from Malaya and I was with my Mother. The war hadn't begun and my Father was alive and well. I had no reason for fear.

That second time I had returned to England. I can remember looking at the approaching port of Liverpool, through a grey drizzle, from that troopship and wondering what the future held. I was alone and not ashamed to admit, I was fearful of the future.

This time, now what? Some thirty odd years later, seeing the cliffs behind Dover looming through a heat haze, from the deck of the ferry, I wasn't fearful.

I had lived a full and exciting life and I had made a modest fortune. Okay, I was still alone but I was now in a position to decide my own future, God willing!

\*\*\*

After National Service, my first requirement was to find a job.

It is strange to recall, that in those days, after the war with a chronic manpower shortage, unemployment was virtually unknown and jobs were plentiful. I had a few pounds saved up and I decided to have a good look round before I made up my mind as to what I would do. The last thing I needed was to make a false start

I was single, had no responsibilities or ties and nowhere to live. The only relatives, apart from my Grandparents and I wasn't sure if they were all still alive, were a sort of Uncle and Aunt who lived in Epping, about ten or twelve miles north of London. In fact, Uncle George had been a distant cousin of my Mother's and I can remember having spent part of one of those itinerant half term holidays with them after Mother had been killed.

They had lost their only son Arthur in the war. He, poor soul, had been the wireless operator in a Lancaster bomber which vanished somewhere in the North Sea after a raid on Berlin.

Uncle George had been a jovial, rotund man who had done well before the war building those rows and rows of houses that mushroomed in suburbia. The war brought a halt to that and his fortunes waned. The loss of Arthur had all but finished the two of them. In a way, I think that they were glad to see me as some sort of link with happier days.

They were very kind and told me that I could stay as long as I pleased. I insisted that I paid a fair sum for my lodgings and moved in.

Uncle George made a modest living by doing odd repair jobs on people's houses. Property had been neglected during the war, not only from the lack of labour but also from the chronic shortage of materials. Timber, bricks, cement, paints even. What had been available had almost all gone to do temporary repairs to houses and factories that had been damaged by the bombing.

Any supplies Uncle George could get his hands on were almost all salvaged from bomb sites. As for paint, that was usually bought from war surplus sales. There were a lot of houses in Epping that were painted a decidedly dreary grey green sort of colour. The result of mixing Army khaki and Royal Air Force blue.

On the odd day when I wasn't job hunting, I would give the old boy a hand. One Saturday I helped him to deliver a load of second-hand roofing slates to a semi-derelict warehouse cum factory.

That's how I met Tony Miller.

The building had been a small factory but it had had its roof removed by the blast from a flying bomb late in the war. It had also killed the tenant and three of his workers. Since they had been engaged on making stirrup pumps and they were no longer needed it had been about last on the list for repair. It had remained roofless, sad and unoccupied ever since. Miller had leased it from the landlord for a peppercorn rent and even that had been waived until he managed to get the roof back on and had made the place habitable.

Materials were his problem. In those days you had to get a license to buy any sort of new building materials. Tony Miller looked elsewhere. That's how he met Uncle.

I unloaded the slates and when I had finished Tony Miller asked if I would like a cup of tea.

To be more precise he waved a mug towards me and said, "Tea?"

That's how we got chatting.

He had been in the Royal Engineers all through the war and had finished as a Warrant Officer. Before he had been called up he had worked as a welder in a factory in Tottenham. No doubt his formal education had been a bit sketchy and he lacked some of what we are pleased to call, the social graces but he was a skilled and clever man.

During the war, he had had what he described as "A belly full of being told what to do by people I wouldn't pay in washers in Civvy Street!"

He had come out of the Services determined to be his own boss in future.

During the invasion of Normandy and the push across France into Germany Tony had spent quite a lot of his time alongside the American forces. One of the things he had seen and tucked the memory away in his mind was something called Polythene.

Odd now, that anyone should stake their future on something as commonplace as we now take Polythene to be but in those days it was virtually unknown in civilian life, even in the States. In Britain, very few people had even heard of it.

One of the first uses for it was the wrapping and protection of spare parts for the American Forces. Since a lot of their operations were in tropical or semi-tropical areas the protection of spares from damp and dirt was important. This new material had proved to be ideal.

Tony had the idea that as it became better known and more in demand, the price would come down, more uses would be found for it and would be a profitable thing to be in.

I thought of the misery of the jungle in Malaya and was inclined to agree with him.

He had taken an important step. He had secured the distribution rights for the UK from the manufacturer in the States. He explained," They don't do any business over here anyhow so it's no skin off their backside. If I can create a market over here, sooner or later they will cut me out but, by then, I will have found something else." How prophetic those words were to prove.

The way Tony got the rights was typical of the man.

"None of the big boys over here was interested so I stood a chance." He explained. "Trouble was they wanted me to go over there to see 'em. I tried letters but, you know the yanks, they wanted me to go and see some vice president or other to sort it out.

a) I couldn't afford to go and, b) if I could 'av., I couldn't 'av. got the dollars."

It seems strange now but at that time we in Britain were only allowed to spend twenty-five pounds a year on foreign travel, that is unless you were very rich and could persuade your Doctor to sign a chit to say that it was essential for your health that you spent the winter in Monte Carlo or whatever your choice was!

Tony's way of solving the dilemma was typical.

He still had contacts in the RAF and a by luck or perhaps good management scrounged a lift on a training flight to Canada. This allied to some low-cost train travel had got him there. His personality and native wit, allied with the American disregard as to class, had secured a five-year contract. The amazingly good timing of the return training flight had got him home!

Looking at things in the long term, the Government, however unknowingly, never made a better investment in a training flight. Tony was to repay them, in exports and in taxation, many, many times over in the next thirty odd years.

He and I seemed to hit it off and it wasn't very long before he asked me if I would care to work for him. He promised nothing and, to be truthful, I expected little, other than the chance to be in on something on the ground floor.

"It will be a long slog and a lot of grief before we're done." He paused to look at the emerging order of the building, "It should be fun though and, you never know, we might even just make a penny or two."

The wage we settled on was just about enough for me to rent a shabby room in a shabby house, which belonged to an equally shabby widow lady, in Forest

Gate. At least it was handy and I could come and go as I pleased.

That was important because I started to keep some pretty unsociable hours. Cycle to what we now started to call grandly 'The Factory' at the crack of dawn and totter back at almost any hour of the night.

I lived on the offerings of a 'Greasy Spoon' transport cafe on the side of the main road or of a fish and chip shop which stayed open late into the night near my 'digs'. Spare time, such as it was, was spent sleeping.

Despite Tony's efforts we barely managed to sell the meagre amount of Polythene sheeting which we did get and that at the slimmest margins we dared accept. Tony's fertile brain, however, came up with another scheme. One which, in the end, was to save our bacon.

It's easy now, to say 'recycled paper' and to have everyone know what you mean. Not so in post-war Britain. True, people had saved old newspapers during the war but they had been recycled back into further newsprint. So much so, that by the war's end most newspapers were almost printed black on very dark grey because they hadn't figured out a way of bleaching out the old ink. Paper was very expensive; most of the raw paper came from Canada and that cost dollars which Britain had not got.

Tony and I built a very primitive plant for turning old newspapers into a crude form of wrapping paper. True, it was still grey but it was strong and it was cheap. Above all, it was a hell of a lot easier to sell to hard-pressed shops and stall holders than Polythene.

We had some pretty strange arrangements with rag and bone men, local dustmen and a sundry host of other scavengers that we would buy what they could collect. It was all in tune with the age of the 'Spiv.' We also paid in cash and that helped.

The plant was made from all sorts of junk. I well remember spending a long time cutting the tops off some aircraft fuel drop tanks to make the vats in which we made the pulp. Those tanks, new, probably cost twenty times what a common or garden oil drum would have cost. However oil drums now cost money, drop tanks were virtually free!

The electric motor, of some great age, which drove the whole contraption was purloined from a bombed-out factory in Dagenham and brought home on Uncle George's trailer behind Tony's apology for a car. It was mucky, smelly and probably dangerous but it worked. Heath Robinson would have been proud of us. We were certainly proud of ourselves!

Of course, you have to have luck. I have always thought that you make your own luck to some extent by working really hard at something and if that's true we deserved some. We got lucky. The factory in Dagenham where we had acquired the electric motor, made concrete paving slabs and curb stones.

These were made by filling a mould with wet concrete and then pressing the water out with a massive hydraulic press. The slabs were then pushed out of the mould and stacked to set for a week or so. In order to enable the stones to come out of the steel mould, a sheet of paper was put in the mould before the concrete was put in. Paving stones were in huge demand for rebuilding war-torn London. The factory made hundreds a day. We supplied the paper. Not only that but once the slab was ejected from the mould, the now sodden paper was thrown away. We got them to save it. We turned it back into slightly less 'newish' paper and back it went. I hate to think how often some of it must have been around the circle.

That hydraulic press gave us the inspiration for our next product. Tony reckoned that if you could press concrete into shapes, why not paper pulp?

Thus was born our version of the egg box.

Eggs were expensive, scarce, rationed and fragile. You bought six, if you were lucky, they were put in a paper bag and if you were very lucky you still had six unbroken eggs when you got them home. Our recycled paper pulp box ensured that you got them home unbroken. It was an instant success.

The hardest part was making the initial mould. True, the shape was pretty simple but it had to stand terrific pressures. By dint of a lot of welding and grinding and a bit of help from a man who worked in the tool room of a well-known car firm in Dagenham, we achieved a fair result. The whole thing was worked by a massive Victorian press we salvaged from a wrecked factory in Canning Town. The boxes were pressed from the pulp, dried overnight in a homemade oven and then bundled up and sold to shops or the egg packers.

By the end of the first full year, we were just in profit, working like madmen but above all, happy with what we had achieved. So it went on. New ideas, new products and better production. It looked as if it were all going to be plain sailing. I should have known better.

***

As I explained, I had to do three years with the Territorial Army as part of my National Service. After I got lodgings in Forest Gate, I had joined the local Royal Engineer Regiment in Woodford. The Headquarters and one Squadron were based on the Drill Hall there, the other outlying Squadrons being based in Braintree and Southend-on-Sea.

We did one evening a week, one weekend a month and a two-week camp every year. Not over demanding and, in the main, good fun. It still provided the family I lacked.

One of the ironies was that Tony Miller, who was still on the reserve, was the Squadron Sergeant Major of Headquarters Squadron. In practice, he was my boss in civilian life whilst I was, in theory at least, his boss in the T.A.

It made no problems because we got on so well together, it became something of a standing joke. Because he was a few years older than myself and he had seen a lot more active service, I treated him with the respect that any young officer treats a senior non commissioned officer. It was always said that the most valuable training Lieutenants get is from their N.C.Os if they have the sense to take advantage of it.

There was a rudimentary Officers Mess in the Drill Hall and it was open most of the time. Since the beer, there was about half pub prices and the company convivial. I spent most of what little spare time I did have ensconced in it.

Our Colonel, Colonel King, was in civilian life a director of a large well-known firm of civil engineers based in London. He had served in the war as a 'temporary officer and gentleman' as the phrase had it, with considerable distinction but he was proud of being a 'part-time soldier'. Not that he didn't take his duties seriously, he did. He was, however, determined that he was going to enjoy it and he was determined that his soldiers would enjoy their time as 'Terriers' as well. Great efforts were made to foster the 'family' spirit and all sorts of activities were laid on to include not only all the ranks but wives and children as well.

Colonel King was also a keen cricketer. Thus we had a regimental cricket team. The fact that I hadn't cared for team games at school didn't mean that I was a complete duffer and as a soldier and a young one at that, you did what was asked of you.

Now I would wish to be clear about this. Cricket is, to my mind, about the best of the so-called team games. For a start, it is played for what passes for the summer in Britain. Add to this that the game is stopped if it rains or the light gets too bad. Hence you are seldom wet or dirty, both of which states I dislike.

Whilst it is indeed a team game, it is made up mainly of individual performances with either the ball or the bat. Lastly, it is a game that frequently takes place, at the level we are considering, adjacent to a public house. Modest drinking of Ale is really part of the total game. Add to this that wives and sweethearts usually come to watch - and to prepare tea - anyone with a balanced view would have to agree that it has a great deal to recommend it.

I wouldn't claim to have ever had any great skill but I had a natural eye for ball games and with the usual opponents we played, I could just about hold my own.

We used to play mainly on Saturday afternoons and wives, sisters, girlfriends and other assorted camp followers would join us for the tea they had usually prepared and at the close of play, as the light faded, we would drift to the bar of some local tavern to talk about what might have been, "If only...."

That's how I met Helen Ford.

Helen was the younger sister of one of my fellow officers, Harry Ford. She was just twenty, slim and dark and very pretty indeed. She was, I suppose, shy. Agreed, she joined in with whatever was going on but she was a long way from being one of the 'Jolly hockey stick brigade'.

We struck up a friendship which developed through that summer into, if not love, something very close to it. I had had what I suppose were 'crushes' on a few girls but, with Helen, it was a form of mutual understanding.

Almost a quiet telepathic agreement of trust. At the same time, it was also, by to- day's standards, totally innocent.

I suppose I was once more, fooling myself, but it was a near idyllic few months. Work was going well, hard work true, but we were starting to see success, I was enjoying the T.A. and I seemed to be doing well in it. Summer, cricket, the odd swimming party, the few opportunities to be alone with Helen when I took her home some evenings in the highly unreliable ruin which I loftily referred to as "My sports car".

Winter came. Christmas with presents and kissing under the mistletoe. The Regimental Dance with dress uniforms and all the traditional trimmings. New Years Eve. It all conspired to add up to what I thought was blissful romance.

Nobody commented. Harry Ford certainly didn't. Helen and I were just two young people amongst eight or ten others who were just a shade more than 'casual' friends among the crowd. There was nothing improper about it all. Most of the time there were several 'young marrieds' with us and don't forget that this was nearly forty years ago when moral codes were much stricter than they are today.

Helen and I saw little of each other during the week. I was still working long hours and Helen went to night school two evenings a week at Walthamstow Polytechnic so it was almost exclusively at weekends when we did get together,

One Friday in early March, Tony asked me to go up to Suffolk the following Monday. We were trying to make a machine that would produce paper pulp trays for some chap or other who thought he could use them to put in boxes of apples to stop them bruising against each other. Tony thought that it wasn't a bad idea and that there might be a future in it so we were going to have a go. The rub was that we couldn't find the bits of machinery we needed.

I agreed to go to see a man who was scrapping old American light bombers on an airfield near Sudbury. We looked at some design sketches he had been making of the machine to press such trays.

"We could do it with a mechanical press like the egg tray one." He studied the sketches.

"But it would be a ruddy sight easier to do it with hydraulic rams. Trouble is we can't get any, certainly not the size we need."

"I guess though, that old aircraft undercarriage rams might just suit. What we need is a big one which will move the die plate about ten inches up and down and four smaller ones that will open and close the guard and turn the bottom table round each time, see?"

I studied the drawings for a bit and made some notes of the sizes he wanted. Then we did a few sums about the pressures and rates of oil flow we thought might be adequate. That's how we went on in those days. Design something and then look for the nearest available cheap hardware that would get as close as possible to what we were after.

On that Saturday evening, I told Helen where I was going and, on an impulse asked if she could manage to come as well.

I collected her very early on the Monday morning and off we set. We got onto the old A12 road and made good time to Chelmsford where we struck off up to Braintree and then north again towards Sudbury. It was a super morning but perishing cold in my old car so we stopped in Halstead for a coffee. Once in Sudbury we asked directions to the airfield which lay to the north of the town.

When we got there it was a sorry sight that greeted us. I suppose there must have been a hundred or so 'planes on the hard standings. All American, light bombers for the most part and the majority had never been used. When the war ended they had been 'mothballed' as they called it; that is, wrapped up to protect them from the elements, parked like sardines and left to await their fate.

Someone somewhere had now decided that they would never be used so they were being scrapped. The engines and all the other fittings were being ripped out anyhow and the rest chopped up and melted down for the aluminium.

We saw men smashing brand new engines that must have cost thousands, with sledgehammers and sorting the metals out into heaps to be sold as scrap. The waste was enough to make anyone weep.

We found the chap we were after and explained what I needed. He waved his hand toward a hanger and said, "You'll probably find most of it in there. Pick out what you want then come and tell me about it and we'll fix a price."

That hanger was stacked with tens of thousands of aircraft bits and pieces and we had a high old time finding the sort of things we needed for Tony's new machine. Eventually, I was happy that what we had, so Helen and I lugged it out and showed it to the chap in charge.

He glanced at our small pile, "That all? Call it a couple of quid."

I thought that at that sort of price we could do with some other bits that I'd seen.

I asked, "Have you got any pumps to go with the rams?"

"There should be hundreds about somewhere; try over there in those sheds." I asked if he minded if we took some more rams. "Take what you want, it's all going to be melted down anyhow so take as much as you like."

We spent the next couple of hours or so picking out what I thought we could use.

Helen went and got the car and we loaded our loot. By the time we had it all on board, the poor old thing was well down on the springs. I paid the twelve pounds asked and promising to be back with a bigger vehicle as soon as possible. We set off, slowly.

We were going to have to go pretty steady if we were going to get home all in one piece. Even so, I managed to boil the cooling water going up  the long hill south of Halstead We just made the top and pulled over and sat on the side of the road while the engine cooled off.

I refilled the radiator with some water out of a nearby ditch, using one of Helen's wellington boots as a scoop, that brought on a fit of giggles. When we got over that, we had another go.

Just south of Braintree one of the back tyres burst. We spent ages unloading everything, changing the wheel and loading up again.

About three miles from the factory the lights packed up so for the last bit Helen drove and I walked in front with a torch. It was very late and we were both exhausted but somehow, ridiculously happy when we finally did arrive at the factory.

Tony, still at work as usual, was well pleased when we showed off our pickings.

To us, the stuff was virtually priceless and even allowing for a new tyre - when I could source one - it had cost so little. We put in hand the borrowing of a small lorry to make another visit later in the week.

I don't really know why but that journey somehow cemented Helen's and my relationship. I suppose, looking back all those years, we were in love but in our undoubted innocence, hadn't quite taken it in.

The trip to Sudbury had been something of an adventure and we had achieved something together. It was from then on that we began to think seriously about the future and to talk about the possibility of getting married.

I was all for going to see her Father and asking him if we could get engaged. That was the done thing and I wanted to do it right. Helen, however, thought that we had best leave it a bit and she would have a word with both her parents before I made a such a formal request.

With hindsight, I suppose that she had known that there would have been trouble but didn't want to tell me. I hardly knew the Fords; the little I had seen of them, calling to collect Helen to go to a dance, that sort of thing, had been fine. They were civil, not exactly friendly but I had assumed that would become so when we got to know each other better.

I was wrong.

# CHAPTER 4

I suppose it's true that I wasn't much of a catch. Certainly, I had a degree but not from one of the better-known universities and my job was a bit precarious.

I think that the real problem was that I had no parents to give me some sort of background. As Oscar Wilde said, "To lose one parent is unfortunate, to lose both looks like carelessness."

The other drawback was the social thing.

I have never understood why, in Britain, many people look down on engineers? They somehow think it's a step down the social ladder from, say, an accountant. God might know why, but I don't! To take it to its limit. If a man is Professor of some totally useless subject at one of the old universities, that's all right and he is socially acceptable. Another man may be Chief Engineer on a massive dam project costing millions of pounds and giving employment and improvement to vast numbers of people and he is thought of as less socially acceptable.

I can remember once hearing a Lieutenant in a famous cavalry regiment referring to the Royal Engineers as, "Mere tradesmen".

I later reminded him of his remark when we built a timber ramp so that he could get his little armoured-car back onto the road after he had fallen down a ravine in it just north of Bathurst. I think that it only served to confirm his view.

All that was as maybe but I hadn't expected the storm that was about to engulf both Helen and me.

Father Ford was, as I remember it now, the Area Manager for one of the high street banks. Shortish, rotund and well aware of his important role in the commercial life of the community. Mrs Ford's main job in life seemed to be to tell everyone she came in contact with of the fact of her husband's place in the order of things or, if they were already aware, to remind them not to forget it.

I received a brief note from Mr Ford asking me to call to see him. I hadn't heard from Helen so I assumed that things were going to be all right. I was in for a shock.

Mr Ford opened the front door himself and asked me into what served as his study. I wasn't asked to sit down. He came straight to the point.

"Helen's mother, Mrs Ford, tells me that Helen has spoken to her about the possibility of the two of you getting married." It was a statement, not a question. "I want you to understand that under no circumstances would we consider such a thing, at this stage."

It was like being hit by an unseen blow. I was stunned for a moment and searched for a reply. It was his adding 'at this stage' that gave me a glimmer of hope.

I rather weakly asked, "Might we at least, get engaged?"

"We think it would be far better if you didn't. Such a step would put Helen under an obligation and at her age that would be unwise."

He stared at me for a moment and went on, "We think it best for both of you that you do not see each other again for a while."

I could hardly believe what I was hearing; it was like something out of a Victorian melodrama. I started to lose my temper.

"That's jolly unfair - we are fond of each other."

"What is fair or unfair Mr Forest has nothing to do with it. Mrs Ford and I have made up our minds that in Helen's best interest you will not see each other again, at least until she gets back."

"I'm sorry Sir, I don't understand .... gets back ....gets back from where?"

"We have decided to send Helen to stay with Mrs Ford's cousin and his family. Portugal, near Lisbon."

I suppose that's where it all went wrong.

I almost spat out, "You can't send her off to Lisbon just because you think I'm not good enough for her."

He became even colder and almost surgical in his manner.

"I will remind you, Mr Forest, that Helen is under twenty-one and she will do exactly as I tell her".

"As for whether you are 'good enough for her' as you put it. Since we have only set eyes on you fleetingly, on the odd occasions, I am hardly in a position to judge."

He paused to collect his thoughts for his next assault. "Whilst my son speaks well of you, I understand that you have no family to speak of - not of course that that is your fault - but it is a drawback. This, however, is beside the point. Mrs Ford and I think that Helen is far too young to commit herself to marriage; it's far too important a decision for a girl of her age. Portugal will give her time to think."

"What does she think of it all - has she agreed to go?"

"As I have already pointed out, what Helen thinks is neither here nor there. She will do as she is told."

I waded in, telling him what I thought - so stupid, sending her off so that she might forget me, meet someone else. I forget now just what I did say but I do remember saying that I would fight to persuade her to stay. He cut me short.

"Mr Forest, there is no point at all in prolonging this conversation, our minds are made up, Helen will leave for Lisbon next week and that's an end to it. It's all arranged."

With that, I was shown the door.

I emerged on the pavement very angry. I was also very ashamed that I hadn't argued a better case in explaining our love for each other. As usual, when I was faced by something really important I had made an almighty hash of putting my side of the story. Just as things had looked so much better I had been smashed down into despair yet again.

I avoided going to the Mess or the Regiment for the fear of the disgrace. Everyone would think we had done something wrong, something outside the code if you like, and we hadn't. I felt I had let Helen down most of all and I couldn't bear that.

Tony Miller made a few sympathetic noises. He said that people had been talking about it in the Sergeants' Mess. That only meant that it would be common gossip all over the place by now. When I did go into a parade people, in turn, avoided me and that made it worse.

Surprisingly, Colonel King did go out of his way to have a private word.

In his direct, no-nonsense language, he attempted to sympathise. "Young Helen's father; stupid old bugger. Don't take it to heart. Means well but does what that dreadful wife of his tells him; not your fault." It was kind and typical of him but it didn't help a lot. Everyone was making a judgement.

I did have a letter from Helen before she left, despite her father's strictures. It was a very sad letter. She said that she had argued that she would be happy to wait until she was twenty-one before making any decision at all. She had pleaded not to be sent away as that would only make people certain that we had been up to no good. In all, she seemed to have made a much better case than I had but it was all to no avail. She was of the mind that her father, urged on by her mother, had made a hasty decision and that he felt that to back down now, would have been a sign of weakness.

She was very firm in her promise that she would stay in Portugal until her birthday and would come back of her own accord. If I still wanted to marry her she would go through with it whatever her parents thought.

In its way, that made me both happy and angry. It was all so stupid that people could behave in such a cruel way for the sake of what I suspected was a mixture of pride, snobbishness and a sense of power. Shades of both sets of my own grandparents.

I couldn't help but think of my maternal grandmother's view. Unwilling to admit that she had been wrong about the suitability of her daughter's wedding, she blamed my Father 'for getting himself killed.' I could see no logic in it at all but her social position, as she saw it, didn't allow for the slightest mistake of judgement on her part.

About ten days later, I had a postcard from Helen saying that she was all right and that if I wanted to write to her that I should send my letters to an address where she could collect them without her hosts knowing about them. She feared that if I wrote directly they would tell her father. All so stupid and senseless.

I wrote that evening. It was a long letter and mainly consisted of me telling her, in just about every way I could think of, that I loved her. I sent it off first thing the next morning to the address she had given me; it seemed to be some sort of cafe in the old part of the city.

On the following Friday, I worked in the factory, sorting out some problem with a press we were building and at lunchtime, I nipped out to the cafe down the road to collect a snack.

When I got back Tony asked for a word in private. That in itself was unusual and I noticed that he was avoiding looking straight at me. Something serious was up.

"The Regimental Adjutant, Peter Hibbert has been on the 'phone. He wants you to go round there as soon as possible and report to him."

"What about?"

"Haven't a clue but it sounded important so you had better cut along there now."

"We haven't finished the hydraulics on that press yet and we promised it would be done tonight."

"Look never mind that, I'll see to it, you get along to the Drill Hall sharpish."

Mystified, I agreed to go.

I was there in about ten minutes. I tried to think if I had done something wrong or had forgotten some chore or other, nothing that I could think of. It never crossed my mind that it had anything to do with Helen.

Peter Hibbert also looked serious when I got to his office.

"The Old Man is in his room and would like a word."

He got up, walked to the Colonel's door, tapped and stuck his head inside, "Robin Forest's here Sir."

I heard Colonel King say, "Thank you, Peter, wheel him in please."

Peter nodded to me and in I went. Of course, I was not in uniform so I just stood in front of his desk, at attention and said, "Good afternoon Sir."

He didn't smile but said, "Good afternoon Robin, you had better take a seat".

I sat; I was relieved he had used my Christian name, always a good sign.

He looked me straight in the eyes and I could see great pain.

"Robin, I'm afraid it's bad news. I won't try to gloss it over, I couldn't if I tried. It's young Helen. I was told earlier today, she was knocked down by a car, in Lisbon. She was killed outright. I'm very sorry."

I don't know really what he said after that. Peter got me to lie down in the little room which was kept for the Orderly Officer and one of the regular batmen brought me a cup of tea. Later, when I suppose I had got over the initial shock, Peter came and told me all he knew.

Helen's brother Harry had phoned Peter with the news because he thought that I should be told. Strictly it was nothing to do with the Regiment but Peter had told Colonel King and he had said, "Find him, wherever he is and I will tell him."

It seemed that Helen had been to a little cafe, quite early in the morning. She had come out reading a letter and perhaps not looking where she was going, had stepped off the pavement into the path of a taxi. She had been killed instantly. There was nothing anyone could do.

I was quite sure then that I had killed the girl I loved. The girl I had intended to marry.

*\*\**

It was that old business all over again. The moment things started to go right, I did something stupid to upset things and my world came tumbling down again. It all seemed so predictable and so unfair. I always landed further down than I had been the last time. Where would it finish?

People were, in the main, kind about it. It was just fate.

Others were less so. Certainly, Helen's parents were adamant, her brother slightly less so, but they took the view that it was my fault. If it hadn't been for me Helen wouldn't have gone to Portugal. If I hadn't written to her she wouldn't have gone to collect my letter. If, ... if....if.

I think at that stage I agreed with them.

The funeral was terrible. I wasn't going to go. I just couldn't face it but the Colonel said that if I didn't go it would look very bad. It would be an admission on my part that I was to blame. In the end, I sat with Peter Hibbert and his wife.

A long time afterwards I heard that Mr and Mrs Ford had said that they didn't want me there. Colonel King said that in that case neither he nor his wife would be able to go. In the event, there was a huge turnout from the Regiment. The old family thing again.

Colonel King asked me to go and see him a few days later and tried to persuade me that my feeling that it was my fault was wrong. He told me a bit about his time during the war and how you could apply the same arguments to the situations he had found himself in.

"Tell a chap to go and do something and he gets himself killed doing it. If someone had got to go and do it and he was the best man, then it's just fate, it can't be helped."

"Old man Ford knows in his heart of hearts that it's rather more his fault as anyone's. If he had acted as a reasonable father, not like some pig-headed tyrant, who knows? We can always look for someone else to blame, just to excuse ourselves. It's never a very profitable exercise. An unfortunate set of circumstances brought about a very sad event and that's all there is to it. You can only put it behind you and press on. You'll never forget it but you must learn to live with it."

His argument was, like him, very kind and thoughtful. However, I wasn't very convinced. Where was that 'Caring God' that I had heard so much about?

The next few weeks were a nightmare.

# CHAPTER 5

Tony Miller's cure was to work me like a dog. A good enough tactic I suppose, in its way, in that it gave me virtually no time to think or to wallow in self-pity. It also made sure that I slept at nights.

Colonel King's ploy was to send me off on detachment for several weekends and evenings to a Territorial Infantry Regiment in Essex to teach them the rudiments of explosive

demolition. It is a good idea to keep your mind on your work doing that sort of thing or you might be responsible for a very nasty accident!

I knew, however, and I think that they both knew, that it wasn't going to provide the long-term answer.

The factory wasn't too bad. The people we employed, by then about eight, sympathised with my side of the story.

Helen's father, besides being an Area Manager with the bank, was a local Justice of the Peace and an unpopular one at that, so local feeling wasn't much on his side.

Working within my own regiment though was still a trial. On the one hand, Harry Ford was a popular chap and everyone, including myself, had sympathy for him. Everyone who had known Helen, and that meant virtually all my brother officers, had liked her and I think that there was certainly a feeling that I was in, at least, some part to blame.

I asked for a move.

Colonel King explained the position. "You have got to do your three years with the Reserve but if you feel you would be happier with a move to another unit, that can be arranged." He went on, "I will give you a very good report, you have done well here and I can see to it that no-one in a new unit will be any the wiser why you have moved."

It was decent of him to make such an offer and I thanked him and asked for a few days to think it over.

He agreed.

I talked to Peter and in passing; he mentioned something which struck a chord.

"As I see the rules, you can certainly move to another unit, as the old man suggests, but you will have to serve out your time." He paused, thinking, "That is unless you were unfit or moved to somewhere where it was impossible."

"How do you mean?"

"Well, suppose you were to go to work overseas, you just couldn't do it could you?"

Again I asked for time to think.

That afternoon I did some checking and I also phoned the firm of solicitors who had acted for Father before the war, Messrs Lewis, Lewis, Lewis and Farr of Lincoln's Inn Fields. I made an appointment for the next day and asked Tony if I could have the time off to go.

I had written to them a couple of times since I had been back from Malaya about the sale of the Rubber Estate after the end of the war. I had received a reply which, in effect said that it was all very difficult. The Malay legal system was still in a terrific muddle, many of the old records had been lost during the war and that while the money from the sale of the Estate was held in the central Bank it would be very difficult to get it back to England.

Added to that, the terms of my father's will were unclear. I was assured that all the Lewis's and Mr Farr were looking into the muddle and that they would keep me informed. They had sent me a copy of Father's will and it stated that all he had was to go to my mother. That was clear enough. It also said that should my mother die first then it all came to me when I was twenty-one. Of course, my father had died first and so far as anyone knew my mother had never made a will.

At ten o'clock the next morning I was shown into the office of a Mr Lewis. Whilst I understood that he wasn't the Senior Partner, to my eyes at least, he must certainly have been the oldest. I think that we both took an instant dislike to each other. He spoke in a sort of shorthand, never quite finishing what he wanted to say.

"All very complicated - Malaya - Far East - war you know - very difficult."

In between each utterance, he either sighed heavily or shook his head.

"Large sum - heavy responsibility - duty to your late Father."

In the long intervals, he either peered at a thick, very dusty file or gazed at me through wire-framed, half-moon glasses.

I tried a question,"Why couldn't the money be transferred back to England?"

"Legal system - foreign exchange regulations - terrible muddle out there."

I explained that I had served in Malaya only a year or so before and it all seemed organised enough then.

Lewis mumbled something about "Impatience - Youth always in a hurry."

We looked at each other for what seemed like an embarrassingly long time. I thought that unless I made a stand now, I would be fobbed off with excuses and I would then go away and blame myself for not having been tough enough. I had been down that route too many times before.

"Could I see the Senior Partner please?"

There was a bewildered look on Lewis's face that was almost comic.

"I can assure you that I am the Partner who has dealt with the affairs of your late Father since well before the

War. I know more about the matter than anyone else in this firm."

I now knew that he could finish a sentence when driven too it.

He glared at me with an expression which he must have expected to quell any further argument. I gazed back and a thought struck me. The last time anyone had looked at me like that had been Helen's father on that fateful day when our fates had been sealed by my giving in. If I didn't stick to my guns now I would be finished. It would be the same old story all over again. I had run away once too often.

"I'm sorry Mr Lewis but I must insist. I wish to see the Senior Partner."

The old chap had one more go, "Senior Partner - busy man - drop of a hat - most irregular."

"Then I will go into the outer office and make a new appointment to see him, and only him."

Mr Lewis sighed, an extra long sigh, slapped the file shut in a small cloud of dust. pointedly put some other papers into a drawer and locked it and with the file under his arm and the key in his waistcoat pocket marched out closing the door behind him.

I sat alone in that dingy office for about a quarter of an hour before I got angry. As I started to walk over to the door a phrase that my mother used to use came into my head,

"Polite but firm dear." Why should that have come to mind just then?

I reached out for the doorknob just as it was turned from the far side and a middle-aged lady nearly pushed the door into my face.

"Mr Forest, I'm so sorry, I was just coming to apologise for your being kept waiting for so long. Mr Lewis has been speaking to one of the other Partners. I don't think they will be long. Can I get you a cup of tea or coffee perhaps?"

I asked for coffee.

Within a very few moments, a much younger girl came in with a small tray with coffee and a couple of chocolate biscuits. I asked if I was going to see the Senior Partner.

She smiled. "I really don't know but Mr Lewis has been speaking to Mr Farr, he is the Senior Partner you know, and then he went to see Commander Black. I think he can see you in a moment."

"I really would prefer to see Mr Farr, if that is possible or make another appointment to see him."

"I think you should at least have a word with Commander Black, he really is very nice." She paused, she seemed to be deciding just how far she dared go. "He is a lot younger than Mr Lewis. I think you would like him." She smiled encouragement and went out.

I took the coffee to the window and studied the world outside whilst I collected my thoughts on what to say to the young Commander Black. I had nothing to lose. If he were another Lewis I could still insist on seeing the elusive Mr Farr. 'So near but so far - no Farr!' Silly but that cheered me up no end.

The coffee bearer was back in very short order and said, "If you'll follow me I will take you to the Commander's room, Mr Forest.

I suppose I must have adopted my 'stubborn' look or she just sensed my reluctance. She smiled. "He really is very nice and I am sure he will help."

I had come this far and I may as well hear what he had to say. I followed.

Black was certainly much younger; at a guess early to middle thirties; big man, dark suit, Royal Navy Volunteer Reserve tie - that helped - and what was then almost the 'hallmark' of his type, the neatly trimmed beard.

I reckoned that I might just get on with Black

Thinking of my first impressions that day, now well over thirty years ago, I was right. In all that time he has not only been my solicitor in England but he has been a staunch friend and he, his wife and his son, have become as near a family to me as I could have wished.

Black came round the desk, hand outstretched, "Mr Forest, I'm Tommy Black, I'm sorry that you have been kept waiting."

We sat and after the usual opening gambit of pleasantries, he got down to business. Tapping the now somewhat less dusty file old Lewis had produced he said, "There seems to have been a bit of a nonsense over this and for that, I apologise. Of course I haven't dealt with your affairs up to now but Mr Farr, our senior partner, has asked me if I would take it on and I will be looking after your affairs, with us from now on, if that is agreeable to yourself?" His very dark twinkling eyes asked the question he hadn't quite stated.

I hesitated and he went on, "I will need a few days to go through it all and I promise I will then treat it as a matter of urgency - what do you think?"

That phrase, 'polite but firm' ran through my mind. I liked the look of Black and I wasn't likely to do better in this firm at least.

"Can I make another appointment now to come back and see you when you've gone through it?"

"Good idea, certainly. I would have thought....." He turned a page of his desk diary, ".... How are you fixed for next Thursday, say about twelve o'clock?"

I agreed.

In the event, it was me who had to postpone the appointment. After a word with Tony Miller, we came to the conclusion that the Friday would be a better bet. I telephoned to see if that would be suitable for Black. He came on the 'phone himself and said that that would suit him fine as he awaiting a reply to a cable he had sent to Kuala Lumpur and he thought that he wouldn't get it until Thursday evening at the earliest.

Tommy Black went on to ask if I had heard from the solicitors who had represented my respective grandfathers and who were the trustees of the fund they had set up for my education.

"I've got the letter they sent when I went to University; I haven't heard since then."

Black went on, "If you agree, I think I will contact them and see if we can sort that out at the same time -

we may as well make a clean sweep of everything all at one go."

I agreed. We settled on eleven-thirty on the following Friday at his office.

I kept my nose pretty close to the grindstone for the next few days - or rather Tony saw to it that I did. I could lose myself in that; it was the time away from work when things really hurt.

*** 

My digs, whilst convenient, had never been anything other than somewhere to lay my head and, in truth, they were pretty dingy. I looked at them and felt that whatever came about it would be better to cut away from the whole wretched mess and start again somewhere else. That was my first thought, my second was that I would just be running away yet again.

Friday came and to tell the truth had a strange feeling that it was 'make or break' day. Looking back now, with the benefit of hindsight, it was the first real turning point.

There was no waiting this time. I was shown to Tommy Black's room. He shook hands and arranged for coffee. We got down to business.

"I have been all through this." He indicated the now familiar file on the desk. "On the face of it, it all seems pretty straightforward enough." I could see the snag coming.

"The main difficulty as I see it is that the monies from the sale of the rubber Estate are still lodged in Malaya.

I asked him to explain. He put the tips of his fingers together in a gesture that I was to come to think of as almost his trademark.

"Let's go back to the beginning of all this. We can reasonably suppose that at the time your late father decided to send your mother and yourself back to this country, just before the war, their assets were comprised of the Estate itself, any money they had in the bank, or in hand, perhaps some other investments, which we have little chance of tracing now  and their day to day effects."

"Like what?"

"Oh, the usual things. Any stock in the business. Raw rubber would be the most likely and his and your mother's things, furniture, motor car, jewellery.... you know the sort of stuff. We know that when you and your Mother came back here he transferred a goodish sum to a London bank, in your mother's name. She would have to have had something to live on and to look after you."

I nodded my understanding.

"There are also records in the bank of money he transferred back each month to your mother's account after that."

"How long did that go on for?"

"Oh, until the Japs arrived. Then, of course, it stopped." He paused to take a drink of his coffee.

"The Japs took or destroyed pretty well everything during the occupation so that by the time the end finally came, all that was left was the land itself and the rubber trees on it."

Black consulted the file again.

"When the war ended the country's banking system had to start more or less from scratch. Most of the records had either been lost or deliberately destroyed. It's one of the effects of a war which we don't tend to think of but, as I said, the land remained."

I asked, "Why was it sold; who said it could be sold?"

"As I dare say you know, as well as anyone, rubber trees don't just look after themselves, so the Government department out there had to take some sort of action in cases like this and there were quite a few. In the first place, they appointed temporary managers, just to keep the places running.

After all, Malaya's chief cash crop is their rubber and they needed to protect the plantations whoever owned them. That was their first priority."

I agreed. "I can see that, but they must have tried to find the owners, surely?"

Black nodded, "I'm sure they did but let's face it, they had a hell of a problem. With most of the records gone and most of the planters either dead or in some other part of the world, in a lot of cases they just didn't know what had happened. In the case of your Father's Estate, they asked the Anglo-Malay company to run it as part of their operation until they could come to a final decision."

"What then?"

"It seems that they made some effort to trace your mother but drew a blank so they took the decision to put the Estate up for sale and hold onto the proceeds until the owner could be traced; it was all quite legal and proper and quite sensible under the circumstances."

"Also I have heard from the Government Agents that the money from the sale is lodged in a special account that they established for these cases and is accumulating interest."

"Couldn't I just go out there and claim the money?" I queried.

Again Black put the tips of his fingers together. "So long as you can prove good title, and I see no difficulty over that. The difficult part is bringing the money back to this country. I haven't got to the bottom of the problems yet but on the face of it I think you would lose a big percentage of the money by doing so."

Black smiled, "That's unless you are going to go in for a bit of currency smuggling that is?"

Funnily enough, something Tony Miller had said a few days ago had set me thinking along those lines myself but not quite in the direction Black meant.

"What if I went out there, claimed the money and then stayed there - to live, I mean?"

Black looked up. "You know the country don't you?"

I explained about my spell there doing National Service. I also told him about the feeling I had about the country and the language. Thinking back now, I realise that Black encouraged me to talk and I suppose I must have gone on a bit. I told him about school, the Army and, rather oddly, about Helen. I also told him about my Grandparents and the feeling I had about trying to get away from the U.K. and trying to make an entirely new start.

"Will going back to Malaya really be making a fresh start, or are you wanting to go back to somewhere where you have been happy in the past?" This chap Black was more perceptive than I had given him credit for.

He went on. "You could afford to do it if you wanted to. Or is it just something of a pipe dream?"

I was stuck for a reply, maybe it was indeed just a daydream but what had started as a vague feeling was growing into something of a certainty.

Black went on to talk about the money which my respective grandfathers had put in trust for me.

"I don't see much difficulty there; it's not a very big sum really. The interest never really met the outgoings in the first place and the capital was eroded even further when you went on to university after you left school.

There's a bit to add. What your mother left.... not a lot but it's been invested and I think I can get them to add it to what's left of your trust. As I see it I think there would be plenty to pay your passage out there with enough left over to pay your way whilst you reclaimed the money from the sale of your Father's Estate."

I thought for a bit and said. "If there is enough to keep me for a week or two I should be able to get a job of some sort to tide me over."

We talked a bit about the legal arrangements which would have to be made and the practical steps I would have to take in order to get the documents I would need, should I decide to go out to the Far East. Although we spoke as if it was just a possibility, I think that by the end of that meeting I had made up my mind to go.

Black looked at his watch and said. "Look, I don't know about you but I'm thirsty, it's just about lunchtime and there's a pub around the corner. How about a beer?"

I agreed.

Over a pint of pretty thin beer and a time-expired cheese roll we talked about a lot of things.

Black explained that he had always enjoyed messing about in boats and had spent most of his University vacations sailing somewhere or other with his father on an old Lowestoft yawl so when the war broke out and he had joined up he had volunteered for the Royal Navy.

He had spent the first half of the war in an escort corvette in the North Atlantic and after that sector had tamed down, he had been posted to a destroyer operating out of Ceylon. This meant that he knew a bit about the Far East and it gave us something in common.

I asked him if he had ever come across my old Housemaster John Longland. He didn't think he had but somehow thought the name was familiar.

Black told me a bit about the trouble he himself had had in adjusting from being a student to a Naval Officer, then back again at the end of the war when he returned to Cambridge to finish his degree. He spoke of the fact that he found help in that many of his fellow undergraduate like himself, had grown up very fast indeed in the services.

He also told of the resultant battles with the university authorities who tended to treat this pretty hard intake in the same way that they had previously treated school leavers.

He also talked of the great change from being part of a 'family' in the services and then with a bunch of ex-servicemen undergraduate to the much more solitary life of a junior solicitor starting out on yet another new career.

I think the things that he said all helped to determine me to make a totally fresh start.

***

The very next day I had a long talk with Tony Miller and whilst, from his own point of view he wanted me to stay, the more so in that it looked as if the business was starting to turn the corner and settle down into a profitable run and he wanted someone he could trust to run the day to day side of things. He saw the sense of my making a clean break.

I spoke to Colonel King and  not only did he understand, he also made a lot of practical suggestions as to the way to go about it, even to the extent of  giving me the names and addresses of friends of his who might well be able to offer me a job when I did get out to Malaya.

"I understand that there's masses of work for civil engineers out there. The whole place has been neglected during the war and there is plenty of damage to put right.

If I know anything, half the companies will be run by ex-Royal Engineers and they are bound to see you right."

As usual, his advice was sound and I was glad of it later. The 'Sapper' brotherhood didn't let me down, ever.

What to do about the grandparents? I had had very little contact with them since I had left school and that had never been frequent even then. However, they were my only close living relatives and they had paid for my education. I owed them something for that at least.

After some hesitation I wrote to both sets of Grandparents, thanking them for their support in the past and telling them that I had decided to go and make a career in the Far East. From my mother's parents who still lived in deepest Gloucestershire, I heard nothing. That was easy to cope with.

From Grandfather Forest I got a devastating reply.

*Helsey Hall*
*Helsey*
*Nr. Knutsford*
*Cheshire*

*Dear Robin,*

*Thank you for your recent letter. Both your Grandmother and I were glad to hear that you are well and we wish you every success in your future career abroad.*

*The tragic loss of our only child, your Father, affected us very deeply at the time and in truth it still does. Your Grandmother has never come to terms with it and it still troubles her very much. In my own mind, I am quite sure that her constant ill health stems from that time. It is a part of our lives which we have tried to put behind us.*

*While we wish you good fortune in the future I think it would be best if you made no further effort to contact us.*

*Kindest regards,*

*Harold Forest*

*P.S. You may find the enclosed cheque a help.*

I am not sure if it was the letter or the cheque for fifty pounds which hurt most. Whichever way you looked at it, it was a very bleak outcome. I had hardly expected a fulsome plea to stay in contact but to be told, in effect, to go and not to bother to come back was a bitter blow.

On balance, no response at all was certainly the easier to cope with. There was clearly very little left to stay for.

I continued with my preparations.

I visited one of the many steamship offices in Lower Regent Street and booked a passage on a general cargo boat which also carried about twelve passengers. I think twelve was the magic number because if they carried twelve or less they didn't need a doctor. If you became ill you were expected to submit to the tender mercies of the Captain. I was certainly glad I had already had my appendix out!

I gave notice at my digs and got rid of most of the clutter I had accumulated. In truth, I think I gave most of it away or dumped it. My car, such as it was, made more than I expected. Virtually every new car in those days went for export and even my old machine had an overinflated value.

I said my 'Goodbyes' and that was surprisingly difficult in some cases. In particular Tony Miller, Colonel King and the Adjutant Peter Hibbert. They had all been staunch friends when I was down.

I went and put some flowers on Helen's grave and sat there for an hour or so. I was then as ready to leave as I was ever going to be. As far as I could see, it was forever.

Tommy Black was kind enough to remember my departure date and came to the docks to see me off. He came aboard and saw me settled in. We had a drink together and he wished me luck and urged me to keep him posted as to how I got on. He also brought some last moment, certified copies of odd papers from the files which he thought might help.

The cry "All ashore" was passed around the ship and Tommy Black shook hands and left. I really did feel very much alone. I vividly remember that journey down river and, as we got further downstream, the shore fading away into the distance and the failing light. I thought it like my past life. Perhaps I was running away yet again but this time I was, at least, doing it at my own pace.

The S.S. Timor Star was not the fastest vessel afloat nor was it the most comfortable but it was adequate and cheap. Compared with my last journey to the Far East on a troopship it was a comparative luxury. I think the

Captain would have been insulted if I had called his ship a tramp steamer but in truth, that was what she was.

We called into Tangiers to offload a consignment of war surplus diesel engines which, even to my eyes, looked decidedly second hand and then headed for Genoa to load six hundred tons of cement bound for Palestine. There, we took on a mass of steel pipes which were to be offloaded at Aden. I was in no hurry however and found the idea of this sort of trade very interesting. It was something that I had never thought about before.

I confess that I did go in for a little trade of my own, however. Something that I admit I hadn't mentioned to Tommy Black. It had stemmed from a hint of an idea from Tony.

Just before I left England I had drawn out all my meagre funds, in cash, and taken myself to the less fashionable parts of the East End of London where I had done the rounds of some of the many pawnbrokers' shops that were a feature of that part.

After much hard haggling, I had exchanged my cash for second-hand gold. I had only chosen items that were heavy for their size and that had really good hallmarks. I think I had about twenty pairs of cufflinks, a similar number of signet rings and a collection of sovereigns and half-sovereigns.

In Aden, I sold three pairs of cufflinks to a very dubious looking chap for about twice what they had cost me in London.

In Bombay, I sold the rest of the cufflinks for about three times their cost price and cursed the man in Aden for a thief. I resolved to sell no more until I arrived in Singapore.

I had the mildest of shipboard flirtations with the only girl of nearly my own age on the passenger list, brushed up on my Malay and got steadily more brown. Above all, I think I relaxed for the first time since I had last been on a ship.

Somehow, ever since that realisation I have always fled, at least to the edges of the sea, when I have felt the need to take time off to take stock of life.

How anyone kept track of the loading and unloading of 'Timor Star' I will never know. Bicycle tyres came and sunflower seed went. Medical stores seemed to be loaded alongside a small shunting engine. Machinery which appeared to comprise an entire cotton spinning mill, changed places with vast quantities of jute sacks. I didn't envy the First Mate, who was forever checking and rechecking the manifest. He told me that I hadn't seen anything yet.

I needed to see what was loaded for the return trip before I could get the real flavour of cargo shipping.

In the fullness of time we arrived in Singapore and as I stepped ashore I will admit to feeling surprisingly more 'at home' than I had felt since I had left after my National Service, some two and a half years before.

Mindful of watching my resources and being able to speak the language I booked into a Chinese run hotel. It also felt very 'comfortable'.

It was a feeling which persisted through the many years I was to spend in the East. The big hotels, the fashionable restaurants, the clubs. They were all full of the same types of people, mainly Europeans, indeed mainly British. Arrogant and ignorant of the country they were in and, for the main part, determined to remain so.

Sometimes, when I did meet them I would wonder if they too were 'running away'. So very few, that I ever met, seemed to be there because they wanted to be there. The vast majority spent all their time complaining.

They complained about the climate, about 'the locals' about the fact that they couldn't get whatever it was that they "Used to have at home." What they really meant was that they were no longer 'at home' wherever that might have been.

I always suspected that, like myself, they had failed for one reason or another in their own country and had decided that making an adequate living abroad would be easier, mainly on the premise that 'They were bound to be superior to the natives'.

For the most part, it looked as if they certainly enjoyed a higher standard of living in the east than they might have expected in Europe. A lot of them would have been hard-pressed to hold down a decent job where the competition was greater.

I suspect that I had an extreme view for there was a stratum of excellent, hard-working people amongst the Europeans but by and large, they were not the type that spent most of their time complaining. Likewise, I myself had 'run away' but at least I was there because I felt at home there.

# CHAPTER 6

Tommy Black had given me the name and address of the firm of local lawyers who had acted for my parents before the war and who had had dealings with the Estate sale after it.

I went to see them.

I think that before the war all the partners would certainly have been British but now they were, by this time, about half and half, Europeans and Asiatics. Firstly I met the senior partner, a chap called Henry Poole. He was cordial and told me that he had met my Father before the war. After the usual opening gambits and his promise that his firm would do all that they could to help me, he handed me onto a middle-aged Chinese Malay called Mr Shak Lin.

I took to him at once. He was Malay born of mixed parents and had qualified in the U.K. before the war. Indeed it turned out that he had been stuck there at the outbreak of the war and had eventually become an announcer for the B.B.C's World Service. His English was, if anything, better than mine. However, he didn't think so. That's where we got on so well. He had, what almost amounted to an obsession, to speak perfect English, whatever that might be. I, on the other hand, was very keen to learn to speak decent Malay and Mandarin Chinese.

Virtually ever since that first meeting, I have spoken to him in Malay and he has spoken to me in English. It has become something of a game and we have been enjoying it for a very long time now.

Whilst the process of claiming the money from the sale of Father's Estate didn't seem to be very difficult it soon became evident that the wheels of the law ground even more slowly in Singapore than it did in London and that the affair would take much longer than I had expected.

\*\*\*

Lewis, Lewis, Lewis and Farr, in the person of Tommy Black, had supplied all the documentary evidence I needed from the U.K., mainly in the form of various birth and death certificates and certified copies of sundry wills and Grants of Probate.

Shak Lin provided all the local evidence in the form of documentation of Father's purchase of the Estate and evidence of his death at the hands of the Japanese.

When I appreciated that I would have to wait months rather than the few weeks I had expected and in order to make my money last as long as possible, I moved from the hotel where I had been staying into a boarding house owned by a delightful, elderly man called Mr Wing.

The old boy was a bit diffident at first about renting a room to a westerner but I think that he took comfort from the fact that since I spoke Malay tolerably well, I knew what I was about.

I suspect that Shak Lin must also have had a word with him so that after a bit of a delay he agreed to my moving in.

The place was comfortable, if a touch noisy. It was very clean and about a fifth of the price I would have to have paid had I rented rooms in a Europeans-only house. All the others in Mr Wing's place were Asiatic and they were polite to a fault. Rather better behaved and hard working, I suspect, than the majority of my fellow Europeans would have been.

Again I felt very 'at home' there and my language skills improved by leaps and bounds.

Those Englishmen I did come across viewed the whole thing with grave doubts. "Going native" was an expression I caught more than once. I didn't care at all. I was happy and solvent.

To keep that way I took a temporary job.

Dear old Colonel King had been right in his assumption that virtually all the civil engineering firms in Singapore at that time, were under the hand of British ex-Royal Engineers. My having belonged to the 'clan' was enough to get me onto the bottom rung of the ladder.

Had I been an artilleryman or, worse still, a cavalryman during my national service, it wouldn't have helped at all. Those sorts of skills have a very limited demand in civilian life. As it was, I got the job of a sort of glorified site foreman rebuilding a jetty in the outer harbour.

Six months to the day since I landed, I banked the Government cheque in settlement of my claim to the Estate. I was by no means rich but I was in a position to take my time to look around to see exactly what it was that I wanted to do in the long term. Meantime the jetty had become something of a challenge and I decided to see it through before I worried about the future.

I have always been glad that I stuck with wretched jetty. It's still there and doing a useful job. I admit to going and passing a 'proprietorial eye' over it whenever I am in that part of the docks.

I was tempted to stick with civil engineering. There was masses of work available and, although there were plenty of applicants for the jobs on offer, I had the priceless advantage of the language and knowing quite a bit about the country plus understanding the mentality of the Malays.

My boss, one Major Frank Stewart, R.E. (Retired) did offer me another job after the jetty was finished. It was helping to repair or, more accurately, to rebuild the railway branch line from Kuala Lumpur to Port Swettenham. The added attraction was the promise of a permanent job with the company if it went as well as the jetty had done.

I was still undecided so Stewart said. "Do the initial survey and see how you feel then."

I agreed.

As it turned out I was glad I had only agreed to do that much. There was some pretty lousy country along the line in those days. Since then most of the land has been cleared and drained but back then what wasn't very heavy jungle was some of the worst swamp land I have ever seen. It seemed to me that if it slithered or crawled and it stung or bit, it lived along the length of that wretched railway line.

I had had my fair share of slogging waist deep in swamps and leeches doing my National Service and I didn't fancy another couple of years of the same. Besides which, I wanted to start and build a business of my own. I had been three-quarters happy working with Tony Miller. We had started from nothing and had just about made it work but at the end of the day, it would never have been mine. I suppose it might just have been 'ours' but never mine. That's what I was after. I wasn't going to achieve that stuck in a stinking swamp.

I finished the survey and went back to Singapore where I spent three or four weeks in the firm's offices writing up the results from a very soggy set of field notebooks and getting the draughtsmen to convert my rough sketches into working drawings so that a quantity surveyor could get too work and get the job costed

It took much the same time for all the lumps and bumps and the wounds and ulcers to clear up.

I couldn't persuade Frank Stewart that my estimates for the general labour costs were not about three times too high. In the end, I suggested, in pretty forceful terms, that he went and "Had a bloody good look for himself".

He spent three days there and came back and agreed my estimates without any more argument. I think that in the event, even my figures turned out to be hopelessly low. It was certainly a rotten place to work.

Then I had a letter from Tommy Black in London. It started with the usual pleasantries and a few bits of news but the meat of the letter ran thus:-

*Now that our Mr Gummer has retired, I have taken on all his Far East clients. As you know we act in the U.K. for a number of firms in both Singapore and Hong Kong and recently I have been handling some work for a company called Angus Findlay & Co who are general merchants of North Dock Street in Singapore.*

*The company was started by Mr Angus Findlay just after the First World War and although they ceased to trade during the Japanese occupation they started up again as soon as Singapore was liberated. I understand that he operates more or less as a one-man band but his reputation is very sound.*

*He seems to trade in virtually anything, both importing and exporting. Although I have never met him, those who have speak very highly of him and say that he is a very kind, polite and above all, a very wise gentleman.*

*If you are still looking for an opening I think that you might do worse than go and see him and seek his advice. I am sure he would help if he could.*

*I have taken the liberty of mentioning your name in my last letter to him.*

It was decent of Black to take the trouble and since I had nothing to lose, I wrote to Findlay that afternoon. I explained something of my circumstances and my ambitions; it was only fair to tell him something of myself in advance of a meeting if he was too offer any advice that might be of value.

Very promptly I received a note in reply, by hand, asking me to call and see him the following Monday afternoon if that was convenient. I shot off a reply saying I would be very glad to meet him as he had suggested.

It was a decision which was to change my life radically and one which I have never regretted for a single moment.

***

The premises of Angus Findlay & Co was a large, solidly built warehouse, facing directly onto the wharf side at the front. North Dock Street ran along the back of the building where a series of double doors gave access for the easy transfer of goods into and out of the building.

Remember that this was all some thirty odd years ago and the warehouse stood out as something large and solid in what otherwise was something of a rabbit warren of sheds and passageways in a very shabby part of the city. Had it not been for my ability to ask the way from the teaming mass of labourers I might well still be looking for it yet.

At one end of the building, an outside flight of iron stairs led to a second floor. A notice on the wall proclaimed 'Angus Findlay & Company. General Traders'. An arrow pointed skywards.

I went up and at the top, through a heavy timer door which opened onto a surpassingly large and airy general office where about eight clerks were busy behind high Victorian style desks.

An elderly Chinese clerk bobbed up from behind a tall reception desk and asked if he could help.

"I have an appointment with Mr Angus Findlay."

He bobbed down again for a moment.

"You are Mr Forest?"

I agreed that I was.

"Mr Findlay is in his rooms at this time; I will get a servant to show you. Sit please."

I sat. It was hardly worth it, for within what seemed like a few seconds the servant appeared. He was, even for those times, like a figure from the past. He was Chinese and looked very old but it was his dress which arrested my attention. It was straight out of an eighteenth-century print. A long, green silk coat, with elaborate embroidery, black silk trousers, a skull cap, forked beard and a pigtail.

He beckoned me to follow him through another heavily made teak door at the far side of the office. This door opened into a long dark passage with a gleaming wooden floor. At the far end a second, similar door opened onto a large, much brighter square hall. My guide opened a door to the right and beckoned me through. To my surprise, as I passed, he bowed. I managed a half bob of my head in reply.

Angus Findlay obviously ran a very traditional ship.

The room I walked into was a complete surprise. The whole of the far wall was taken up with a huge window which looked out over the harbour. The brightness of it made me blink after the darkness of the passage and the relative gloom of the hall. The furniture was what I think you would call 'Oriental Victorian' but lighter and more colourful than that might indicate. The curtains and the carpets positively glowed with rich reds and golds.

Angus Findlay stood up as I went in, rising from a huge desk directly under the window. He stretched out his hand and said, "Mr Forest. I am glad that you could come."

His voice was deep and there was no mistaking the brogue. God knows how many years in the East hadn't robbed him of that. We shook hands and then studied each other for a few seconds, strangely I had the feeling that there wasn't a trace of embarrassment on either side.

Findlay's age was difficult to judge. From my mental calculations I guessed that he couldn't be much less than seventy but somehow he seemed younger. A full head of heavy, wavy, gleaming white hair and a neat, trimmed beard contrasted sharply with the skin of his face which was tanned to what I could best describe as a dark shade of yellow ochre.

It was a skin colour which you might imagine as typical of an elderly man who had long lived in the tropics - but seldom came across in real life.

He was tall; I guessed somewhere about six foot two and possibly a touch overweight. He wore a cream linen suit of a rather old-fashioned cut and a tie whose colours spoke of being the badge of some organisation; a school or a club perhaps.

His eyes were arresting. Very bright blue, set in sockets that were heavily creased at the corners and decorated with some of the most luxuriant eyebrows I can ever remember seeing. "Please, sit down." He waved a large hand in the direction of a heavily carved chair of apparent antiquity. I sat. It was, rather to my surprise, very comfortable.

He picked up two letters from the desk and studied them in turn for a few moments. Despite the fact that I knew he must be over seventy he had the mannerisms of a younger man, the way he looked at the letters and the way he turned to face me.

"So you're Captain Forest's son?" He smiled.

I agreed that I was, "Did you know my father Sir?"

"Indeed I did, we did quite a bit of business together between the wars. What is more, since I understand you were his only son, you and I must have met before!"

Perhaps I looked puzzled, "I don't remember.....".

"Since you were in your perambulator at the time, I doubt that you do."

The way he said the word 'perambulator', rolling it off his tongue, almost savouring it, gave him away. I placed him from well north of Edinburgh.

"I was visiting your Father, buying his latex in fact and your Mother very kindly gave me tea." He reflected for a moment. "I'm afraid it's a world that's gone forever - all such a tragic waste." He smiled again, "No good dwelling in the past though. Never does any good."

He gazed out of the window with its view of the bustling harbour for a few moments and them turning to me again he said. "To business though. I understand you want some advice?"

I started to explain about wanting to make a life and a career in the East. He said little apart from the odd encouragement to amplify my thinking of 'How' or 'Why'?

Thus he coaxed me into telling him the thick end of my life's story. I suppose the turning point came when he asked, "Why choose Singapore?"

"Mainly because I speak the language but, above all, I feel comfortable here, somehow I feel at home."

His eyes positively lit up, "That's the main thing Laddie; that's just what I wanted to hear you say."

He went on to go through his reasoning why that attitude was so important. The more he expanded on his thinking the more I found that I agreed with what he was saying.

"People coming out here thinking that it's easier to make a go of it than it would be in the at home - that's nonsense. Ignorance and a dislike of your surroundings is a handicap that only makes life harder and, believe me, it's hard enough without adding to the difficulties. But if you can understand the minds of the people you trade with you have a priceless advantage."

I didn't think I needed to reply.

He was interrupted by a faint knock at the door. He called "Come in." and the servant who had shown me in brought in a tea tray.

We sipped our tea and he continued to probe with his questions. As the light faded and the lights came on across the harbour he made the suggestion that I should leave the matter with him and that I should come and visit him again in a week's time.

"I need time to think over all that you've told me, if my advice is to be worth anything to you."

I suppose that some disappointment must have shown.

"You're talking about a new life Laddie; best make sure that you get it right."

His logic was flawless. We fixed a time.

***

One week later I was back in that same room but with almost a different man. Gone was the slightly rambling idealist. Here was Angus Findlay the Trader.

"The first thing you need to do is to learn. You haven't got a great deal of capital so I suggest that you invest it in something safe for the moment and then spend all your time looking, listening and above all, learning.

If you set up now - on your own - as an independent, you will lose your capital within six months. Learn to think like a trader, learn to tell the difference between the good and the second rate. Learn who to trust and who not to trust."

I agreed that all this was sensible but it didn't tell me how.

Angus Findlay gave me a pretty steely look. "I'll make you an offer laddie."

"Come and stay here and work for me...." I started to disclaim that I had come with any such intention.

"Hear me out; it's not all good news." I kept silent.

He repeated himself, "Come and stay here, there's plenty of room, Lee Yew can look after you, he's hardly enough to do just now. You can pay something for your keep if you insist but I won't worry about it."

I started to protest but he waved me to silence.

"Work for me and I'll teach you; I'll pay you what I pay a clerk, which isn't a lot. Give it six months and we will talk again with no promises on either side."

I thought for a little while whilst Angus seemed to inspect the harbour with more than usual interest. It was an offer I would be a fool to refuse. I agreed. Angus rang a little bell and Lee Yew brought in a tray of drinks, ready prepared. The old boy had been pretty sure of his ground.

I moved in with my kit two days later and started work at dawn the next morning.

If I thought I was going to be some sort of trader straight away, I was wrong. I was given into the charge of 'The Goods Inwards' clerk Li Wan. He was a middle-aged man of seemingly indefatigable energy and no English whatsoever.

I spent the next six weeks checking goods coming into the warehouse and entering figures into one of the massive ledgers in the office. The main thing was that not only did Li Wan and I check for quantity but he checked for quality and trickery. I learnt something of the ways of trade.

The difference between good and poor latex. The virtues of Javanese versus Cambodian rice. The differences between good and second-rate teak. Not much I grant you but I did start to get something of the flavour of the general business. At least enough to whet my appetite to learn more.

After six weeks of Li Wan I moved to the office of the Import Clerk. No one had any greater title than Clerk, even though in reality these men were the managers of their own departments.

I raised the question one evening with Angus. "Call them Manager and they will want paying as one." was a somewhat brusque reply. I did take the trouble, however, to find out how their wages compared with other similar local employees. It was evident that Angus paid for and got good men whom he could trust. All important in a world where graft and corruption were rather more the norm than the exception.

We soon fell into a routine so far as domestic life was concerned. Socially, Angus and I had virtually no contact during the day. Of course, he was around most of the time talking to the clerks and constantly checking on pretty well everything. He had an almost infallible sixth sense which could detect when anything wasn't just as it should be. It was all strictly business.

The evenings were however different.

Our domestic arrangements were fairly simple but of excellent quality. There were three servants. Lee Yew combined the duties of a butler, waiter, valet and general housekeeper. A cook, who hardly ever appeared did the marketing and managed to produce excellent meals, all in the Chinese manner with the single exception of rice pudding, of which Angus was exceptionally fond.

He liked his rice pudding virtually solid whereas I liked mine very milky. 'Bairns pap' as Angus called it. Thus, the cook always made two individual ones on the frequent occasions when it figured on the menu.

There was a middle-aged Malay lady, My Lee, who did most of the cleaning and the laundry. When asked, she also did the little sewing we needed. None of them ever seemed to take time off but they did their jobs very well indeed. If my contribution to the housekeeping bill was anything to go by they also did it very cheaply.

We worked a long day, starting at six o'clock in the morning and, apart from a short break at midday, going on until six in the evening unless we were very busy when we worked later. After work, I had tea in a little dressing room alongside my bedroom and then had a bath and changed into clean clothes for dinner.

At seven thirty I would go to the big sitting room for a glass of sherry with Angus and talk about the day's work. We ate at seven forty-five on the dot and the rule was no more talk of current business but Angus would talk of the past and the way he saw the future. Not bad for a man of his age.

After dinner, we would talk or perhaps play a game or two of chess. He was a much better player than I, but I suspect he put up with my standard just in order to get some sort of game. Almost invariably we would have a largish measure of Dalwhinnie single malt and go to bed fairly early.

It was a life of hectic activity by day and modest relaxation in the evenings. It was a way of life I enjoyed. In those days almost all our business was carried on by letter, typewritten on an ancient Underwood machine by the junior clerk. Only infrequently did we resort to the telephone.

Angus used to spend quite a lot of his time going to see suppliers or customers, sometimes staying away for a night or two. On those occasions the Chief clerk, Mr Li was in charge but as time went on he developed the habit of seeking my opinion if some difficulty arose. I confess that I usually fell in with his suggestions. Thus we went on. As promised Angus reviewed the situation after six months and we agreed to a further six under slightly improved terms.

After a year we settled on a further year but at a higher salary for myself and an obligatory two weeks annual holiday. Angus said that I should get 'out and about' otherwise I would end up a bachelor like himself. I took that first holiday in Penang and came back with a contract to supply the Georgetown Police Authority with thirty bicycles. It seemed to give Angus a great deal of pleasure.

It began to be a comfortable life with security and predictability and it began to worry me. It was one Sunday afternoon when that comfortable world, so much in the manner of the past, came crashing down around my head.

***

It was Angus's ritual that he would stay in bed late on a Sunday. That in itself was a relative expression because his idea of 'late' was half past seven. This was followed by breakfast and then the Presbyterian Church in Connaught Road.

Angus was not only a regular attendee but, I learnt afterwards, one of its chief benefactors. The church was for him and a good many others of the large Scottish community in Singapore, not only an obligation but a convenient meeting place where they could talk about 'home' and I suspect, exchange the gossip which to an extent is the lifeblood of trade. It has never ceased to surprise me how many of the traders that I have met in the Far East have been of Scottish descent. They formed a very effective 'Hibernian old boys' network'.

Sunday lunchtime had become an almost invariable ritual.

Angus and three or four of his cronies would gather in 'Rothney's Restaurant', a mock Tudor establishment near the church in Connaught Road, for a traditional Sunday Lunch. God knows why anyone would want to eat roast beef and all the trimmings in that heat but, for some reason, it was their treat of the week.

I had a standing invitation to go and I did so on two or three occasions but it wasn't really for me. I have always preferred to stick to the local food which seems to fit the climate so much better than European cooking. Besides which, not being a Scot, I felt a bit out of it anyhow.

I had recently bought an old Morris Ten car, a convertible and had got into the routine of spending Sundays doing a bit of sightseeing.

That particular Sunday I had been across the causeway into Jahore to look at a temple near Bahru. I had stayed rather longer than I had planned and didn't get back to North Dock Street until just after seven. The place was in turmoil.

It took some time to sort out the story but the gist of it was that Angus had got back from his lunch at just after three o'clock and had gone to his room to take a nap. Lee Yew had taken him a cup of tea at just before a quarter to five only to find that he had died in his sleep.

The local Doctor had been called, a fellow Scot and he had confirmed what everyone already knew, that Angus had had a massive, instantly fatal heart attack.

The impact of his death on his staff and his friends was traumatic.

Common sense dictates that none of us is immortal but there are a few people whom we consider might well be. We have great difficulty imagining life without them. Angus fell into that group. Remember, this was an age when what we now could call 'colonial influence' was becoming more and more resented around the world and the record of a percentage of Europeans wasn't all that it might have been. No one I ever met put Angus into that category.

What is even more remarkable is that what we now think of as 'racial prejudice' never seemed to enter his head. He was always equally scathing about Europeans who failed to do their job properly as he would be about an Asiatic. I have heard him berate an English banker who tried to pull a fast one in exactly the same terms as he would the skipper of a trading junk who tried to deliver a short cargo. On balance I think he did it better in English though!

From rubber planter to tin miner, from rice farmer to civil servant, a very fair cross section had dealings with Angus Findlay & Co. and I never heard one who complained about the way they were treated. Complain about the prices asked or given, of course they did - for that's the very nature of that sort of trade - and Angus was a trader to his fingertips. Complaints about his honesty or his treatment of his business associates or his employees were unknown.

For my own part, his death was a very considerable blow. Not only had he given me a home and a job but he had encouraged me at a time when I needed it most. He had not only been kind and considerate but he had been a teacher who was not above telling you of your faults, occasionally in pretty colourful terms. By the same token, he had handed out praise when earned.

Once more I was a sad man.

Of course, in the two and a half years I had been with Angus not only had I learnt something of the job of a trader but I had gained some confidence in my own judgement.

Angus was not the type of man to mollycoddle his pupil.

"Never mind what I think, what the blue blazes do you think?" He would thunder.

"Laddie, can you see a profit worth the work involved in doing the deal?"

There were times when I would reply, "I think so."

"Then don't bother doing it. Wait until you are quite sure you *know* so and then go in with both feet."

Not, of course, that you really ever knew for certain, it depended on the deal. Take rice, for example; high weight and volume but comparatively low value. The deal was virtually certain to make money but not very much.

Others like timber were much riskier; however, if all went well the profits could be considerable. The fates that can befall a consignment of teak between its felling in north Burma and its eventual loading into a freighter in Rangoon harbour are legion. For a start, it could be re-sold several times to dealers trying to make up larger lots. They, in turn, could re-grade part of a consignment if they weren't interested in poorer quality timber. With a single log worth several years wages to a forest worker theft was always a possibility. The risks were there all right but so was the profit if you could get it all right.

Angus's tuition and his guidance helped me to avoid a lot of mistakes but I still made plenty.

"Never mind Laddie, the trick is not to make the same one twice. That's another bottle of Malt you owe me!"

I tried very hard not to lose too many bottles.

***

A very few hours after Angus's death, I was in the thick of it. The Chief Clerk, Mr Li, always called by his formal title, wanted to know what to do. His certainty seemed to have deserted him along with several of the others. I resorted to the old army maxim when you didn't know what to do next.

"Carry on as normal Mr Li. Carry on as normal, as if nothing had changed."

He didn't look very convinced but took the cue.

I also arranged to send messages to all our principle clients telling them formally of Angus's death and of the funeral arrangements. Also, working on the principle that if you don't tell your associates the truth they will invent their own version, I put a covering note in saying that business would, for the time being, continue as normal and that all contracts would be fulfilled.

I was a bit unsure as to the last bit, in that I doubt that I had the authority but there was no point in going off 'at half cock' and it seemed to me that the preservation of our clients' confidence in the firm had an overriding priority.

I sent a long cable to Commander Tommy Black explaining the circumstances and asking him to get in contact with the people who acted for Angus's family, such as it was.

I made urgent appointments with the company's local solicitors, our Bank Manager and our accountants.

I was lucky with the local Bank Manager, in that he was one of Angus's Scots cronies and we had met several times already.

After a hectic round of meetings with all and sundry, we came to a 'stop-gap' arrangement. We agreed, or rather, the Bank agreed, to freeze the company's accounts but to allow a 'float' that I could use to continue the day to day business, until such time as we could obtain further agreements, or instructions, from the executors of Angus's Estate.

For the next week or so we carried on on this very sketchy basis. Mr Li, looking after the routine work, which normally he did very efficiently anyhow, and me sanctioning new deals as they came along. I admit to turning several down that under normal circumstances I would have accepted but at this stage, I wasn't going to stick my neck out further than was very prudent.

There was one deal that sticks out in my memory from that 'twilight' period and it concerned one Archie Ruston, the owner of a palm nut plantation up near Butterworth. We had dealt with him in the past and he hadn't been very reliable. As I recall it now, he had agreed to sell us a hefty consignment of palm nut oil at a fixed price per ton. We had sold it on forward, to a soap manufacturer in the U.K. In the event, he only delivered about half to the dockside at Port Wing near Taiping. In order to fulfil the contract with the buyer, Angus had bought in the balance at a higher price, from another supplier. We hadn't lost on the deal but we didn't make anything for our trouble either.

Archie Ruston was very put out when I told him that I didn't want to handle his current harvest as he had let us down the previous season. He got pretty rude about my refusal. In the end, somewhat against my better judgement, I agreed but on the condition that if he didn't supply the correct amount, the price we paid for his crop would reflect any shortfall.

It was this deal, I think, that got me the reputation of being a hell of a lot tougher to deal with than Angus. In the event, I don't think it was any bad thing. At least it scared off those sharks who thought that they could take us for a ride now that Angus wasn't at the helm.

A cable arrived from the Commander in London. It was, as I read it, fairly reassuring.


*'Your present action most sensible -- suggest you keep on as normal -- local agreement with bank agreed by us and London Bankers. Same message put out at your end being circulated to suppliers and customers this end. Have been in contact with next of kin & their advisors -- awaiting further instructions. Will advise soonest. You are now very much in deep end -- good luck, Black.'*

I had been so busy with the firm that I had hardly had time to think of Angus's family but it was pretty plain that our fate would rest with them in the end. As far as I knew, he had only got two living relatives. They were elderly, spinster cousins who lived somewhere near Aberdeen. I couldn't see them being very much interested in keeping the business going.

Looking dispassionately, I suppose that the firm was, even by the standards of those times, fairly old-fashioned. For a start, we were both exporters and importers whilst most others had begun to specialise. We dealt with a wide diversity of different commodities whereas, again, most of our competitors had narrowed their interests down to, perhaps, tin or rubber or timber.

We were small, very small by comparison with the major houses but we had two assets which many other firms would have given their eye teeth for, our reputation and the minuscule costs of our overheads. Angus and I had been the only Europeans on the payroll. All our other staff had been Asiatic and while they had been paid well by local standards they still cost a fraction of European wages.

We lived over the shop as it were and had not only no lavish offices to upkeep but there were no other shareholders wanting a dividend at the end of the year.

As Angus pointed out more than once, "I would rather be my own master, laddie." A view I still aspired too.

There is a great deal to be said for a small company making a decent profit rather than a socking great big one, with hundreds of employees and shareholders and a massive turnover and yet barely breaking even. Apart from anything else you sleep easier at night.

Our main imports, at that time, were the better brands of malt whisky from Scotland - where else! Bicycles from both the U.K. and from India. Textile machinery from Yorkshire and Lancashire. A couple of makes of motor cars but these were in small numbers and in decline. The days of the small volume, specialist motorcar maker were even then ending, most of them falling to the giant companies.

To a large extent we had replaced that particular trade with reconditioned, American, war surplus Jeeps. Angus had located quite large numbers of these which had been stored in various places throughout south-east Asia after the end of the war. They had gradually been sold off at disposal sales. By buying in big lots he had been able to get them at knock-down prices and we employed an up and coming Chinese ship owner who owned a very second-hand, very gradually sinking, ex-American tank landing craft, to bring them to a place near Malacca where an enterprising Malay, who went under the engaging name of Lye Low Fook, had them stripped down and rebuilt. Despite his name, he did a good job and they were very well done. Somewhat like Mr Ford, you could have any colour you fancied, so long as it was jungle green.

Not only did we sell a lot in Malaya but quite a number found their way to Burma and Thailand and many other destinations. I wouldn't be surprised if a good number of them are still doing a useful job even today.

On the export side, the range was virtually endless: rice, copra, tin, raw rubber latex, palm oil, mainly what could be described as 'raw materials' but we did export almost worldwide.

On both sides of the business, the rule was if we could get it and someone wanted it, we will deal in it if there was a decent margin in it for us. I really couldn't see one of the large trade houses wanting to take us over. What I could see however was someone buying the company, selling off the parts they didn't want and then selling the principal asset, the warehouse site itself.

The site was leasehold true but crafty old Angus had taken a long lease which still had about forty years to run. What's more, when he had obtained the lease from the Colonial Government, he had been happy to pay a relatively high ground rent in return for the fact that the rent was fixed for the life of the lease. That now meant that the rent was absurdly low by present standards and certain to become even more attractive as time passed.

The next development was a long and detailed letter from Tommy Black in London. The news was, from both my own and the firm's standpoint, good.

The ladies in Scotland, understandably, had no wish to have any part in the running of the enterprise, as might have been expected. However, neither did they wish to do anything that might cause it to cease to trade. Reading between the lines they wished it to continue, under the same name, in some way as a lasting memorial to

Angus. They were, it seemed, financially quite well off but, not surprisingly, they wanted some reasonable income from their inheritance. With guidance from their own man and, I suspect, from Black no doubt, they had come up with a proposal in the form of a question.

"Would I like to purchase the business as a going concern at a fixed price over a period of five years?"

The price suggested was, by my reckoning, fair but by no means a gift. My own capital which Angus had urged me to invest had done well but at best it would only really suffice as a basis upon which to try and persuade the local bank to allow an overdraft for working capital. Money for the purchase price would have to come from profits and to do that over a five year period would take some doing and a lot of careful management, not to say a fair slice of luck into the bargain.

I embarked yet again on a long series of meetings, not only with my chief clerk, Mr Li, who did all the day to day bookkeeping but with the bank and both my own and the firm's solicitors and, of course, the accountants. The latter was a mainly European-run firm and to my mind, was less than totally on my side.

It was the old story again. 'Can you really expect to run a successful firm with just yourself as the only European?' I told them, "Yes! You run your business your way and I'll run this one mine."

After a long string of meetings and a good number of letters to and from the U.K., I managed to extend the term of the purchase from five to seven years. I had wanted ten but they drew the line very firmly at seven on account of the age of the legatees.

One afternoon, I was sitting at Angus's desk under the window, gazing out over the harbour, trying to come to a final decision.

Did I want it enough to risk everything I had?

The answer had to be 'Yes'. Here was the chance which I had craved. To prove to anyone who was interested but above all to myself, that I could make a real 'go' of something.

Did I think that I could make it, not only work but work well enough to be able to fulfil the contract? I was pretty sure that I could.

Did I think that I would enjoy doing it? If I could make it work then I thought that it would be the most satisfying thing I could possibly do. Above all, it would be my own 'show'.

The conversations I had had with Angus came into my mind. I could hear him saying, "Wait until you know so and then go in with both feet Laddie."

I reached out and put my initials at the bottom of the draft contract which I had been studying. I went to the door and called for the junior clerk and sent him off to the solicitors with that paper which would determine how the rest of my life would turn out.

A few moments later a knock at the door heralded the arrival of Mr Li. He did something he had never done before. Without a word, he came across and shook my hand.

At first, we went on much as before. It was that solid trade which, after all, paid everyone's wages, including mine. However, I had this constant niggle at the back of my mind that we needed to change to a degree in order to have a fair chance of meeting my obligations.

It seemed to me that a quick trip back to London was unavoidable. If the plans I wanted to put in train were ever to get off the ground I would have to sort out a whole mass of detail and by letter and cable that would take forever. No! London it would have to be and I certainly couldn't afford the time to go by boat.

Extraordinarily, I seem to remember that in those days it took five or six days to fly from Singapore to London. Flying by day and stopping over at night. Sounds silly now of course but in those days it was a pretty daring exercise.

I've forgotten the detail now but I remember a night in Calcutta and then flying right across India to Dum Dum near Karachi, Habbaniya in Iraq and then the long haul over the Mediterranean to Rome. Then the final leg from Rome to London. Besides the overnight stops, we seemed to be forever putting down to refuel at various places along the route.

I spent the best part of five days in London, the bulk of it with Black in his office. At the end of the third day, I was feeling pretty jaded. The flight had been something of a trial. Remember that then, the aircraft were unpressurised and powered by very noisy piston engines.

Black suggested that I take the following morning off whilst he had all the paperwork sorted out and we would have another go the following afternoon and evening. I took up his suggestion and also the kind offer of the loan of a car.

I went to see Tony Miller.

What we called 'the factory' (in reality a rather tired old shed), had gone. In its place a modern, airy, purpose-built factory designed for the job. He was still in the recycled paper business, mainly making egg boxes but other applications of the same principle as well. It was, however, the plastics side which had really taken made the difference.

Tony Miller had made four visits to the States over the last three years and each one had been fruitful. The Polythene side was at last showing real growth. He imported sheet from the manufacturer in the form of massive rolls and had built a machine which converted a great deal of it into polythene bags. These he seemed to be selling in huge numbers to a disparate variety of users. A great many seemed to go to the food retail trade.

Being Tony, he had already decided that the job would only be short-term in that he thought that the American suppliers would soon open a factory producing basic sheet in the U.K. and other firms would start up in opposition to himself. He had decided to get out of converting sheet into bags himself but concentrate on building and selling the machines to make the bags. He was also in the middle of developing a machine to make gloves out of the sheeting as a cheap alternative to rubber gloves which were very expensive and difficult to get at that time.

"I think the way to go is not to make things yourself but make the machines and sell them to other people to make them."

I suggested that there must be a limited market for such machines. He gazed out of the window for a moment and then looked at me and smiled.

"By the time we have sold as many as the market can stand, I will have come up with a new machine that will do the job better."

After another moment he went on "There are going to be whole new types of plastics which will do things we have never thought of up to now. We will be able to make machines to convert them into all sorts of things."

I gave some sort of reply - I forget what it was now but perhaps I seemed sceptical.

"Don't you worry about it Robin, your Uncle Tony has a hundred ideas fermenting away and all of them will need specialist machines."

I think it was the gleam in his eyes and the way that he said it persuaded me that he was right.

The upshot of my visit was that I left with an informal agreement that if I could find customers in the Far East who needed such machines then I would handle their sale.

\*\*\*

After I left Tony, I called to see 'Aunt' Daisy. I had had word about a year or so before that 'Uncle' George had died. He was mending someone's roof and he either had a stroke and fell off or had fallen off and then had a stroke. No one seemed quite sure which but the upshot was the same. Daisy was pretty well lost without him and had moved into a small flat quite close to where they had lived. "Near me friends and handy for the shops, dear. Not that I've got many friends these days, they've mostly died orf now."

I thought of her and George much as I did of Tony Miller and Angus Findlay, kind people who gave help more or less without question and asked only loyalty in return. Not a bad principle really.

I went to visit both my mother's and Helen's graves.

I told my mother what I had found out about Father's death and I told Helen what I was trying to do with my life. In the cold light of memory, that sounds rather sad but it made me feel more contented. I also felt ready to go back to face the task I had set myself.

I finished my work with Black by dint of our both working some very long hours. I went back to what I now regarded as home with the contract for my buying Angus Findlay & Co. all signed and sealed, tucked in my briefcase. Once again, Black kindly came to what was then called London Airport, to see me off. By the time I was back in the warehouse in North Dock Street I was physically tired out but I had a head seething with ideas.

Whilst I had been away things had gone well. Most of it, fortunately, had been pretty routine and Mr Li had coped easily. There had been a couple of minor problems but he had overcome them well. I thought to myself that he had taken extra trouble, along with the rest of what was now, my staff, to ensure that things had gone smoothly in my absence. After we had finished going over the details of what he had done whilst I had been away I showed him the contract I had agreed with Angus Fraser's sisters and their solicitor.

Apart from the small matter of paying the instalments for the business, I was now the owner. Mr Li seemed pleased and assured me in his rather stilted and pedantic English that he and the others would "Have honour in serving you in the same manner in which we had served Mr Fraser." I thanked him and suggested that the first change I would be making was to promote him to the post of Manager.

One thing you get to learn about Asiatics is that they don't show emotion the way westerners do. It is rare that you catch them off their guard as it were. That day I caught old Li well off his.

He stared at me, saying nothing. Very gradually a tear formed in the corner of his eye and he was obviously not keen to wipe it away with me watching. I got up, turned around and looked at the view over the harbour. When I turned back he was again composed.

"That means that you had better decide which of the others should become Chief Clerk."

He protested that he could do it all himself.

"I don't think so. I'm going to have to spend quite some time going to see customers and suppliers and I will need someone to be in overall charge here. For the next few months we will do my job here together and you can get the feel of the task."

Mr Li agreed to do his very best.

After that, I took him completely into my confidence. We discussed every contract and every decision in depth. I explained the reasons for taking each deal, who was a good risk and who wasn't and why. We talked about the financial side and my need to make the progress payments on the purchase contract. Mr Li was never going to be an adventurous trader but he was sensible and very reliable and that's what I needed.

He also had a few suggestions of his own on the finance side. One of our constant problems was going to be a limiting shortage of working capital with which to finance deals. This was caused, to an extent, by late payments into our account from people we had supplied and a desire, on my part, to preserve our own reputation by paying our debts to our suppliers exactly on time.

Mr Li had two suggestions. The first was to introduce a discount for prompt payment to those who owed us money. This must sound less than revolutionary now but in those days it was a novel concept as a regular arrangement. Of course, you had to set the discount at a figure that was equal to, or better still, be a bit less than what we would have paid the bank in interest on our overdraft.

The second idea was slightly more novel. Many of our clients were trading with us both ways. By that I mean that a grower who sold us his cash crop, often spent a good deal of those proceeds back with us, later on, to purchase further supplies for his next crop.

Mr Li thought that a number of them could be persuaded to leave their credit balances with us if we paid them interest on their money. He pointed out that we could offer them a rate of interest which would be slightly better than they could get from the banks but less than we were paying the bank on our own borrowings.

I thought about this for some time before agreeing to try it with one or two of our long-standing customers and after explaining to them why we doing it. It worked well and within a couple of months, we had several other clients asking us why we hadn't made the same offer to them. Naturally, we were happy to oblige.

Much to my surprise, Mr Li didn't suggest the next senior clerk as his replacement as Chief Clerk but the next man below him. I asked why.

He explained that whilst the second man was very good at his job, which was in essence, the supervision of the arrival and despatch of consignments, he had not the ability to oversee the office in general, besides which he was quite old and would find the change difficult. The suggested man, Loo U Fin was forty-two, wanted to get on and if he was promoted would probably stay for a long time. I left both the decision and the implementation to Mr Li, He was pleased.

We got the new system running well and I started to feel happy about going away on trips to see customers and suppliers. A couple of days at a time at first but then three or four, sometimes a whole working week. When I did this I would come back on Friday evening or Saturday morning and Mr Li and I would spend the afternoon going over the previous week's activity and planning for the next week. He was always very good about telling me all that had gone on, warts and all.

One of the unexpected gains which came out of having Li as Manager was that he was better informed about the goings on in the quite close-knit trading community of Singapore than I, or perhaps old Angus, had ever realised.

Every community has its 'Old Boy Net' and ours was no exception. The vast majority of the clerks were Asiatic. They drew up the paperwork for the deals between the various trade houses and it was apparent that not a great deal went on which wasn't common knowledge between them.

In no way am I suggesting that they were disloyal to their respective employers but like all souls, I expect they gossiped in their own time just like the rest of us. The point was that I don't think that many of the old-time traders would have asked their opinion-or even thought that they might have one.

# CHAPTER 7

The appointment of Mr Li to the post of Manager led me into a spot of bother again. I had been a member of the European Club since just after I started to work for old Angus. He had suggested that I join. Indeed, he had proposed me. He didn't frequent it much himself, he was much more at ease in the church with his Scottish cronies but he suggested that I join. I think that he thought I might meet a 'suitable' girl there.

In truth, I never really seemed to feel comfortable with the people there - always talking about 'home' or 'the locals', two attitudes I disliked. My infrequent visits were usually to play snooker, a game which I enjoy and at which I rather fancy my skill. A hang over from my time in the army, I suppose.

However, one Saturday evening I was at a bit of a loose end and I suppose I was looking for a change so, quite early, I went along to the Club and found a chap I knew slightly who was willing to play a few frames. We decided that the winner of the best of three frames should pay for the drinks, a common enough bet in those days. I won the first frame and think I was in a fair way to winning the second when Calender, the chap I was playing with asked, "How are you getting on with your new Chink manager?"

I suppose I overreacted but the remark annoyed me, "Mr Li is settling in very well, better than I had expected really but I would be grateful if you didn't refer to him as a Chink if you don't mind." I suppose I was a bit stuffy about it and he came back, "Keep your shirt on old boy, I only asked because everyone is talking about it - pretty unusual to give the job to a local, you must admit."

I was just lining up to pot a longish black so I concentrated on the shot and made it. I don't know if it was anger or the satisfaction at having made the shot but I hit out.

"Look, Li is a good man, years of experience, speaks the language and knows his way around far better than some idiot straight from England. If we want to stay out here and do business we should give better jobs to Asiatics. Everyone, as you put it, should think about that and then mind their own bloody business."

Perhaps I should have remembered that Calender had not been out from the U.K. long himself. He studiously chalked the tip of his cue. "I'm sorry if I spoke out of turn but it is true about everyone talking about it. At lunch today people were saying that it was typical, you live down on the waterfront, right amongst the locals and now you have a Chinese Manager."

"God, bloody bar gossip, I expect they will be saying next that I'm going native?"

Calender smiled, "Don't take offence old chap but I think they have been saying that for a long time."

We finished the frame which I won. I made damn certain that he paid for the drinks!

*** 

The response I had from the Bank Manager could not have been more different.

As I have said he was an old pal of Angus', a Glaswegian and as solid as could be.

"I'll no deny that I have heard talk about your giving the manager's job to old Li but I think it's a shrewd move."

I let the word 'shrewd' go without comment. If he mistook my reticence to give the job to a European whom I wouldn't know a great deal about and probably couldn't afford, as 'shrewd' then who was I to argue.

"You will hear a lot of silly talk about 'giving jobs to locals' and 'undermining the system' but it's all nonsense. Malaya, with our help, has seen off the Japanese and the Communists and they haven't gone through all that just so we can stay here as their masters forever. Mark my words Forest, the harder we hold them back the faster they will be rid of us."

I did mark his advice, then and several times later. When he did retire his successor was indeed a Malay and he turned out to be the best Bank Manager I have ever dealt with.

The visits to clients proved to be successful. Gradually they started to trust me and my word. Angus was a hard act to follow but I made a point - some said an obsession - of doing what I said I would do and expecting the same in return. It certainly paid off in the long run.

We increased the imports of bicycles from India quite a bit and gave up on the English versions altogether; they were just too expensive and frequently late on delivery. That, in turn, led to many a long day in Delhi arguing and cajoling our supplier to keep to the specifications for quality but once we established that we were not prepared to mess about they, in response, stuck to their word.

I decided to get out of cars altogether. I know Angus had made it work well in the years before the war but things had changed both out here and in England. The British industry seemed to have an attitude that they had a God-given right to overseas markets but weren't prepared to make sure that they delivered the right goods at the right price at the right time. I hadn't the energy or the inclination to try persuading them that they hadn't.

One good thing came out of my snooker playing, however. I went into a small joint venture with young Calender. I had met him several times since the 'Chinky' affair and one day he came down to the warehouse to see me to ask my advice. We sat and talked, very much as I had with Angus several years before. I encouraged him to tell me about himself.

Rather like me, he had done his National Service in Malaya in the Royal Army Service Corps. They were the people who provided the heavy transport for the Army in those days. He had gone back to England when his time was up and had got a job with, I think, Pickfords, whose major function was house removals. He had stuck it for a bit but he wasn't really happy and since he had few family ties had decided to come back to Malaya.

Calender had got a job working for the Singapore Omnibus Company and by all accounts had made a fair stab at it. He was however possessed by a devil. One that I knew all about. He wanted to start something himself and be his own boss. He had one other factor in his favour so far as I was concerned. He was learning Malay.

I grilled him about this pretty thoroughly and whilst he still had a lot to learn he was doing well. He seemed to have the same feeling about the country as I had myself. He felt 'comfortable' there. The idea he had was to import some sort of very light motorcycle that the Japanese were now making. Perhaps that doesn't sound very much of an idea now but then what thirty-something years ago, it was pretty daring.

Don't forget that the recent war was not that far back in peoples' minds and the Japanese had been savage in the extreme in their conquest of the Far East. They had treated the local Malay population very badly and anything Japanese was viewed with very considerable mistrust. Add to this that the machines themselves were quite primitive. Little more than a heavily built bicycle with a small two-stroke petrol engine bolted to the frame. They were also noisy and smelly. Their appeal, it seemed was that they relatively cheap to buy and very cheap to run.

The roads in Malaya at that time were really awful and outside of the bigger towns, there was virtually no public transport other than the railway and a very few trucks that carried people, if they had room, on top of their normal load.

Add to this, young Calender had very little money saved up. I told him to stick with the Omnibus Company, move into a Malay boarding house to conserve his money and improve his language and I would think about it.

I had myself been in touch with a Japanese export firm a few weeks before. We had had an enquiry about cultured pearls from a company in America who manufactured jewellery and I had made some tentative moves to see if we could do anything. Angus had dealt with both cultured pearls and mother of pearl before the war and it seemed possible.

In the event, via my Japanese contact, Akida San, I made a few enquiries about these motorcycles.

The upshot was that I purchased three machines and arranged for them to be shipped to our warehouse in Singapore. The day after they arrived I sent a message to Calender. The arrangement I offered was that if he sold them well and at a suitable margin, I would import another batch of twelve. He was to pay us the manufacturer's price, plus the transport, plus a smallish margin. In each case, we would extend sixty days credit.

I thought it a pretty generous deal. Much to my surprise Calender turned it down.

"I don't think that would work," he said frowning. "I would rather pay you a bigger margin and take ninety days credit."

I must have looked unhappy. He went on, "I need to do this properly, the three you have bought are fine but you haven't bought any spare parts with them. If I sell them and they break down not only will I have lost a sale but I will have lost goodwill."

I could see the logic in that.

In the end, he bought one machine with his own money and rode it all the time that he could whilst not doing his job with the bus company. I kept the other two in store and sent for a batch of spare parts which arrived about six weeks later. Calender sold the remaining two within days of the arrival of the spares and I sent off the order for a further twelve.

That's how it started and it went very well. Calender sold the batches of machines in specific areas and appointed a local agent who stocked spares and did simple repairs. Within twelve months he had agents in about ten of the bigger towns and had sold something like two hundred machines.

Six months ago, when I left Singapore, Calender had become the main importer of three makes of motor car and owned the biggest car and van hire company in the country. True, my company made a lot of money out of it as well, but I am proud of Calender and count him as one of my most valued friends.

***

The association with Tony Miller paid off in the long run as well. On a trip to Jakarta to see one of our raw materials suppliers, I met a man starting up in the plastics trade. After a lot of haggling, I sold him one of Tony's polythene bag converting machines. Within a few months, he came back for two more. Within a year we had sold fifteen to various people in the Philippines and another eight in Hong Kong. I suppose in the end we sold about two hundred of the original type. As Tony predicted, by the time they have absorbed their first ones they needed replacements which work faster and produce a wider range of goods. Miller now makes, and we sell, a machine which makes a polythene raincoat. The last time I was in England and went to see Tony's new factory, I could hardly believe it.

The second factory has now been replaced by a very modern plant which turns out machines for all the branches of the plastics business. He told me that he exports to over thirty countries besides the ones where we represent him.

So it went on for nearly twenty years. After about ten years Mr Li retired and I appointed the Chief Clerk again as Manager. Whilst we hadn't expanded our premises a great deal, the staff now occupied most of the old warehouse. The trend had changed from our actually handling the goods ourselves. Most of the stuff we rarely saw. We would get the import orders and the goods would be supplied directly to the buyer from the producer. It was the same with the raw materials we exported but that side of things had changed from the high tonnage, low value products, like rice and raw rubber latex to smaller quantities of higher value.

We had always done quite a bit of trade with Mother of Pearl since old Angus' time and a few semi-precious minerals for the costume jewellery trade back in the U.K. I had been asked by a London supplier to the trade, a man called David Canin, whom I met when he was on a buying trip to Singapore, to keep my eyes open on my travels and let him know of any likely contacts. I never liked to work like that, apart from anything else there would be little in it for my firm, so I told him that if he cared to tell me what to look for I would see what I could do.

I think he was a bit out of his depth, travelling in the East. He didn't speak the languages for a start and he was too heavy a man to stand the heat well. He showed me several samples of a mineral called Spinel, both in its rough form and some that had been cut and polished. I had never seen the stuff before, or if I had, I hadn't known it as such. Most of the best of it came from Burma, it seemed. Canin would buy it in its unpolished form and then send it to small firms in Birmingham, or sometimes Antwerp in Belgium for cutting and polishing.

Now I was no expert in such matters but I had a thought that it could be done a sight cheaper in Singapore. I asked if he had ever thought of having it done in the East but he said that he had always dealt that way so that he could be sure of getting his own material back from the cutters. "I'm never sure with these people; if they are honest."

Now I have never thought that the average European is any more or less honest than most of the people I dealt with in the East. Were you to see some of the strokes that big, reputable London firms, household names some of them, have tried to pull over me in my time I would very much doubt it. It was that old 'colonial' prejudice again. Overall, I think I'm inclined to think the reverse.

Looking for supplies of all sorts, I travelled quite a bit in Burma and Thailand and occasionally to the more distant parts of Borneo and New Guinea. Sumatra and Java were thought of as almost our home beat. I decided to keep my eyes open for minerals whilst I was about my normal business.

I will say I quizzed Canin pretty closely as to what he needed as a finished product; I even went as far as getting him to draw a few sketches and asked if he would be prepared to leave a few of the finished stones with me. The poor man was a bit reluctant at first but in the end, handed over about ten various shapes and sizes with a note of the prices he would expect to pay.

Over the next few weeks, I talked with several contacts and found that most of what Canin was looking for were pretty readily available and at prices well below the figures he had quoted, which I suspected he had pitched on the low side anyhow.

I took the trouble to learn quite a bit about spinel. The various colours and qualities. The samples Canin had left me were mostly a sort of ruby red. I gather they were used instead of real stones on occasions, but I saw others, both green and blue which were less common. I purchased a small selection and sent them to Canin in London quoting prices a little below the prices he had suggested but which left us with a very healthy margin. His first firm order came back by return of post.

We executed that order within a month. We have traded with each other ever since. In that time we have supplied increasing quantities of all types of stones, not only to Canin but to other dealers all over the world. Beryl from Korea, topaz, aquamarine, alexandrite and peridot from Burma besides the original spinel which we started with.

Japan has furnished us with rock crystal and a great number of both cultured and imitation pearls. Our contacts in these places suggested other lines that we might take on. Coral and, in the early days, ivory beads came from both Japan and India. A lot has gone to Italy where it seems the bulk of the European costume jewellery trade is based.

As time has gone on and we have learnt the trade we have done a lot of very good business with proper gemstones as well, mainly rubies and sapphires from both Thailand and North Burma. It has been an exciting development and has given me a new interest in learning not only about the materials themselves but the demands of the markets.

As I said, we supply far more dealers, however, David Canin was the first and to be fair, with his help we have made it a major part of the business. Frequently, suppliers of stones have, in effect, been paid for by trade goods in return. Our contacts in Japan, for instance, have supplied mining machinery to mine operators in Thailand which has enabled them to cope with the increased demand for their outputs which we have helped to develop. I am very glad to say that we have had no hesitation in taking our proper commission on both halves of the deals.

About three years ago David Canin's son Lawrance took over their firm from his father. He is a very capable young man and has the right sort of 'get up and go' which I like to see in trade.

# CHAPTER 8

I don't really know why, when or even how the first seeds of doubt started to take root. I think, looking back, that it was a combination of advancing age, the climate - which can become a bit of a trial if you live in the East long enough or perhaps it was that I was just running out of steam. I suppose an increasing personal fortune had something to do with it but I like to think that wasn't a prime reason. If the truth be known I think I had achieved most of what I had set out to do when I 'ran away' to the East, all those years ago.

Not quite like old Angus who was a respected, if slightly eccentric, trader in his time; I was becoming an anachronism.

The style of Trading Companies had changed. I was well aware that I was thought of, amongst the Europeans anyhow as a bit of a throwback to a past age. Modern houses were all computers and written contracts and seemed to be run by men in shirt sleeves with a lurid necktie pulled half way down their shirt front.

I wouldn't say that the majority of houses were wrong but there were still far too many Europeans who had no sympathy with the locals. The pressure for the local population to take charge of their own affairs was irresistible and I couldn't see much of a future for businesses like mine that were still being run by men like me.

Don't get me wrong, there was nothing wrong with Angus Findlay & Co. as a company. We had an expanding and very profitable business. The problem was with the man running it. Me.

My style of trading was out of date. I suppose if I had still been in the first flush of enthusiasm I could have changed it all. There was possibly a case for restructuring the whole show by issuing shares on the local market or turning it into a Partnership but then it would no longer be mine. I would be responsible to others. No longer free to stand or fall by my own decisions or come and go as I pleased.

That last bit wasn't strictly true. Over the years we had progressed past that state. I prided myself that one of the reasons for our success was that I had a totally Asiatic staff and many of the decisions were taken by them. They knew the markets as well if not better than I did and I valued their input but, in the end, the Company and the responsibility were mine. I also had the feeling that they could get on just as well without me!

After having mulled things over in my own mind I had a long talk with Lee Fin, my Manager, and explained my thinking. At first, he showed the concern I had expected but gradually as the alternatives, which I am sure he had already thought of, were laid out, he became more receptive to my plan for my own retirement. I suggested that he discussed the options with the other senior staff and that we would talk again.

A week later Lee Fin asked if I would have a meeting with him, our Bank Manager and two other Chinese businessmen. I agreed.

We held that meeting in the big room overlooking the harbour where I had first met Angus Findlay, so many years ago.

Their plan was simple; to purchase the Company outright. How they did it was of course up to them so long as the price was right and the figure they suggested was about what I had in mind. Out of politeness, they told me that Mr Minn and Mr Cheng would take a third share each and the senior staff, headed by Lee Fin and supported by the Bank would take the remaining third.

The snag of that situation was that I reckoned that my staff would be in hock to the Bank for quite a while and that might well prove to be a problem for them. I did some quick mental arithmetic and suggested that if they were in a position to up the offer price I would leave a slice of my own money in the new business at an interest rate rather less than the banks.

The thinking behind this was that I well knew that Minn and Cheng could well afford it and it would be easing the future burden on Lee and his chums. Minn and Cheng weren't too happy and the Bank Manager could see some of his profit going out of the window but it was a sensible proposal and in the end, they agreed.

They surprised me at that point. They said that in recognition of the way I had run the Company over the many years I had been in charge, the company would pay me a pension for the remainder of my life. It was a touching gesture. We had all but agreed on the final terms and I was happy with them, so it wasn't a case of a final sweetener to clinch the deal but a genuine expression of their feelings; I think that that was as valuable to me as the main deal.

The actual process of handing over wasn't as painful as I had thought it might be. The financial part went through on the nod so to speak and my domestic arrangements had never been complicated in any case. My servant, now well into his seventies, decided to retire and I bought him an annuity. The furniture, much the same as I had taken over from old Angus was put into store to await a decision as to where I would settle.

I said my goodbyes to the few friends I still had and I flew to Auckland in New Zealand.

"Why New Zealand?" you may ask. Well, I suppose I had the thought that it was a fair imitation of Britain but with a better climate. Added to which I had some monies invested there, as indeed I had in several other countries. All legal and above board and placed as a form of insurance.

What Europeans tend to call 'The Far East' is a pretty turbulent part of the world. If you run down some of the conflicts which have taken place out there just since the Second World War it makes a long list. Malaya itself, Korea, French Indochina, Borneo and Sarawak, Laos and Cambodia to say nothing of the disaster of Vietnam and that's beside problems in Java and Burma and even China itself. People have now largely forgotten the tensions of the old Formosa question and the Philippines.

For years, Colonial powers tried to keep the lid on simmering pots all over the region with varying degrees of success and when they have eventually gone, it has usually led to some pretty strange forms of Government in their place. Freedom has never been a synonym for democracy.

Thus then is it any wonder that the prudent man has provided himself with alternatives. I did so, after Angus' fashion, by salting away a few pennies in various corners of the more stable world. Hence the first port of call in my search for a 'Shangri La' was that region north of Auckland called the Bay of Islands.

It was all that I had remembered but I hadn't been looking at it through the eyes of a man bent on retirement when I had been before. I had seen it then as a short-term place to relax and, I might add, a place where you could buy some very good Macadamia nuts - which we bought and re-exported to Japan and the United States. I was always one for making a holiday pay for itself!

I hired a car and toured the North Island to see what else it might offer. The Bay of Plenty, Poverty Bay and Hawks Bay were all fine places for holidaying but I was after a place to live. After the rush and bustle and the confines of Hong Kong, I needed a certain space and freedom to be quiet. What I found was a feeling of isolation which wasn't what I was after at all. I didn't bother to go to the South Island fearing it would be even more so.

Australia next. Sydney - too busy and full of non-Australians (of which I was one). Plus the flies.

Melbourne - too suburban. Perth - too far away from the rest of the country and too new.

Should it be thought that I was being 'picky', let me add that I looked at a whole range of places in the course of nearly two months visit but nothing was quite what I had in mind. I had enough money and time to look around and I was happy looking. I was not sure I would be so happy making a decision.

I spent the next month in the United States. I think I would have stayed longer but for the fact that it wasn't the country which put me off. It was the Americans themselves. That may sound hard as a generalisation but I was looking for the option to be alone and that, I discovered, is almost impossible in the States. American hospitality is so overwhelming that it can soon become a burden. I was almost entertained to death.

I hastened to London. This wasn't because I had thoughts of settling there, for I find that my own countrymen can be as irksome as anywhere else but I did need to set some affairs in order and doing it face to face is always the best way.

The firm of 'Lewis, Lewis, Lewis and Farr' of Lincoln's Inn was still going strong but now Commander Black was semi-retired after having relinquished the post of Senior Partner some three years previously. He was still hale and hearty for his age but the death of his wife about four years back had made him take stock of his life and he had decided, very sensibly in my opinion, to take things easier.

He had sold up the house, one of those pretty places down by the river in Chiswick, and moved into some rather old-fashioned service rooms in Westminster. He had also bought a cottage down in Bosham so that he could spend more time messing about with the old cruiser he kept there. Black still went to the office about two or sometimes three days a week and looked after the affairs of a few of his old clients. I am glad to say that I was one of them.

Whilst we hadn't seen each other much over the intervening years we had corresponded quite regularly on all sorts of matters besides business. Black and his wife had only the one child, a son, Harry, to whom I was Godfather and I had followed his progress with great interest. I liked what I had seen of him and he was making a name for himself as a Barrister in Chambers in the Inner Temple. Like his father, he was slightly unconventional, which is a good thing in any young man.

Black had offered to put me up in London but I thought it a bit of an imposition so I had booked into a small hotel where I usually stayed on the odd occasions when I was in London. Again, it was a throwback to a previous age but it suited me well enough.

We dined together several times and talked of the old days and of our changed and changing lives. On one occasion I took Black, Harry and his wife to dinner at the Savoy. It was very enjoyable. I think it must have been the first time for about thirty years that I had danced with a young woman. I enjoyed it but perhaps my dancing was a bit rusty.

A few evenings later, Harry invited his father and me to dine with the Benchers at the Inner Temple. I sat next to a well-known politician who seemed to represent, to my mind at least, all that was wrong with Britain.

This worthy soul spent the entire first two courses telling me what was wrong with the attitude of industry and commerce. "Have you ever worked in commerce?" I asked politely.

"Good God no!" Here was a man who made decisions that would have considerable influence on the prosperity of the country, yet who seemed to look down on the people who generated the wealth he so generously 'redistributed'.

I spent the rest of the meal talking to a very amiable old gentleman, on my other side, about his passion in life, fly fishing.

I hadn't intended to spend long in London as I wanted to have a good look at the Continent. In particular, I wanted to tour France. I have always had a, perhaps unfashionable, regard for the French. I'm not sure what it is about their attitude to life. They have always seemed to take serious things unseriously but unserious things very seriously. An engaging trait.

I bought a small but very comfortable sporty motor car and took myself off to France.

***

The next month was a joy. I drifted where the muse took me, staying in small hotels for a night or so at a time and then having poured over my maps and the guidebooks, move onto another area which took my fancy.

At one stage I rather took to the idea of buying a rather run down vineyard and getting it back up on its feet. I found such a place to the west of Cahors and spent several days trying to work out the pros and cons of such a scheme.

The conclusion I came too was that the regulations governing such a venture were formidable. At the lowest level, the local Mayor would have to be 'persuaded' of the merits of the scheme, for without his 'say so' nothing would ever get done. The list of bureaucratic fences seemed endless. The local Département, Central Government, the E.E.C, The Appellation Authority, the Food and Drink Office and, not least, the Office of Employment.

I decided that I would be better employed sampling the outputs of numerous vineyards rather than trying to rescue one.

I retreated to the banks of the river Lot to reconsider my next move. It was at that point that I received the telephone call from London which would, in the event, take my life in an entirely new and unexpected direction.

# CHAPTER 9

At the appointed hour, on the following Wednesday, after my dash across France, I presented myself at the Holborn offices of Harper & Swinburn, Solicitors. I told the young lady at the reception desk who I was and that I had an appointment with a Mr Charles Harper.

She consulted a diary and agreed that I had such an appointment and added that "Mr Charles was running a little late." The visual impression amused me slightly and I agreed to take a seat in the waiting room.

I didn't have to wait above a few minutes until I was ushered into the mighty presence.

My first thought was that Harper hadn't run - late or otherwise - for a good many years. I had the impression of a small, round, pink head, which looked far too small for the body it was attached to.

He greeted me in the same nasal, exaggerated, Home Counties accent which I had remembered from our 'phone call three days earlier.

"My dear Mr Forest, so glad you were able to come so quickly."

I refrained from reminding him that I had been in middle France not the upper reaches of the Niger, restricting myself to, "You said it was fairly urgent."

Harper explained that the first urgency of the funeral was "Very regrettably past."

However, at "Harper & Swinburn, we do like to progress our clients' affairs with expedition."

I had a feeling, born of much contact with the U.K. legal system, that the man was lying through his teeth. I produced my passport for inspection so that Harper knew I was who I claimed to be and we got down to business.

After a deal of legal mumbo jumbo and general disclaimers we arrived at the fact that I was, very much to my surprise, the residual inheritor, 'after a number of lesser beneficiary recipients' of the Estate of Augustus Forest - my late paternal grandfather, sometime of Helsey Hall in Cheshire and more lately of Locklate House in the county of Gloucestershire.

All this information and a great deal more Harper produced rather in the manner of a magician. Unlike a magician, however, he seemed not to want to produce the actual rabbit. Several interjections from myself along the lines of, "How much are we talking about?" sent him off into further labyrinthine quasi-legal reasons why he was unable to mention a figure.

In the end, I could see that, at this meeting at least, we wouldn't get much further, I asked for a copy of the will and told him that since I had still 'no fixed address' I would contact him once a week until such time as I had.

Harper didn't seem overjoyed by either idea but I pressed the point and he gave in.

I stood on the pavement in Holborn not knowing if I was either now seriously rich or if the modest fortune I had made on my own account would vanish in settling up the affairs of the grandfather who had so plainly explained, in his final letter, all those years ago, that he wanted nothing more to do with me.

In something under half an hour I was seated in Tommy Black's office in Lincoln's Inn whilst he perused the copy of Grandfather Forest's will.

"Looks all right Robin. Of course, at this stage nothing's sure but I would have thought that the wording of 'My Estates in Gloucestershire and Scotland ....' sounds promising. Have you any idea what they consist of?"

"Not the faintest Tommy. I've had nothing to do with either side of the family since I went East." Tommy Black put his fingers together in the gesture so typical of him when he was thinking.

"Leave it with me; I'll get in touch with Harper and Swinburn's and tell them to do it all through me here if that's what you want."

I agreed that I did.

"In the meantime, I'll get one of our chaps to nose about and see what he can come up with. Now, much more importantly, what are you doing this evening? How about dinner together and then, if you've nothing planned, why not come down to Bosham for a few days and I can try to fatten you up a bit - I've seen more meat on a pedal cycle."

I agreed to the dinner but declined the offer of Bosham. Tommy's idea of a 'good day' down there was to spend it soaking wet and half frozen on his wretched boat.

I had other plans.

We dined that evening at the Travellers and, if anything, slightly over enjoyed ourselves, never mind, it was only once in a long while.

The next morning I packed my bag, paid my bill and by half nine o'clock I was headed westwards thinking myself lucky that I wasn't part of the mass of traffic heading into London. I stopped for a coffee at about eleven and again for lunch at about one. By mid-afternoon I was over the ridge of the Cotswolds and through that somewhat confused area on the borders of Worcestershire and Gloucestershire.

Eventually, I managed to park my car and by three o'clock I was in the Gloucester branch of the Bank which I used in Britain asking a pleasant young woman if it would be possible to have a few words with the Manager.

I explained that I was a customer of the Bank but not of that Branch. She asked if she might have my account number which I gave her and she asked me to wait. Within a few minutes, she showed me into the Manager's office. He was a Mr Hall, middle-aged, well dressed. It was good to see that standards hadn't slipped in this bank at least. He stood up to welcome me.

"Good afternoon Mr Forest. How can I help you?"

Now there is no sense in beating about the bush on these occasions so I told him that I was recently returned from the Far East and that I was the inheritor of an Estate in the area. I produced the copy of Grandfather's will which I had got from solicitor Harper. He read it.

He looked up. "I am afraid I don't know the Estate myself. Your grandfather wasn't one of our customers and Locklate is a bit outside my area. I'm not sure how I can help you."

He went on, "I think that perhaps the solicitors, er...." He looked at the will again, "Harper and Swinburn may be able to tell you where he banked."

I explained that wasn't what I was after. "If you could just give me the name and address of a good local firm of Land Agents, I would be obliged."

He looked relieved that my request was so straightforward, I went on,

"If you could also help me with the name of a decent hotel it would save me time and the risk of choosing a dud."

Hall smiled; he pulled a piece of paper across the desk and as if dictating to himself, wrote the names down for me.

"A Mr Turner is your man - very good - he does quite a lot for the bank ..... valuations, that sort of thing. Please tell him that I sent you." I assured him that I would.

He added, "Should you move to this area perhaps you might consider moving your account to this branch."

I thought for a moment, "Mr Hall, I don't know what I am going to do; I haven't seen the place let alone know what it consists of. I might well sell it. I just don't know at this stage but I'll certainly bear it in mind."

I thanked him for his help.

Out in the street, I asked a traffic warden for directions to a good bookshop where I studied the large-scale Ordnance Survey maps and bought the sheet which featured Locklate. I collected my car and drove to the hotel Hall had suggested. It was what you would call a 'Country House' type of place and looked well kept. The lawns were newly mown and edged, always a good sign I think. They had a room which I took for three nights.

I had a gin and tonic sent up, a long soak in the bath and then lay on the bed studying my maps.

I had a goodish dinner with half a bottle of Chateau Potensac '82, a glass of Graham's Malvedos Port and went to bed.

Next morning I telephoned the Land Agents and made an appointment to see their Mr Turner at noon and then went to the main Library in Gloucester and did some research into the history of the area of Locklate. It seemed that it had figured more frequently in the story of England than you might have suspected for a place by no means on the beaten track.

At five to twelve I was in the Offices of the Land Agents and being shown into the office of Tim Turner.

He was a tall, dark, thin man, somewhere in his early forties, who seemed to know what he was about. I told him as much as he needed to know about my interest in the Locklate Estate. He admitted that he knew nothing of it, other than the fact that it was there but that he would make it his business to find out all about it should that be what I wanted.

He studied me for a moment, probably calculating just how far he wanted to get involved. "What do you propose doing with the Estate Mr Forest?" he asked.

I told him quite frankly, "I don't know, I'm no agricultural expert and I know nothing about Estate management, I'm what you might call a commodity trader and have been for most of my life. I need to know all the facts before I can decide anything and I think you, when you have done your homework, will be able to give me the view from the outside."

He was in front of me at that moment at least.

"While you get the facts from the inside?"

"Precisely."

We briefly discussed fees and I told him where I was staying.

I retrieved my car and drove the few miles to the village of Locklate and then stopped at a small cross roads to study the map. It looked as if I had already passed what seemed to be the main entrance but I had certainly not seen anything that might have been it.I turned the car around and drove very slowly back the way I had come. At a bend in the road which corresponded with the map and was near where the gateway should have been, I pulled the car onto a rough grass verge and started prospecting on foot.

Within thirty yards I found what I was looking for and no wonder I had missed it the first time. I had assumed something grander. Wrought iron gates, hung from brick piers I supposed. All that gave it away was a fair sized hillock of vegetation, brambles mostly, set back about fifteen yards from the road. The tip of an ornate chimney pot poking from the top of the mound of lush growth gave me the clue. The only trace of the entrance to Locklate House was a very overgrown ruined lodge which I presumed had stood guard over a now vanished gateway. The omens were not looking too good.

I re-consulted the map and decided that since there must be an entrance of some sort still in use, I should try what looked like another entrance which could be reached via a series of small lanes which ran around the edge of the Estate.

After a couple of false starts, I managed to find what I was looking for. A rather hidden farm entrance which led to a collection of obviously old but solid, well-maintained farm buildings.

The only person in sight was a young chap who was working on the engine of a large tractor which stood in the yard outside what looked like a well-equipped workshop. I parked my car and walked over. "Good afternoon, could you help me? I'm looking for the farm manager or whoever is in charge."

He seemed a cheerful sort of man and grinned, "That would be Mr Pearson and I think you'll find him in the Estate office, along there and the last door on the right." I thanked him.

"That's all right, you can't miss it, it's got a sign on the door."

I walked to the office, tapped on the half-open door and walked in.

A big burly man, dressed in a tweed suit was behind a table covered with plans of some sort.

I asked if he were Mr Pearson. He agreed he was, stood up and holding out his hand asked what I wanted. I shook his proffered hand and introduced myself.

"I'm Robin Forest."

This got no reaction so I explained.

"I am the grandson of Augustus Forest." A light dawned in his eyes, "Ah! So will you be the new owner of the Estate then?"

"Mr Harper of Harper & Swinburn tells me that I am, or rather, will be when all the legal formalities are completed."

I went on before he could make a reply, "I haven't come to interfere with the running of the Estate but rather to gather facts. I'll put my cards on the table; I know virtually nothing about agriculture or about Estate Management. I've spent most of my working life in the Far East as a trader. What I plan to do whilst the legal people do their job is to find out as much as possible about the affairs of my late grandfather."

Pearson looked worried. I smiled. "What I suggest you might do is 'phone Harper and check that what I say is true and ask if he is in agreement that I can do just that."

He looked a bit happier at that.

I went on, "If Harper agrees then I would think that we can have a proper meeting and you might be kind enough to brief me about this place and how it's run."

Pearson looked more relieved at the suggestion. "How long are you staying down here Mr Forest?"

I told him I had booked into the hotel for two further nights. He thought for a moment and then said, "How about if you come here the day after tomorrow, say at about eleven o'clock, that will give us time to run over the facts here in the office and then I can show you the land in the afternoon?"

"That would be very kind of you; will you have time to get everything together by then?"

"No problem, everything is here, I just need to get it all laid out."

I thanked him and said that would do very well but that he should check with Harper first.

He said he would do that before he did anything else.

He paused for a moment and then went on to suggest that, if I cared, I might like to look over the house the next day, if I hadn't anything else planned. "I'll get Mrs Barker to show you around if you like."

"Who's Mrs Barker?"

"She was Mr Augustus' housekeeper when he still lived in the house and since he went into the Home she had carried on, a few hours a week as a sort of caretaker, keeping things 'looked after'."

I agreed to that and made a time.

I thanked Pearson and he walked with me to my car. I drove off with a happier heart than when I had arrived.

I spent the remainder of the afternoon exploring Gloucester. I bought a couple of local history books from a fascinating second-hand bookshop, had a good look round the Cathedral and went back to the hotel.

I found a quiet corner in the lounge and indulged myself with a couple of large glasses of a very good Manzanilla and a dip into the history of Gloucester and its surroundings. A bath, another sherry and a very passable dinner with a glass or two of Chiroubles and I was ready for bed and another run at the history.

In the morning, after a leisurely breakfast, I telephoned Pearson and agreed about looking at the house and then Turner, the land agent and he agreed to come round in the early evening and bring me up to date with what he had found out about Locklate.

I got the car out of the garage and set off for my meeting with Mrs Barker.

She was waiting with Pearson when I got to the Estate Office. She resembled a cottage loaf: jolly, short, quite stout and I would have guessed nearer seventy than sixty.

After introductions by Pearson he suggested that it would be best if I took Mrs Barker up to the house, which was about half a mile away, in my car and bring her back to the office when we had finished. I had doubts about my car's suitability for a lady of Mrs Barkers age and build but agreed.

The good lady managed to ease herself into the passenger seat whilst I surmised about her ability to get out. As I went round to the driver's door, Pearson told me that he had spoken with lawyer Harper who had been surprised at my visit but had told him to give me any information that I might need 'concerning the Estate.' There was a slight emphasis on the 'concerning the Estate' part and I guessed there had been a bit more to the conversation than Pearson was letting on. Never mind, I'd spent a good part of my life dealing with the Harpers of this world. I made a mental note that it was much more important to get Pearson 'on side' than worry about treading on the lawyer's toes.

I drove slowly alongside a small wood and as we reached the end of it the house came into view.

I stopped, sat, and looked.

My first impression was that it belonged there. Some houses look as if they are placed in a landscape. Locklate Hall looked as if it had grown out of it. It was long but only two clear stories high with some smaller windows let into the roof but it seemed to nestle into the land around it.

Tudor-ish, I suppose, would have summed it up; mainly very mellow dark red brick, quite a lot of timber work, stone dressings to the windows and doors and some tall elaborate chimneys stretched above a tiled roof. The windows were larger than I would have thought fitted Tudor but they were elaborately leaded, with some panels of stained glass. Overall it was as attractive a house as I think I had ever seen.

For the first time since getting into the car, Mrs Barker spoke, "Lovely don't you think, Mr Forest?"

"It certainly is, do you know when it was built, Mrs. Barker?"

"I couldn't really say, Sir. Parts are very old but I've heard that some bits have been knocked down and rebuilt; some more than once." She paused for a moment, "Seemingly the gentleman who owned it before your Grandfather, old Squire Parslow, he had a lot done to it." "Electricity, heating and running water.... you know, modernised."

"Did Grandfather alter it much do you know?"

"Not the house much, I don't think, but he did a lot to the grounds."

I couldn't see any formal garden so I asked, "How do you mean?"

"He had most of the old gardens done away with Sir. All the flower beds and such like, he had 'em all ripped out and had lawns instead."

I looked at Mrs Barker, she looked a bit uncomfortable, as if she felt she had overstepped the mark.

"Go on." I urged.

"Well, I think it was because of the work it took to keep 'em up. The wages you see."

"Four gardeners the Old Squire had, very fond of his garden he was, both him and Mrs Parslow."

I smiled at her, "Do you think Grandfather couldn't afford to keep them?"

"Well, I wouldn't say that Sir, I think he was a bit careful about money; if you take my meaning." She looked more uncomfortable.

"I am quite sure you're right Mrs Barker, I always found that he watched the pennies." I thought back to the arrangements which had been made to provide for me, when what I had really needed was affection, not 'providing for'.

I slipped the car into gear and drove slowly the final hundred yards or so to the front door.

Oddly enough the house didn't seem as large inside, as it had appeared from the outside. True, the rooms were quite large but to the left of a generous hall, which was floored in black & white marble tiles, was a long sitting room. With three windows looking out to the front and a vast floor to ceiling window in the end wall, it had a surprisingly light and airy feel.

The floor was of fine, well-polished oak planking, partly hidden by a number of rugs, rather faded but which looked to be of good quality. There was a heavily carved oak staircase at the back of the hall and to the right another, smaller sitting room which went through to a panelled dining room. Beyond that was a smaller room which I supposed to be a study.

Behind the hall was the usual kitchen and an old-fashioned scullery. Another room off the kitchen, which I thought might have been a living room for the several servants, which there must have been at one time. Behind that again were various pantries and storerooms, one of which still had an old copper boiler in it.

Mrs Barker had shown me around, displaying pride and, I think, affection for the house and pointing out various pieces of furniture, most of which hid under dust covers. I remarked on the absence of pictures and smaller items and she told me that all the more portable stuff had been crated up and put into store some four years before, when it became apparent that Grandfather would not be returning from his Oxford nursing home.

"The old gentleman was never quite the same after old Mrs Forest died." She commented.

"When was that, Mrs Barker?"

"Just seven years before he went." She seemed very precise. She went on, "The same month as my Arthur passed on." The memory obviously triggered a memory and her eyes grew quite moist. I made the usual sympathetic noises and to avoid her embarrassment asked, "Is that all on the ground floor?"

"Everything bar the cellar Sir, do you want to go down there?"

"May as well see it all whilst I'm here," I said rather too cheerfully.

"If you don't mind Sir, I'll stay here, the stairs are quite steep, I haven't been down there for years. It's that door under the stairs, you'll need the keys, Sir, it's kept locked."

I took the bunch of keys and looking more carefully saw the door, which wasn't, at first glance obvious, it was partly camouflaged, by the ornate carving on both it and on the staircase surround. I unlocked the door and peered down a very steep flight of brick steps.

"The light switch is on the left - please be careful." I assured her that I would.

My first impression was that the cellar was much older than the rest of the house; the bricks were quite small and very neatly laid. It seemed too deep for a normal cellar and when I reached the bottom of the steps I was surprised by the beautifully vaulted roof. More like the sort of thing you see in a church building rather than in a house. It was all clean and dry and the space was dominated by a very large, old-fashioned boiler which, judging from the pipework, drove the central heating. Along the left-hand wall there was a range of racking which held all the sort of detritus you might expect to find in such a place. Some massive cooking pots, clearly from an age when you had twenty or so to dinner, a bedpan, a few tools, a croquet set, in an elaborate box. A picnic basket which would have taken two to carry and several trunks. All stuff of a bygone age.

I had half expected to see some sort of wine storage but there wasn't any. Rather disappointed, I turned to go when I spotted another, smaller door in the middle of the end wall. It was locked but one of the keys fitted, I pushed the door open, against the creaking resistance of very little used hinges.

Another light switch enabled me to see inside. I had found the hoped-for wine store. It took me a moment or two to take it all in.

About twenty-five feet long and some fifteen wide. It was lined down either flank by slate 'bins' with a double row down the middle. That    splendid    line from

Galsworthy's 'Forsyte Saga' came to mind when Uncle Swithen says that 'Robin Hill' would be a nice house but the cellar was too small, "Only room for a few hundred dozen."

True, the majority of the bins themselves contained few bottles. Those few, however, were gems. The labels were in good condition, apart from a good coating of dust and I spent quite a time looking at what amounted to a roll call of most of the great names of viticulture: Mouton, Las Cases, Bechaville, Palmer, Margeaux, Barton and further on Graham, Cockburn, Warr, Dow. The bulk seemed to be Bordeaux and Port but there was a good sprinkling of the best of Burgundy. There was Maderia, Tokai and some curious stone bottles which I took to be German.

Stacked along the top of the central bins were unopened cases, I suppose thirty or forty, with names branded on their ends which I could only gaze at in wonder. Thus I stood, to some extent stunned by the display, when I became aware of a plaintive voice asking if I was all right. I had forgotten poor Mrs Barker. I assured her that all was well and that I would be up in a moment. I had a last good look round, switched off the light and retraced my steps, carefully locking the doors behind me.

Mrs Barker was relieved to see me safe. "I feared you might have slipped and fallen, Sir. But I didn't dare come down. Look you've got yourself all dusty."

I brushed off the sleeve of my jacket and asked if I might go upstairs. I would have preferred to go on my own but she insisted on coming with me.

A long landing reached out in either direction from the head of the stairs. There were five bedrooms, two with small dressing rooms, only one bathroom, with a very antiquated bath and toilet and a linen cupboard which would have housed a small troop of soldiers. There was also what Mrs Barker described as 'The cleaning room'. She explained it was where a valet or a ladies maid would have brushed and ironed clothes and where the other maids would keep their cleaning materials. All again, evocative of an age long since passed.

I went up into the attic rooms on my own. Two quite decent bedrooms, each with a tiny fireplace, probably for the housekeeper and the cook; then six more very small rooms, more like cubicles, for the lesser staff. Mrs Barker explained later that only female staff were allowed on the attic floor. It was strictly out of bounds to men. The butler, if you had one, lived in the butler's pantry, just off the kitchen, the footmen and the chauffeur would live across the backyard above the stables or what later became the 'Motor House'.

I had a quick scout round outside and then took the good Mrs Barker, who was clearly tiring, back to the Estate Office. I offered to run her home but she improbably had her bicycle at the office. I thanked her for her time and bade her 'goodbye'.

Pearson asked if I had seen all I needed to see and I asked if I might go back to the house and wander around the grounds for a while. He had no objection.

"Mrs Barker, quite a lady, what's her history?"

He smiled. "Her father worked for old Squire Parslow and May started as a kitchen maid up at the house when she was about fourteen. She married Arthur Barker, who was late head cowman here on the home farm, when she was about twenty-five. Lived in the lodge down by the main road."

He paused for a moment. "They had a boy, Robert but he died; she worked up at the house, on and off, ever since. She more or less kept house for your grandfather after his wife died. Her Arthur died about the same time and I think she was glad of the interest."

I made my 'goodbyes' promising to keep my appointment with him the next morning. As I turned to go, a thought struck me. "Why is the front entrance onto the main road all overgrown?"

Pearson gave me a long look and shook his head. "Mr Forest, I suppose you will have to know sooner or later and it's better if I tell you rather than you hear it from someone else. May & Arthur's son Robert was killed on the drive outside the lodge by your Grandfathers car. Not long after your grandmother died in pretty strange circumstances. She died of a heart attack in the garden. About two weeks after that Arthur Barker hanged himself at the back of the lodge."

"Good Lord, are you saying that Baker was responsible for grandmother's death?"

"Nothing ever came to light. She was a very old lady, she was alone and only Arthur was nearby. I don't know if anyone has ever been accused of frightening someone to death; be hard to prove I'd have thought."

"Was there an Inquest on Grandmother?"

"No, as I said, she was old and your grandfather didn't want any talk; wealth has some advantages you know. The local doctor signed the death certificate and that was that." He looked at me again as if deciding how far to go. "But Arthur doing himself in did encourage a lot of speculation.

Your grandfather had the front drive closed off and the Lodge boarded up. It's never been used since."

I repeated my goodbyes and postponing my look round the grounds, drove back to Gloucester.

\*\*\*

Tim Turner, the Land Agent arrived on time and we settled down in a quiet corner of the lounge. I asked him if he wanted tea or a drink and he chose the tea.

To save him any embarrassment, I decided to tell him what I had found out before he had his turn. "I've looked at the house and I've learnt that Grandmother's death may, or may not, have been something of a mystery."

He looked relieved.

"I'm glad about that Mr Forest; I've spoken to several people who've known the Estate for years and two of them mentioned something about rumours at the time. I wasn't looking forward to telling you if you didn't already know."

"Would you have told me?"

He hesitated for a moment. "Yes.... I would. You asked me to find out all about the place and I supposed you meant 'warts and all'."

I smiled, "You understood quite rightly. If we go along on that basis we will get on splendidly. Now, what else have you found out?"

Tim Turner had done his task well. All the factual information he been able to glean. Something of the Estate's history, acreages, types of crops, types of soils and the like, he had set out in a quite formal report. Well written and presented. The non-factual stuff: how well the place was run, did they pay their bills on time, what did the locals think. That was all put down in narrative form on a couple of separate sheets.

I read through it all quickly whilst he drank his tea and made inroads into the cake.

I reflected that young Mr Turner must have some very good connections in the district to have turned up so much in so short a time.

"Excellent, just what I needed. Now give me your thoughts, you must have formed  some sort of picture in your own mind?"

He took time to collect his précis.

"Overall it's not a bad set up; from what I hear the Manager, Mr Pearson, is an efficient and scrupulously honest man. I think that he's  is a bit out of date with modern farming but that's perhaps because of his age, he's nearing retirement, about a year or so to go I think."

"The Estate itself is sound. It's a large enough unit to be viable in present conditions but the minimum economic size is rising all the time and it could certainly do with being larger."

I stopped him there. "That means buying more land and surely that is expensive; would that make economic sense?"

"The historic book cost of the land you do have is probably very low and if you averaged the cost of further land over the whole Estate it would still make sense, yes."

"On the other hand if the book cost is low on the present land, if it were rented out it would be a good return?"

"That's one way certainly Mr Forest." He thought for a moment.

"I don't know your circumstances and I don't know what you want for yourself. There are lots of different ways of handling this. If you wanted you could live in the house, employ a good Manager and the Estate would go on as it is, making a very modest return on the capital."

"You could sell the house and the land, either together, or separately, and invest the capital. You might, however, run into tax problems if you did that right away."

"You could do a bit of each; keep the house, sell some of the land and perhaps rent out part. I doubt that would be the best course though; it's usually better to keep a place as a whole. It depends, in the main on what you want to do."

We talked about the various possible ways of going on for a while. He declined my offer of a drink - he had some way to drive home - and said his wife and children would soon forget what he looked like if he didn't try and get home once in a while.

I told him about my appointment to look round the Estate the next day and we talked over a few things I might make a point of probing into. Before he went I asked him to have a note of his fees sent round to the hotel the next day.

He looked a bit crestfallen so I explained. "Look, I don't know what my immediate plans are, either for myself or the Estate. It will be some time before probate is granted and I can have any say. I am in the hands of the executors to a large extent and since one of them is Grandfather's solicitor, Harper, I expect it will be a pretty drawn-out affair. At this stage, I am fact-gathering so that I can come to a sensible decision when I do come to have to decide what to do. After I have finished here, I am off to Scotland to gather a few more facts."

I paused to decide how far I should commit myself; "No matter what I decide to do with the Estate here I will in all probability need you again. You can be sure of that; in the meantime, I would rather be out of everyone's debt."

He agreed to send the bill round in the morning. I walked with him to the front door.

I got a half bottle of Taittinger from the bar, took it upstairs and drank it in the bath.

*** 

In the morning I saw to a few routine things and then got the car from the garage and was in Pearson's Estate office on the dot of eleven. He was all ready for me. A good sign.

I will say that he had prepared well. On the table, he had laid out the big scale maps of the land and his notes on what crops were planted where. His accounts for the last five years were to hand and all the other paraphernalia that is needed to run a fair sized farming operation in this day and age.

I confess that a deal of it was so much mumbo jumbo to me but the accounts and the day to day books I did understand. I was impressed by the way they were organised and kept but less impressed by the bottom line. True, the Estate was profitable but the return on the capital was pretty low. I was interested to see that Tim Turners 'guesstimates' had been very near the mark.

I also noticed that Pearson's salary was, at best, ungenerous.

I mentioned it to him.

He smiled, "I won't say that I wouldn't like a bit more Mr Forest but I get a house rent free and there is a pension scheme but I haven't had a rise since your grandfather went into that home. I have mentioned it to

Mr Harper a couple of times but he hasn't done anything about it yet."

I made a note on my pad to speak to the solicitor. The part I couldn't quite grasp was the 'chain of command' that had been in place.

Pearson explained.

"While your grandfather was still living here, I used to see him most days and tell him what was going on. Usually, we would talk it over and he would give me the 'go ahead'. For the last few months, before he went into the home, he lost interest a bit and would say, 'Whatever you think George, whatever you think'. I still made a point of telling him what we were doing though - it seemed to keep him interested and he still signed the cheques and agreed any major costs."

I cut in, "What were the arrangements after he went to Oxford?"

"We carried on much as before. Mr Harper came down a couple of times and we fixed up so that I could draw wages each week from the local bank and draw small sums for petty cash, that sort of thing."

"Who pays the bill now?"

"I write a list each week, send it off with relevant the invoices to Harper & Swinburn and someone there signs the cheques and sends them off. It's a bit long winded but it works all right."

"And what about money coming in, you know, if you sell grain or whatever?"

"Mostly they pay London direct but if a cheque comes here I bank it.

At the end of each month, I send a report and an account of what I've spent or received; they look after the rest."

I thought for a bit, "Not very satisfactory from your point of view, I would think?"

He smiled again, "Not really, when Mr Forest was here I had much more control."

He added, with a wry smile, "I'm not sure that Mr Harper is happy to trust other people."

I turned back to the accounts for a few minutes. Perhaps a bit more trust and the Estate wouldn't be paying the hefty 'Management Fees' which cropped up each year in the profit and loss account!

George Pearson had, with the help of May Barker, I suspected, laid on some very decent sandwiches and a couple of bottles of beer for lunch. We ate and drank and talked of what he thought should and could be done with the Estate.

I asked him about retirement. He was quite open and said that he was in good health and if the chance presented itself he would be happy to carry on for a few years yet. He was realistic though. "If you decided to keep the place on you might feel that a younger and perhaps better-qualified man might do better."

I was rather beginning to like George Pearson.

When we had eaten and drunk he suggested that we went and had a look at the land itself. He found me a pair of wellington boots and we climbed into his elderly Land Rover.

Now I've said that I am no expert in such things but what I saw looked well.

Hedges and ditches, gates and farm roads. The woodland and the arable land, they all looked neat and tidy and well cared for. Better than I would have imagined. I was impressed by the plant and machinery. Two big combine harvesters were parked in a large shed together with a plethora of other agricultural machines. There was a clean and neat, well-equipped workshop in a smaller building at one end. The four staff I met, all dressed in green coveralls, seemed cheerful and interested. There was a room for them to put their gear, wash and make a hot drink.

There were two farmhouses. The smaller, near the main yard, was where Pearson lived. He asked me to go in but I said that I would be pleased to after all was settled up.

The larger house, which we passed at the far end of the land, was let to a surgeon who worked in Gloucester Hospital. There were eight cottages, five occupied by farm staff, one by May Barker and two let out. All looked, from the outside at least, well maintained and neat and tidy.

We spent three hours looking around and everything I saw, I would have found it hard to have found fault with. The one exception was what had once been the front entrance with its very overgrown lodge and the drive that led from it to the house. It was so out of keeping with the rest of the place that I felt there was some other reason for its being so neglected.

"I can only say." Pearson explained, "Old Mr Forest gave me very specific orders that it was to be left and no one has ever said different, so it's stayed like that."

I gradually formed the impression that whatever concealed faults the Estate might have, they wouldn't be found in George Pearson's department.

Back at the Estate office, we went over a few of the notes I had made and I asked if I could have copies of the last three years Estate accounts. Since there was no photocopier and there weren't any spare copies, George Pearson agreed to have copies run off the next day.

I stared out of the office window for a bit and thought about what I had learnt. I had decided that I had found out about as much as I could at this stage and would move on. Now I wasn't trying to be devious and I certainly had nothing to hide from Pearson but I did want to keep Harper in the dark so far as my actions were concerned; I was beginning to get an uncomfortable feeling about the stout Mr Harper and decided the less he knew, the better.

"I am moving on tomorrow so perhaps you could post them on to me."

He agreed. I gave him Tommy Black's address. Not his Lincoln's Inn one - that was rather obviously the address of my solicitor. I gave him the address of Black's rooms in Westminster.

I had one further request. I asked if I might have another look round the main house.

"I'll come with you," said George.

"I think I would prefer to have a mooch around on my own, if you have no objection." I smiled to soften the request. "I need to do a bit of thinking."

George hesitated. "I've no objection, of course, Mr Forest, it's just that the burglar alarm will be on and needs switching off first and then resetting when you've finished."

The result was that he took me up to the house and let me in and agreed that he would be back in about an hour to lock up and take me back to the yard. He opened the front door, saw to deactivating the alarm system and gave me the keys. I watched him drive off.

I spent twenty minutes or so wandering around the ground floor and the thing that struck me was the sheer quality of the place. True, it was showing signs of long-term closure but that seemed superficial. The walls showed patches of a different colour where pictures had once hung. Definite wear on the curtains, the odd sign of damp on the ornate plaster ceilings. Nothing very serious but which could only get worse and more expensive to remedy if they were left. The very air had that smell that you get in a building that has been empty for a long time.

Inexorably I was drawn to the cellar.

In the main part, I studied the huge old boiler for a bit. How on earth had they got it down those steps in the first place? How would anyone get it out to replace it?

I spent rather longer than I had meant to in the inner part dusting off and reading the wine labels. This in itself was a veritable treasure; had anyone stopped to think what it was worth?

In a small bin at the far end, underneath a dozen bottles of a very passable Barsac, Chateau Coutet 1963, were eighteen bottles of Chateau D'Yquem of 1937. They alone, I suspected, would be worth more than a new boiler, with something to spare.

I warned myself not to start counting chickens. The condition would be the critical factor but the cellar seemed to provide just about perfect storage.

Looking at my watch I saw that George Pearson would be back in about ten minutes. I locked the inner door and after a moment's hesitation dragged three of the cabin trunks and the smaller sections of racking in front of it. To anyone who wasn't in the know, it looked as if the cellar had just the one section.

I was sitting on a stone bench outside when Pearson came back. He locked up and we drove back. We went over a few details and I gave him the number of my new mobile telephone which I had bought a couple of days before.

I told him I would be in touch from time to time and that he should only try and contact me if it were urgent. I made my farewells and drove back toward my hotel.

I called in on Tim Turner on the way and settled up his account, which was somewhat less than the work he must have put in justified but he was adamant that he was happy. I asked him to look into another few matters before I saw him next. He readily agreed.

\*\*\*

Back at the hotel, I decided to take life seriously. I had a short conference with the head waiter who, I was discovering, knew his wine list well, as any head waiter worth his salt should. I settled for a half bottle of a New Zealand Sauvignon Blanc, Oyster Bay, to take with me to my room and after deciding on a starter of smoked eel followed by the venison, we settled for a glass of very cold, dry Madeira and a half bottle of Jayer's Vosne-Romanee '79. to be got ready for dinner at eight o'clock.

I bathed and then, enjoying the Oyster Bay and spent twenty minutes on the phone talking to Tommy Black. As always he had got most of the answers I needed and I went down to dinner in a much clearer state of mind.

If you take the trouble to decide what you want in advance, talk it over with the expert and then put your faith in them, you are usually not disappointed. I wasn't that evening. If you were being super critical, I suppose the eel could have been a fraction less oily but the venison was as near perfect as I could have wished. The cheese, a double Gloucester with a glass of Graham's Malvedos and the pudding, a simple apple tart with Calvados matched my mood of overall wellbeing. I arranged for an early call, breakfast and the account to be ready and went to bed a contented man.

\*\*\*

The morning was fine and I made good time, north of the Potteries, however, the weather closed in and by the time I had got north of Lancaster I had had enough. I bore off to the west and by early evening I was ensconced in a comfortable looking hotel on the shores of Lake Windermere.

Sad to say that the cooking wasn't good and the service was of the 'take it or leave it' school of incompetence. So it was with a sense of relief that I set off again the next morning on the last leg of my journey to see what the words, in Grandfather's will, 'My Estates in Scotland' really meant.

I stopped in Fort William, had a bite to eat and sought out a shop which catered for hikers and climbers. They were very helpful and I emerged three-quarters of an hour later with some workmanlike waterproofs, a decent pair of boots and a small rucksack. I also bought a few odds and ends which I felt I might need if I wasn't to get hopelessly out of my depth in some of the wilder country hereabouts.

The road from Fort William to Mallaig is not meant for high-speed motoring and I had decided that I needed to establish some sort of a base from which to explore the country to the north. I found what I was looking for in the shape of a very promising country house type of hotel which faced down the Sound of Arisaig. The place looked well kept and since it was both off the main road and out of the high season for tourists I had the pick of several rooms. I admit that I was rather too tired to do justice to the very acceptable dinner they served me and I was glad to get to bed.

In the morning I woke to a complete contrast in the weather. It was still pretty windy but the previous evening's near horizontal lashing rain had been replaced by that hard northern sunlight that made the world look as if it had just come back from the laundry.

I had a substantial breakfast, including, I must tell you, porridge served not with milk but with Drambuie. A combination which would not have sprung readily to mind but which was, in the event, very bracing.

Fortified and dressed for walking I drove back a few miles the way I had come and then turned north up a very secondary road. Well into the hills I found a spot where I could park the car without causing anyone any inconvenience. I shouldered my rucksack, locked the car and set off to approach Grandfathers 'Scottish Estate' from the rear. Tommy Black had done his work well.

When Grandfather had retired from practice he was a wealthy man. He had made a good living before the war but it seemed that the real benefits had come after it. While Grandfather Harold Forest had lived in Knutsford his law practice had been mainly in Manchester.

# CHAPTER 11

The war, as wars always do, had caused great distortions in trade and industry. Many businesses which had been on the slippery slope to closure just prior to the outbreak of the Great War in 1914 had been kept going because of the incessant demand for their products despite the costs. Economics had gone out of the window in the drive to produce whatever the country needed.

Government contracts were placed on a massive scale, providing profitable work for lawyers. The real bonanza came however when the war stopped. Many government contracts were cancelled, virtually overnight with resultant court cases over the cancellations. One firm alone, in Trafford Park who had spent huge sums of money on a new factory to produce equipment for the Royal Navy found that their investment was worthless.

There were factories full of half-built aircraft that no one now needed. Stockpiles of raw materials, priceless whilst the war raged were now virtually worthless. The legal ramifications provided lucrative pickings on a scale never seen before for those with the contacts and the skill to exploit the situation.

Many employers had stayed on past retirement age because of the war. Now that it was ended and they had made considerable sums of money from war contracts they decided to call it a day and sell up. Many factories, with plant that had been kept in production, despite being long since obsolete, were forced out of production because the government finance tap had been turned off. War damage claims, shadow factory breakups, claims for repairs to buildings requisitioned during the hostilities all provided a legal feast that fuelled Grandfather Forest's practice and it's expansion.

All this, however, was only a prelude to the main course of redevelopment. Old man Forest had used the money from his legal activities to invest in land and property. When the restrictions started to come off in the early fifties and the price of land had escalated mainly because of the new planning laws, the old boy had made a killing.

Now there are two things you can do with surplus money. You can either spend it on having a high old time or you can reinvest it. Grandfather took the latter route but he also was very aware that there was a loophole in the tax laws in those days.

If you had two businesses you could offset the profits of one against any losses of the other. Like many other people, Grandfather took up farming. With his surplus cash, he bought the land in Gloucestershire. He didn't move there then but spent most of his profits on improving Locklate and no doubt a fair sum went into renovating the house against the time when he retired from practice. When he had spent as much as he thought the Inland Revenue would stand for in the south he turned to Scotland.

I don't suppose the fact that the modest Fannich Estate was situated on and owned the riparian rights to, the south bank of a modest river, with a good reputation for both salmon and sea trout, detracted from its appeal. There was a farmhouse with good buildings and some improved pasture. There was also a modest Estate house with views over the sea loch.

The theory was that hardy stock raised on the hill grazing could be sent south to finish profitably in the more lush surroundings of Gloucestershire.

This all coincided with the fact that Grandfather's only outdoor pursuit was game fishing and a little rough shooting and Grandmothers liking for periods of peace and tranquillity, which she found, more frequently when she was in Fannich and Grandfather was in Manchester or more latterly at Locklate.

This had all been the theory anyhow. Seldom, if ever, does theory match up in practice. According to Tommy Black, all had gone well with the new agricultural arrangements and when Harold Forest retired, he sold Helsey Hall in Cheshire, for a considerable sum to a chemical company, to which he was the legal advisor at their new head offices and decamped to Locklate.

In the early days, he and Grandmother had paid quite frequent visits to Fannich, sometimes staying for several weeks at a time. He had a farm manager in the farmhouse who also acted as a factor for the Estate and one of the farm workers looked after the fishing and acted as ghillie as and when needed.

Even the arrangements for the stock had worked for a few years. The young blue-grey Galloway cattle, sent south by rail had fattened well on the Locklate land. Times had changed, however, as they always do and with it the demand for leaner beef and the reluctance of the railways to transport livestock, the enterprise became less profitable.

Added to that the Fosters, with age, became more set in their ways and as Grandmother's health failed, they became more reluctant to make the journeys. Eventually, the house had been let to a retired Judge but the farm was kept on. The original Manager had retired about five years ago and had been replaced by a man called Swan.

Whilst Tommy Black had found out pretty well the history of Fannich there didn't seem to be much up to date news of its progress. I intended to rectify that. I had a feeling in my bones that something was not quite what it should have been.

Pearson at Locklate was the Manager but he seemed to have little say in the overall financial management of the Estate. He was really directly responsible to Harper. Who was Swan responsible to and what degree of control did he have? Who was Harper responsible to, if anyone? Since Harold Forest had become incapable of running his investments and had gone to live in the home in Oxford there seemed to have been a general lack of control.

On the basis of a simple 'back of an envelope' calculation, the return on the capital invested in Locklate looked low. A view backed up by Tim Turner's opinion. What was the situation at Fannich?

Whilst I had been pondering on these matters I had been making steady progress up what had now become a very third rate track to the summit of the land between the main road and the next valley. I was discovering that perhaps I wasn't quite as fit as I had thought I was. The weather, however, was holding up and despite a keen wind, I was sweating pretty well by the time I reached the crest.

I will say that it was an effort well worth making. The view from up there was superb. To the west and north, the open sea and the Isle of Skye and to the northeast, the Highlands. I tried to pick out some of the other, closer features but my map was too localised. I did manage to work out however that the loch to my front was the one which the river at Fannich drained into the sea and once I had got that Fannich House itself was quite distinctive in the landscape. It also looked further than I had thought from the map. However, in for a penny in for a pound. I put the map back in my jacket pocket and pressed on.

Fortunately the track, which at one stage had been barely discernible as such, steadily improved as I got nearer the bottom of the valley which ran across my front. As I got closer it seemed that there was a collection of about ten or a dozen houses where the track met the line of the river and the narrow, very second-class road which ran alongside it.

Fannich House lay to my right, almost at the point where the loch drained into the river. There was then a gap of about half a mile, then there was a cluster of buildings which I took to be the farm. Then a smaller gap to the group of buildings clustered where the track I was on joined the road. Almost like a small scale village.

I stopped by a gateway off the track, at a point which gave a good view of the valley in front of me and got out a plan of the Fannich Estate, provided by Tommy Black. The bigger house to the right and the farm buildings were all part of it. The boundary ran along the river frontage past the little village which wasn't included. The land however which I had crossed was. As was the land on the far hillside on the other side of the valley.

According to Tommy's note, the total came to a little over three thousand acres. From where I was standing, the part on the far side of the river looked pretty rough going but the land in the valley bottom looked neat and well cared for.

I folded up my plan and walked the last few hundred yards to the riverside road. From down in the valley bottom it looked a sight more inviting than it had from part way up the hill. It was obviously quite well sheltered and the land on the far side of the river didn't look quite as steep. There was a small bridge over the river from the farm buildings to the land on the far side and in front of the cluster of cottages, there was a little quayside where a couple of purposeful-looking inshore fishing boats, I suppose about twenty or so feet long, lay on the sandy river bottom.

I leant on a railing which separated the footpath from the top of the quayside. To the left, the river broadened out into what I took to be a sea loch. On the far side of which there seemed to be a collection of some sort of floating rafts.

The only signs of life were at one of the cottages almost opposite the quay. On closer inspection, it looked as if it were some sort of shop. There was a van parked outside and a dog sat with its head half out of the window.

As I started across a man came out of the door, clutching a loaf of bread and got in and started the engine. As he moved off I saw a faded sign which proclaimed that the place was, 'The Fannich Superstore'. It was pretty dark inside after the bright light outside. As my eyes adjusted it was evident that it was, in fact, larger than I had thought. There were shelves, stocked with a somewhat bizarre assortment of goods and a small counter at the back where a lady of uncertain age but considerable girth was pricing up tinned foods with one of those pricing guns which print little sticky labels.

She looked up with some surprise.

"Good morning to you." She had that soft accent that goes with the west coast.

I bade her, "Good Morning." and then, "Could you tell me is there anywhere I can get anything to eat?"

"Not if you're wanting a proper meal but I can find you a bread roll, if that would do for you."

"That would be most kind."

"Would you want anything in it? I have ham or corned beef."

I chose the ham.

Whilst she got it ready she asked, "Have you come far?" and I told her that I had walked over the hill from the Fort William road.

"Och, a tidy step." she commented. "On holiday is it you are?"

I made some sort of non-committal reply and asked if there was any form of transport I could make use of. I was not looking forward to walking all the way back over the hill to my car.

"Not really, the Post Bus will be through about three o'clock but that only goes back to Mallaig. I resigned myself to the long walk. Mrs Rothney finished making my roll and I asked if I might have a drink of some kind and chose a tin of beer. I paid the very modest bill and took my makeshift lunch and sat on the edge of the quay. The roll was very good, filled with thick slices of what I suspected was home-cooked meat.

I sat and contemplated the undeniably splendid and very peaceful view. The thought that I was now, or soon would be, the owner of a great deal of it had a strange but somehow disturbing effect. I was well lost in thought when a discreet cough behind me brought me back to reality.

The kindly Mrs Rothney asked, "Would you take a cup of tea?"

Now the thought of tea after drinking a largish tin of beer didn't really appeal but I had come here to find out as much as I could. It was also evident that Mrs Rothney didn't perhaps have many callers in a day and might be inclined to furnish some of the local gossip at least. I accepted and we walked back across the road to her shop.

We sat in the little room behind the counter and she told me some of the local news I wanted to hear. How she had lived in Fannich since she had married, some forty years. She had stayed on after her husband, who had started the shop when he gave up 'the sea' had died. Her son who was married and lived 'at the end of the village' had been in the Royal Navy but had come back and ran the salmon farm with a partner.

She pointed to the floating rafts that I had seen on the other side of the loch.

"Hard work it is but he makes good money at it." She assured me in an almost conspiratorial tone.

At that point, someone came into the shop. As she went to serve them I started to get up.

"You bide there, I'll not be long."

I looked around the room. Whilst it wasn't luxury it was comfortable and had all the memorabilia of a long life. One of a number of faded photographs caught my eye. I stood up to get a closer look. It showed a well-dressed man holding a fishing rod in his hand. By the side of him stood another, shorter man who was holding up a very large salmon. If I wasn't very much mistaken the taller man was my grandfather, Harold Forest.

As luck would have it Mrs Rothney chose that moment to come back.

To cover my embarrassment I said, "That is a huge fish."

"Aye, that's my Neil, my husband you know, with the old Laird, Mr Forest and the fish was the biggest he ever caught in the river here, forty-eight pound it was."

I could see that I was getting into deep water myself here. I certainly didn't want to deceive this good lady at all and someday I would have to admit to her who I was. I decided to put my cards on the table. It would have to be done carefully, however. I thought that in a tiny place like Fannich, news would travel fast.

"Mrs Rothney, the Mr Forest in that photograph was my grandfather, Harold Forest; my name is Robin Forest."

I had thought that this revelation would cause a degree of surprise but I had underestimated the lady. She looked at me very shrewdly and said, "I had a notion that you might well be at least related. You have the very look of your grandfather about you."

It was me that was surprised. I suppose that because I had never spent much time with any of my grandparents and anyhow what little time I had spent with them had been so long ago that no one had ever commented that I resembled any one of them. I had never thought of it as even a possibility.

I took another look at the picture. I could see what she meant. There was something about the man in the photograph, not the face perhaps but the way he was standing. It was a very odd sensation to think that this good lady had detected a likeness.

Her next question surprised me further, "How is the old gentleman?"

When I told her that he had died a little while ago she told me how sorry she was to hear the news. I was at something of a loss to understand why the fact wasn't known locally. I would have thought that the news of the death of the owner of the Estate would have been important to anyone living here.

Mrs Rothney chatted on about 'the good old days' when Grandfather came for the fishing and the shooting and how 'her Neil' had helped. She told me something of the times when she had 'helped out at the big house' when my grandparents had people to stay.

I asked about the retired Judge who lived there now. It was her turn to look puzzled.

"Och! Him, he left several years ago; went to live near his daughter in Dundee."

"Who lives there now then?" I asked.

"It's empty most of the time but a couple from London come two or three times a year, with their friends, for the sport you know." The tone of her voice spoke of a degree of disapproval.

I asked, "What's their name." But I suspected I already knew the answer.

"Mr and Mrs Harper, Charles Harper."

"And the farm manager, Swan, is he still here?"

Mrs Rothney's face was not one which was capable of a great deal of deception; her opinion was evident before she spoke. "Well I don't know what to say Mr Forest but most of the managing is done by old Angus Farr."

"I thought that this chap Swan was in charge?"

"So he is but he's no a farmer, I dare say that he's got the position because his wife is Mr Harper's daughter."

I let out a long breath. There was, as the Chinese say 'dead fish on the wind.'

At this point, another customer in the shop claimed Mrs Rothney's attention and she seemed to be away quite a long time. After a long hushed conversation in the shop, she came back and said. "Young Hector Farr is in the shop and he is off to take some boxes of fish to Fort William. If you don't mind travelling in his van he says he can drop you anywhere along the road."

The news the old lady had imparted about the Harper Clan, had pushed the matter of getting back to my car from my mind but I still didn't relish the thought of walking.

"I would be very grateful for a lift."

Thanking Mrs Rothney, and very nearly offending her by offering to pay for my tea, I set off with the 'young' Hector.

He was a big strapping man of nearer fifty than forty and it transpired the son of 'Old Angus' who was the nominal foreman at the farm. Hector told me that his father had worked there for a great deal of his life, a fair slice of it for Grandfather.

It was evident that Mrs Rothney had told 'Young Hector' who I was and of the news of Grandfather's death and he couldn't restrain his curiosity.

"I'm sorry to hear about old Mr Forest. Mind you, we haven't seen him for a few years now." He paused. "A stern gentleman he was; always fair though."

I told him it was kind of him to say so.

He concentrated on his driving for a bit and then asked. "Will there be any changes do you know.... on the Estate.... that is?"

It was my turn to think carefully of my reply. Firstly, I was fact-finding and the few facts I had found thus far didn't encourage me to think that all was well with the stewardship of the smooth Mr Harper. Secondly, if I kept the Estate which I would seem to have inherited, I would have to work with the people on it. From what I knew of the west coast of Scotland, which in all truth was precious little, if I wanted harmony which I think I craved almost above all else, I would have to treat them openly and honestly. Much as I had tried to do with anyone I had worked with in life.

"Mr Farr, I really don't know. I came up here to get a feel of the place and to try to decide what I should do for the best.

I have spent virtually the whole of my life as a trading merchant, living and working in the Far East and I know very little of things like Estate management."

I gazed out of the van window at the rolling hills before continuing, "It could be that both the interests of the people who live and work on the Estate and my own interests might best be served by letting things go on as they are.

On the other hand, it might be best to sell up to someone who could improve and develop it. Alternatively, I could just start and find out what I could do to improve it myself."

Hector Farr replied "Aye" to my long reply and went back to concentrating on driving his van.

I liked that.

He confined his further conversation to pointing out features of the landscape and commenting on the very few vehicles which we passed. The Post Bus, something I had never come across before and a couple of lorries laden with timber going to the mill at Fort William and the ownership of several cars.

He asked if I would like him to take me right up to where I had parked my car up the side road and I agreed that I would indeed be grateful if it wasn't too much out of his way. He waved the thought away, saying it would be "Nae trouble".

As we came in sight of my car he slowed, turned his van and then asked, "Might I offer a word?"

I told him I would be glad if he would.

"Fannich used to be a bonnie place in the days when your grandparents came here. The land was well looked after and the sport was very good. These last few years it has gone down. No-one seems to take any interest any more. There is little work about and the youngsters all leave. It could be just as good as it was before, with a bit of trouble."

He added, "I hope you don't think I have spoken out of turn?"

I assured him he hadn't and that I was glad of his thoughts. He paused again and probably feeling he could go a bit further without offence, he added.

"I spent a couple of years in Hong Kong in the Royal Navy so I know a bit about the East, if you ran a successful business out there you'll be nobody's fool. Nothing can survive forever if you don't put back a part of what's taken out."

"For too long Fannich has been paying out and getting nothing back, if you get my meaning!"

I thanked him for his candour and for the lift. I promised I would be in touch before too long and headed for my car. I drove back to the hotel mulling over what few facts over in my mind. The more I thought about it, the less I liked it.

On the face of it, Harper. The smooth, rotund, urbane solicitor had been using Fannich at least as something of a private domain for the benefit of his family and probably himself. Did the same situation apply to Locklate?

The receptionist at the hotel asked me if I had a pleasant day and I arranged for a pot of tea to be sent up to my room.

# CHAPTER 12

The Hotel was run by a young couple called March. The husband, Peter was the chef and the wife Helen oversaw the running of the place. They were young and enthusiastic and seemed well up to the job.

Helen March came into the hall just as I was about to go to my room and after the usual pleasantries, I asked about dinner. She produced a menu from the reception desk and after a little discussion we settled on smoked fresh scallops and bacon to start with and local lamb as a main course. I chose a half bottle of Chiroubles to have with the lamb.

I drank my tea and had a soak in a deep, hot bath and emerged feeling tired but happy that I had had a useful day. Whilst I was contemplating the superb view down Loch Arisaig, a knock at the door heralded a young girl come to collect the tea things and to ask if I needed anything else. I asked for a half bottle of Champagne which she returned with very promptly accompanied by a dish of, what I took to be, potato crisps. Now I am not a great lover of such things but I tried one and found it to be very tasty indeed. Later I found out that they were, in fact, deep fried filo pastry. I would suggest that all half decent establishments should adopt them at once!

I lay on the bed and reached for the telephone.

Tommy Black was at home and after telling him where I was and how he could contact me I gave him the facts as I had found them. I think I was beginning to feel angry that Solicitor Harper, on the face of it at least, had been running the Fannich Estate as his own domain for the benefit and profit of himself and his family.

Tommy was as usual full of common sense. "Now look Robin, we certainly don't know that for sure. Your grandfather may well have sanctioned everything he has done."

I admitted that was possible.

"We don't know what instructions he gave Harper - he might have given him carte blanche to find a new manager when the old one retired. The fact that the new manager appears to be his son-in-law might not look too good to you but I can't see anything criminal about it. We just don't know."

I 'mummed' a sort of reluctant agreement down the phone.

After a reflective pause on both sides, he went on. "The best thing we can do is for me to go and see Harper and, as a first stage, ask for the full accounts for both Fannich and Locklate for the last five years say?" He put the suggestion in the form of a question awaiting my approval.

"I'll go along with that, but will that tell us anything?"

"It will give us a good pointer as to if he's just taking advantage of the situation or if he's actively dishonest."

"All right, you win. When will you go and see him?"

"I'm up in the office tomorrow; I'll try and get an appointment to see him as soon as possible. Are you staying up there for a long?"

"Not sure, I don't think I can do much more unless I go and make a formal call on this chap Swan."

"Tell you what, I'll tell Harper tomorrow that you are in the area and that you are going to call in and see Swan - then it's all open and above board - but I think you would be better to wait till you hear from me."

I agreed to wait and gave Tommy the number of my new mobile 'phone. He chaffed me about such modern trappings, "You'll be a Yuppie before you're finished. Call you tomorrow."

I finished my Champagne and got ready to go down to dinner.

The meal was really very good. The scallops were locally caught and were first class. The lamb was excellent if a fraction on the underdone side. The only slight disappointment was the vegetables. The potatoes were fine but the peas were of the frozen variety as were, I suspected, the baby carrots.

Halfway through, Helen March came and asked me if all was well with the meal. I asked her if she would join me in a glass of the Chiroubles. She looked round to see all else was well, fetched another glass and sat down.

I answered her question about the meal. She was quite happy that I was so honest, explaining that while fresh fish and meat were no problem to get, the difficulties getting top quality vegetables, especially green vegetables, were formidable. All to do with a lack of local production and the distances involved. I could see the problems.

I commented on the few people in the dining room. Helen March explained about the season and the difficulties of running a high standard hotel in the more remote parts of Scotland where they were virtually totally dependent on tourism. She also touched on the problems of staffing such an enterprise when all the local youngsters tended to leave for the brighter lights of the big towns.

I quizzed her gently about her and her husband's history and she told me that they had met when they were both working at a large hotel in Stirling and that they had been able to branch out on their own as the result of coming into some money when her mother had died. She didn't say so, but I deduced that they were finding the going quite tough.

I decided against the cheese and opted for a quite excellent apricot tart. I had my coffee in the lounge with a very decent glass of Calvados and thumbed through a weighty tome which seemed to explain the many diseases of the red grouse. So many, in fact, that I began to wonder how the poor creatures survived at all to the point where they could eventually present themselves to be shot.

I gave up such a sombre pursuit and took myself to my room. I tried the late news on television but that was no improvement in entertainment value consisting, as it did, of various political leaders telling the nation that the 'current problems' were either the peoples own fault or that of the 'previous administration'.

Why do such people never try telling the truth and saying, "Sorry, we made a cock up, we will try and do better?"

I retired to bed and a study of the local maps.

***

The next day was, to put it politely, bracing. Whilst the sun still shone the wind from the south-west was pretty keen. I had a quick walk around the grounds of the hotel to develop a sharpness for breakfast which I assuaged by way of a pair of very tasty kippers.

I got the car out of the garage and set off for Fort William.

I did a round of the few Estate agents, suggesting, perhaps by default of direct answers that I was looking for a place to retire to. There seemed a number of rather dreary bungalows and cottages but larger properties were notably missing from the selection. I decided to move upmarket.

The Fort William office of a large London based firm of 'property consultants' - so much more gentile than 'Estate agent', I supposed - provided an eager young man who seemed to know something of the upper end of the market and plied me with questions about my needs and how much I had a mind to spend to meet them.

I mentioned a figure which produced a somewhat less enthusiastic response. Was I not aware that the market was very buoyant for the type of property I had in mind? I admitted ignorance in such matters.

When I mentioned such trivial desires as a few acres of rough shooting and perhaps a few yards of fishing rights his eyebrows shot up to new heights. Such desirable features were only obtainable at figures far in excess of the one I had hinted at.

It would seem that from this source, at least, that the sort of property I had envisaged was in very short supply and being sought after by virtually every and any sensible person with a few hundred thousand pounds to rub together.

I got the distinct impression that for 'few' it would be better to think in terms of 'many'.

To give the poor chap his due, he did arm me with several very glossy brochures of impressive barrack-like houses, all of which mentioned the phrase like, 'would benefit from a degree of modernisation' or 'potential for improvement'. Estate agents speak for 'semi-derelict,' I suspected.

I tried another couple of places with much the same results, except for one little piece of information I gleaned. At a long established firm of solicitors who acted as Estate agents as well, I asked if there were any properties for sale on the west coast, somewhere in the Mallaig area and that got, if not a bite, a little nibble at my bait.

"Nothing specific in Mallaig itself, but I did hear of a possibility that there could be a place for sale in that general area in the near future."

I asked him if he could point out the rough location on the map on his wall. He put his finger virtually on top of Fannich. Without any emotion, I asked what sort of a place it was.

"Well there's nothing definite at the moment but we were asked our advice on the likely sales potential for a moderately large house in that area."

"What would you class as moderate?"

"I think it had six or seven bedrooms; I'm not sure exactly."

Fannich House had six bedrooms. I decided to ride my luck a little further. "Is the present owner moving away do you know?"

"I couldn't really say Sir, the enquiry was from a London firm of solicitors, something to do with inheritance tax I think but I really don't know."

The man asked if he could have a name and an address so that he could send any information on. I stalled by saying that I was staying in the area for a while and would call back in a few days and let him have an address when I had found somewhere to stay. He didn't seem very happy at that and the thought occurred to me that should the property indeed be Fannich House and if Harper should be in contact again they might mention that someone had been asking after the place. If they hadn't a name it might arouse a suspicion. I gave him the first name that came into my head, Bird.

I was just getting into my car when my 'phone rang. I confess that it took me somewhat by surprise and it was several moments before I found it in the glove box. It was Tommy Black.

"That you, Robin?"

I assured him it was. "I've been trying to get hold of you for the last hour but there was no reply."

I confessed that the phone had been in the car and I hadn't.

"Look, the whole idea is that you carry the wretched thing with you, switched on!"

I promised to be a better Yuppie in the future.

"I've spoken to Harper, had quite a long conversation in fact. He's not too happy about us wanting accounts but I told him you needed them to help you decide what to do with both Locklate and Fannich."

"Was he happy at that?"

"I think so, he tried to pump me as to what I thought you might do but I told him I had no idea, as indeed I don't."

"Neither do I at this stage."

"I also told him that you were in Scotland and intended calling at Fannich."

"How did he take that?"

"Not too enthusiastic I would say. He said that Swan, the Factor was away and there wouldn't be anyone to answer your questions. I told him I thought you would go anyhow."

"Did he mention that Mr and Mrs Swan were his son-in-law and daughter by any chance?"

"No. He didn't and that omission might just bring me round to your way of thinking."

"How do you mean?"

"Well if it was all open and above board, you would have thought that he would have said something to make the situation clear. I believe I would have done so."

"What you are saying is that you think, like me, that the man is a crook?"

Tommy Black took his time with his answer. When it came it was forceful.

"Look, Robin, I said no such thing and I don't even think it. What's more as your legal advisor I must urge you not to say things like that. You'll get yourself into trouble."

I took the somewhat less than subtle warning.

"So what do you think then?"

"For a start, Harper's no fool. He is a successful man with a big and reputable firm. I don't think he's would be outright dishonest. Looking after your grandfather's affairs must have been a profitable account over the years.

I think, perhaps he has let things slide a bit over the last few years - perhaps given too free a hand - he hasn't given it as much attention as he should but I would be very surprised if he was milking the Estates, either of them. The risks would have been too high and the profit too small.

At the end of the day, I think that we will find evidence of a certain amount of ill-judged behaviour, putting his son-in-law in charge, that sort of thing, but not fraud."

I laughed, "That's what I think I like most about you Tommy, think the best about people until the worst is written out in black and white."

His somewhat stuffy reply was, "Robin, it's an attitude that's served me well over a long life; you could do worse than think the same way."

"Point taken, Tommy."

"One other thing, Harper made the point that he was chief executor to the will and as such, until everything is settled, he has control over the running of the Estates. He asked me to remind you of that. Of course, in that, he is quite right."

"What did you say?"

"In turn, I reminded him that you, my client, were a rich man in your own right and had been a very successful businessman over many years. You would be looking for the whole thing to be wrapped up efficiently and quickly, with as little hassle as possible. I also said that you would not tolerate unnecessary delay or expense."

I paused, that was about as stout a support as I could want or, indeed, need.

I told him I was touched by his support.

"Well, I'm not quite the pushover that he might think."

"Oh! the other small thing, there is a package come for you, I think it's the copies of the working accounts from Pearson at Locklate that you were expecting, do you want me to send them on?"

I suggested that he opened them and kept them till I came back south.

"Any idea when that will be?"

"Not sure, a few days I think. I'll keep you posted."

We bade each other 'Goodbye' and rang off.

I drove slowly back to the hotel anticipating a long bath and a decent dinner.

I thought that I might 'phone Swan and make an appointment for the next day. Then I had second thoughts and decided that he might just put me off, I decided just to turn up on his doorstep and see what transpired. Not perhaps, the best manners but I wasn't worried about being too popular. I had the feeling that I wouldn't be anyway!

A dish of warm goat's cheese on a splendid salad followed by a modest Aberdeen Angus steak, done to perfection and a near perfect crème brûlée, fortified me sufficiently to see me through to a breakfast of cold, home cooked ham with a poached egg on top.

Thus in some good humour, I set off for Fannich.

It was just after ten o'clock when I drew up outside the home farmhouse halfway between the hamlet and Fannich House.

My first impression was that it was pretty untidy, why farmers spend good money on equipment and then leave it lying about wherever they last finished using it has always defeated me. There was a dirty, newish Land Rover parked outside the front door and the nose of an even newer Jaguar poked out from a barn. No shortage of money then.

I rang the doorbell. I waited some time and had the distinct impression that I was being inspected from a window.

# CHAPTER 13

The door was eventually partially opened and a female face, still half hidden behind it, regarded me carefully.

"Yes?"

"Good morning, my name is Robin Forest, I have called to see Mr Swan, if he's in."

The door opened a bit further.

"What about?" The question was put in such a way that it implied that I was something of an irritant.

I considered my reply carefully, "I've come to talk to him about the Estate." Then added, "And you are?"

There was a pause of some moments while she thought over her options.

"I'm Marion Swan, Cedric is my husband. I suppose you had better come in." The reluctance was teetering on the edge of studied rudeness.

She opened the door fully. A well-built woman of, I suppose, forty-something, dressed in what might be called 'Scottish gentry' style: cashmere jumper, plaid skirt and sensible shoes. She had one of those green padded, sleeveless jackets on over the jumper. A string of real pearls - if I wasn't much mistaken - and a hair band completed the ensemble.

The hall was bigger than I expected, two yellow Labradors sprawled on a rug at the bottom of the stairs. Marion Swan indicated a door to the right at the same time as she called out "Cedric, it's Mr Forest, about the Estate," and then to me, "We won't be a moment."

I stood and looked about. Well furnished, quite newly decorated, an old but good Indian carpet and some attractive paintings on the walls. They looked as if they had new frames. The window looked down towards a good view of the river and the hills beyond it. Very attractive.

Marion Swan came back and in her wake, Cedric.

They were certainly a pretty ill-matched couple. After Marion, I had expected a semi-military figure in a hairy tweed suit. What I saw instead was a thin, bearded man dressed in faded jeans and a rather dirty tee-shirt. He said "Hello." and didn't come close enough to shake hands.

There was an awkward silence and I got the impression the ball was firmly in my court.

"Mr and Mrs Swan, I am Robin Forest. I'm Augustus Forest's grandson. As you know he died recently and I am told by his solicitor, Mr Charles Harper, of Harper and Swinburn in London, that I am to inherit his Estate, of which the Fannich Estate is a part."

I pause for breath and to watch for any reaction. I got very little.

"Has Mr Harper been in touch?"

Cedric Swan looked as if he were about to make some sort of reply but a look from wife Marion prevented it. She was going to do the talking obviously.

"He rang to tell us that your grandfather had died, certainly, and he phoned to say that you might call. We were rather expecting you would telephone and make an appointment though."

I let the implied rebuke pass. If they wanted to play it like that it would be tedious but I could cope with it.

"I was passing so I called in on the off chance. What I would like to do is to have a look round the land in general and, of course, Fannich Lodge and this house so that I know what I am dealing with."

I had been going to add "So that I can come to a decision what I will do with the place once all the formalities have been completed." but I never got that far.

Cedric started to say something but he was overridden again.

Marion said, rather too quickly, "Quite impossible." then thought better of it and added, "At the moment."

I looked directly at her eyes and said, "Why!"

"My husband and I are far too busy just now; perhaps if you came back in a week or two we might be able to arrange something."

I looked out of the window to collect my thoughts and to steady my temper.

"Look, it's a perfectly reasonable request, I too am a busy man and I'd like to see around the place whilst I am here; I'm happy to come back tomorrow to look at the houses. I've got a plan of the land and I am quite happy to look at that on my own."

Marion Swan looked as she had just bitten into a lemon but perhaps something at the back of her mind urged her to keep her tongue in check. But not quite enough. "Our lease doesn't say anything........" She trailed off to silence.

I went on, "I will take a walk round now and I will be back tomorrow at what, let's say ten-thirty and I can look round the two houses then." Before she cut in I decided to rub a bit of salt in the wound.

"If you are not happy at that I suggest you phone Harper today and see what he thinks. You might also ask him to send a copy of any lease you may have to my solicitor - he knows who he is."

I had the impression that mighty Marion was going to burst.

"Our lease! What on earth's that got to do with you?"

"Everything, Mrs Swan, everything. For one thing, it will have a bearing on the sale price should I decide to sell the place."

"Sell?" she said it as if it were a swear word.

I decided to offer a truce. "Look, let's be reasonable about this, I just want to judge what it is I've inherited. I don't want to create trouble either for you and your husband or the people who work on the Estate but I have got to have the facts."

"Harper has already been asked to produce the last few years accounts for the place and, when I have got all the information, I need I will make a decision. Fair enough?"

Marion Swan certainly didn't think so but I pressed on.

"We can either do it amicably or we can do it the hard way, it's really up to you. Ten-thirty tomorrow then?"

Marion's mouth was fixed in a cold hard line, Cedric's open as if he were about to say something but couldn't. I saw myself out.

*** 

I could have left the car where it was and started my tour but I thought that would be going a bit far. I think I could hear Tommy Black somewhere in my mind. "Steady Robin."

I drove out onto the lane and turned up the valley. I went a few hundred yards and pulled in onto the verge to look at the plan of the place. Roughly speaking, the road up the valley formed the southern edge of the Estate land; most of the cultivated land lay between the road and the river with a bit more on the far side. Another, smaller lane ran along the other side of the river and the loch and on the far side of that to the north lay most of the grazing land, climbing away to the crest of the hills. As far as I could see the only way across the river was by the bridge near the farm buildings.

I drove about another half mile or so up the valley to see where, what I was starting to think of as 'my land', finished. It coincided with the end of the cultivated land

and was marked with a cattle grid, beyond that it was rough heather and bracken. I turned around and drove back to the bridge over the river.

I parked off the lane and changed my shoes for boots and swapped my jacket for my anorak. I hung my field glasses around my neck and remembering Tommy's advice put my mobile phone in my pocket.

I stopped at the middle of the bridge and took in the view.

To the west, the river, once past the bridge opened out quite quickly to form the estuary and the sea loch, with the cottages of Fannich itself to the left. I could see the little quay where two boats lay moored, afloat now on the tide. To the right the loch stretched away to the hills and with the glasses I could see the square shapes of the fish farm tanks near the far shore.

Turning and looking upstream the roof of Fannich Lodge was just visible over a stand of pine trees. The farmhouse was almost to my right and from here it looked quite a decent sort of house. If you believed the Estate Agents dictum of 'Location, Location, Location' both houses were well worth inheriting. Certainly with the green of the fields, the browns and purples of the hills and the sunlight glittering on the water, it was pretty well perfect. A second thought made me wonder what it was like in winter, especially with a sharpish westerly gale blowing.

I turned left over the bridge where the track ran along the shore of the widening sea Loch. I was under the impression that I would have to retrace my route to go upstream but I found the beginning of a smaller rougher track which seemed to cut back across the flank of the hill.

A careful study of the plan revealed a dotted line which I hadn't noticed before and it was drawn so that it was shown as running parallel to the crest but about a third of the way from the bottom. It dropped back to the bottom track about a mile above the bridge. A rough measure told me that the round trip would be about four miles. In my condition, say a couple of hours or so. The exercise would do me good and sharpen me up for a decent dinner.

In truth, it proved to be steeper than I had thought but I made it to where the track started to run along the hill before I took a rest. The view was magnificent. I got the glasses out again and I could see for miles to the south and west. About halfway along the track, when I was opposite the farmhouse, I had another rest and studied it from this high vantage point.

As I watched, I caught a flash of light from the back of the house. It was apparent I wasn't the only one with a pair of binoculars. I dropped down behind a bit of cover and shading the lenses with the hood of my anorak studied the farmhouse carefully. Marion was sweeping the hillside with what looked like a telescope.

I suppose I should have known better but I couldn't resist the temptation. I stood up and waved to her. All right, I must have been about five or six hundred yards from the house but with a telescope, she could hardly fail to see me. I don't think she waved back.

It was only after I stood back that the chilling thought, that she could just as easily have been holding a rifle with a telescopic sight, entered my head.

I had found out why the track was there. There were two lines of shooting butts stretching from the road in the valley up to the track. Another line went from the track up toward the crest. It must have been put in at some time to get sportsmen up onto the slope as well as to make it easier to manage the grazing stock.

I made it back to my car in just over the two hours and since I still had plenty of time I decided to call on the redoubtable Mrs Rothney. I parked by the quay and crossed the road to the shop.

Mrs Rothney, as round as ever, greeted me warmly. "Och! It's young Mr Forest, are you well?"

We both agreed that we had never been better which was, I suppose, either a deliberate untruth or wishful thinking on both our parts.

"Will you take the tea?"

I agreed that that would be 'Most kind'.

"Come through..... come through." She lifted the flap in the counter and we went into the room behind the shop.

We chatted about inconsequential matters while she brewed the tea and ferreted about amongst some tins to find "An odd end of cake" which turned out to be a substantial slab of fruit cake with a fruit content of about eighty percent. Eventually, her curiosity got the better of her.

"Is there any news of the Estate then?"

I told her that I had been to see the Swans and that I had had a look over some of the land but what I needed was a word with Mr Farr senior.

"I don't know where he's working just now but young Hector will be by soon, I'll ask him."

"Do you know what time Mr Farr will finish work?" She looked surprised.

"When whatever he's doing is done I suppose. We don't keep regular hours out here you know."

I accepted the faint rebuke.

"I'm coming back tomorrow, I'm looking over the Lodge and the farmhouse; maybe I could have a talk with him then if he's about."

"What time will you be here?"

"I'm due at the Lodge at half past ten."

"If I can, should I tell him to be here at one o'clock?"

I agreed that would be fine. I took Mrs Rothney's telephone number and told her I would give her a call in the morning to check. I drove back to my hotel happy, slightly less hungry than I should have been but still determined to do justice to dinner.

When I got back Helen March had got a list of people who had telephoned. Seemingly, I had just missed the latest call, from a Mr Charles Harper. He wanted to contact me as soon as possible; Helen had told him that she expected me soon and he had agreed to call back later.

Tommy Black had left a message to call him but it wasn't urgent.

A Lester Porter had called at lunchtime but had left no message, nor a contact number. So far as I could recollect I didn't know a Mr Porter.

I armed myself with a half bottle of Taittinger and headed for the bath.

I told Helen that I didn't talk to people whilst in the bath and if anyone rang in the next half an hour would she be kind enough to take a number and I would return their call after my ablutions. She said she would take pleasure in doing so; especially if it were Mr Harper. I gathered that he had been less than polite when he called before.

True to form, efficient girl that she was, she rang the bedroom phone just after I emerged from the bath, said Harper had phoned and gave me his number. I gave it another ten minutes and dialled it. He replied at once.

"Harper."

"Forest. I'm returning your call."

"Ah! Good, I've been trying to reach you for some time. Some girl told me you were in the bath and wouldn't be disturbed?" He put it as a question to which he didn't believe there could be an answer.

I replied, "Very true."

He sensed my mood, which I dare say was aided by the excellent wine of Maison Taittinger.

"Well, I've got you at last. Look, I've had Mrs Swan on the telephone and she is rather upset about your visit this morning." Still no mention of the fact that Marion Swan was his daughter. Odd!

"I can't think why."

"She says that you were insistent on looking around the place although it wasn't convenient and that you were somewhat rude."

I took time out to consider my reply.

He was impatient, "Mr Forest, are you still there?"

"Umm, yes, still here. I was wondering how she thought I was rude?"

"She says that you demanded to see her lease."

"That's quite untrue, I didn't know until she mentioned it that they had a lease and since that would affect a sale price it must be taken into account. I merely asked her, very politely, if she would arrange for a copy to be sent to my solicitor; I can't see anything wrong in that, can you?"

Harper conceded the point but quickly took up the mention of a sale.

His tone changed noticeably to that of the persuasive man of affairs.

"If you have decided to sell I'm sure I know of a potential buyer for the whole Estate!"

I decided to have one more go at the reasonable approach.

"Look Mr Harper. I have already explained several times to everyone, I need to know all the facts about all my grandfather's affairs before I come to any decision about what I am going to do. I may well decide to sell everything, on the other hand, I might sell off some parts and keep some. I really don't know and can hardly be expected to decide unless I am in possession of all the facts, you must see that."

To give Harper his due he tried. "I quite see your point Mr Forest - very wise - will do everything I can to help..." He trundled on but I was only half listening. There were several thoughts running through my mind and none of them induced me to let Harper or his insufferable daughter get away with anything.

I cut in. "Look, I've arranged to go to Fannich again tomorrow morning and look at the farmhouse and the buildings and The Lodge. I will talk to Swan, if his wife will let me, and I may want to take another look round the land, probably with the foreman who I understand is called Farr."

Harper 'hummed', his equivalent I presumed to Tommy's 'Just so' when he was being non-committal.

"As soon as I have finished this call I will phone my chap, Tommy Black, and I'll get him to liaise with you tomorrow and arrange a meeting of the three of us and we can go through all the questions I have."

I added as an afterthought, "I may well need to bring my accountant to the meeting as well- he might as well be in on it - I shall need his advice and it's better if he's in the picture."

I smiled to myself that the only accountant I employed was a chap called Li Wan and he was, to the best of my knowledge, still where he lived, in Hong Kong. I would have to find someone quick.

Harper wasn't exactly over the moon at my suggestion but there was little he could protest at but he tried. Phrases like, "Rather too soon." and "A great deal of work to do to gather all the information."

I had had enough. I suggested, "Early next week would be fine. I will be in London briefly. I'll leave it to yourself and Tommy to fix it up between you."

I bade him a pleasant evening and rang off.

Now I had been longer on the phone to Harper than I had thought and I didn't want my dinner to spoil so I made a quick call to Tommy and very briefly explained what had transpired. I got the feeling that he thought I was going at it a bit strong but agreed to arrange a meeting for early after the weekend.

I added, "Look Tommy, I know you have reservations about all this but there is something not right about the whole thing - I can sense it - I honestly don't think it's just a case of Harper being sloppy or the Swans feathering their own nest. Something is going on and I want to know what it is."

Dear old Tommy gave me one of his very non-committal 'Just so's! "What do you want then?"

"What we need is a jolly good accountant, a chap used to ferreting about a bit. You must know someone?"

He thought for a bit. "I still think you're barking up the wrong tree Robin but you are the client after all and if you think that's what's needed, so be it."

"Do you know anyone then?"

"There is a chap we use from time to time. He's really an insolvency practitioner but if he's got the time he would be your man."

"Ask him, at least, to make the time to come to the meeting, we can take his advice after that, see what he thinks."

"I'll ask him Robin, I can't do more than that." He added, "He'll cost you though!"

I told him it would be money well spent.

Tommy asked if I would stay with him in Westminster, I accepted and rang off.

Dinner was a delight. Having been used to Oriental food for so long, I much prefer quality to quantity and that evening I was not let down. The quail pâté was sublime, accompanied by a glass of Cadillac Chateau La Bertrande '82. It was very good. A locally caught lobster with a half bottle of '83 Bâtard-Montrachet from Sauzet and a raspberry concoction, which must almost have classed as a work of art, rather than a pudding.

I sat in the sitting room afterwards with a coffee and a glass of a very superior Hine Antique a contented man.

# CHAPTER 14

Next morning I took the precaution of borrowing a rather official looking clipboard from Helen March and after a short hunt, a long tape measure from her husband. Thus armed I set forth for Fannich.

As I arrived at the Swans' I sensed a change in manner, if not in atmosphere. Madam Marion was on the doorstep to meet me and she was as near civil as I thought she ever managed. Someone, I suspected, had had a word with her overnight.

I asked after the non-appearance of Mr Swan.

"Cedric has had to go into Fort William, I'm afraid. Urgent business you know, sorry."

I didn't know but could well guess.

"When will he be back?"

"Not until late I'm afraid - he's seeing some people this evening as well, he might well stay over until the morning."

I suggested that we would deal with that matter later.

Now Marion Swan had got the wrong idea about what I meant by 'looking over' the property. She had in mind a quick look round. I had a different plan, hence the tape measure and the clipboard. I started by making a meal of measuring up the hall and sketching out a plan.

Her irritation was wonderful to behold.

She 'tutted' and sighed. Purposely, to annoy her, I asked her to hold the end of the tape."At this rate, this will take all day," she complained. I assured her that I expected that it well might.

"If you have other things to do I am quite happy to do it on my own." That seemed to shut her up.

In stony silence I progressed from room to room making my plan in some detail. I assured her that, yes, I would need to do the upstairs as well and even that the attic would need a visit.

By twelve o'clock I had seen all there was to see of the farmhouse. By one o'clock I had 'done' the farm buildings. I told her that I would be at the Lodge at two. I offered to take the keys and look at it on my own but she said she would see me there.

I got in the car and went back to Mrs Rothney's shop.

Her greeting was warm and she told me that Mr Farr was waiting in the back room for me. I went through.

Angus Farr was just about what I expected. A big man, slightly stooped with age but still an imposing figure. I judged that he must have been very near seventy but looked younger. He stood up and we shook hands.

He had that same soft burr of the west coast as Mrs Rothney.

"I'm pleased to meet you, Mr Forest, I'm sorry though to hear the news of your grandfather. What can I do for ye?"

Mrs Rothney, still hovering in the doorway, said, "I'll leave you men to yourselves, I've work to do."

There was a plate of sandwiches on the table with a bottle of malt and a couple of glasses. A kind thought.

We sat. I started the ball rolling by explaining why I was there.

"Now I don't want to get off on the wrong foot, Mr Farr but I do need to know something about the Estate before I decide what I must do."

"Ay, I understand that."

"On the other hand, I don't want you to think that I'm going behind Mr Swan's back in talking to you like this."

He gave me another, "Ay." Not indicating whether he thought I was or wasn't.

"I'm not asking what you think of Swan but I do want to know about the Estate. Is it a viable agricultural proposition? If it isn't, could it be one in the future? What does it need that it hasn't got now .... that sort of thing."

I wasn't going to get any instant answers out of Angus Farr, that was certain. He poured himself a small measure of whisky, tasted it and helped himself to a sandwich, bit into it and studied his glass.

I did likewise and waited. After munching his way through half the sandwich he said, "Money Mr Forest, that's what's needed. Money and someone who cares what goes on."

I asked him to explain further.

"I hear what you say about Mr Swan - and I mean no disrespect - but the man knows nothing about how to run an Estate. He doesn't seem to realise that these days ye need to keep up to date and that takes money. I don't know the figures but I've a good idea what they might be and I'll wager that the place only just about holds its own."

"Who runs the accounts?"

"Again I don't know, Mrs Swan does the wages, that I do know, but beyond that you'll have to ask Mr Swan."

"Do you think, Mr Farr, that the Estate could make a decent profit?"

He looked at me steadily for a moment and went on, "That I do."

"How?"

"On the farm, you need to spend on things like decent machinery, better quality animals, fertiliser, better seeds - all those things; a poor animal costs just as much to rear as a good one!"

He resumed eating his sandwich. I suspect he hadn't composed such a long sentence for some time.

"You said 'on the farm'.... what about 'off the farm'?"

"Well, there's the sport; the Estate should be making money from that. Rich people will pay good money for the fishing and the shooting."

"Aren't they let out then?"

"Not that I know of. That Mr Harper comes up once or twice a year and usually brings a friend or two but we should do it on a proper scale. Meoler, that's the place over the hill, they make a good thing out of it."

"How do they do it?"

"Och! they have an agent and he lets it out for them; Germans, Americans, all sorts; they pay big money for it, so I'm told."

I thought to myself, 'I'll bet they do'. Despite Tommy Black's strictures I was going to have a few questions for Charles Harper and I was prepared to wager a few pounds that he would have a job answering them, to my satisfaction at least.

I thanked Angus Farr for his frankness and his time and promised I would be in touch as soon as I had sorted things out.

He hesitated and then, looking me directly in the eyes said. "Mr Forest, there's plenty people round about who'll be worried, waiting to see what you decide, think on them before you make up your mind.... that's all we ask."

I assured him that I would certainly do just that.

I was a few moments late arriving at Fannich Lodge which didn't seem to endear me any further to Marion Swan, judging by the way she rather pointedly looked at her watch as I drove up.

We went in, in a somewhat stony silence.

The place was much larger than I had expected. There was what can only be described as a spacious hall with an impressive staircase and two big reception rooms at either side. A dining room that would have seated twenty with no problem was at the left rear and a good sized library to the right. In all, a bigger house than the outside would have led you to imagine.

I measured and sketched to Mrs Swan's annoyance. There was a big kitchen reached from behind the stairs and that, in turn, led to a number of smaller rooms, larders, sculleries and the like. My measuring got a bit sloppier. I, too, was feeling that it was a bit of a waste of time but as an argument for seeing everything, it was unquestionable.

Upstairs, there were certainly six principle bedrooms, all of a size that you don't see in modern houses but there were another six smaller rooms which I suppose had been for the staff and hardly counted when writing the 'Estate Agents' details of such a place. All the smaller rooms were quite empty.

In a sort of annex, built to one side of the frontage there was a gun room and a very much larger room which I surmised must have been built as a billiard room. In fact, if you looked hard you could see where the legs of the table had stood at some time.

Politely I asked, "What happened to the billiard table?"

The mighty Marion, looked at me as if I were making an indecent suggestion.

"What billiard table?"

"The one that must have been here."

She was stupid enough to try to bluff it out. "I don't remember there ever having been one."

I pointed to the leg marks and then to the place where the overhead lights must once have been. I looked round and then showed her where the scoring board must have been screwed to the wall.

"I said I didn't ever remember there ever having been one; I didn't say that there had never been one." She said it with an air of a tennis player serving an ace.

I let it go for the time being. My reckoning with the Swans would come later.

"Now is there anything else to see Mrs Swan?"

"I rather think you have seen it all.... at least twice."

I made a pantomime of thinking for a moment. "Ah! I know, the cellar."

She, in turn, looked puzzled, "Is there one, I really wouldn't know."

"I think there must be. There's central heating but we haven't seen a boiler and it must be a big one for a place this size, ergo there must be a cellar.

I went in search of a door that had been overlooked.

Funnily enough, it was a bit like the cellar door at Locklate; semi-concealed by the panelling round the bottom of the staircase. It was locked and there wasn't a key that fitted it on the bunch that Marion Swan had!

"Look, Mrs Swan, this is getting silly, very soon there will have to be an inspection and a probate valuation done of the house and its contents. Now there *must* be some sort of inventory of the contents and I would very much like to see it."

If hatred had anything to do with it I would have been dead meat.

"I don't know of any inventory, as you call it."

"Then I suggest you ask your husband, after all, he is supposed to be in charge and he must have some sort of list at least."

218

Mighty Marion had another attack of the hates and said, "Are you accusing us of stealing the wretched furniture now?"

I gave her my most placatory smile. "Of course not, but you can see for yourself that from the patches on the wallpaper there must have been several pictures that have been taken down, the small rooms upstairs are all empty, they must have had beds at least."

"The floorboards show where rugs and carpets must have been at some time; I would suspect that either they have been put in storage or else perhaps, put in the cellar for safety's sake. Just look, there's hardly a vase or an ornament in sight, they must have been put away somewhere and since I have been all over the house and not found them, either they are in store or in the cellar, it stands to reason."

The poor woman didn't know if she should argue and make matters worse or agree.

"Look." I went on, "I've got my mobile phone in the car, why don't you ring your husband and ask him if he knows if the stuff is in store with a removals firm or put away somewhere safe here and ask if he's got a list?"

She protested that she wasn't sure where he would be, as I expected she well might.

"Otherwise, I'll leave it for now and check with him tomorrow when he gets back. There must be a sensible answer."

She had to be content with that. She seemed deflated, to have lost her immediate anger, if not the look of pure loathing she gave me. She locked up, I went to my car and she to her Land Rover.

# CHAPTER 15

I didn't think it worth calling in on Mrs Rothney at the shop for the one piece of information I needed. I stopped the car just where the road ran alongside the coast and whilst I dialled in her number on my mobile, I was well aware of just what a beautiful part of the world it was.

"Mrs Rothney, it's Robin Forest. Sorry to trouble you but I have a question you might be able to answer."

"Mr Forest, halloo, it's no trouble, what is it?"

"Can you remember when you last saw the billiard table in Fannich Lodge?"

You could hear the amusement in her voice, "Is it billiards now? Let me think. It was certainly there when the old Judge left - he was very keen on the snooker you know - but the cloth was torn, it will need a new one, I'm thinking."

I thanked her and rang off.

I drove back to the hotel in a thoughtful mood.

I armed myself with a large Pimms and retired to my bath to mull over the day's events before I phoned Tommy Black and found out if he had a man lined up for our meeting with Harper and to arrange a session with him beforehand to talk tactics.

I explained, in some detail, to Tommy what had transpired during the day and that I was now firmly convinced that there was some sort of fraud going on, certainly as far as Fannich was concerned. About Locklate I was much less certain.

It seemed to me, that the retirement of the previous Factor at Fannich, had given Harper the opportunity of putting Swan in the job and that they had just deliberately run the place for their own benefit and not for the good of the whole Estate. I also thought that Cedric Swan and his wife had systematically stripped the Lodge. What had become of the loot was anyone's guess. Probably a not too near saleroom.

I think that at last Tommy was beginning to agree with me. You can take the business of thinking the best of people too far!

He had been in touch with his insolvency accountant, a man called Nick Conway and he would take on the job of looking at the affairs of the whole Estate. He would also come to the meeting with Harper and have a meeting beforehand so that we could pass on what we knew. Things were looking up, at least in that direction.

Sad to say that dinner that evening was a bit of a letdown. Maybe I wasn't in the mood. Somehow, nothing quite came up to expectation. I don't think it was all the fault of the food or the wine, though I didn't much care for the wild mushroom and dill soup and I thought the Rully, a Clos Saint-Jacques '82, which I had with the capon, was past its prime. No, somehow the feeling that there was something rotten about the Fannich Estate spoilt the whole flavour everything.

I still didn't know what the likely outcome of my inheritance would be, there still could be undisclosed debts hiding away somewhere, but I doubted that they would be major. It was the feeling that the gloss had gone off it somewhere along the line. There was also the growing feeling that I was going to be responsible for the future of a lot of people who were dependent on both Fannich and Locklate.

It wasn't just myself and my search for that elusive Shangri La that was at stake. I went to bed somewhat dispirited and sad at the thought of what might lie ahead.

True to form I had a rotten night. I lay awake till very late, mulling things over, unable to sleep. When, in the early hours, I did sleep, I dreamt of my mother and father and death and loneliness. Things which hadn't troubled me for a long time. I woke stale and disinclined to get up. I rang for toast and coffee in my room.

It must have been about ten past ten when I eventually made it downstairs. Not my usual habit by a long chalk. I was cheered up, however, to an extent by Helen March. She really was an attractive, vivacious woman. Someone who took a degree of joy in life whatever the outlook. She reminded me a bit of that other Helen, Helen Ford, who I had lost so many years past.

"You look worried."

Was it really that obvious? I confessed I was.

"What are you planning on doing today?"

When I didn't answer she went on. "When I've got the blues I take a long walk along the shoreline.... somehow it helps."

In the event, that's what I settled for. Helen produced a small packet of food and a hip flask and on the big map in the hall, she pointed out a decent walk which I reckoned would take me about three hours. I set off without any great hope of a cure.

In the event I was wrong. It was a glorious day and gradually my spirits rose. The scenery was superb, as anyone who has walked along that stretch of coast will testify. I stopped for my makeshift lunch on a rocky outcrop well above the level of the water and looked out towards Muck and Eigg with Rum in the background. Life couldn't be all bad when you had moments like that.

I decided to extend the walk further than Helen had suggested with the result that when I did arrive back at the hotel I was pretty well done in but I came back a very much happier man than when I had started.

I had tea in the sitting room - the full works - which reinforced my mood.

Somewhere along the day, I had almost heard old Angus Findlay's voice,

"Laddie, can you see a profit worth the work involved?"

I suspected that the work would be stiff going for a while and that the profit might well not be by any means financial. With age, however, came the knowledge that there are other forms of profit and they can be just as rewarding in the long run.

Tonight was decidedly a Champagne evening so I armed myself with a bottle of vintage Ayala and headed for my room.

I put in a call to Cedric Swan, without much hope of getting him but, to my surprise, he answered the phone.

"No doubt Mrs Swan has told you that I will need some sort of inventory for the contents of the Lodge and of anything that had been moved from it into the farmhouse."

He was silly enough to tell me that nothing had been moved into the farmhouse.

"I would suggest that if you stopped and thought for a bit, you might just think of a few things at least."

"The same goes for the farm. For a proper valuation I will need to know all about the machinery and the livestock, then there will be the values for growing crops and work in hand; it will all have to be taken into account, Mr Swan."

"Tell me, is the Jaguar yours or the Estate's?"

He told me that he wasn't quite sure.

"Who pays for the servicing, the insurance; who pays for the petrol it uses?"

He said that he thought the Estate did. Clearly, the man was either a total fool or a liar. I had had enough of the charade. I can stand people being sharp in business, that's part and parcel of everyday life but I do get annoyed when people assume that you are a fool as well.

"Look, Swan, when the legal details are all complete I will be having a very close look at the Estate in general and your stewardship of it and I will be looking for proper answers so I advise you to start thinking about it."

I put the phone down.

I drank some of the excellent Champagne and dialled Tommy Black's number. At first I thought that he must be out but at last, he answered.

"God I knew it would be you, I was in the bath. Why do you always ring when I'm in the bath?"

I apologised. I knew how annoying it could be. "Just rang to say that I'll be down to London the day after tomorrow. Is the offer of a bed still open?"

Tommy assured me that it was.

"Thanks. Look, if you're free in the evening, get that girl in your office to book a table for us at the Travellers for dinner.... my treat."

"What are we celebrating?"

"I've made my mind up about the Estates. I'm starting up a new business!"

"Oh Lord! All right then. See you on Saturday."

I rang off and went downstairs, clutching my Champagne to share it with Helen and husband Peter.

I explained a little of my thinking to the two of them. They were receptive listeners. I delayed having my dinner until the dining room was virtually empty and then the three of us sat down to a delightful dinner of what was left from the menu and talked late into the night.

***

I was away not long after dawn. I made good time down to Glasgow where I hit the morning traffic. On down the motorway to Penrith and the A66 to Scotch Corner and then the Great North Road. I decided to call a halt and cut off to Ripon where I found a quite decent hotel.

I had an hour to spare before getting ready for dinner and spent it in the splendid Cathedral, trying to fathom what strength of faith inspired men to undertake such work so very long ago.

I took it easy down to London. I was in no hurry and I stopped off near Stamford and had a look round Burghley House and then went on and had a drink at the Bridge in Huntingdon then the A14 and the M11 into London. I was sitting in Tommy's place in Westminster by five o'clock.

# CHAPTER 16

We had a good evening at the Travellers. You can nearly always be sure of meeting someone interesting there. In the bar, I saw Ewert Brook who was a director of London's biggest marine insurers. A nice man but with a very talkative wife, happily not with him, who was known to most of her friends as 'the Babbling Brook'!

Tommy introduced me to one of his lifelong friends, Arthur Monro. Now, Monro was the man who had been chairman of the Government report into the economic outlook for the Highlands and Islands about four years back. He probably knew as much as anyone alive about the problems involved. We had a long chat in the bar and since he was to have been eating alone Tommy suggested the three of us joined forces.

In the event, I think Tommy must have got bored by my quizzing Monro but he didn't complain. For my part, it was as good as a crash course in rural economy. I enjoyed every moment and before he left, Monro invited me to go and see him at his house near Strathpeffer when we could find a suitable date.

When we got back to Westminster we sat and talked well into the night about my thoughts on the way things could go.

We had our meeting with Nick Conway at eleven the next morning. Tommy had previously sent him the rather sparse accounts we had got from George Pearson, the Locklate Manager, together with the report I had got from Tim Turner, so that he had a chance to go through them.

Tommy did the introductions.

At first, I think I was a bit disappointed in Conway. He was about thirty-two or three at a guess and certainly didn't look the part of a thrusting, go-getting sort of man. Thin, bespectacled and rather untidy, with an irritating habit of constantly shuffling his papers, he looked more like an eccentric schoolmaster than an accountant.

I was rapidly to change my opinion.

Nick Conway had a very good brain indeed and a dogged determination to find the truth. It was only much later that I learnt that, when he wasn't accounting, he was one of Britain's top glider pilots.

He started by asking me a very direct question. "Mr Forest, before we begin can we get a couple of difficult questions out of the way?" I said I would do my best.

Commander Black asked me to come to this meeting because you think that there has been some sort of malpractice going on concerning the management of your late grandfather's affairs. Is that right?" I said that's what I thought.

"Are we talking about a bit of petty thieving or do you suspect it's much bigger than that?"

I paused to assemble my thoughts.

"I can only point, at the moment, to rather more than petty thieving but I am worried it goes very much deeper than that."

"Why?"

"It's the whole set up. Harper seems to be playing things very close; he hasn't come up with any figures and seems very reluctant to do so. The control of both Locklate and Fannich is too centralised to be transparent. Pearson, at Locklate, is an honest man. I'll bet money on that but all he can see is the day to day story. He has no idea of the overall picture other than what his common sense tells him. I also get the feeling that he thinks there is something seriously wrong as well."

"What about? Conway turned several pages of his notes, "....ah! yes, Fannich?"

"Well that's easier, I think that's petty pilfering on a grand scale, if you can have such a thing, but that's down to the man there, Swan. He is certainly a liar and very much under the control of his wife, Marion. She is Harper's daughter, as you know, something that Harper has so far failed to mention. That in itself isn't a good sign.

The other point about Fannich is, if Swan is the Manager and, I presume, paid as such, why does he get a lease on the farmhouse?"

Nick Conway went into his paper hunt routine again. Eventually finding whatever he was looking for he went on.

"The point about Marion Swan is a fair one..... though there could be an explanation - one comes readily to mind but we will have to ask, won't we?"

He didn't elaborate on a possible reason for Harper's secrecy. "Your second point about the lease. It might well be that Swan is managing the Estate in return for the use of the house. It would save on a manager's salary."

I wasn't wearing that and said so. "That can't be right. Firstly, you would only make a deal like that if you were getting a first class man in return and Swan certainly isn't that, secondly, do we know that he isn't getting a salary? He seems to be getting a company car - a new Jaguar - and his wife is driving an up to date Land Rover which I'll bet is on the Estate as well."

Conway smiled. "Another few questions for our list."

I noted the use of the words 'we' and 'our', a good sign. Conway had already decided to act for us.

He asked, "What other reasons do you have for your suspicions?"

"Lots. Both Locklate House and Fannich Lodge have been empty for some four and a half years at least, that's if you don't count Harper using Fannich from time to time. Why haven't they been let? If Harper wanted to go fishing at the Estate's expense he could have stayed with his daughter; the farmhouse is plenty big enough?

Why hasn't the fishing and the shooting been let off? That alone must be capable of bringing in a very tidy sum. Fannich and Locklate together must represent capital of several million at today's prices and I bet that they don't make anything like a half decent return."

Tommy Black cut in, "Robin, that could be said of almost any agricultural holding in the country these days."

I conceded the point.

Conway took over again. "You see, Mr Forest, what we have so far, is possibly all due to bad management and let's face it Harper isn't an Estate Manager, he's a solicitor. Okay, there's probably a bit of dishonesty on the part of his son in law but Harper might not even know about that side of it."

I looked at them both. "He's got your disease Tommy, see the best in everyone until it stares you in the face. If Harper was halfway a decent solicitor, the first thing he would have done is to hand the whole lot over to a proper firm of Land Agents."

Tommy smiled and said nothing. Conway looked a bit shamefaced.

"I don't think that's quite right Mr Forest. I've thought about this a bit and I can see one angle that you might not have considered."

It was my turn to smile, "I'll bet you I have. My real worry is the rest of Grandfather's Estate. I would be prepared to bet that the old boy wasn't silly enough to put all his eggs into one, or even two baskets. Somewhere, under the thumb of Mr Charles Harper, there must be a tidy sum in investments of one sort or another. What's more, I don't doubt that, at best, we will find that they have been managed with the same self-interest as the property has been."

Tommy Black laughed out loud. "You never fail to amaze me Robin. The point you make was the one which Nick here made when we first spoke about this the other day."

My touch of anger subsided and to ease the tension I said, "It's all right for you city types to scoff but just because some of us have been slogging our guts out in the sun for years our brains aren't totally addled, you know."

At that point, we had a break. Come about midday and my body craves refreshment and since the coffee in Black's office is little better than cold brown Windsor soup, of an inferior sort, I had taken the precaution of slipping the girl, who looks after him, a bottle of Bollinger with strict instructions to cool it down and produce it the moment she heard raised voices.

After she had gone we settled down to draw up a list of points for our meeting with Harper.

That evening, Tommy took me to the Savoy and we did the idle thing and went to the theatre next door. I can't tell you now what it was about but we laughed quite a bit and enjoyed ourselves. Later we went to the Oriental Club where I was assured by the Porter that I was still a member and arrived back at Tommy's place at an hour which might be thought disreputable for two such ancient old men. All in all a good evening.

\*\*\*

The next day I took the car and went into Essex and visited first my Mother's grave and, on the way back, that of dear Helen Ford. I had also made an appointment to call and see Tony Miller at his wonderful factory. He was, as always, very kind.

He showed me, with some pride, a batch of laser cutting machines that were destined for the Far East and I was very happy to see that the order had been placed by Angus Findlay & Co.

Tony's private life, as ever, was going through yet another rough patch and I hesitated to ask if this was the third or the fourth divorce. Since he was hardly ever at home, I suppose it didn't really matter. He did explain that it was the company he missed. I knew what he meant.

On the way from Helen's grave to Tony's factory I passed the place where the Territorial Regiment had been based. It's now a supermarket. Sad.

Tommy had an engagement that evening and I decided on a night in. I ate in what passes for a restaurant in the building where Tommy has his place. It was like being back at school.

I raided the bookcase and went to bed early.

\*\*\*

Tommy and I went to Harper's office in Holborn. We had arranged to meet Conway there.

We were shown into a sort of boardroom by a secretary who said, "Mr Harper will be with you in a moment."

Tommy had told me that the firm of Harper & Swinburn was, in reality, just Harper who had a couple of clerks as foot soldiers and three or four secretaries. For such a small firm, the premises were quite impressive. The word was that the firm specialised in looking after the U.K. affairs of either foreigners who had business in this country or British people living overseas.

How he had come to be Grandfather's solicitor wasn't known.

After a wait of seven or eight minutes, Harper came in. He took the chair at the head of the table. He had no papers or files with him.

When the rest of us were seated he began.

"This is a somewhat unusual meeting at this stage in the handling of the Estate of my client, the late Mr Augustus Forest. It was requested by your solicitor, Mr Forest, but for what purpose I am not quite sure. I can only say that at this stage very little has been resolved and such questions as to the worth of the Estate and the time scale of the legal formalities are, as yet, not clear. However....." He paused for effect and smiled reassuringly. "However.... I am here to look after the interests of both my late client's affairs and the beneficiaries so, of course, I will do what I can to help."

Very smooth.

He went on. "I would remind you though, Mr Forest, that since I am the executor to the will I am, at this stage, in charge of the administration of the Estate as it now stands."

He smiled at me. "Now how can I help you?"

Tommy looked up from the block of paper he had taken out of his briefcase and on which he seemed to be making copious notes. Nick Conway, by comparison, had half his end of the table strewn with a mass of papers which he had taken from a sort of large satchel which was still on the table.

Tommy opened the batting.

"As you know Mr Harper, I am Robin Forest's solicitor, have been for many years, and since I requested this meeting, which I grant you is perhaps a trifle unusual, I will explain the reasons. By the way, you don't mind if I make a note do you?"

Harper said he didn't mind but couldn't see the need since the meeting was quite informal.

"My age Mr Harper, I find it wise these days, the memory you know." Tommy was putting on his doddering old buffer act; he said it always made the other side more comfortable.

I was expecting him at any moment to pretend to lose the thread of what he was saying but he didn't go quite that far.

"My client, as you are well aware, has considerable business interests in various parts of the globe. He is a busy man and travels a great deal. He has recently retired from his principal interest in Singapore and is currently looking at various options as to where he might settle and to what new ventures he might put his talents."

Certainly, Tommy was thus far technically correct but he was laying it on a bit.

"Bearing this in mind, he is anxious to make an assessment of the size and the exact nature of the legacy from his late grandfather so that he can be in possession of all the facts before he comes to any final decision. Is that quite clear?" he asked the question as if addressing a small boy.

From the look on Harper's face, I don't think that he was deceived for a moment by Tommy. I guessed that he recognised a shrewd man when he saw one and Tommy was certainly well known in the City as no pushover.

"I can see the problem and I would love to help but there are a number of difficulties as you might well imagine." Again the theatrical pause.

"Accounts to be drawn up, valuations to be obtained, capital transfer tax to be calculated and paid - and that will be considerable. We will certainly have to dispose of some of the assets to meet that bill, I can assure you."

Black chimed in.

"That is one of the problems we face. Thus far, we don't know what the assets consist of. "He left the question hanging in the air. "We can make an informed guess at the worth of the two main properties but are there others? There must be other investments and securities and we would be grateful for at least some indication of their nature and their worth."

Harper's face turned a slightly darker shade of pink.

"All in good time gentlemen, all in good time. Here at Harper and Swinburn, we are busy people and your affairs are not the only ones we have to deal with. You must understand that it will all be very complicated and in a case like this it will take time." He was now floundering.

From the bottom of the table, Nick Conway put his pennyworth in. In the event, it was more like a broadside.

"Do you run separate accounts for Fannich and Locklate?" He posed the question without the normal pleasantries.

"Certainly, .... of course we do. They are run by the respective Managers."

Nick went on, "I don't know about Fannich but I have here copies of the Locklate Manager's accounts and while they are well kept and, as far as I know, accurate, they are little more than petty cash accounts, a record of some of the banking and the wages."

"We do the main accounts here, in this office, our.... rather one of our bookkeepers does them."

"Excellent, and are both Estates separately registered for Value Added Tax?"

Harper couldn't see where that one was leading and his "Yes" was hesitant.

"So the main accounts must be made up quarter by quarter in order to obtain the balances for the Customs and Excise?" Harper could see it now all right.

"So it would only take a few moments to obtain the last quarter's figures at least?"

"Possibly."

"Let's leave that one for the moment. Do you administer the main bank accounts for the Estates? I understand that invoices for payment from Locklate are sent here to be paid so I presume someone here authorises payments and sends out the cheques, if you use cheques?"

"That is the way we do it, yes."

"So you must hold the bank statements as well?"

Harper started to fight back. He turned to Tommy. "Commander Black, I'm not sure where this is all leading and I must say I don't care for this young man's tone.... not at all."

He glared at Conway, who, not the least abashed went on. "So far as the other investments are concerned, do you have them in a managed fund or do you see to them 'in-house' as it were?"

Harper, reluctantly agreed that he, himself, managed the funds with the advice of a Broker.

"And the Broker's name please?"

Harper did get angry then but Tommy poured oil on things and Harper relented with the name and the address.

Nick Conway laid several sheets of paper on the table and announced that it was a list of the information and the documents he would need in order to be able to agree the Executor's account when it was presented.

Tommy added a further sheet listing such items as the inventories for Fannich and Locklate and the details of leases, rental agreements, contracts of employment and a host of others which, to be truthful, I had not even thought of.

Up until then, I had said virtually nothing, under instruction from Tommy, but I couldn't resist just one question. I might have asked it so that Harper had the opportunity to come clean. If he didn't then I was certain that he was a crook.

"Could you tell me, Mr Harper, did you appoint Swan as Manager at Fannich."

He went a darker shade of pink. "Certainly, ..... your grandfather..... he asked me to find someone."

"And Swan is qualified for the job?"

"I thought so."

The man was a crook, of that I was now certain.

We went back to Tommy's office and didn't say a word until we were seated round his desk.

I started. "Well, what do you two think? For myself, I am now certain the man's a crook!"

Tommy, with elbows on desk and index fingers making a 'steeple' on his lips - a sure sign that he was displeased with life - "Reluctantly, I think that I have, probably, to agree with you."

"Oh! Come on, I'll bet you the man's been milking the Estate for all he's worth, it stands out a mile. What do you think Nick?"

He went through the paper shuffling routine to give himself time to think, I suspect, and then said, "I have to agree with Commander Black."

He hesitated, "But I think that the implications might well be far more serious than we have thought at this stage."

"How do you mean?"

He replied slowly, thinking as he went along. "For a start, it could be that the only thing you might inherit is debts. Just suppose that this has been going on for a long time, by now he may well have mortgaged both the main Estates and spent the money."

I looked at Tommy, "Could he have done that?"

"Robin, it may well not be as bad as that." He paused but before he went on I asked.

"But to do so, either he'd have had to persuade old Augustus to sign something or he'd have had to forge his signature."

"Not necessarily, he might well have an overall power of attorney over your grandfather's affairs. We don't know but we will take steps to find out."

"But look, we're looking too much on the black side, it may well not be anything like as bad as we think. I admit, on the face of it, it would seem that there has been every possibility for fraud and human nature being what it is, Harper might well have taken the opportunity to commit it."

"So far, however, we have no direct evidence that that is the case."

"We will have to give the man the chance to come up with the details we want and then we can decide what to do."

This was Black at his best: solid, sound, reasoned argument. To be fair it had stood me in good stead more than once and I was inclined to listen. But I needed a clearer picture of the risks I faced.

"Look, just suppose that Nick here is right, the whole thing's a dog's breakfast - Harper's fiddled the books, mortgaged the property and runs off with the petty cash.... what then? Will I be liable for the debts or will he? Could I, for instance, back away and refuse to have anything to do with it?"

"If it could be proved that there was fraud involved then the debts would be down to Harper, not you. As far as refusing to have anything to do with it, that's doubtful because in the end it would be you who would be owed the money."

"Say he has got a power of attorney and fraud couldn't be proved; say it was all down to bad management .... Would I be responsible for all the debts?"

"Only to the realisable value of the remaining assets."

A dark thought crossed my mind. I'd have the contents of the cellar at Locklate away well before anyone counted them in the sums.

I thought about Harper and the Swans for a moment and then said,

"Can we sue him?"

Nick raised his head. "I wouldn't have thought it was worth it; as I see it you won't be the only victim if it is a swindle. We know that Harper & Swinburn specialise in what we could call 'absentee clients'. People who live abroad but who have property or investments in this country.

It could be that he saw your grandfather as just another absent client. After all, the main beneficiary of Mr Forest's will - you - have been living abroad and have had no contact with the family for years. It's possible that you might never have been traced and the fraud, if there is one, might never have come to light. There might never have been the likelihood of any really close scrutiny of the valuations or of the accounts put forward, if you hadn't turned up. Harper, if he is a fraudster, might well have got away with it."

My mind went into overdrive.

"That leaves the one thing I don't understand. Why did Harper get in contact with me in the first place? What's more, how did he know where I would be staying? I've not thought of that before."

Tommy Black looked puzzled. He got up and went into his secretary's office. He came back a few moments later with a big desk diary. What date did they first contact you, Robin?"

He flicked over the pages, "Ah! Here it is.... I thought I remembered something."

"Does the name Santobaldi mean anything?"

I said it didn't.

"Well, a Mr Santobaldi of a firm called Santobaldi and Musso of Milan - said they were jewellery manufacturers - rang and asked if we knew where you were. They apparently had a query about buying some stones and needed to get in touch with you as quickly as possible."

"Did you take the call?"

"No, Mrs Driver did. She checked with me and I told her to tell him that we didn't know where you were." He looked troubled and added, "What I actually said was that we didn't know where you were other than somewhere in France, somewhere along the river Lot."

"He couldn't have found me from that, surely."

Nick Conway said, "Don't you believe it. Given that, with a couple of girls on the telephone and a decent hotel guide, I could have found you in a few hours almost certainly."

# CHAPTER 17

I had a picture in my mind's eye of a hillside in France, at the back of a near-derelict farm that was for sale. I could recall exactly the crack of a high-velocity bullet as it whipped past my head. At the time I had put it down to a stray shot from a careless hunter, not something unknown in rural France. Now I began to think again. It was all too fanciful though.

Fraud was something I had come across before and could understand. Deliberately killing someone to cover it up, needed a leap of the imagination which I was unwilling to think about, even though the intended target might have been me.

Then, I remembered the drunken driver who had so nearly run me off the road. It was only because I had reacted quickly and had a car with anti-lock brakes, a novelty then, that I had avoided what could have been, a very nasty accident. If I had been hit by that van coming down the hill I would have gone over the edge of a long drop.

Despite the sick feeling that welled up in my stomach, I still thought it all too fanciful.

"Robin, you're miles away." Tommy Black's voice brought me back to the present.

"Sorry! I was thinking about something else. What did you say?"

"I said, can you check with Singapore to see if they know of Santobaldi & Musso?"

Now, there's no better place than a solicitor's office in the City of London for doing such things and within a few moments the good Mrs Driver, Tommy's secretary, had sent off a fax to Findlay's. Considering the time difference, we wouldn't get an answer until the next day though.

Tommy and Nick Conway talked on about what we needed to do but I confess that I didn't take it all in. The idea that someone might well have tried to do you in, tends to make you think a bit - and I was doing rather a lot of serious thinking.

All right, one or two communist terrorists had had the same thought a good few years back during the war in Malaya. I had been shot at once or twice but they hadn't cared who I was as an individual, only that I was one of the so-called 'enemy'. This was a very different concept, that someone might have tried to get me out of the way because I was the one person who might spell disaster to a very comfortable fraud.

I still found the whole thing unbelievable. I decided not to say anything to the others in case they jumped to conclusions. Conclusions that I feared might be correct but which I couldn't either take in, or prove.

Tommy was trying to solve a dilemma of his own.

As a solicitor, he was, technically, an officer of the court and, as such, had a duty to report any serious suspicions he had over legal matters. Were there grounds for such a report? It was the sort of thing that he took very much to heart. To him, the letter of the law was very important. Me. I took the opposite view.

"Look, the only thing that we know for sure is that something at Fannich smells."

"While we wait for Harper to come up with the stuff we want let's concentrate on that; I can't see that there is much else we can do."

At least Nick agreed. "I can run a check on the Swans if you like and while we're at it, it wouldn't hurt to have a closer look at Harper! If you want I can also have a sniff round and see if I can dig up anything on the stockbroker Harper uses."

Dear old Tommy looked sideways at Nick, expressions like 'sniff round' and 'dig up' weren't part of his everyday vocabulary but he didn't press the point. Nick asked if I minded him getting in touch with Tim Turner, the land agent in Gloucestershire and I gave him his telephone number and said I would phone him and tell him to expect a call.

As soon as Nick had gone, I spoke to Turner in his office and said it was all right for him to let Nick share any information he had. He also, in turn, asked if I would be down that way soon as he had a couple of things he wanted to discuss. I told him I would let him know as soon as possible.

Tommy and I went back to his place. I declined his suggestion that we eat in what I referred to as 'his canteen' so we went to a pleasant little Chinese place I knew of and had an excellent meal.

During dinner, I broached the matter of my staying at his place. We were both used to having a place to ourselves and were of an age where we were set in our habits. I didn't want to outstay my welcome but I didn't want to offend him either.

In the event, the problem solved itself in that Tommy needed to go to his place in Bosham, something to do with alterations to his wretched boat and thought he would be away for two or three nights and that I was welcome to stay on in his rooms if I didn't mind being alone.

He went off the next morning in what served him as a car. It was almost as old as he was. He said that's why he kept it. "Don't make them like this now!"

I didn't bother to tell him that proper, modern cars have things like heaters and radio sets, engines that don't need servicing every couple of weeks and are smaller than an average battleship. It would have been a waste of time, on a man who lavished time and money on a dreadful old boat. One which was nearly as old as his car.

As I was at something of a loose end, I spent a couple of hours in the public gallery at the House of Commons, listening to the political buffoons taking themselves seriously. Disenchanted with that, I walked up Whitehall and across Trafalgar Square and had a look in the

National Portrait Gallery. Funnily enough, there didn't seem to be much difference between the two places!

When I got back, there was a message on Tommy's answering machine. It was his secretary, Mrs Driver. Would I ring? There was an answer from Singapore. No, they didn't know of anyone called Santobaldi or Musso, or any combination thereof. The only call they had taken was someone who needed to know how to contact me urgently and they had given them Tommy's firm's number. That was on the day before the call from the supposed Santobaldi to London. Things were falling into place and I didn't care much for the obvious conclusions. I spent an hour or so in Tommy's sitting room, overlooking the river, thinking things through.

Let's assume Harper was on the fiddle. His best solution would have been that I should vanish without trace. That would only work though, if there was no direct connection between me and the news of any inheritance. I had been in the habit of wandering about the world as the whim took me, for the best part of two years. If I had vanished from France suddenly, perhaps no one would have been worried for months, by which time the trail would have gone cold.

I started to think how it could have been done. Say that I had been shot dead in that deserted farm or, for that matter, deliberately killed in a fake accident on a remote mountain road. Someone could have buried my body with the fair expectation that it would never have been found, driven my car to, perhaps, Italy and sold it cheap, with a nod and a wink to the sort of people who bought such cars. It would never have been traced.

Someone could have gone to my hotel, settled the bill and collected my luggage, told a tale about my having been called away on urgent business and I doubt that anyone would have been any the wiser for a long time. Perhaps never.

Sooner or later Tommy would have started to get worried but by then I would have been just another unexplained mystery.

That still didn't explain though, why Harper had told me that I was Grandfather's heir in that first call. Was it a bait to get me back to the U.K? Why, if someone had tried to get rid of me and failed, why hadn't they tried again?

I thought of that very early start I had made to my dash across France. Perhaps I had just got up earlier than they had!

I also recalled the message I had left for Tommy Black, with the girl in his office. I had dictated it to her and got her to read it back. I had told Tommy about the call from Harper and asked him to contact him and tell him that I was on the way back and that if he needed to contact me he should do so through Tommy's office.

Once Harper had got that message (and I had spent an extra night in Montreuil, so he must have got it before I got back to Dover), the chance would have gone.

It's one thing for a person to vanish. It's a different matter if he vanishes a day or two after he has told his solicitor that he stands to inherit a great deal of money.

My message included Harper's name and Tommy phoning him would have confirmed the connection. If I had died after that connection had been made, then the fat would have still been in the fire. Tommy would still have had an interest, as my solicitor, because the legacy would have formed part of my Estate. No, my call to Tommy and his subsequent one to Harper would have been my protection against another attempt at murder.

I was, I suspected, luckier than I'd deserved.

I still couldn't believe it though. It was all very well to sit, in comfort, in a very civilised flat, looking out over the familiar scene of the river and dream up 'who done it' theories. It just didn't happen to people in everyday life. Or did it? What about Santobaldi & Musso? What about that shot? Why had no one come to see if they'd killed me?

That last one was easy. Corpses don't shout. The moment I shouted, they would have known.

That's if there was a 'they'.

The one thing I couldn't get away from though was that Harper was a 'wrong un'. Years as a trader, as I had been, had given me an instinct and I had very little doubt that we were dealing with a crook. Tommy, bless him, would give him the benefit of the doubt. "Poor judgement" or "didn't give it the attention it deserved." You could hear him saying it. Ever reluctant to think that a member of his own profession wasn't as straight down the line as he was himself.

No. If my theory, improbable as it seemed, was correct then Harper would have to rely on a smooth tongue and some nifty bookkeeping to get him out of trouble. I thought the only way round it was to prove him to be a crook and then do a deal. It wouldn't be the popular route, especially with Tommy but I was happy to wager that it would be the easiest and the cheapest in the long run.

That miscalculation nearly cost me my life.

# CHAPTER 18

Having come to the decision I felt a much happier man. I helped myself to a large dry sherry, had a bath and took myself off to the Asian & Oriental Club. The great thing about the A & O is the cooking. You can't get better Far Eastern cooking anywhere else in London to touch it. Added to which, whilst you can't be sure that you will see someone you know, you can reckon on meeting someone interesting.

That evening I met a chap who had been in the Navy and had served in the East. Later in life, he went into politics, didn't get to the top though - I suspect he was too honest - said what he thought. The fact that everyone else thought the same but hadn't the bottle to say it out loud, didn't endear him to the great and the good of his, or anyone else's party. Shame really.

It was a coincidence that he and I were leaving at much the same time. I collected my hat and my overcoat from the cloakroom, said "goodnight" to the Porter and walked off down the road toward the main road to find a taxi.

The next thing that I knew was that someone behind me had his forearm around my neck, pulling my head backwards and I felt a burning sensation in the right-hand side of my ribs. In the next second, whomever it was had let me go and I was on my knees on the pavement.

I half turned to see what was going on and saw a man with his hands clutching his head and the chap from the club raising his umbrella for what I took to be a second swipe at my assailant. I don't know which way round he'd held it for the first go but he now held it by the point and he brought the handle down with a fearful crack across the man's arms. If he'd hit him on his unprotected head, I dare say he would have split his skull open.

The man gave a yelp of pain and took to his heels down the street a hell of a lot faster than either of us was going to manage.

"Are you all right? Bloody muggers!"

He said it with the resigned tone of a man who knows that such things happen.

He helped me up and leant me against some railings to recover my wits.

"Can you make it back to the Club? That'll be best - they'll sort you out - ring for the police."

I assured him that I could make it.

Part way back we were joined by the Club Porter who had come to the door to see what the noise was about. The two of them got me through the front door; anyone passing would have thought I was some poor old drunk!

The Porter helped me off with my coat and as he did so, a knife fell onto the floor. Now that did give me quite a turn. They eased me down onto one of the hall chairs. Everyone was very kind. My politico friend eased my jacket off to reveal a large bloodstain on my right side and when he gently pulled my shirt back, there was a nasty gash across my lower ribs.

He was all for calling an ambulance and the police but I protested that I didn't need either. The Porter went off and in a moment or so came back with another club member who was a medical man. He looked at the wound and said it needed proper cleaning and several stitches. Thank the Lord it wasn't bleeding much though and he put a sort of pad on it from the first aid kit in the office.

By this time the Club Secretary had turned up and when I was recovered a bit and made slightly more presentable, he called a taxi and sent me, accompanied by the Porter to the Accident Unit of the hospital around the corner.

Everyone assumed that I had been the victim of some opportunist mugger and were all for calling the police but I wouldn't hear of it. I suppose they might well have been right but I wasn't so sure. The whole thing had shaken me up rather more than I was prepared to admit and the last thing I needed was half the night spent answering silly questions I didn't know the answers to.

A young chap at the hospital poked about for a bit, making me wince somewhat and then put some sort of clips in to hold me together.

The Porter, whose name I had learnt was Charlie Morris, tried to get me to back to the A & O but I insisted that I went back to Westminster. He was very good and saw me in and bedded down, before I sent him off in the waiting taxi back to his duties. I did make a note of the name of the member who had saved my bacon so that I could thank him and buy the poor man another umbrella!

I spent a miserable night. My side stung pretty much and my mind kept going over the event. Was it just a coincidence or was I still a target for someone. I still had a great unwillingness to believe that was the latter. I spent most of the night trying to find a comfortable position and doing a lot more serious thinking.

As soon as it was almost a civilised hour I put in a phone call to the farm at Fannich. Much as I expected Marion Swan answered. She sounded as if I had woken her up; which was what I had intended. She didn't seem too pleased.

"Good morning Mrs Swan, Robin Forest here."

Before I could continue she snapped, "Do you know what time it is? What do you want?"

"I need to speak to your husband - rather urgently."

"What about?"

"Well it's an Estate matter and I would like to speak with him myself if that's possible."

She sighed. "Well it isn't, what is it you need to know so urgently that you ring up at this hour? He's gone out early.... he isn't.... he isn't here.... I'll give him a message."

I decided to string her along a bit further.

"Sorry Mrs Swan, I really do need to speak to him as soon as possible, will you ask him to ring me the moment he gets back?"

Reluctantly she agreed and I gave her my mobile number. No sense in advertising where I was, even if he already knew.

I couldn't find any bread so I made do with some time expired biscuits I discovered lurking in a tin and made a cup of instant coffee. Half of which I poured down the sink. Next, I sat down and, on some of Tommy's notepaper, I wrote out a factual account of the near road accident I had had in France, the rifle shot which had so very nearly caused me to be the late Robin Forest and the story of last night's attempted stabbing. Dates, times, places. As much as I could remember about all three events. I added the fact and time of the phone call to Fannich and Cedric's non-availability. I signed and dated it, sealed it in an envelope and addressed it to Tommy firm.

I went downstairs, found the caretaker and giving him some money, which included a big tip, got him to ring a courier service and have it delivered.

Back upstairs I phoned the good Mrs Driver, Tommy's secretary and asked her to open it, make two sets of photocopies and send them back, again by courier. The original was to be given to Tommy when he was next in the office.

Mrs Driver didn't seem put out by these strange requests, said she would do as I asked and added that she expected the Commander back 'About midday, the day after tomorrow'.

"Does he usually come to his rooms before he goes to the office?"

"Not normally, if he's got an early appointment he comes up the evening before but normally he comes straight here from Bosham."

"I thanked her and rang off."

Next, I wrote a note of thanks to my deliverer of the night before and said that I was arranging to have a new umbrella sent round to the Club for him as soon as possible. I then phoned an order to a firm in Jermyn Street to do just that. They assured me it would be there by lunchtime.

With the aid of a mirror, I examined the site of the wound in my side. The dressing was a bit bloody but I decided to leave it as it was for the time being.

I thumbed through a Michelin guide, selected a hotel with three stars near Morton in Marsh, rang them and booked a room for two nights. I then packed a small bag of belongings.

The Caretaker came up with an envelope from Mrs Driver with the copies I had asked for. I wrote a note to Harper saying that I thought I should let him know what had happened and that I had sent a copy to Tommy Black's firm and that a third copy was on its way to my bank for safekeeping. I didn't explain further why I had sent it. I thought that if he was the swindler I reckoned he was, he could work it out for himself. If he wasn't then I was just keeping him 'in the picture' and no harm done. His reaction, or lack of it, would speak volumes anyhow.

I tried to ring Tommy but there was no reply. I left a message on his machine saying that I was going away for a couple of days and would ring later. I didn't say where I was going. Putting on my overcoat I felt something in the pocket. It was the knife that had stuck in the material of the coat. I don't know how it came to be in the pocket. I supposed that someone had picked it off the floor when it fell and put it there.

It looked like a very ordinary kitchen knife with a serrated blade about five or six inches long, a very sharp point and a black handle, riveted to the blade. Without really thinking, I put it on the mantelpiece in Tommy's sitting room and promptly forgot it.

Having laid my plans, I sent off the letter to Harper by yet another courier and, after having a good look round before I came out of the building, took a taxi to Paddington station.

By that evening I was comfortably installed in an excellent room in Morton in Marsh with a half bottle of Taittinger Champagne and the anticipation of a good dinner. When I had arrived, I had asked about a doctor and they had arranged, for a fee, for a local man to come in and see me.

He had been a bit surprised at having to treat what not only looked like a knife wound but which was described as such in the note the hospital man had given me for my own doctor. This, despite my admission that as yet, I hadn't got one. He cleaned up the leaks a bit, put on a fresh dressing and said I should have it looked at again in two days time. I promised I would.

Dinner lived up to expectations although the dressing on the globe artichoke was a fraction over powerful. The guinea fowl was, I think, the best I have ever had. I treated myself to a wonderful Nuits-Saint-Georges from Robert Dubois. I didn't bother with the pudding, settling for cheese. One shouldn't overdo these things!

A good night's sleep and I was feeling well rested. The side was distinctly better; the sharp sting had subsided to a tolerable throb which only caught me out when I forgot about it.

I had a packed lunch put up and spent the day walking the countryside toward Bourton on the Hill. I was back for my evening's preparations for dinner and again the hotel didn't let me down.

The next day I repeated the treatment, getting a taxi to take me up to Long Compton and walking back.

By the morning of the next day, I was feeling a great deal better and ready for whatever was coming my way.

I had phoned Tommy the previous afternoon and told him I would be back the next evening. I suggested that I stayed at the Travellers but he wouldn't hear of it. We arranged to meet at his place. He had heard from Nick Conway and he wanted a meeting. I suggested that we all went to the Travellers for dinner, my treat.

# CHAPTER 19

I got back that next evening to hear two startling pieces of news.

The first came from Tommy. Harper's offices had been gutted by fire on the previous evening. That was something of a shock in itself, although, bearing in mind the circumstances, not wholly unexpected.

The second was news from Nick Conway. He had promised he had got someone to look into Cedric Swan's background and they, whoever 'they' were (I thought it better not to ask) had come up with what might be called 'The Goods'.

Dear old Cedric Swan had been born in Plaistow, where his father was the manager of a newsagents. Mother had run off, when Cedric was thirteen, with a local insurance salesman. From all accounts he had not been a happy youngster. The school he had gone to was pretty tough and Cedric had suffered the disadvantage, in the eyes of the bulk of the other pupils, of coming from a comparatively middle class background. He was also something of, what would have been called in my school days, 'a swot'. Nevertheless, he had done well enough at school and had gone on to the local Polytechnic. He had studied Computer Sciences.

Nick Conway paused in his story. "You have to remember something here. Swan must be forty three or four now, so he must have been studying computers about twenty five years ago. We forget, but they were in their infancy then; no such things as home computers, let alone 'laptops'. They were massive things.... had to be housed in special air-conditioned rooms.... very expensive and only used by big organisations."

Since I am a real duffer when it comes to computers, this was an angle that I hadn't thought of.

Nick went on, "So the young Swan was pretty early in the field and anyone who understood computers and more importantly, programming the things to do what people wanted them to do, was in demand."

It seemed that a smallish London company of Currency Brokers called Kutners, had decided to invest in a computer system and they took Swan on as their programmer. All went well to start with and the Company, having stolen a lead on the rest of the currency market traders did very well but the others soon caught up and of course tried to lure Swan to pack up his job with Kutners.

They responded by upping his salary and he stayed.

Nick's informants were unsure about quite when Swan saw the possibilities of milking the system – simple, as virtually only he knew how it worked. Nonetheless, milk it he did.

If you buy a million French francs and pay for them with Danish kroner, which you had just bought in exchange for Italian lira and you then translate all that back to pounds sterling, most people would have trouble with the maths. Hence the use of computers.

When you have been using them for a while and all goes well, you tend to trust what the wretched machine tells you. If you understand the system, and are clever enough with the programme which tells the computer what to do, you can adjust the multiplication tables which the thing works on so that you can cream off a percentage. If you are not too greedy and allow say, five hundredths of one percent, the odds are that no one will ever notice. The trick is to remove the 'cream' without leaving a hint that it has vanished.

Nick also pointed out that whilst a quite small fraction of one percent didn't sound much, it amounted to several pounds on every million that went through the system. Bearing in mind that the turnover was of the order of very many millions a day then it became apparent that cunning Cedric was onto a good thing.

As time went on currency regulations were relaxed, international trade expanded and the so-called Common Market made a bigger and bigger impact, thus the size of the currency markets grew ever bigger. More importantly, from Swan's point of view, the perfectly legal electronic transfer of money from country to country became an everyday thing.

His big problem was how to conceal his ill-gotten gains?

Enter Marion Harper.

Up to this stage in the story the events were well documented. Not least in the transcript of Swan's trial, on a charge of embezzlement from his employer. Just how far it went was another matter because, for a start, Kutners didn't wasn't their credibility in the market to be undermined, secondly, the money which Swan admitted to having stolen was paid back and thirdly, that no one could really calculate, with any degree of accuracy, how much had indeed, gone missing.

The upshot was that he had been given three years in prison and, with remission, had served just over sixteen months.

Swan had met Marion Harper well before this all came out. Charles Harper did a lot of his business with overseas clients and thus frequently moved money, in various currencies, from one country to another. That's how he first came in contact with Kutners. Subsequently, Harper had taken his daughter, Marion, to a Kutners' corporate hospitality party at Goodwood races where she had met Swan. For reasons known only to the chemistry of romance, they had fallen for each other and had married with near indecent haste.

The Mighty Marion had herself not been without blemish. As an only child, overindulged, expelled from a leading school for young ladies for conduct which, today would hardly have raised an eyebrow, and an abortion at a time when such things were still illegal. All this made her a difficult item to place on the marriage market.

Swan came along and although he might not have been the catch of the season, he was more or less presentable, had a good job and seemed to have the resources to keep Marion in the manner which she felt was her God-given right. Charles Harper had not been slow in giving his blessing for what, on the face of it, seemed an unlikely, if convenient union.

The grade three rumour went on to suggest that at some time after the marriage Swan and Harper discovered that they had more in common than they had at first realised. They were both involved in financial dealings of a dubious but dissimilar nature.

I thought to myself that the process of such a discovery between a Father in Law and a Son-in-Law must be an interesting one. Since, however, I had never had been in either position, it was no doubt my ignorance that was perhaps my own difficulty.

I also mused that if the rumours were true, it would have been a good match of interests. Harper would have had the knowledge of offshore investments and 'creative' bookkeeping and Cedric would have had the knowledge of the untraceable moving of money from place to place beside that added bonus of a regular cash stream.

All however, as always, was to end in tears.

Messrs Kutners got taken over. Not only that, but they were taken over by a Japanese company who did, very well, understand computers and the misuses to which they could be put. The new combine of Kutners Osaka had Mr Swan's card marked about two months after the contract was signed.

How the money that Cedric admitted to having purloined was paid back, no one seemed too sure but the rumour had it that Charles Harper found it. Whether it was the right amount, no one knew because it would have taken a huge effort to trawl back through all the transactions and anyway the trail had been very well concealed.

It was suggested that Harper did a deal with Swan that he, Swan, took the rap in return for the repayment of the money and for keeping Harper out of the proceedings.

When Swan did get out of prison, father-in-law found him a steady little sinecure at Fannich, well away from both publicity and temptation.

Nick Conway had told his story well but added a rider.

"We know the first part, about Swan is true because he admitted it in open court, everything else is supposition and we've no proof that Harper is, or ever has been, on the fiddle."

"However, I must say it all seems very likely."

Tommy Black had listened without a single interjection, fingers in that familiar gesture.

He cleared his throat. "I think we can take the affair of the defrauding of Kutners by Swan as quite accurate, after all it's in the court records but anything else is mere supposition and we should treat it as such. All we can say with any degree of certainty is that Harper might have been very lax in his administration of your grandfather's affairs.

As for the suggestion that he colluded with Swan to conceal moneys which either he or Swan obtained by deception; it is totally without foundation. That's not to say that it's impossible. I would go so far as to say it's quite likely but there is not a shred of proof as far as I can see."

Having delivered a judgement worthy of Solomon he sat back and gave us both his best 'I told you so look'.

Nick said, "So where do you suggest we go from here?"

Tommy thought for a moment and then went on. "I think our best course of action is for me to report the whole matter to the Law Society and ask for an investigation."

I cut in, "And what about this fire in Harper's office Tommy?"

"That's one of the reasons I would favour a formal investigation. I really do think there are sufficient grounds."

Nick looked at me, "What do you think Mr Forest?"

I confess that I had spent the last two or three days thinking of the answer to that very question.

"Do a deal!"

Tommy Black looked a bit shocked and Nick looked puzzled.

"How do you mean?"

"I have little doubt that Harper is a fraudster and has probably been one for a long time. That doesn't bother me too much."

"As for anyone other than Grandfather and myself - that's a red herring - if any other of his clients can't take the trouble to look after themselves, that's their problem, it's not ours. If we go down your route Tommy, we will end up fighting a court case for ages, spend a fortune on legal fees and get precious little out of it in the end."

I looked at Nick, "Did you find out if there was a mortgage on Fannich or Locklate?"

"Nothing that I can find."

"Well that's one mercy anyhow. What do you think the two places are worth; a ballpark figure?"

He had done his homework, "Together.... somewhere between five and seven million, I would think."

"Let's work on that then; I retired with enough money to see me out for the rest of my life, all of a sudden I learn that I am the heir to a great deal more. Okay, there are snags. Some crook has been taking my grandfather for a ride when he was too old or too ill to either know or do anything about it. Despicable, I agree, but life is too short to go back over all that. Now though, it's not Grandfather who's being done down, it's me and that makes me very cross.

I suggest that we write to Harper and tell him in no uncertain terms that we think he's been, at best, negligent. That he has installed at Fannich a man, his son-in-law, who knows nothing about farming or Estate management and is a convicted swindler.

I would go on to make a deal with him. The rough terms would be that if he comes to a very quick agreed valuation for probate and gets the Swans out of Fannich at once and hands over the running of both places to me. We will then undertake to forget the past and take no further action. If he won't play along those lines then, I personally, will ruin both him and the Swans."

Tommy asked," And just how would you go about that Robin?"

I grinned, "Stir up as much of a stink as possible."

"How?"

"Well, there's your idea of a complaint to the Law Society, we could also complain to the Inland Revenue that the accounts are perhaps not all that they might be. Oh! I don't know. The VAT man, anyone we can think of."

"Look." I went on, "If, as we suspect, we might not be his only victims.... if you were in his shoes.... would you risk going down that route? I bet he would cave in and do what we wanted. If he's in the clear, then he might well fight but I doubt that's he in any position to risk being looked at too closely."

Poor old Tommy looked quite shocked by my proposition.

"Aren't you overlooking a few things Robin? From what I gather from the letter you sent me you have been shot at once, stabbed once and someone seemingly tried to kill you by running you off the road."

It was Nick Conway's turn to look a bit taken aback.

Tommy explained about the notes I had sent to him.

When I added that I had sent a copy to Harper as well they both looked surprised.

Tommy said, "Why on earth would you do that?"

"So that he knew that I suspected he was involved, or more probably it was Swan who was the instigator and Harper didn't know. Certainly Swan wasn't available to talk on the phone the morning after, he might well have come down to London and had a go at me outside the club."

Nick hesitated and then said, "If it's getting that serious then I think I agree with Commander Black, perhaps we should go to the authorities and lay a formal complaint."

I smiled, "I have been shot at before for a hell of a lot less than several million pounds."

"If I remember rightly, we got four shillings and sixpence a day in Malaya, not counting the leeches."

Tommy laughed, he had a right to; he had seen a lot more action in the war than ever I had doing National Service. "Think yourself lucky, Robin, we got rather less than that."

We discussed the fire at Harpers and came to the conclusion that either it was a very convenient coincidence or someone was trying to delay the inevitable. Whatever it was, and anyone in their right mind would think the latter, we could do nothing until we had been in touch with Harper.

In the end we decided on a preliminary meeting, the three of us with the wretched man to see if a deal was possible and then, if it was, a fuller one to thrash out the numbers.

Nick and I left to go our separate ways, leaving Black to get on with his 'in' tray which, for a semi-retired man, looked well filled. He and I arranging to see each other back at Westminster later.

# CHAPTER 20

I bathed early so that I wouldn't interfere with Tommy's use of the bathroom when he did get back and I was just getting dressed when I heard the unmistakable cacophony of his ancient car arriving. Just as he was letting himself into the flat the phone rang. It was Tim Turner for me.

I waved my hand to Tommy and putting my hand over the mouthpiece said, "Tim Turner!"

Tommy said, "Sherry?" I nodded and turned back to the telephone.

"Sorry Tim, I'm with you now."

"Mr Forest, do you think we could arrange a meeting, I've quite a few things I would like to talk to you about."

"Is it urgent?"

"I wouldn't say urgent.... but I would like to pass on what I have found out.... some of it is a bit worrying." After hesitating for a moment, he added, "I would prefer it if I could see you rather than talk about it on the phone. Should I come up and see you?"

He sounded less sure of himself and certainly sounded worried.

I asked, "How are you fixed for tomorrow, if I can come down?"

"I've got a valuation to do in the morning but I should finish that about twelve."

"Right. I'll drive down in the morning and see you at about, what.... one o'clock?"

He sounded relieved, "That would be fine; will you drive straight back to London?"

I felt there was no sense in rushing back so said, "No, I'll stay over. Could you do me a favour and book a room for just the one night at that place I stayed at before? And while you're at it, book a table for the two of us for lunch."

"I'll book you in for the night certainly but do you think we could skip lunch and perhaps have a sandwich in the office here, it'll be easier with papers and things?"

I said that that would be fine by me and we fixed that I would try to be at his office by a quarter to one or thereabouts. I rang off and turned to Tommy who was slumped down in one of the armchairs with a sherry in his hand. He said, "Yours is over there."

He looked about whacked and under the 'wind' tan that he usually had, his face looked unnaturally pale.

"You all right Tommy, you look done in?"

"This business is all a bit of a worry Robin. I'm really only used to dealing with the affairs of dear old ladies these days. Swindlers, attempted shootings and stabbings aren't part of my daily fare. What's more, I don't like people in my own profession who break the rules and by rights I should do something about it."

I asked, "Would you like me to get someone else to deal with it? Is there someone else in your firm who could take it on?"

He smiled, "Not really, in either case Robin, I've looked after your affairs ever since that row you had with old Lewis and it would be a pity if I didn't see you through this."

For a moment I was puzzled, "Lewis?"

"Yes, Henry Lewis.... don't you remember.... he was dealing with you and you stuck your toes in and demanded to see old man Farr, the senior partner in those days.

Farr suggested I saw you, nearer your age he said.... reckoned he didn't understand youngsters any longer.... said it was the war that had made young people too independent - probably right I suppose."

It all came back to me. Trying, for the first time really, to stand up for myself. Insisting that I saw someone other than that dry, dusty old stick of a man whose only advice was to 'wait, it will all come right if you wait.'

I had been waiting too long. Not for someone else to do something but for the notion to get into my thick head that it was up to me to make things happen. I suppose in a way I had been waiting to grow up. Funny really, plenty of people had tried to get me to grow up: John Longland, my old housemaster, Tony Miller, my first employer and perhaps most of all, in the Army, the redoubtable Major Blood and later Colonel King. But it had taken a long sustained campaign by Angus Findlay to get the message to stick.

Tommy broke into my thoughts, "You still with us Robin? More sherry?"

"Sorry Tommy, I was thinking about the past." I explained my theory about growing up being the time when you decide to think for yourself and make things go your way.

"Life's great lesson Robin. It's a difficult thing to grasp, some people never do and they drift through life without ever really catching on. Some of our generation had the war to thank for driving the lesson home.... I certainly did. It was one of the very few positive things that came out of the war."

I said, "Explain!"

"One night, on a Carley float in the North Atlantic, six ratings and myself. The notion that if I didn't do something we were all going to die. Concentrates the mind, that sort of thing."

He tailed off, unwilling to explain further.

I didn't press him on it, some things are best left.

He went onto another tack, as if to stop the thoughts that must have been running through his mind.

"A great thing, positive thinking; the ability to decide for yourself, to question your elders and supposedly betters, the habit of looking at things from all sides. I suppose there's some trendy modern name for it but it's all the same thing. Whatever you call it, you never get far without it."

We had drunk our fair share of his excellent dry sherry and I decided positive thinking was needed now. I went down to the canteen which Tommy referred to as 'the dining room' and grabbed hold of the so-called head waiter and invaded the kitchen to beard the man who did the cooking.

The result was a half passable dinner, served in Tommy's rooms. I rummaged through his wine rack and found a bottle of Chateau Cantemerle which I seem to remember having sent him some years back as a present. There was a very good bottle of brandy on the drinks tray and we made do with that as a digestive.

At least we went to bed content men rather than maudlin ones.

*** 

I had set the alarm for six and crept round the place so that I didn't wake Tommy. He really had looked a bit off-colour in the evening and I was worried that it was all a bit too much for him.

I was up and dressed and making a cup of tea in his tiny kitchen when he stuck his head round the door and said, "I'll have one of those if there's any left in the pot."

I stood drinking mine and he sat, in his dressing gown, on the corner of the table.

"Robin, after I went to bed last night I was thinking about what you said about finding someone else to do the day to day legal work you're going to need doing."

I was about to say something but he put his hand up and said,

"Wait a moment, hear me out."

"I am supposed to be in the process of retiring and I've given up the Senior Partner's job and my 'old ladies' keep me just about as busy as I want. Would you think it unfair of me to hand over the routine stuff - probate - leases, that sort of work, to someone else?

If you would prefer to go somewhere else I wouldn't be upset. However, this way, I could let one of our people do the donkey work and I could still keep an eye on it."

I gave it a moment. "I think that would be a very good idea, Tommy. Given the choice I would rather stay with your firm, if you'll put up with me. The fact that you would be in the background would be an added comfort."

I added, "Have you a particular 'donkey' in mind?"

He smiled. "I haven't got that far yet, I just wanted to know how you felt in principle."

"If we can pick on the right person, I'm all for it." Tommy looked relieved that I had taken to his suggestion.

If I was going to make Turner's place on time, allowing for any traffic hold-ups, I was going to have to make a start.

We arranged to see each other the following evening and I suggested dinner out. I didn't think that I could face another session with the head waiter downstairs. Tommy said he would lay it on and I took myself off to the lift to collect my car from the underground garage.

In the event, I had a good run down to Oxford but then the traffic built up and I was only just about on time when I parked at the back of Turner's place.

I was shown into his office and he had been as good as his word and had laid on some imaginative sandwiches and a couple of bottles of first class local ale. He had a lot of papers laid out on a table by the window.

We got down to it.

To start with he was somewhat diffident and I knew what was coming. I decided to make things easier for him. "Look Tim, I've been up to the Estate in Scotland at Fannich and it stinks; I've come here expecting to hear much the same from you, am I right?"

He looked relieved. I added, "I'm not going to take it out on the bearer of bad news, just how bad is it?"

"Well, the Estate itself seems to be quite well run really, you know. The standard of cultivation is very good, the crops themselves are good quality, the buildings.... reasonably well kept. All that side seems to be fine; it's the end result that just doesn't add up."

"Go on!"

Turner turned over a sheet of paper. "Take the arable, for instance. I know what sort of yields you should expect from the sort of land on the Estate, I've been and looked at it and if the job's done right and I think it has been, then I could make a decent guess as to the tonnage you might expect."

He looked worried.

"From the accounts I've had from your solicitor, the money received from the grain sales just doesn't add up to what I would have expected."

"Anything else?"

"It's not just the grain. Take cattle. From what I can gather from asking around, Pearson, the Manager, is good with beef. The Estate used to win quite a few prizes in your grandfather's day but the returns from the suckler herd is only just about at the break-even point."

"Even allowing for poor markets, they should be much better than evens; they aren't even up to the average for this part of the country."

He added, "I've looked at the beasts and I would have said they are a very decent bunch, I can see no reason why they don't do better."

I looked young Mr Turner in the eye. "You mean you can't or don't want to see a reason?"

It was his moment for biting the bullet. He went slightly pink and said.

"Mr Forest, I think someone is milking the place left, right and centre."

I agreed with him, somewhat I suspect, to his relief. After that things went better. Turner went through everything, the fixed costs, cost of sales, depreciation, the wages bill, fuel, fertiliser, chemical sprays - the lot.

On the other side, he detailed the returns. Grain, livestock, fodder, he had even taken into account what the Estate's income from the sporting rights should or, more importantly, could have been. There was no mention in the accounts of any such income.

We talked through his findings at some length and I asked him to write me a report on what he had found out and his conclusions. He had a bit of difficulty with that, and I could see his point. Without a really free run at the place, with full access to all the figures he was, to a certain extent, guessing. I had told him to try and find out as much as possible without causing local rumours. Hardly a free run.

He could see that this all might end in court and he might have his guesswork called into question. I promised that were it ever to come to a formal hearing then he would have the opportunity to do it all again with all the information he needed. I also asked Turner to do a full scale valuation of the Estate which we could use for comparison with any probate figure that might come up.

That's when I got the really big shock of the afternoon.

I'm sure he hadn't any idea what sort of a bomb he was exposing.

"It's a pity about the land on the Upton road. That would have made a big difference."

It was obvious that I didn't understand.

"The eight acres, by the village.... along the main road. It was to have been a garden centre but it got sold on to a developer."

I assured Tim Turner that I hadn't any idea what he was talking about.

He explained in detail.

Almost four years ago the Estate had sold eight point three acres of pasture land on the edge of the village of

Upton. It had been sold to a man who wanted to open a garden centre. It was alongside the main road and at the furthest part of the Estate from Locklate House. Not long after the sale, he had sold the land on to a firm of property developers, claiming that he couldn't raise the cash funding to build the shop and the glass houses that he needed.

The developer had applied for and been granted planning permission for twenty-five, so-called, 'executive homes' and had also agreed to donate part of the land for the use of the village. Seemingly, it was a generous gesture. Not only was the firm giving the land, they also proposed building a village hall, a playground and a sports pitch complete with a pavilion free of charge. Not surprisingly there had been few local objectors to the scheme and since the land was adjacent to the village, the scheme had got approval.

"When." I asked, "Is this all going to go ahead?"

Tim looked uncomfortable. "About half the houses are already up."

"Are any of them sold yet?"

"I don't know but I would have thought so."

"Who are the Estate agents selling the houses? Are they a local firm?"

Turner picked up a telephone and asked someone in the office downstairs the same question.

He said, "Thanks." and put the telephone down.

"A firm called Abbott and Clerk, in the Shambles."

"Do you know them?"

"Yes, a perfectly proper firm, we've used them ourselves, several times. I know Nigel Abbott quite well."

"Do you know the name of the developer?"

"No, afraid I don't but I can find out easily enough."

He picked up the phone again and asked the girl on the switchboard to get him Abbott & Clerk.

He asked to speak to Nigel Abbott. He waited. I, of course, only heard the one end of the conversation.

"Nigel, Halloo! Sorry to bother you, look, those houses you are selling out on the Upton Road. Can you tell me who the developer is?"

All I heard was a muffled response.

"Oh! Nothing really." Turner pulled a face. "Land drains, a slight problem, it looks as if they have blocked off one of the land drains from the ditch."

Another reply.

"Okay. I've got that." Turner pulled a pad towards him and jotted down a name. "Do you have their address as well?"

"Thanks Nigel, nice to speak to you, thanks.... bye."

Tim Turner passed me the pad. On it was written, Harrep Modern Homes, their address was in Birmingham. I took off the top sheet of the pad and put it in my pocket.

Tim finished his report but I confess to not really having my mind on it.

# CHAPTER 21

I drove to the hotel where I had stayed before; I was half angry and half delighted. If instinct was anything to go by, I thought we had Mr Charles Harper just where we needed him.

As on my previous visit, the hotel did me quite well and I enjoyed a far better dinner than the 'canteen' offering of the night before. The wine, by comparison, was no better than the bottle I had given to Tommy and had never expected to taste.

By nine o'clock the next morning, I was on my way to Birmingham.

By eleven o'clock I was speaking to a very dumb young lady who manned the counter of small newsagents which, according to the address the good Mr Abbott had given Tim Turner, should have been the offices of Harrep Modern Homes.

Patently it wasn't.

The young lady who, I was not surprised to learn, was called Tracey, did say that they had a lot of post for Harreps and, no, she didn't know what happened to it.

"You'll 'av ter talk to Amzi."

I asked if he were 'available', which was silly of me. I tried again, "Was Mr Amzi in?"

"Not Mr Amzi - that's just what we call 'im."

After some further cross-questioning, I was satisfied that the gentleman who went by the name of 'Amzi' was probably called Amziman something or other.

I thanked the less than desirable Tracey and sought out a public library.

The electoral roll yielded nothing but by the use of a five-pound note, a computer and a 'Quick Address' programme in a not so nearby cybernet cafe, I found out that the resident at the address purporting to be the offices of Harrep Modern Homes was one Amziman Mahmud.

Birmingham could yield no more. I drove to London.

Tommy's news was good. He had been in contact with Mr Charles Harper and had arranged a meeting for the next afternoon at Lewis's offices, those of Harper and Swinburn being, for the foreseeable future, uninhabitable.

Tommy described how the good Harper had been reluctant to attend a meeting, saying that because of the fire everything was on 'hold'. I gather he had been persuaded by talk of, 'my client's unease at the situation' and 'thinking about going to the Law Society'. Anyhow, the meeting was on.

Tommy was a bit vague about dinner but assured me that all was well and that he had asked someone else to join us. I was a bit disappointed about that because I was rather more intent in talking about the meeting on the morrow.

When we were ready, we took a taxi and Tommy gave an address which was well off the usual beaten track that we tended to stick to. Some part of Islington which I had never heard of. On arrival, it turned out to be a small, quite discreet Italian restaurant just off the Essex Road. We were expected and stood having a drink in the tiny bar awaiting our guest. Tommy still failed to explain.

I was looking at the menu when a lady, forty-five or so, walked over and greeted Tommy. She was quite striking, tallish, red-brown hair and brown eyes. She was exquisitely dressed in a smart, silk suit of a colour somewhere between green and blue. That tone of colour that you see sometimes in tropical seas, or perhaps on a peacock's neck.

Tommy did the introductions. Her name was Mrs Anna Hudson.

The reason she was there was that she was a partner in Tommy's firm, Lewis, Lewis, Lewis and Farr. I chided Tommy that it was about time that they changed the name. All the Lewis's and Mr Farr had been dead for years. Tommy looked horrified and Mrs Hudson laughed. She laughed well. So many women adopt a sort of half-hearted smile and utter a strangled cough. Mrs Hudson's smile was broad and accompanied by a deep-throated chuckle. I thought her quite charming.

I also learnt that she lived a few hundred yards from the restaurant, in Cannonbury Close and this was her local watering hole. We had a serious discussion over the menu and it was obvious that Anna Hudson was both an expert on Italian food and well known and respected by the staff. She also spoke what I took to be fluent Italian.

After we had chosen food, the wine waiter proffered the wine list. Tommy gave it to me saying I was 'an expert'. I countered by describing the definition of an 'expert' as a 'has-been drip under pressure'! Again that chuckle.

I handed the list on to Anna Hudson commenting that I knew nothing of Italian wine and it was her pub anyhow. She ordered a Barolo.

There was no mention at all of why she had been invited.

We had a very good meal, a pasta starter, which normally I would not have chosen but it was good, followed by veal done in a sauce which I think had Marsala in it. The vegetables were rather overdone I thought, but not bad.

The Barolo was full and rich and had enough power to make its mark against the sauce of the veal.

I opted out of the pudding and had some excellent cheese. Tommy and Anna Hudson had a cream and chocolate concoction which must have been good judging by the way they cleared it away. At one stage I thought Tommy was going to lick his plate!

When it came to the coffee stage Anna Hudson said, "Look, may I make a suggestion?"

We assured her she could. "I only live about three hundred yards from here".

"I walked here; I usually do, but I usually take a taxi back, safer than walking on one's own, this late. Since I have the company of two gentlemen, why don't you both walk me home and I will make you coffee?" She added by way of persuasion, "I have a very good bottle of brandy as well."

Tommy, the ass, asked, "What sort of brandy?"

"Hine Antique."

Tommy said, "Done"

I think we would both have been happy to walk her home, brandy or not.

It was quite warm and we strolled back to Anna's house, she in the middle, both of us taking an arm. It was very pleasant. Her house was one of those tall, three-storied, semi-detached houses where you go over a basement area by a sort of front door bridge. I calculated in my mind that Mrs Hudson must be either a very good solicitor or married to a rich man.

Inside it was comfortably furnished rather than being smart. Good quality furniture, well used. Good lighting and tidy enough for entertaining visitors without making them feel guilty about messing it up. The type of place I liked.

She vanished down to a basement kitchen and came back bearing a tray with brandy and some very nice Venetian glass balloons. She went back for the coffee. Now, I'm no expert on coffee but this was quite strikingly different. She explained that it came from Vienna and it had a proportion of ground figs in it. I rather liked it.

After a second round of coffee and brandies, we made a move. Anna called a taxi which came in a few moments and she kissed Tommy lightly on the cheek. She shook my hand and said that she was delighted that we had met.

I could hardly wait for the taxi to set off before I demanded of Tommy, "What was all that about then - you old fox?" Laughingly I added, "Are you matchmaking? Or perhaps having an affair yourself? What are you up to?"

Even in the uncertain light of the street lights, I could see that Tommy looked shocked. "I'm doing no such thing, Robin. I'm merely trying to find you a suitable donkey."

I couldn't stop myself laughing. The combination of Tommy's serious look of concern and the thought of Anna Hudson as a donkey, of any sort, was too much. He was however not to be put off his argument by my amusement.

"I am suggesting that Anna Hudson takes on the routine legal backup that you will need to see this through. I can assure you that we think very well of her."

I bet they did! So did I - and I'd only just met her.

"Look Tommy! If you think she can do the work then that's good enough for me. I have no doubt that we can get on together, apart from anything else she's a sight better looking than you are."

Typically he went off at a tangent. "I suppose it's because you've never married that you're so flippant about women Robin. Never taken them seriously I suppose?"

I admitted that it was probably that I had never had very much to do with them for the last thirty odd years. This earned me a well reasoned but concise lecture on the ever-growing importance of women in the modern world, which lasted until we arrived back in Westminster. As we let ourselves into his flat, I reflected that Tommy, dry old stick that he seemed on the surface, was a long way ahead of me in, at least, this part of his thinking.

We made the serious decision that we could probably manage another small brandy. When we were settled, Tommy came back to the specific question.

"I think Mrs Hudson would suit you. She's very good on criminal work and on property. She looked after that business of old Sir Henry Block's will. The family contested it on the grounds that he had gone stupid in his old age. Well, the old boy was as sane as anyone I ever met - right to the end. The trouble was that they were all too greedy."

"What was the outcome?"

"The court decided that they had all been well provided for and the rest of the will stood. He left a big endowment and his house in Suffolk to a charity running a school for orphans. Anna dealt with the whole thing very well. She can be quite firm but she manages to be so with a good deal of tact."

He peered at me from under his, still, heavy eyebrows.

I protested faintly. "I can be tactful when I need to be!"

It was Tommy's turn to smile. "My dear Robin, you have made a very good job of being a trader; I doubt you would ever have made a success as a diplomat!"

# CHAPTER 22

The next morning, I had a long meeting with Mrs Hudson in her office. I told her the story as I saw it and she told me what she thought and advised from her reading of all the papers. I was relieved to find that she wasn't totally against my idea of a deal with Harper provided that we could find conclusive proof that he had strayed over the indistinct boundary between 'poor management' and fraud. I was quite sure that the evidence provided by Tim Turner would be enough to make the outcome of any deal a foregone conclusion.

I had a snack lunch with Tommy and Anna Hudson in their conference room. Nick Conway joined us and we went over the arguments we would put to Harper.

It was pretty clear that Tommy was the only one of the four of us who wasn't in full agreement over the tactic of making a deal designed to get Harper off our backs as swiftly as possible. Clearly, it offended his sense of 'the rights' of the matter but he could also see the sense in bringing, what might possibly turn into a protracted and expensive court case, to a quick end.

"If he admits nothing and pleads that any poor management, as you call it, was just that - I think you might have a job to get him to agree to any sort of arrangement."

In my head I was thinking about the development of 'executive style homes' on the edge of the village of Upton. Was Harper involved in this?

Harper arrived just a few moments late, pleading 'pressure of work'. He beat Tommy to the opening of the meeting. He smiled round the table and raised an eyebrow when he took in Anna Hudson.

"Madam, I don't think we have met, are you taking part in this meeting?" He made the question sound as if he was saying, "What the devil are you here for?"

Tommy was studying the ceiling at that moment and continued to do so. He was going to let Mrs Hudson fight her own corner.

She returned Harper the benefit of a dazzling smile. "Mr Harper, I'm Anna Hudson. I'm a partner here in Lewis, Lewis, Lewis and Farr and I look after the routine affairs of Mr Forest".

She didn't elaborate.

Harper rushed on like a politician trying to deny anyone else the stage.

"I have come today because you asked me and I always try to help in any way I can." He paused for effect and gave us all another smile.

"However there is very little I can add to what I told you at our earlier meeting; these things take time. It's the system - we have to abide by the rules that are laid down." He nodded towards Tommy, "As no doubt, Mr Black has explained. Add to this a most unfortunate fire, in our own offices and, as you might expect, further delays will be inevitable."

I began to feel angry. I wasn't going to let this miserable man dominate a meeting we had called so that we might put him on the spot.

"Rubbish!"

Harper pulled up short. "I beg your pardon?"

I repeated the word. "Rubbish!"

He appealed to Tommy. "Mr Black, I have come to this meeting to explain the legal position. I didn't expect rudeness .... perhaps your client doesn't understand ...."

Tommy gave up his study of the overhead plasterwork and gave his attention to Harper.

"Mr Harper, I can assure you that Mr Forest understands a great deal about this business and this has caused him to raise a number of pertinent questions which he would be obliged if you could answer."

I was going to interject but Tommy waived me into silence.

"My client is concerned that the Estate of his late grandfather has not been run, in the past, as well as it might have been. This may well have caused the value of his legacy to be very much depressed."

Harper assumed a look somewhere between offence and pity.

"I am a lawyer, as Mr Forest well knows; I had the privilege of serving Mr Augustus Forest for many years in that capacity and I think, to his entire satisfaction." He paused to give effect to his sonorous tones.

"I am not and I have never claimed to be, a Land Agent. If he thinks that the running of the Locklate or the Fannich Estates has not been properly carried out then I suggest that he takes the matter up with the relevant managers."

He sat back as if he had won the day.

Before Tommy could shut me up I repeated my challenge. "Rubbish!"

Harper said nothing for a moment but a change came over his face. Self-satisfied complacency gave way to something that looked very much like malevolence.

"Mr Black, if your client can only say 'rubbish' to everything I say then I think there is little use in our continuing this meeting." He started to gather up his things.

I decided to play it softly. "George Pearson runs the farming of the Locklate land very well, as far as I can see - but he has no control over the finances. You do that surely. You told us the other day that the books were all kept by your bookkeeper at your Holborn office."

Harper looked at me directly. "That may be true but I hope that you are not hinting that there's any malpractice so far as the books are concerned?"

He looked to Tommy. "I would say that if this is what your client is suggesting then you advise him not to repeat it, certainly not outside this room."

Tommy retreated into the standard non-committal, "Just so."

I went on, "So far as Fannich is concerned, old Mr Farr seems to run things as well as he can but Swan's useless as a manager and I understand you appointed him."

Harpers colour deepened a touch. "As far as I know, Mr Swan is quite capable. Your grandfather asked me to find someone in a hurry and he was available. I kept him informed and he raised no objection." Still no mention of their relationship!

I pressed harder. "Have you any proof that you consulted Grandfather?"

He decided to hit back. He turned to Tommy. "Am I to be cross-questioned by Mr Forest? That's not why I came here; I came to explain why it would take time to complete the formalities.... not to be harangued by your client."

Tommy played the diplomatic role. "Just so, however, if you could show that you consulted your client it might well help us along.... Umm?"

Harper glared round the table, "Very well then, if it will help but I think it disgraceful that my word isn't sufficient."

He delved into his briefcase and produced a thick green file. He sorted through the contents for several moments and then said, "Ah! Here it is." He pushed the file over to Tommy who read the brief letter and pushed it onto me.

A copy letter from Harper and Swinburn, addressed to Grandfather at the nursing home outside Oxford, stated that a replacement manager had been found for the position at Fannich. His name was Cedric Swan and he would take over as soon as some minor repairs had been made to the farmhouse.

The letter was initialled by someone over Harper's name.

I read the letter out, half under my breath as if reading to myself but I wanted Nick Conway and Anna Hudson to know the contents.

I looked up. "Would you say, Mr Harper, that this letter really constitutes 'consultation'?"

He stared back. "Of course, it's there in black and white."

I sighed, "What's not there is the fact that Marion Swan is your daughter and Cedric's your son-in-law; is that not so?"

Harper's face didn't inspire me to think that this was going to be easy.

"What's on earth's that got to do with it?" "I didn't write that letter myself, one of the clerks did, I instructed him to tell Mr Forest that we had found a manager for Fannich and he did. The fact that we were related wasn't relevant, if it had been we would have mentioned it."

"Perhaps the same with the fact that your son-in-law had just done a prison sentence for fraud?"

My question didn't have the impact I had been expecting. Whilst Harper's went further up the colour scale towards purple he continued to bluster.

"Cedric Swan was tried and convicted for a stupid deceit; the money he borrowed was repaid in full and he served his time. Are you going to hold that against him for the rest of his life?"

I was about to tell him that I wouldn't if he had the Swans out of Fannich in very short order but the man was a fighter, I had to give him that at least. I could see that I had to play harder still.

"Who sanctioned the sale of the eight acres of Locklate land for a garden centre?"

There was a noticeable downturn in the colour scale.

"It was a decision I reached in conjunction with Pearson, the Manager. The land was too far out from the buildings and, before you ask, we used the money for a new grain dryer."

I decided on bluff.

"The land wasn't ever used for a garden centre was it?"

Harper said he had no idea.

I went on, "Does the name Harrep Modern Homes mean anything too you?"

I think it was that question that started to turn the tide so far as he was concerned.

Sullenly he said it didn't. If nothing else I had everyone's attention now.

"Is the fact that Harrep is an anagram of Harper relevant?"

"No."

I decided to put all my cards on show.

"Look! I just don't believe you."

"I have someone looking into Harrep Homes. So far as I know, the development at Upton is the only one they've done, that in itself is strange. Stranger still is that their office address is a tobacconist in Birmingham. We are talking to Mr Amzimam Mahmud to find out where he sends the mail. Mr Nigel Abbott of Abbott & Clerk Estate Agents of The Shambles, Gloucester, as I suspect you already know, are the sellers of the houses.... they will tell us all they know about the man who appointed them as agents.

Last but not least, we are looking for the would-be garden centre owner who bought the land in the first place only to find that he couldn't raise the money to build it. It was your son-in-law, Cedric, wasn't it?"

In a way, it was an odd sensation to watch this man seemingly grow smaller the further I went. I had expected a sense of triumph but in reality, it was one of sadness.

"I could go on. Some of the things are probably sidelines, thought up by your daughter and Cedric, like the sale of the furniture from Fannich. Some.... you must have known about.... like the granting of a lease to them. Where did about a third of the corn crops from Locklate finish up? Likewise, a good number of the fat cattle? A distant market in the south-west, under a different farmer's name?"

Harper had given up trying to reply. He sat with his head bowed.

I had a last go. "I propose a deal." His head came up slowly.

"One. Get the Swans out of Fannich by the end of the week and they only take what they can prove is theirs.

Two, agree, with Nick Conway here, a set of figures for your payment of a lump sum in compensation for the fraudulent sale of the Locklate land.

Three, hand over all the documentation for the stocks and shares in Grandfathers Estate to Nick by this time tomorrow.

Four, with Nick freeze all the Estate accounts as of tonight.

Five, agree with Anna what she wants done about deeds, leases, any agreements, powers of attorney.... all the legal stuff.

You will also work with the two of them to wind up your executorship as soon as possible, under their supervision.

In return, I will agree that if you do everything I ask and don't try and wriggle, we will forget everything else that went wrong before the date of Grandfather's death."

Harper looked uncertain. I added a sweetener. "I will also overlook the three attempts on my life."

He gave himself away altogether, "That wasn't anything to do with me."

"Good, that clears the air a bit anyhow; if you deny your involvement at least you are admitting that you knew someone had had a go!"

We had better add another condition. If ever I see you or the Swans anywhere near anything I own from now on, the deals off.... clear?"

Harper nodded agreement.

I turned to Tommy Black who was looking at me with a strange expression. "Come on Tommy, I've had enough of this, let's leave the rest to Nick and Anna, I'm sure they can take it from here."

When we were settled in Tommy's office, he produced the bottle of brandy he keeps for clients in shock when he announces the scale of his fees. He said, "You can play pretty rough when you want to can't you?"

I smiled.

"At the same time your 'deal' as you call it, will have cost you a small fortune."

"Not really Tommy, think about it. Whilst old Augustus was alive he was robbing him, not me, that was down to Grandfather. I never expected a brass farthing but when it comes to robbing me.... that's another story. What's more, think of the tax we won't have to pay!

The land hasn't made money for ages, ergo that valuation must be lower than if it had been making a whopping profit. Look at it another way, if you have traded in the East for as long as I have, you expect a bit of graft and corruption.... it's part of business life."

We went back to Westminster.

The next morning, both Nick Conway and Anna Hudson declared that after a very long session they had come to suitable agreements and, better still, they had Harper's signature on a 'letter of intent' whatever that might be, to cover the points I had outlined and a good few others they had dreamt up for themselves.

I was well satisfied that we would overcome the major problems.

I suppose I was getting naive in my old age or perhaps the sense of relief that it had all turned out at least as well as I had expected, dulled my suspicions. Whatever the causes, that assumption was to cost us all dearly.

***

I didn't want to impose on Tommy any longer than was strictly necessary. He was looking decidedly jaded and, I think, wanted to go down to his place at Bosham Harbour and spend a few days doing what, in his terms, passed for rest.

I decided to go down to Locklate and start the process of getting it back onto its feet. I telephoned George Pearson and told him that from now on I would be taking overall control instead of Harper and that I would like to open up a small part of the house, just sufficient, at this stage, to make life to tolerable. At this stage, I would be quite happy to 'camp out' in some makeshift quarters.

He came up with a more sensible suggestion. It would take time to get the house adequately ready for any sort of occupation but there was, what was called the 'Motor House', a small flat over what had firstly been the stables and, in Grandfather's latter days, the garage.

Seemingly, his driver had been a married man and the old hayloft had been made into a place for him and his wife. It had last been used for an agricultural student about three years ago.

George Pearson sounded a bit uncertain. "It's not very grand by any means.... but it could be got ready quickly and I could get some basic stuff, sheets, blankets, that sort of thing, moved in from the main house."

I told him that I thought that would fit the bill very well for a start. I thought I would assure him on the most important point so far as he was concerned.

"George, there is one thing I want to make quite clear right from the start. I know nothing about Estate management and clearly, you do. I've no intention of doing your job but I do want to reorganise things so that you're the overall boss of a well set up place. As things stand, you run the day to day farming side but you don't have any financial control and you don't get much chance to change the way the place is run."

He agreed that that was the case.

"We will thrash out the whole thing and then decide how much I need to pay you to do it? That is if you feel you want the job?"

I think that I could hear a sense of part relief and part joy in his reply.

"Mr Forest. It's the best news I've had since your grandfather was here."

We arranged a few practical details and I said I would see him sometime in the afternoon two days hence. I then phoned an excellent Chinese restaurant in St. James' and booked a table for six for the following evening.

I was lucky that both Tommy and Nick Conway agreed that they could come. Nick phoned back later to say that his wife would be free as well but I got a surprise when I spoke to Anna and asked if she and her husband would care to come.

"I'm sorry, Mr Forest" she sounded serious and I feared a refusal.

"I thought you knew. I'm a widow; my husband died eleven years ago.... didn't Commander Black tell you?"

It was my turn to be embarrassed. "I'm terribly sorry Anna, Tommy didn't say anything and I'm afraid it just didn't occur to me ask."

She let me off the hook with that chuckle of hers.

"If you will have me on my own, I would be delighted to come."

I telephoned back to the restaurant and changed the booking to a table for five people.

In the event, I needn't have worried about it working, I think it was one of the happiest evenings I have spent in a long time. Nick's wife Miriam was a very ebullient young woman and she and Anna Hudson had a lot in common, notwithstanding the gap in their ages.

Tommy, who despite his somewhat forbidding face, added to by his beard (I always thought of him as a doppelganger for King George the fifth) regaled us with some of his wilder legal stories which not only had us all in fits of laughter but I think, caused Anna to see him in a completely new light.

I got the restaurant manager to call three taxis and when Tommy and I had seen off my guests we took our cab back to Westminster. Driving past the end of Horse Guards Parade, Tommy thanked me for the evening and then said that he had a request.

"Look, Robin, I know you all too well and I want you to promise me something!"

I told him that I would if I thought I could.

"Don't go mad at this thing, heaven knows you don't need the money."

I assured him that I would if I was going to make something of Locklate and Fannich, to get them back to some sort of decent order.

Tommy said. "That's what I'm afraid of. Why don't you sell the lot and relax. You could afford.... haven't you've been looking for.... several of them if you wanted.... a house in France, one in Scotland say and perhaps another down this way. Why not set yourself up and then enjoy life?"

I told him he was a fine one to talk.

"No, Robin! I mean it. I do just about as much as I think I want to and I do enjoy life.... except when some silly beggar like you comes along and upsets my routine. That's why I want Anna Hudson to do your work for me. Take it a bit easier. I don't want to see you finish as the wealthiest man in the graveyard you know."

I told dear old Tommy that there was no fear of that.

By the time we arrived at the front of the block where he had his rooms we had agreed that I wouldn't go at things 'like a bull at a gate' to use his phrase and that I would keep him in the picture as to what I was up to. We had a smallish large brandy to celebrate our agreement and then another as a night-cap.

# CHAPTER 23

I had planned to set off early the next morning but I was a bit later than planned.

Tommy, at some time during the night, had wrapped up a present for me to take with me. You didn't have to be very clever to tell that it was a picture but despite my efforts to see if there was one missing from his rooms, I didn't have the slightest idea what it was. I had strict instructions not to open it until I had somewhere permanent to hang it. That condition I did promise to stick too.

I pulled into the Locklate Estate yard just after three o'clock that afternoon.

George Pearson had been busy.

He took me up by the main house and then round the back to the old stable yard. The entrance to the flat he had told me about was up a flight of outside stairs at the end of the garage building. I must say I was pleasantly surprised.

So, granted, it was small; just one living room with a tiny kitchen behind it and a door to a bedroom plus a bathroom which had quite a decent bath and a lavatory.

I asked about hot water.

"It has its own electric immersion heater." George Pearson assured me. Thank the Lord for a bath anyhow.

Pearson explained that he had had May Barker and a younger woman, the wife of one of the stockmen, clean the place and bring some things over from the main house. Looking around, they had done a good job. Even to a bowl of flowers on the table. He had also had a few basic food things put into the tiny refrigerator - milk, butter and a few other odds and ends. It would certainly do for a stop-gap answer.

George Pearson hesitated to see what my reaction would be.

"Thank you, George; it's a very sensible answer for the time being. I intend to sort things here and then move onto Fannich and do the same there."

He asked anxiously, "Have you decided if you are going to keep Locklate on, Mr Forest?"

For him, it was the key question of course.

I looked out of the window of that little living room, across the yard to the back of the house. I turned and said, "Look George, at the moment nothing is settled. I certainly want to keep the agricultural part on but I must have it run efficiently. I know it's nothing to do with you but, for the last few years, it's hardly broken even."

He looked surprised and I notice his brow furrow deeply, "I think, Mr Forest, we've done a bit better than that." He said it in a defensive tone.

I reassured him, "Not after our Mr Harper has had a go at the accounts it hasn't.... but that's certainly not your fault."

I told him that whatever the outcome, he would not be the loser by it but that we would have a proper meeting sometime the next day and thrash out the bare bones of a plan of action."Would you ring young Tim Turner and ask him if he could come as well and, if he can, arrange a time and place.... your office would be best if he can manage it. Let me know what you've fixed up later this evening."

Pearson said that he would do that and then asked what I was going to do about eating.

"I had thought of going to a pub somewhere but perhaps I'll spend the time having a look round and probably make do with a boiled egg or something here."

He seemed worried about that. "Would you care to eat with us? It won't be anything special but you'd be very welcome."

I thanked him and added, "I'd be very happy to come and eat with you one evening George but I think this evening I will make do with something here, I want to get a bit of a feel for the place again before we meet tomorrow."

He promised to let me know about the arrangements for the next day and handed me two sets of keys. One set for the stable block, including the flat and the other for the house. He explained about the alarm system and offered to get my luggage up from the car but I said I only had a small bag and would manage.

After he had gone I had a good look round, opening cupboards and drawers. Not only was everything very well cleaned but there were spare blankets and pillows, some towels and a good stock of basic foods. There were also four bottles of quite decent wine. Either George or Mrs Barker had used their brains.

I made a cup of tea and then went down and collected my kit from the car.

I opened the big double doors of what had been the old coach house and put my little car away. As I locked it I noticed, in the gloom at the far end of the building, a large shrouded shape under a dark blue dust cover. Intrigued, I walked over and lifted a corner of the cover. It concealed an old Rolls Bentley touring car, also dark blue and in seemingly good condition.

I was to learn from George Pearson the next morning that it was Grandfather's and it had been standing there ever since it had taken him to the home in Oxford.

Back upstairs, I unpacked and changed from the suit I was wearing into some cotton slacks and an old shirt. I went exploring. I had decided to leave the house until later so I walked round to the front and tried to follow the line of what had once been the main drive from the road. I reflected on how rapidly the wild growth had taken over what had once been a major feature of the landscape.

I was impossible to walk down the old drive at all, what I supposed were saplings from the trees that lined the road were now grown to a considerable size, they, in turn, had been invaded and smothered by a massive growth of ivy.

Part of the route, less overgrown with trees, had been taken over by brambles that formed a totally impenetrable entanglement. Convolvulus hung in great swathes from the original trees that marked the edge of the drive, some of the stems being nearly as thick as my wrist. The only way to make much progress was by walking on the arable land alongside the drive, where a post and rail fence divided the wilderness from the neatly tilled land.

About, I suppose, four hundred yards from the house, there was a sharp little valley running at right angles to the line of the drive and about forty feet deep. The fencing turned along the flank of the valley and beyond it was a line of much older mature woodland. I climbed the fence and pushed on downwards.

I didn't appreciate what I was looking at was what, at one time, had been a small lake, until I nearly walked straight into it, so thick was the undergrowth. Shades of Malaya.

I turned right to gain the drive and found myself faced with a very steep bank. I thrashed about for a bit and after much slithering and sliding and not a little bad language I gained the now-defunct drive and was able to make out the general picture.

The road crossed the valley on the top of what was in effect an earth dam. The lake at the top, two or three times the size of the lower one, was virtually silted right up and only a very sluggish stream of water about five or six feet wide meandered across what had once been its surface. It seemed to be a haven for moorhens judging by the noise they made.

There were the remains of a weir which once had drained it, under the roadbed, into the lower lake. The weir was now so blocked with rotten timber, weeds and silt that the water had backed up and now flowed over the road itself and had washed away a great gap in its surface. The only option for reaching the far side of the drive, without getting very wet and muddy, would be to go around the top lake and I didn't know how far that would be. I forced my way back through the wood lining the valley wall and eventually regained the arable land on the upstream side.

I must confess to being fascinated by that drive.

I still remembered enough of my Royal Engineer training to appreciate that it would be a big undertaking to restore that entrance to Locklate House. Big and probably expensive. Clearing the two lakes would be a job for a dragline crane and they certainly didn't come cheap.

I cut off to the north, following the top edge of the valley, curious to see if I could find the source of the stream that fed the lakes and gradually, as the valley became shallower, I came to a series of pasture paddocks, some with young cattle feeding contentedly. They took little notice of me as I crossed their fields, just pausing to raise their heads and to study me with huge brown eyes fringed with eyelashes that gave them an almost 'pantomime dame' look.

Like an idiot, I hadn't brought a plan of the Estate with me so I was unsure where the boundary ran. When I came to a stream that looked as if it was the source of supply for the lakes I turned back for my temporary home.

As is so often the case, an indifferent day had turned into a very glorious late afternoon and I walked slowly back thinking that maybe this was what I had been looking for, for the last year or so. As I got back to the front of the house I was overcome by one of those urges that you know that you should resist but that equally, you have no intention, whatsoever of so doing.

A relatively harmless kicking over the traces that gives infinite pleasure particularly when shared with no one else. Deliberate solo hedonism.

I fished out the keys of the main house and let myself into the hall. I punched the code into the alarm and crossed to the staircase. It took me a moment or two to locate the cellar door. I unlocked it and descended to the depths. I was pleased to see that the door to the wine store was still concealed by the racking I had dragged over it on my last visit. I pulled it to one side. Unlocked the door and turned on the light. All was just as I had left it.

I now had a greater problem than I cared to contemplate. I have a theory. Not one that is shared by expert cooks, I will confess. A 'serious' dish should not be accompanied by a really great wine. If you make the mistake of choosing such a wine, you lose from both ends. Each competes with the other for pride of place in the memory.

You should either have really good food to remember or a superb wine, not both at one and the same sitting.

My dilemma was half solved by both my ability as a cook and the restricted selection of foods that were available in the flat. There were plenty of eggs and I thought I could just about manage a competent omelette. Since this didn't, by any measure, come into the category of 'Great Dishes' when cooked by me, I could claim that I could serve myself a 'Great Wine'. Now, which great wine to go with eggs?

Selection was difficult.

I inspected those wine bins until I was totally bemused by over choice. In desperation, I settled on an Alsatian Gewurztraminer by a producer I had never heard of but it's inclusion in such rarefied company promised quality.

I retreated to my lair bearing the fruit of my search. The good Mrs Barker or someone had provided a corkscrew and a near suitable glass.

I was not to be let down. Nectar. Spicy, lemony nectar. I only had a small sample to ensure against disappointment once I had produced the gastronomic delight of my omelette. As is always the case, I had to retry the wine several times whilst I made my dinner.

I set a place at the table and served my offering as well as I could. It still ranks as one of the best meals I have tasted.

I was reflecting on the way we should tackle the huge task I was about to undertake when a telephone rang. It took me a moment or two to find it. I hadn't thought there would be one in the little flat. It was George. He had arranged for Tim Turner to come at ten o'clock the next morning.

# CHAPTER 24

I was up and about early. A quick slice of toast and a coffee and I was ready and eager to face the new challenge.

I walked down to the home farm and early though I was, found that George Pearson was there before me. Since he had just given his instructions to two of the men and they were climbing into their tractor cabs, to set off for their various tasks, it was apparent that an early start was the norm. A good sign.

I wanted to see the far end of the main drive and George suggested that the easiest way was for me to take his Landrover and go round the lanes back onto the so-called main road and tackle it from that end. I told him of my excursion the previous evening and we went back into his office and he pointed out the boundaries and the main features on the big plan on the wall. A moments search in a file and I had a smaller version.

When I reached the Lodge I wasn't much the wiser. It had virtually vanished under what was now a mass of brambles. They were spiteful and, kitted out as I was, impenetrable.

I did, however, manage to follow the line of the old drive from the site of the Lodge as far as the causeway between the upper and lower lakes and although it wasn't by any means easy, it was slightly less overgrown than the part from the lakes to the house.

Returning to the Landrover and studying the plan George Pearson had given me, I tried to drive right round the outside of the Estate. I managed to get lost in the web of tiny lanes that surrounded it. By the time I had got that sorted out and stopped a few times to look at things that caught my eye. I was surprised to see that if I didn't get a move on I would be late for our meeting. Three hours had vanished in what seemed to be seconds!

\*\*\*

Tim Turner was already with George in the office when I pulled into the yard. We started, by my watch, at a few moments past ten and we were still hard at it at one o'clock.

I had drawn up a very rough agenda. Not that we stuck to it by any means. I started the ball rolling by laying down the aim as I saw it. The enterprise must make a profit in the long term. I could, and would, find the capital for investment on the agricultural side to achieve that. Over this, there didn't seem to be too much trouble. Both George and Tim were quite sure that the place was already in profit even if the books didn't reflect it.

All right, improvements could and would be made. One of the most pressing needs was for a lot of the machinery to be updated but there was no basic problem. We decided that the beef herd should be upgraded. It costs just as much to rear poor cattle as to rear good ones!

We also decided to put some of the farm work, like the deep ploughing, out to contract. That would save on machinery costs and free up labour for some of the improvement work which needed doing.

We turned our attention to the sporting potential of the Estate. The place had been noted for the pheasant shooting in Grandfather's early days but it had gone downhill as he lost interest and it had been virtually neglected after he had gone to the home in Oxford. One of the older men we employed would be willing to become a full-time keeper and I sanctioned adding a youngster to the payroll as an under-keeper.

We went over the potential of all the buildings and we decided that by a process of overhauling the cottages we would have a better chance of retaining a workforce of the best standard.

We came to the difficult problem of the original entrance.

Here, at first, I came on some resistance. George argued that to put it back into a decent state, to clear the lakes and restore the Lodge, would not only cost a great deal of money but it would divert the labour from jobs that would show profitable returns more quickly. Tim Turner agreed with him.

However, when we came to the most difficult question on the agenda, Locklate House itself, and I explained the very outline of the plan I had in mind, they saw the sense in the proposal. To soften the blow, I made the proposal that I would make the required money available from my own resources, at this stage. If all went according to plan then I would recoup the money from the Estate at a later date.

The last major matter we had to settle was a valuation for probate purposes. The value, upon which the executors and District Valuer would need to agree, would be the figure used to calculate the Inheritance Tax.

I explained the situation with lawyer Harper. I told them what I had found out about the land at Upton which had been sold on for development and of my visit to Birmingham to the supposed offices of Harrep Modern Homes.

I asked George a straight question. "Harper said that he had discussed the sale of that land with you and that you had agreed to it; was that true?"

Poor George looked uncomfortable. "It's true that we talked about it, yes. He told me that he had had an offer from a man who wanted to build a garden centre. On the face of it, it looked sensible because it was right at the far end of the Estate and, to tell the truth, it wasn't very good land but he had it all cut and dried before he ever asked me."

I smiled reassurance. "That's what I expected. Did you get a new grain dryer?"

George pulled a face. "No.... we revamped the old one." He paused. "It isn't too bad now.... we can cope with it for a few seasons yet I dare say!"

I made a mental note to remind Harper of his lie the next time I spoke to him.

In the end, we arranged for Tim to get on with the valuation of everything at Locklate and for him to get a firm he knew in Oxford to cover the stuff in storage there; there was no sense in bringing it all back until we had somewhere safe to put it.

We went on for a bit about the fine detail: getting quotations for clearing the old drive and cleaning the lakes, getting contractors to give us some idea of prices for the heavy cultivation we would need, that sort of stuff.

Tim agreed to have a good look at the cottages and start a programme for their modernisation. I didn't forget the home farmhouse either, where George Pearson lived. He hurried to tell me that both he and his wife were quite happy with the place as it was.

I asked one question. "Has it got central heating George?"

He confessed that it hadn't. "Then it will come under the renovation programme just like all the other buildings. I suggest you ask Mrs Pearson what she thinks and then tell me if you still want the place left off the list?"

He had the grace to blush slightly.

The meeting broke up and we saw Tim off back to his office with his long list of 'things to do'. I scrounged a clipboard from the office with some paper and spent a happy few hours thrashing through the undergrowth along the line of the drive and round the lakes. It reminded me of the survey I had made of the old railway line from Kuala Lumpur to Port Swettenham all those years ago. Luckily, rural England doesn't have as many 'nasties' in the undergrowth as Malaya. I reflected that such things in England, tended to wear suits and come with letters after their names!

In the event, I spent almost two days on that little job. I don't pretend that I produced a working plan of any sort but I did get a pretty good idea of what would be entailed and felt I could then sort out the most realistic proposal from anyone who applied to take the task on.

I was glad I took the trouble.

Some weeks later I interviewed three people who were prepared to quote for the work. The first young man was from quite a large firm of civil engineers and came up with a price that made me think he was going to build a short length of motorway. The second hardly looked at the land and quoted a price so low that I knew he hadn't the faintest idea what was involved and that he would overshoot the price by miles before he was through.

The third chap, who came from over Monmouth way, spent a day looking at the land and then came and said that he didn't think that he could give us a price at all.

I asked, "Why is that?"

His explanation was honest in the extreme. "The lakes are no problem, we've got the right equipment and we've done lots of similar jobs, we can do the work on the embankment and the sluice as well but the driveway itself is the difficulty."

"Why, I don't understand?"

"Well! There's a lot of clearing to do and it's going to have to be done very carefully if we're

not going to damage the old trees that were there in the first place.

They really need a proper tree surgeon to get them looking decent again. By the time the clearing has been done, I think you will have to remake the drive itself from scratch if you want a proper job done."

I assured him that that was what I was after.

"We don't really have what it will need in the way of tackle or experience."

I thought about it for a bit.

"If we got someone else to do the clearing and to see to the old trees would you take on the lakes and the embankment and the spillway?"

"Certainly but what about the roadway itself, it will be in a hell of a mess by the time the rest's finished?"

"I think we'll have to get a specialist firm in to do that as well."

In the end, after a bit of strong-arming from me, the Estate workforce cleared the site and a brilliant tree surgeon did the work on the old trees, lopping off overhanging branches and reshaping the crowns. David Morgan's firm made a super job of the lakes and the embankment and I got a chap in from Worcester to relay the roadbed and finish it with tar and shingle.

At that stage, we decided that we should go the whole hog and replace the fencing on both sides of the drive. That we did ourselves.

It may have well cost a small fortune but it looked well worth it. By the time we had finished rebuilding the Lodge and the gateway by the road it would surely have added at least its price to the value of Locklate.

The one drawback I didn't think of was its effect on dear old Mrs Baker. Sadly, she decided that my opening up the old drive again and restoring the Lodge reawakened too many memories and she moved to live with a relative near Temple Guiting. It was a reaction I hadn't expected. The upside was though, that with her going and the Lodge restored, it gave us two more cottages to use.

I wasn't sure if we had won or lost. Much later I can look back at that time and think that it was about then that I decided that material gain wasn't the only yardstick for measuring one's profit in life.

After my surveying of the work for the restoring of the front entrance, I thought it time to move on to Fannich again.

I phoned Anna Hudson and she told me that, as far as she could ascertain, the Swans had left. I checked with Angus Farr and he said that they had gone but that a removal firm was due in two days time to shift their belongings. He didn't know where they were going.

I felt I needed to be at Fannich.

After a very long drive, I arrived late in the evening. I called in on Angus and asked for the keys to the main house. He didn't have them. He told me that Marion Swan had still got them and had insisted on keeping them until they had 'collected their things'.

I was not in the mood for messing about.

I drove to the house, parked my car by the front door and went round the back and forced a door. From what I could see things were much as they had been when I went round with the mighty Marion when I was last there and as far as I was concerned they were going to stay that way.

I checked to see if the electricity was still on and went back down to Mrs Rothney's shop to see if I could get a few things. By this time all was locked and barred but a good banging on the door got results and after her prudent enquiry as to who was getting her out of bed at this time of night - it must have been about ten o'clock! - I explained who I was and what I wanted.

She offered to feed me, kind soul, but I declined with as much good grace as I could muster and instead went round her stock collecting up the things that I thought I needed. Her till was locked away and she said that I could pay later. I left some notes and said that if there was any change to come back I would collect it the next time I was in.

By the time I had got back to the house I was just too tired to bother with anything. I broached the bottle of Scotch I had bought and, finding a couple of blankets, made the best of a bad job on a settee in the sitting room.

I must have been a sight more done in than I had thought. I awoke once in the early hours and lay for a while wondering where the hell I was. Slowly it came to me and after banging about for a while finding the light switch and then opening various doors until I found the lavatory, I went back to my makeshift bed.

The next thing I knew was that I was laying, at a distinct disadvantage, confronted by Marion Swan, wanting to know 'What the hell I thought I was playing at?'

It has been said that I am not at my very best when I first awake. Add to this the fact that I was being harangued by a woman I certainly didn't care for, in a house that was now mine in all but legal detail and I was not disposed to bandy polite conversation.

I told her to go away and that I would see her when I was up, shaved and breakfasted. "Say in an hour."

She didn't seem to appreciate that the subject was not open for negotiation. I insisted and eventually she went.

The prescribed hour later, abluted and fed, I was ready for the fray. The only snag was the wretched woman was gone. By going upstairs and looking from a window, I saw that a large pantechnicon was parked at the farmhouse down the road.

I drove down there. It was going to be a stressful day!

I made it quite clear to Mrs Swan that she was only collecting anything that she could prove was hers and her husband's. She was insistent that everything in the farmhouse came under that heading. I disagreed.

The crew of the removal van looked from one of us to the other, much as spectators at a tennis match. In the

322

end, they retired to the depths of their vehicle to drink tea and read the newspapers whilst the battle raged.

As on previous occasions, I suddenly got fed up with the game and told her that unless she played it my way I was calling the police. It wasn't until I had actually got the station at Mallaig on the other end of my mobile telephone that she semi capitulated. After that, the crew removed items which we agreed on were hers - or I couldn't see that we would have any use for - and they left items which I insisted were part of the belongings of the Estate.

Fatigue on both of us brought an end. I did agree to go with her to the main house and see if there was anything there which she might legitimately lay claim to but we couldn't agree on a single item. She decided to call it a day.

Back at the farmhouse, I had a quiet word with the foreman of the removal team and in exchange for a five-pound note was informed of the address in Montrose where the cargo was headed for.

The final straw came when just before the lorry left Mrs Swan headed for the Jaguar parked in the driveway. Through the open car window, I told her that she couldn't take it since it was undoubtedly the property of the Estate. She enquired if I proposed that she rode in the van. I assured her that that was exactly what I was proposing. She very nearly ran me down.

# CHAPTER 25

Before the dust of Mrs Swan's wheels had died down, I was talking to Anna Hudson instructing her to inform Harper that the deal was all off and that she was to contact the police, the Law Society, the fraud squad and anyone else she could think of as soon as I had rung off.

Her chuckle made me smile as well. "Am I to take it that you are in Fannich?"

I told her I was.

"If you told me exactly what the problem is then I could tell Harper why you are taking this action - couldn't I?"

I agreed to that as well. Somehow that well modulated, dark chocolate voice, took some of the tension out of the day. I set about explaining why I was so angry.

"I have a suggestion," she said. "You go and look at the scenery and have a cup of tea or something and I will see what I can do. I will ring you back in.... let's say.... half an hour and we can see where we have got to, all right?"

I took her advice. I rummaged about and found the makings of tea and went and sat on the bank of the Loch.

As good as her word, it was exactly half an hour later when she phoned back. Harper had sworn that he didn't know his daughter was taking anything from either the farmhouse or the main house. He promised, for what it was worth, that anything not theirs would be back within the next forty-eight hours. That applied to the Jaguar and, for that matter, the Range Rover.

A prickle ran up my neck. "The wretched man's lying again Anna."

"How do you know?"

"I didn't even know the Range Rover wasn't here and I certainly didn't mention it to you, did I?"

"True.... but how does that mean he's lying?"

"He must have known they had taken it, otherwise he wouldn't promise its return. He's been talking to them.... or at least her.... before you rang."

"She could have rung him at the same time as you rang me!"

"Only if she had a mobile phone as well."

Again that laugh. "People do you know.... some of us have had them for ages."

It was my turn to laugh. "Okay. I take your point. Oh! and thanks for calming me down."

"All part of the service. Just try and take it slowly.... you did promise Tommy you know."

That blasted Black had told her of our talk. I'd a good mind to phone him as well. I had to have the last laugh.

"Anna, it's just occurred to me. Marion Swan's mobile; if I know anything, that will belong to the Estate. Tell Harper that it had better come back with the Jaguar or the deal really is off."

She was still laughing when she put her phone down.

I retrieved the keys to the farmhouse from the drive where angry Marion had flung them and locked the place up. I drove back to the big house and found the keys to that were still in the lock in the front door where, again, she had left them. I went through to the back kitchen and secured the door I had forced the night before by the simple expedient of jamming a chair back under the doorknob. Hardly grade one security but it would have to do until later. I locked everything else and went to find Angus Farr.

I eventually saw him on the other side of the river, at least I saw a tractor and trailer and went across the bridge to look closer.

He was repairing a stretch of fence using old rusty barbed wire and some posts which had also seen better days. I told him what had gone on but he didn't say very much. I got the distinct feeling that he knew more than he was letting on but didn't want to get involved in any argument.

I tried a different tack. "Wouldn't it be better if you got some new wire and posts for that job?"

He looked me directly in the eye and said in that distinctive west coast lilt, "Where do you think I should get them?"

"Isn't there a merchant in Mallaig?"

"I doubt they would supply Fannich - unless for cash - and perhaps only then if we paid the bills still owing."

I said I was sorry.

He went back to his work and I stood looking out over the view across the Loch to the sea.

Fannich had sunk a deal lower than I'd thought, that was clear. It was going to take a very determined effort to reclaim it. Was it worth it? Did I need it and the headache it was bound to be? I certainly wasn't sure about anything.

One thing was certain, Angus Farr was not going to be the man to drag it round, if that's what I decided. A good, loyal and probably honest foreman he might be, but it would take massive energy, brains and money. I suspected a very great deal of money. I bade the old man 'good afternoon' and re-crossed the bridge, got in my car and drove back to the March's hotel on Arisaig.

*** 

Helen March seemed as fed up as I was. That was unusual. Over a cup of tea and a couple of slices of delicious fruit cake that I was going to live to regret, I ferreted. Despite her protestations which I think stemmed from pride, I got the feeling that all was not well between Helen and husband Peter. I also got the impression that it stemmed from a poor run of trade in the hotel.

I have no real knowledge of such things but I've often found in other friends I've had, that a problem in one area - say money - generates problems in relationships. This must be axiomatic and I would bet that psychologists have a name for it. Not that that solves anything, but it does prove cause and effect.

I tried to get Helen to admit that perhaps that was the root cause but she had lots of reasons why that wasn't the case:

'We knew that it would take time to build up the trade.'

(It's slower than we thought)

'If only we had more money to spend on publicity.'

(We didn't have enough capital in the first place)

'We haven't yet matched the service we offer to the client's needs.'

(We are doing what we think they should want not what they actually need)

I tried to point out that these were the sort of problems that faced pretty well any business you care to mention and they are all curable but it didn't seem to be much help. In the end, I retired to my room with a half bottle of Bollinger, a plate of cold green olives stuffed with anchovy and a severe case of the blues.

Helen knocked on my door a few moments later with a plate of her special 'crisps' - very thin filo pastry deep fried in olive oil and allowed to cool and dry.

"On the house, Mr Forest."

I protested but she added, "You are one of our few guests who knows precisely what they want, who wants the best and above all is prepared to pay for it."

She vanished smiling and pulling the door shut before I could reply.

I bathed and then phoned Tim Turner. He was still in his office.

"Tim, I'm up in Fannich and if you can spare about three days, I need you."

He was very hesitant. "Mr Forest I'm pretty busy, with your valuation for one thing and we seem to have a bit of a rush on with all the other stuff just now."

"Well, part of it is the probate valuation. We need to get this place done as well and I would like you to do the whole lot if possible."

"You say part, what's the other part?"

"I need someone to look over the whole place and try and work out if there's any future in trying to pull this place round as well?"

He sounded as if he was on firmer ground.

"Mr Forest, I wouldn't try and mislead you on that one. I know something about Estate management here in the south, more specifically the south-west. I'm not sure I'm your man for Scotland.... it's very different you know."

"Tim, firstly if I thought you would mislead me, as you put it, I wouldn't have asked. Secondly, bring someone with you who does know; I'll foot the bill. Better still, do you know anyone up here who you think might be our man?"

He hesitated for a bit. "I know a chap in Inverness.... I was at college with him.... we could try him."

That sounded better. "Look Tim, see if you can take say four days, fly up to Inverness or wherever and hire a car. Arrange to see this chum of yours and bring him as well. While you do the valuation he can look over the place and let us know what he thinks. I'll make all the arrangements here, bring your wife and children as well."

Tim sighed. "If only, Mr Forest, they've just gone back to school."

I realised I was a bit out of touch with family life and its patterns.

"Sorry Tim, silly of me."

He laughed, "Thank you for the offer anyhow.... very kind of you."

In the end, we decided to leave it for a couple of days and see what we could cobble together. I thought that if we could have a really serious look at the whole picture and try and come to a sensible conclusion we would all be better placed to see how to deal with Locklate as well. It seemed obvious to me that we should look at the problem as one.

Helen perked up a bit when I asked if she could cope with two more guests for a few days, probably next week. Since the hotel was less than half full, it was no problem.

I had an excellent dinner and read a book on the Highland Clearances for a bit. Not a very edifying period in British history.

*\*\**

The next morning, I donned my walking outfit and went back to Fannich.

Angus Farr was in the yard at the side of the farmhouse sorting out some hurdles and loading them onto a trailer hitched to the same old tractor I had seen him using for repairing fences the day before. I told him that I was going to spend the day having a good look round. He didn't seem very interested. I told him to carry on with the run of the mill work, just as he had been doing and that if anything came up he couldn't handle, to come and find me.

There wasn't a proper Estate office at Fannich, unlike Locklate and I thought the first move was to find a temporary home for one, for the time being.

There was a small room at the end of what had once been a range of four loose boxes. I thought that it had probably once been a tack room. Anyhow it had the merits of appearing to be water and wind tight and had electricity laid on. The downside was that it was full of rubbish and was filthy dirty.

I stood in that yard that morning and tried to size up the magnitude of the task that I was facing. There was no doubt that both Fannich and Locklate were beautiful places. Very different. The soft rural tranquillity of Locklate contrasted totally with the rugged grandeur of Fannich. Grandfather, if nothing else, had had an eye for landscapes.

If I had continued my search for that ideal place I had in my mind's eye for so long, I doubt that I would have found anywhere that would combine the potential advantages that these two places possessed. I was lucky that they had fallen into my lap and I suspected that if I didn't try to make a go of both places I would spend what years were left to me regretting it.

Likewise, I had a sinking feeling that the task was so daunting that I would know times when I would curse the day I had decided to try. On the other hand, it just might be a hell of a lot of fun.

I walked back to where Angus was still loading hurdles and asked if he knew of anyone who might take on a few days work to try and sort out the old tack room. He didn't have anything to suggest other than the jobbing builder who had always done what little work had been required in the recent past. Somehow I wanted to cut off the past.

I drove down to Mrs Rothney's little shop and after she had insisted on settling up my change from when I had bought my provisions earlier, gave grave consideration to my question.

She ticked off the possibilities on her fingers. The little finger of her left hand, Andy Duncan, was working in Mallaig building a new bungalow for someone from Glasgow who had pots of money but no sense. The third finger, the oddly named Pablo Whatshisname, was doing a job at Millburn for the council. The second finger, George Mulvein, was away down south. Her index finger, Colin Mc Bain was in hospital after falling down a sewer.

She thought for several seconds before choosing her thumb and exclaiming that that only left Cathy Muir and I wouldn't want her because she was trying to run the business on her own since her father, a widower, had taken up with a woman, much younger than himself and gone to live with her in Stonehaven.

I asked where I might contact Miss Muir. After asking if I was sure, she found the telephone number of N Muir & Daughter. The address was in Mallaig. I telephoned from my car. Miss Muir, luckily, was in and what's more, would meet me at Fannich Farm House at two o'clock.

As I drove back to the yard I saw a convoy of three vehicles turning into the drive in front of me, the Jaguar, the Range Rover and a very well worn saloon with a taxi sign on the roof. Puzzled, I prepared for a verbal fight but I needn't have taken the trouble. The Jaguar and the Range Rover were driven by two youths and the taxi by a middle-aged man. They were all strangers to me.

It transpired that they were a father and his two sons, engaged for the day to ferry the two cars back to Locklate by Marion Swan. They came from Montrose, where the father, a chap called Doug Haig, operated a taxi in the town and had been phoned by Marion to see if he would deliver the cars to Fannich. The money on offer had been fair so he had got his two sons, both of whom were 'between jobs', to help him. They had collected the vehicles from outside a house in Union Place in Montrose.

In the Jaguar there were two mobile telephones.

Haig produced a typed note in the form of a receipt which Marion had told them to get signed; it was for the safe return of the cars and the phones. I pointed out that I could hardly be expected to sign for something which was my own in the first place. Haig said that they had only been paid half their fee for the delivery. The other half was dependent on their producing the signed receipt. It wasn't their fault, indeed they didn't know who's the cars were. I signed the wretched note and advised the Haigs to make sure they got the balance of their money before they parted with the paper.

After they had left, I parked the Jaguar and my own sports car in the open fronted shed in the yard and took the Range Rover, checked the fuel and set about a bit of exploring.

In the next three hours, I think I saw most of what comprised the Fannich Estate. True, I didn't make the very high land along the top of the hills that lay to the north of the river but I did get up along the track that must have been built to ferry people to the shooting butts and, for the first time, I got to the eastern boundary of the high ground on the north face.

The higher ridge ran west to east and was quite a sharp feature for most of its length but at the inland end, judging from the map, it flattened out and split into two. Between these two ridges there appeared to be a large basin which had a small lake at its centre. On the map, it was named as Loch Coira. I made a mental note to get up there some time and explore.

# CHAPTER 26

When I got back to the farmyard there was a small van parked by the house and a young woman was knocking at the front door. I instinctively checked my watch. Cathy Muir was bang on time. A good sign.

I don't know what I had expected of a lady builder but not what I saw. She was somewhere in her early twenties, twenty-four perhaps, a good six feet tall and sturdily built with it. A bird's nest of bright ginger hair pulled back with one of those giant plastic clips added to her height. She wore brown 'Doc Martin' boots, faded jeans and a tee shirt with a bust born slogan which said, "Hands Off." Judging by the overall size of the girl I was not inclined to argue!

We introduced ourselves.

She was certainly forthright.

"Are you the new owner of this place?"

I agreed that I was.

"What are you going to do with it?"

I told her that, as yet, I hadn't decided but that I needed a temporary office space so that I could get everything sorted out. I showed her the old tack room.

She hardly looked inside. "It's too small," she said.

"It'll do to start with; I only need room for a desk and a chair, somewhere for the telephone, nothing elaborate. Could you clean it out, colour wash the walls.... just make it habitable for the time being?"

She looked at me. "I could. It needs a new door though and the window frame is rotten.... you'll need that replacing, and.... what about the floor?"

I hadn't even noticed the floor. It looked as if it were made of bricks, that is, where you could see through the dirt.

"Looks all right now but wait till the winter - damp, draughty - you'll never stick it - cost a bomb to heat - waste of money if you ask me."

I don't think that I had ever come across anyone who tried to talk themselves out of a job with such candour. It was certainly a new line in sales talk. I wasn't sure it was one that would lead to her financial success.

"Why not use a room in the farmhouse there?" She nodded her head in the appropriate direction.

"If I decide to keep the place on, I might want to put a manager in there."

"So why not wait till you've decided before you do anything?"

The logic of her argument against my spending my own money was impeccable. I conceded that it hadn't been a very bright suggestion in the first place.

"I'll be off then," she said without any dwelling on small talk and started to make her way to her van.

"Hang on a moment will you?"

She stopped, and turned around, "Och! There's more?"

I was very unwilling to let this strange builder go just like that. All right, I suspect that had 'she' been a 'he' I might have left it, but she certainly had a manner which was, not so much attractive, as arresting.

"The locks on both the farmhouse here and the big house, want changing and there's a window at the back up there which needs repairing." I added that I had had to break in. "We may as well get this place cleared out anyhow and, as you say, it needs a new door and a window."

She gave me a long stare, lips pursed, while she thought.

"Determined to spend our pennies, are we? Hang on a sec."

She went to her van and came back with a notebook and pulled a pencil from the ginger mass that did her service as her hairstyle. By the time we had been round the farmhouse, we had noticed a gutter that was falling down, a couple of slates off the roof and a leaking tap. We checked the locks on the front and the back doors and a window that wouldn't fasten.

She drove me in her van up to Fannich House and we looked at locks again and the window which I had forced. I asked her if she could have someone check over the central heating.

"I could.... if you want to spend more than you need, otherwise I'll do it!"

I asked politely if central heating was one of her fortes.

"You don't need a heating engineer for this one; you need an antique dealer.... or, more likely, a scrap merchant!"

I gave up and let her drive me back.

Cathy Muir promised to have a quote for the work in the post by the next day. I suggested that she just got on with the work. I was unlikely to quibble about the bill. Again, that long look with the lips pressed into a straight line.

"I think we will do it properly if you don't mind. That reminds me.... how will you pay?"

I got the wrong end of the stick. "Are you saying that there's a different price for cash?"

Her lips compressed into an even tighter line.

"Mr Forest, I run a proper business and I charge and I pay the tax on jobs I do. If you think otherwise you'd better find someone else for your work. Why should I risk my neck to save you money? I'm not a cowboy."

She said it with a finality that allowed for no argument.

I apologised and asked in return, "If you were not meaning the tax, I don't understand?"

She paused for a moment as if deciding how far to go. "Round these parts the Fannich Estate has a reputation for arguing over every penny or not paying at all, my dad refused to work for them."

She waited to see what reaction I would show.

"I'm sorry Miss Muir, I didn't know it was that bad. I will pay by cheque as soon as the jobs are done but.... if you want something on account for materials.... I can give you one now."

She smiled. "I reckon that's fair enough, I'll send my bill when I've done but it'll be ten per cent extra if you call me Miss Muir again - it's Cathy."

Just as she was leaving I couldn't resist one more question.

"Tell me, if your dad wouldn't deal with Fannich, why did you come?"

She laughed outright. "Firstly I need all the work I can get.... it's not easy being a girl builder around here. Secondly, someone said that the new owner of Fannich was quite a nice old codger. I wanted to check for myself."

Before I could reply to her cheek she let the clutch out and shot off down the drive waving out of the window.

\*\*\*

I spent the remainder of the afternoon exploring the Estate land to the south of the river. It was softer, not nearly as steep as the far land. A fair proportion, probably half of it, had been reclaimed in the past, with the expenditure probably, of a great deal of money and effort.

It was the part of the Estate which held most of the beef animals and would give shelter for the sheep in hard weather. It was the most sheltered land right at the bottom of the valley, alongside the river and the Loch shore where what arable crops there were, were grown mostly, to my untutored eye, grass for silage and some oats.

I drove up and south along the track I had walked over when I first set eyes on Fannich and from the crest turned back to survey almost the whole of the Estate. It was an impressive sight. The water in the Loch was an unexpected and unlikely shade of blue, with the shadows of the few clouds running across its surface. The spit of sand which ran out from near the little jetty by the shop was that shade of palest lemon yellow which you normally only see in tourist brochures.

Where the cloud shadows ran across the far hillside the greens, purples and browns went dark for a few moments before regaining their individual bright contrasts. My heart was telling me that I would be a fool to turn my back on such a place, however, my commercial instinct said, "Look at the figures."

I took a few steps to my right to get a better view of the big house and, in doing so, put up a grouse which must have been sitting tight. It flew off along the hillside making a 'clattering' noise.

It was probably at that point that the voice of reason started to fade.

That evening, at the hotel I asked the owners, Helen and Peter March if they would dine with me. Because, for once, they had a near full dining room they accepted on the condition that we could eat a little late - after the rush had subsided. I was quite happy with that and took my Champagne out into the garden which ran down to Loch Arisaig. I needed time to think and to make some phone calls.

I was bathed and changed in good time for our meal. A simple dish of home potted shrimps cooked, I suspect, in sea water with a little Madeira added. We drank a New Zealand Oyster Bay Sauvignon Blanc and to my surprise, it was rather good. This was followed by medallions of wild boar with a potato dish done with eggs and milk. With that, we had an '84 Ch. Palmer. I was taking no further chances in one evening. Cheese and then a pudding made with local bilberries and served with whipped cream finished off a super meal.

I must confess that it is something of an insult to the chef to talk business over a first-rate meal. I, for one, prefer to devote my attention to the skill of the cook and the excellence or otherwise of the ingredients. After the last course is cleared away and the cloth cleaned is time enough to think of other things.

We were all settled with our coffee and whatever drink we chose when I started.

"I am not quite decided yet but I have a mind to go into the hotel business and I want some advice."

I had their undivided attention. They looked at each other and then at me, puzzled.

Peter said, "Why?" and Helen said, "Don't!" at almost the same time. Peter added the supplementary question, "Where?"

I explained that I thought the only practical use for Fannich House would be to develop and extend it to create a sporting hotel. They looked dubious. I had suspected that Helen was the one of that pair with the entrepreneurial brains and that evening she confirmed my thoughts. Peter was a first class chef - as the meal had just shown - and he could run a good sound kitchen but I think that was the limit of his interest. He saw cooking as an art form in itself, which he wanted to practice for its own sake.

Helen was the one with the wit to create a business which turned his 'art' into a profit-making enterprise that would sustain them both. The trouble was that the unremitting grind of running an underfunded and limited appeal hotel was beginning to sap their morale and, I also suspected, to destroy their marriage.

Helen and I had spoken before about the different types and aims of Hotels. The country house place which offers nothing other than good food and comfortable rooms is one of perhaps hundreds and is at a disadvantage compared with the same sort of hotel which can offer, say, shooting/fishing/tennis/snooker, the list can go on.

I told them that I had heard recently of a hotel on the edge of Dartmoor which will not only put you up and feed you but will do the same for your horse if you care to bring one. If you don't, or haven't got one, they will provide one should you so wish. Such a hotel multiplies the number of people who might be attracted straight away.

Helen was still doubtful.

"But what about the rest of Fannich?"

I smiled, "That's what the people I am bringing here to stay for a day or two will help me with. I think that the two could run together very happily; the agricultural side should be able to be made to run at some sort of profit and if we can add the income from the sporting side, it should do quite well."

I went on to explain that I would like them to go with me to Fannich and have a look and see what they thought.

Helen was full of questions. Was there enough room? Where would any staff live? Who would I get to run it? Peter had gone pretty well silent but in a pause in Helen's rush of queries said, I think to both of us, "You realise that it would probably put this place out of business, don't you?"

I had thought of that and I was reluctant to tell them of all my plans, at this stage but I was going to have to if I was going to keep them on side. I told them of Locklate and the similar plans I had for that Estate. I also told them that if the plans for Fannich did go ahead then I would be in the market for someone to run the place. I added that the atmosphere that they had created in their hotel was exactly what I would want for mine. Helen saw the implications at once. I don't think that Peter was too keen. I decided to let Helen work on him.

I spent the bulk of the next day sorting out the Estate affairs and paying off all the outstanding bills I found lying about in the farmhouse room that Marion or Cedric had used as an apology for an office. It cost me a tidy sum by the time I had finished.

I rang everyone who, till then, had been owed money by Fannich Estate and explaining who I was and that I had taken over running the place until I could find a new Manager.

I drove to Mallaig and had a meeting with the Bank Manager of a different bank to the one the Estate had used and got him in the picture. I asked him to check with my chap in London and satisfy himself that my own credit was sound.

I called on the manager of the bank the Estate had used in the past and found that the account had been frozen on the instruction of a Mrs Hudson of Lewis, Lewis, Lewis & Farr and had been confirmed by Harper at her insistence. Nice to know that she was well on the case! I gave verbal instructions that the account would be moved to the bank's competitors. The Manager didn't seem too upset but asked for instructions in writing from Lewis's.

The remainder of the afternoon I spent looking at what Mallaig had to offer.

Perhaps by chance - or perhaps not - I found myself outside the small builder's yard that bore the name of N. Muir & Daughter.

I went in.

I caught myself just in time. I didn't want to pay a ten percent penalty on my bill!

"Cathy."

She looked up, "Ah! I can save the cost of a stamp. It's the new Laird of Fannich himself."

She said it with a laugh and a very cheeky smile that robbed it of any offence.

I laughed as well. "Cathy, I don't know that I approve of your sales talk but it seems to have some advantages."

She looked puzzled, "Is that a compliment? The last laddie who paid me one of those turned out to want to borrow a concrete mixer, for free!"

Laughing I took the proffered envelope and tore it open.

The quotation was well inside what I had expected. Looking at the itemised list I saw that there was no charge for new locks.

"I think we'd better have brand new locks on both the farm and the main house. The Swans may still have a set of keys for both."

Cathy grinned, "Did yer no see those locks? They're beautiful, they must be a hundred years old, it'd cost a fortune to replace them and I doubt we could."

"If we can't I'll have to alter the doors."

They're both the same so it'll be cheaper to swap some of the levers around and have new keys. If the Swans kept a set they would'na fit anyhow."

I told her that she was a genius.

She told me in return that she would start in two days time.

I said that her selling technique might not be so bad after all.

She stuck out her not inconsiderable chest and said, "Ha yer not heard my slogan? Yer get more with Muir."

I chuckled most of the way back to the hotel at Arisaig.

# CHAPTER 27

During dinner, Helen came and sat at my table for a while. Peter didn't put in an appearance. She started hesitantly. "Mr Forest..... we've talked about what you said last evening.... Peter and I, that is."

I waited for her to have her say. She fiddled with a piece of bread, then looking up at me directly, went on.

"Of course you're right. We had pretty well decided that we would run this place till the end of the season and then try and sell it. Not that that will be easy.... we will be lucky to get what we paid for it let alone what we have spent on improving the place." Helen looked worried. "The accounts aren't too good and that's what someone, looking to buy a place like this, will look at first."

She was very close to tears.

"We've tried very hard.... but we're not much different to plenty of other places. The restaurant is better than most.... that's Peter's doing but it just not enough to keep the place making a real profit. We would be better off working for a bigger place and have less worry."

Her smile was now a very sad one.

"When are you planning on making your final decision?" I asked.

"I think we have already decided to give up but we are going to carry on while we can - say about another two or perhaps three months, at a stretch."

"Are you all right for money?"

She looked slightly shocked at my question but did smile a little more convincingly.

"I won't say we're rolling in the stuff but, yes, we're keeping our heads above water - just - that's Peter again.... he hates debt and I think that's his biggest worry."

She stopped to think, wondering how far to go.

"Don't tell him I told you, will you?" I nodded agreement. "His Mum and Dad used to run a place like this once, in Devon. They got caught out in the recession in the eighties and they went bankrupt - he's never forgotten it - I think that's part of the trouble.... he worries so much, .... it makes him angry in a way."

She looked so very miserable. "He thinks people don't understand what it is to be in debt."

"Especially someone like yourself!"

She looked up to see if she had offended me.

I explained that I knew very well indeed what it was like to owe a sight more than you had; I had been there for a fair part of my life as a trader, especially after old Angus Findlay died. I think it helped.

My final advice was that she should hang on for the rest of the season, as they had planned, and that I would put some sort of proposal to them if we did decide to go ahead, before they put the hotel on the market. She seemed happier at that.

\*\*\*

We were expecting just Tim Turner and his pal from Inverness to come that next evening but I had a phone call at breakfast time from Tommy Black. It seemed that things had been moving a pace and he thought that I needed keeping up to date. He proposed that Anna Hudson should fly up to Inverness with Turner. They would pick up a hire car and then Turner's contact. He thought they would be with me in time for dinner.

The plan was that they would stay three days and then do the whole thing in reverse. I agreed with some enthusiasm. Seeing Anna would be a bonus. I let Helen know the change of plan and she said it was no problem. I went into a huddle with Peter and he promised to produce something a bit special for their evening meal.

I spent most of the day flogging through the mass of papers I found in the farmhouse. They were in a sorry state. The pay records, together with those for tax and national insurance were so bad as to be incomprehensible. I only hoped that our deal with Harper might not reveal the same state of affairs with the value added tax.

Helen had very kindly put me up a packet of sandwiches and at lunchtime, I took them and sat on the river bank and took in the view.

By the time I had finished my lunch and drunk the thermos of coffee and was ready to rejoin the fight against the paperwork. I was quite sure that any arguments for abandoning Fannich would have to be very good to stand a cat in hell's chance of winning me round.

Partly because I didn't enjoy the day's work and partly because I wanted to be at Arisaig well before the others arrived, I cut off early and was bathed and ready to greet them in plenty of time.

They pulled into the forecourt just on six o'clock. Anna looked marvellous. Why is it that some women have that wonderful ability to look the part wherever they are? I used to notice it in the East. Well educated girls, who should have more sense, would turn up at a Malay party, if they turned up at all, looking as if they were off to a ball at Buckingham Palace. They ended up looking foolish whilst their hosts would be embarrassed.

Anna wore a brown skirt, an orange blouse and a paisley shawl that picked up the colour of her hair exactly.

Tim Turner introduced his Estate management expert friend from Inverness.

David Dicks was one of the biggest men I have ever seen. I would have thought that he would well have topped six foot six but it wasn't just his height that impressed. I guessed he weighed eighteen or nineteen stones and didn't look as if there was an ounce of fat on him. Younger than I expected, perhaps thirty, he was almost an archetypal Scotsman. The thought crossed my mind that I couldn't wait to show him to Cathy Muir. I had a feeling that he was her sort of man.

I suggested that we had tea or a drink and that they then went and changed for dinner. I thought that if we met in the sitting room at about seven forty-five it would give us time for a drink before we sat down.

Anna had other ideas.

"Would you mind Robin, if I had a walk round the garden first? I have sat in an aeroplane or a car for most of the afternoon and I'd like to stretch my legs before I go and have a bath."

Tim Turner and David Dicks settled for tea and I took Anna off to see the garden and the Loch side. I was as happy as a schoolboy in a tuck shop. We chatted about the conventional things, the flight and the drive till we were down by the Loch. It really was a magnificent view out across the Sound towards Rum and Eigg and an almost perfect late afternoon.

Anna put her hand on my arm and said, "I wanted to get you alone for a bit before this evening. I thought you should know that I've some good news and, I'm afraid, some bad as well."

I played the old game. "Try me with the good first!"

"Nick Conway and I have been through the whole business of your grandfather's investments. It's not all clear yet because it's so complicated and Harper's records are by no means complete."

I had the feeling that I knew what was coming.

"And?"

"We think." she paused, "We think that the final total will be very much greater than we first thought."

"How much.... as a round figure?"

The figure she came out with actually stopped me in my tracks.

"How much?"

She repeated it. I was in something of a whirl for a moment and held onto her arm. Concerned she said, "Robin, are you all right.... come over here and sit down for a moment."

I shook my head. "I don't understand. I knew the old boy was well off but I didn't think it would come to anything like that. Where did it come from?"

She smiled, "Land basically, or rather property, in the forties and fifties he bought up masses of old industrial land very cheaply, most of it wasn't worth a light then; run-down old factories and mills which nobody needed. He bought it all up and just sat on it."

I thought for a moment. "You said there was bad news as well.... what's that?"

She laughed, that deep, throaty laugh which had attracted me the first time I had met her.

"No gain without pain, as they say, the problems are going to be horrendous."

"Explain."

"For a start, all the records are in a dreadful state." "We suspect Harper has deliberately let them get into a terrible mess, we also suspect that he must have defrauded your Estate out of several millions of pounds, however, it will be virtually impossible to prove anything."

I looked out over the water for a bit and said, "I don't really care a lot."

I think that made her a bit angry. "Well, you jolly well should. This is mega money we're talking about, apart from anything else the tax bill is going to be astronomical. We'll have to sell off all sorts of things in order to meet it."

I calmed down a bit; I certainly didn't want her to think that I wasn't well aware of the time and effort she must have put in during the last couple of weeks.

"Look, I made a bargain and I will stick to it. Okay, when I made it I thought we were talking about much smaller figures but just because the sums are bigger I'm not going back on the deal."

Anna Hudson made a face that spoke of disagreement.

"Men! We're not just talking about cheating a little bit here - we're talking serious fraud. Nick Conway thinks two and a half million at least and he's still digging. The man should go to prison!"

She hurried on. "Young Nick thinks that he can prove at least two cases where he has sold land, forged the documentation and pocketed the proceeds."

She waited for my response.

"Okay then, let's do it this way. Put it all down on paper, names, places, dates, the lot. Then confront Harper with it and suggest that when we made the deal we had no idea that it was on the scale we think it is now, threaten the wretched man with whatever you like.

I dare say that he might cough up a bit more - if it isn't already spent."

The smile on Anna's face was a picture. "Nick can play very rough when he wants to Robin. I think Harper will find a way of paying up."

She added, "I thought you might see it our way... come on, I want my bath and a half decent dinner."

I somehow got the feeling that I had been conned yet again, but in the most enjoyable way possible.

That evening was memorable, strange to relate I can't really remember all the detail but the meal itself centred round a delectable fillet of venison. I remember we drank perhaps too much Champagne before we sat down and a very acceptable Côte Rôtie with the meat.

Peter came and saw that we were all happy and he shared a glass of wine, as did Helen. I thought they looked happier than I had seen them for some time. I even noticed them holding hands. Not that holding hands is a sign of anything much. I held Anna's when we had a stroll in the garden after Tim Turner turned in followed just after by David Dicks. I promised a nine o'clock start in the morning.

We didn't talk about much down in the garden, we were happy enough to enjoy the peace and quiet after what had turned into quite a party. Something about the moon and the stars up in Scotland perhaps - brighter than London certainly. There didn't seem a great deal that needed saying. I saw Anna to her door and she thanked me for a super evening. She put her hands on my shoulders, gave me the lightest kiss and vanished.

I lay in bed for a while thinking what a lucky man I was. I realised that I hadn't felt so happy for a very long time, perhaps since those far off days with Helen Ford.

*** 

The men in the party looked a shade jaded in the morning light, me included. Perhaps I was getting a tad ancient for partying! Anna, needless to say, looked as bright as a button. I put it down to the fact that she'd the sense not to drink too much.

After breakfast, we drove to Fannich; Anna and me in the Range Rover and Tim and David in their hire car.

First of all, we had a session in the farmhouse. Sitting round the kitchen table, I laid out what I wanted from both Tim and from David. I lent them the Range Rover so that they could get over as much of the land as they thought necessary and gave them the keys to all the buildings. I explained about the door locks and that they might come across our 'Lady Builder'.

As luck would have it, as we went out to do our various tasks Cathy Muir pulled up in her van to start on the farmhouse front door. I introduced everyone too her. When David Dicks stepped forward to shake hands her jaw dropped perceptibly. Her tongue didn't seem affected, however, in as broad an accent as I had heard her employ, breathlessly she said. "My Gord! yon's a bonny wee laddie.... where der'r fin him then?"

I explained he was here to see if the Estate could be made to pay.

She ignored me totally, "Are yer married?"

Confused by this girl, built to the same scale as himself, he blushed furiously and admitted to being engaged.

"Ach, thas na problem." she then added, "Look he's shy as weel." which only made it worse. Not content she pressed on. "What yer doin' this e'ning? I don alway look like this. I've got a frock yer ken."

I decided she had had her fun and once he had regained his composure I was sure that David could look after himself.

"I need him this evening Cathy.... sorry!"

I got the answer I hadn't thought of but should have guessed at. She fluttered her eyelashes outrageously and said in a mock shocked voice. "Och Mr Forest, I'm sa sorry, I'd never ha guessed - an him such a big felly too!"

It was Anna's laughter which saved the situation from getting worse. Controlling herself she said, "Cathy, it's not like that at all, I promise you, take my word."

Cathy Muir feigned coyness, not easy I'd have thought in a girl like her. She looked at me with a very knowing look and replied, "And he never even wanted to borrow my mixer. I'll be about my work then." giving poor David a very seductive smile, "Never yer fret, I'll catch you later laddie."

A bemused David Dicks and an amused Tim Turner went off to do their surveying and valuing.

Anna, chuckling, asked, "And what's this about a mixer then?"

We spent most of the rest of the day going over the paper work which I had got into some sort of order. She suggested that she took some back with her for Nick Conway to troll through. We bundled up what she thought might be needed.

That done, we had the packed lunch that Helen March had provided and in the afternoon explored the two houses and the grounds near the big house. She was just as enthusiastic as I was. I found that a great relief.

Eventually, we collected up the papers we had decided to send south and were waiting for Tim and David to get back when Cathy Muir's van drove into the yard. She got out and walked across.

She looked a bit contrite. "Mr Forest, Mrs Hudson. I've finished the work you wanted and I'll be off." She hesitated, unsure of herself. "Also, I'd better apologise for this morning, I think I was perhaps a wee bit rude." She now had a very winning bashful look. This girl, I thought could make a fortune as an actress.

Anna stepped in, "Nonsense Cathy, it was just a bit of fun that went a tiny bit too far.... that's all.... forget it."

I could have kissed her.

The irrepressible Cathy went on, "Did you ever see such a chappie though?" She then made a noise like a tiger growling.

Anna laughed again. "You didn't spend half the day yesterday in a car with him! I could fancy him myself. I think I'm a bit too old though."

Cathy drew herself to her full height and said, "I'm not though - I'm a big girl now. Bye!"

After she drove off I did kiss Anna on the side of her head. She put her arm round my waist and snuggled saying, "Mummm." We had just about regained our composure when Tim & David turned into the yard from the road. They reported a successful day and that they thought they could agree on a valuation for the land itself. Tomorrow, Tim was going to do the houses and the buildings and David was going to draw up his suggestions for improving the running of the place. We had discussed the possibility of using the main house as a hotel earlier in the day and we spent some time up at the house looking at the site and seeing what could go where.

David thought that we would be well advised to seek expert help about that side of any plan because he had little knowledge of the hotel side. Tim, of course, had none.

Back at Arisaig we had tea and then decided on a working meeting after changing. For part of it, Peter and Helen joined in. Luckily they had had some quotations a year since for building extra bedrooms but it had proved far too expensive for them to pursue but the information gave us some sort of basis to work on.

David quizzed us all pretty closely about how we saw the Estate developing. This puzzled me a bit. I had assumed he would come up with the ideas but as he pointed out he could think of several different ways to run the place but the only viable plan would be the one that suited the way we wanted it done.

I took his point. Hotel or not, David seemed to think that the most undervalued assets we had, which were being totally neglected, were the sporting opportunities. He quoted figures for shooting and fishing which made me quite angry with the way Harper had let things go to rack and very near ruin.

Tim, I think, was better on the farming side, despite his protestations he clearly had a very good grasp of the likely future of agriculture all over the country and as he pointed out we could do what Grandfather had thought of when he first bought Fannich, raise stock and move them south to finish before they went to slaughter.

He made several points which made me think that we should be treating both places as one enterprise. I had several rosy visions of our serving Fannich beef and lamb to discerning customers at Locklate, not to mention salmon, venison and grouse. Likewise, Locklate game in Fannich.

Tim brought me back to earth with the mention of refrigerated transport costs. It did, however, spark a response from Anna. Two sporting country house hotels sharing a promotional budget. A big item in the cost of running such places. Would visitors like the thought of having, say, a week or so in one and then another week in the other? It was an idea worth thinking about.

I made a vain attempt to stop shop talk over the meal but it was on everyone's mind and that's what they wanted to talk about. I let it ride. Brainstorming it may be, but there were worse surroundings in which to do it.

After dinner Tim and David went to their rooms to do sums, leaving Anna and me to drink a little brandy with our second or possibly third coffees.

We talked of this and that, past lives, past loves, past sadness. The sort of thing that people speak about when they are trying to get to know each other. We compared tastes in books, music, art, wine and food. All, what I consider to be the important things. We avoided religion and politics and perhaps, most importantly, money. We were sated with turnover, bottom lines, gross margins; the means by which we can afford the important things.

In the end, talked out I think, we gravitated to the garden. There was a bench where we could look out over the water and breathe the scents on the night air. It was as near to tranquillity as I have known in many a long year.

# CHAPTER 28

The next day, Tim Turner finished off his valuation of the houses and their contents, so much as they were after the 'scourge of the Swans' and David Dicks was at the farmhouse drawing together his recommendations for the future running of the Estate and his thoughts on its possible viability.

For I was still in no doubt that, unless we could see our way clear to making a viable business of it, we would certainly sell off some or most of it. However, I wanted to keep it going as a unit if at all possible.

Anna and I, having nothing pressing to do until the meeting we had planned with the others at three o'clock, decided to go and explore the northeast corner of the Estate. It was the highest part of the east-west ridge that ran along the northern boundary. I wanted to go and see what Loch Coira was really like.

Anna had very sensibly brought some trousers and a pair of stout walking shoes with her and I took my rucksack with a small packed lunch and the other things I thought we might need. We drove the Range Rover across the bridge to the north side of the river and turned along to the east.

I suppose the track ran out about three-quarters of a mile from the Loch but about eighteen hundred feet below it. Looking up from where we parked the vehicle, it was a daunting prospect and I was having second thoughts but Anna was all for having a stab at it.

There was even some suggestion, on her part, that the last one to the top paid for a bottle of Champagne that evening. I thought to myself that I would be very glad to buy it, provided I was still in a fit state to enjoy it!

We did have the sense to stop and take a good look at the hillside, trying to work out some sort of a route. There was a cleft which ran at about forty-five degrees across the slope from about a third of the way up and it seemed to run out onto bare hillside quite near the top. It had some stunted trees growing in it and that seemed the way to go.

The stretch to the corrie wasn't too bad, steep but a hard walk rather than a real climb. When we reached the first of the little trees we found that the cleft in the slope was deeper and steeper than it had looked from the track, so we stuck to the bottom edge of it.

There were parts where it was much more of a scramble than we had appreciated. One bit, where another little valley ran off, was about as difficult a bit as I thought we could tackle. What had seemed from the bottom as a minor stream was, in fact, a dry stream bed about ten or so feet deep and I had to push Anna up the far side and then, in turn, she had to help me up with the aid of a length of old branch we found.

We stopped for a breather just after that and whilst I looked south out over the valley, Anna was studying the remainder of the climb that still faced us. Suddenly she put her hand on my shoulder and said in a whisper, "Quick.... Look."

I turned just in time to see about six or seven deer, moving swiftly up the slope.

"Where on earth did they come from?" I asked.

"I'm not sure. I think they must have been further up this gully."

"Come on; let's see where they have gone."

Privately, I thought that they'd be miles off by the time we got to the top but kept my opinions to myself, the look of excitement on Anna's face was encouragement enough, to urge me on. The first stretch after the top of that gully was enough to dampen my enthusiasm. For about twenty or so feet it was one solid slab of granite. As luck would have it there was a way around it to the left which was, by comparison, a fairly easy scramble but you didn't want to look down. You would have bounced a devil of a long way if you'd slipped. After that, it was safer if not easier going.

What had looked from the bottom a stretch of steep but smooth ground was anything but smooth. As Anna described it, "Some of these rocks are bigger than a double bed."

I think we thought we were at the final crest about five times but each time there was another ridge a bit higher than the one we were on. Finally, we made it and all we could see in front of us was a great big basin-shaped stretch of land, about four or five hundred yards across with a lake of about three or perhaps four acres in the bottom.

We had made Loch Coire.

Not much to my surprise, the deer were nowhere to be seen but there was something we hadn't expected. By the west end of the Loch was a small stone building. All right, there was no roof left, just the dry stone walls with an opening for a door. Inside it smelt appalling. Sundry bones and filth littered the floor. We decided that a fox was probably using it as a place to bring its dead prey.

The only sign of life, other than birds that we could see was one very thin and bedraggled looking sheep, which ran off the moment Anna made a move towards it. The only other sign of human activity up there was three spent cartridge cases from some sort of shotgun. The brass at their bases looked quite bright, as if they hadn't been there for very long. The tube part though was plastic so it was difficult to tell. I put one in my pocket meaning to ask about it. The others I threw into the Loch. Somehow man-made objects like that seemed to be out of place in such a remote place.

We sat by the little Loch and ate our lunch and drank coffee from our flask. Apart from the noise made by a bird, that we couldn't see, and a vapour trail high in the sky, we could almost imagine that we were alone in the world.

If I had been looking for solitude as opposed to loneliness I had found it.

We didn't linger over our lunch too long. We had arranged the meeting with Tim and David for three o'clock and I was worried about the descent if we went back the way we had come up. Often going down is just as difficult, if not more so than the climb. The stretch over the rock slab at the top of the gully was very exposed and a slip there could well end in serious injury if not worse.

Looking from the crest we couldn't see the middle part of the way down but it seemed that if we tackled it further to the east it would be easier. It was, however, a lot further and we were likely to be late. I decided that we'd try it and if we were going to be late I'd ring Tim on my mobile phone and let them know where we were.

We all make mistakes. We got about a third of the way only to discover that the next stretch was a convex slope so it got steeper and steeper the further down you went, until the last stretch was as near vertical as made no difference.

Rather wearily we retraced our steps to the ridge and tried again nearer where we had come up. That was not a great deal better but after several blind starts, we found that by going part way down and then traversing along to the west we gained the gully we'd come up, bypassing the rock slab that guarded its top entry.

By the time we got back to the Range Rover, we were both pretty well done in. We were also a lot wiser about the dangers of wandering about the hills without being properly equipped. We had been lucky. If the weather had turned nasty, as it can do, very suddenly, we would have been in real trouble.

I phoned Tim and let him know that we were on our way back and would be about a quarter of an hour late. We met the others at the Farmhouse and after we'd had a cup of tea and told them about our climb to Loch Coire, we settled down to hear what they had to say.

Tim's report was short and to the point. He had finished his valuation and would work out the final figures back in his office in Gloucester. He would then have to talk with the relevant District Valuers and reach an agreed total for probate. That, together with the figures for Locklate and for the other stocks and shares and the property, would form the basis upon which tax would be paid.

Tim was taking advice from David, who was better informed as to local values, for the figures on the Fannich land. They were going to talk to an associate of David's about the values that could be put on the sporting possibilities. These were an unknown area since they had been so neglected and would need money spending on them to make them any sort of asset. With the tax, being at forty percent on virtually all the agreed values, it was important to agree a figure as low as possible.

David's main report was a much more involved. His brief had been to assess if the Fannich Estate could be made to pay as an agricultural enterprise. His report as to the present state of affairs was not very encouraging.

The standard of management had been so poor as to be virtually non-existent. Cedric Swan, or more probably Marion, had been very poor stewards.

The land, the fences, the buildings, the machinery and the stock itself were all in a poor state. David thought that the real troubles were ignorance and a lack of spending. That didn't surprise me. Money had very obviously been spent on non-productive things like motor cars but there had been virtually no spending at the productive end. Once again, I heard the mantra that 'It costs just as much to feed a poor animal as it does a good one.'

One case in point was that, due to bad management some of the land reclaimed at great expense in years gone by, was reverting to gorse and bracken. Rushes were growing in some of the lower land because the drains had been allowed to fall into disrepair. Those crops that were harvested were deteriorating because the buildings were not maintained. His list of defects was not encouraging.

I asked, "So what's your verdict David, get rid of it?"

He pulled the lobe of his ear. "I wouldn't go so far as to say that."

He paused for so long that I thought he had finished but I let him have time to think.

"Fannich's a bonny place.... a handy size.... a wonderful location, it'd be a pity to see it go."

"So what do you suggest?"

He looked up and smiled, "Whatever I say, it's going to cost you a fair bit to pull it round and it'll take time. I think first you've got to decide if that's what you want?"

"David, let me be the judge of that. Things worth doing are seldom easy and usually not cheap. What I need from you is a plan to make the place profitable and an idea of how much it will cost."

He was cautious, "I'll need more time to come up with a firm plan as such. I'll need to talk to people, do my sums and get it all written down properly but it's my opinion that the place can be made to pay, and pay well."

I was a bit disappointed by his reply. I had expected him to come up with something of an instant answer. Thinking about it he was almost certainly right to be reluctant.

"Have you no thoughts that you can tell us about now?"

He looked at Tim Turner who nodded very slightly.

"Tim and I have been talking about this and we think the first thing is to get the legal structure right first."

I was puzzled at that. "I'm sorry, I don't follow!"

"I know you didn't ask me to take your other interests into account but I.... we...., Tim and I, think that you might do best to consider Fannich and Locklate all as one business."

"Why?"

"Well, Tim says that Locklate really is in profit." He looked uncomfortable. "The suggestion is that it only looks as if it's not making a profit because the books don't reflect the real state of the place."

I understood his difficulty. "Look, David, I know the mice have been at the accounts and Tim and certainly George Pearson think that it is all right but I don't see how it ties in with Locklate."

Tim had a go. "Look at it this way, Locklate has a good Manager, George, and we think that if the accounts were run properly it would be showing a decent margin. Okay, it could be better if more money was spent there as well, but it's sound."

"Fannich has the potential but hasn't had a decent Manager."

"If we ran the two as one company the profit from Locklate could be used to improve Fannich, cut the need for new capital and be tax efficient as well."

I started to get the idea. It appealed to me. It was along the lines I had thought of but much bolder. I turned to Anna. "What do you think; could we do something like that?"

"I don't see why not, I'll check of course.... but why stop there?"

"Please explain!"

"What about the property holdings? If they were treated in the same way would that not make the whole thing more sensible?"

We talked round it for a bit and then decided to call it a day. We would all do further homework and then have another meeting, perhaps in London. Tim would go back to his office and finalise his figures for the Valuer, David would write a proper report and a costed plan. Anna would try and sort out the property end and I would decide the overall plan of campaign. We didn't consider the hotel idea at this stage. We had enough to think about to be going on with.

Tim and David went back to the hotel at Arisaig to continue their deliberations and Anna and I decided to linger for a bit and perhaps see them in the dining room later but not to wait for us.

We drove the short distance up to Fannich House and spent a while wandering through the rooms. If the truth be known, I was thinking if it would be a waste to turn the place into a hotel or if it would be better to renovate the place and live in it.

It was the same old question, loneliness or solitude? On my own, loneliness. With someone to share it, solitude perhaps - but the happy solitude I had spent my time looking for.

Standing in the sitting room, looking out over that view across the loch to the hills we had climbed that afternoon, I came very close to asking her if she would consider sharing my solitude. I think she felt it too. It was almost as if I were back on that slab of rock at the top of the gully. Frightened of going back and still more frightened of going on.

I put my arm around her shoulder. We stood like that for several moments; me back to that old state of not having the determination to go on and Anna not wanting to prompt me too hard. She seemed to sense the difficulty I was in and put me out of my misery.

"Come on, we can't stand here all evening. Is there anything to drink in this place?"

I found the bottle of whisky I had bought and a couple of dusty glasses.

We drank a toast to Fannich and its future.

# CHAPTER 29

It was quite late when we got back to Arisaig. Helen March said that the other two had eaten and were talking business upstairs but the two of us were still quite all right for dinner if we didn't take too long getting ready.

I can't remember what we ate that evening but I do know that we talked long after everyone else had given up and gone to bed.

Helen left us with a pot of coffee and a drinks tray. I tried to persuade Anna to stay for another couple of days and go south with me in the car but she insisted, in the most charming way, that I wasn't her only client and that she'd meetings arranged for the rest of the week. She did agree, however, that we should meet for dinner as soon as I got back to London.

Eventually, we called it a day and I saw her to her door. She kissed me on the mouth lightly and I returned her kiss with less restraint. After a few moments, she pulled away and said. "Robin, this will never do, my kissing my clients - you could have me struck off you know." Again, that deep-seated, throaty chuckle.

"What would Commander Black think?"

I replied, "Bugger Tommy!" and kissed her again.

When she disentangled herself she said, "Language, naughty. Even if you haven't, I've got packing to do. God bless" and was gone.

***

We were all in high spirits the next morning when we sat down for an early breakfast. I think we had achieved a lot and we'd somehow become something of a team. I noticed that everyone was talking about 'we' would do this or 'our' best plan. From the business point of view it had worked, from my personal point of view I had seen the opportunity that could be there if only I had the sense to make it work.

When they drove off from the Hotel, I stood waving at the back of the car and I knew I had missed my moment. I determined not to let it pass again.

I drove back to Fannich in a reflective mood, thinking about the possibility of turning Fannich House into a hotel. I had arranged to meet Helen and Peter March at the house at three o'clock when they had finished the lunchtime rush. Funnily enough, neither of them had ever been to Fannich although they lived quite close. The road to Fannich was, of course, a dead end when you got to the top of the Glen and few people went up there out of curiosity.

As I pulled into the farmyard I saw Cathy Muir's van parked by the old stables. She was just finishing putting the finishing touches to the new door, on what had been the old tack room.

Mock-seriously she asked, "What have you done with that David Dicks then Mr Forest?"

"I've sent him home to Inverness - to get him away from being tempted by you!"

She laughed, "That'll be the day, a great big laddie like him. He's the one doing the tempting." She went on, "I could'na get away frae him yesterday, in my way all mornin' he was."

I let it go at that. There was no arguing with this one.

"Cathy, can you spare an hour? I'd like you to come up to the big house with me."

She assumed her most coquettish look, "Why, Mr Forest, is it you I'll be having trouble with now?"

"Be serious for once Cathy, I want to ask your advice."

"If you're paying, I'm yer gel."

We got into my car and started up the lane.

I asked her why she had joined her father in the building line. She told me that there wasn't a lot of choice if you wanted to stay on the west coast.

"I never fancied being a hairdresser or a waitress and I turned down the chance at ballet - I'm too small you ken. Besides which, I like building. You can see what you've done at the end of the day."

I decided that her jocular style was, in reality, just a defence against her improbable height and build.

"Did you do any training?"

"Och! Didn't I spend three years at college. I'm not just a pretty face yer know."

I declined to comment that pretty wasn't the adjective I would have used, arresting, attractive, yes. Pretty was just the wrong word.

We pulled up outside the big house.

I asked the question. "If I wanted to turn this place into a hotel it would need more rooms. If it were your decision, how would you go about it?"

She looked at me and twisted her mouth into a grimace. "Are you serious?"

"Perfectly."

She got out of the car and walked across the front of the building. She then walked down the west side towards the Loch. I let her wander, hands deep in the pockets of her jeans, shoulders hunched. After several minutes she turned and walked back to where I stood.

"What you need is an architect. I'm just a builder."

"I know I'd need a qualified architect but I wanted to hear what you thought."

She kicked at a stone in the drive. "There's a hotel neat Loch Milfort, same sort of house as this. They've built an extension, about ten extra bedrooms on the side of the house."

"What's it like?"

"It's good. They didn't make the mistake of trying to make it match the house. It's sort of Scandinavian; a two-storied chalet building but in local stone. I like it.... very much."

"Do you know who the architect was?"

"I can't remember his name but he was from Oban. I can find out though."

"I'd be glad if you could, now.... the big question. If I decided to build something like that would you're firm be big enough to take it on?"

She looked at me seriously. "No, not as a whole job but then I wouldn't go about it like that anyhow."

"How do you mean?"

"I'd subcontract most of it - cheaper that way - no one firm round here would be big enough to do it all anyhow so that would be the way to go about it."

I told her that I wasn't making any promises but that if I did decide to go ahead she would get the chance to tender for the project if she wanted. Somehow I had the thought that she would do it well. Behind the 'I'm one of the lads' facade, there was a rocky determination which I thought I could trust.

"One thing though.... not a word to anyone.... otherwise the deal's off. Okay?"

She promised. On her Girl Guides honour!

I was about to take her back to the farm when she said, "Oh, by the way, there's a mystery about your house there."

I enquired, "How so?"

"I had a good look at that antiquated heating system of yours and I can't make it out.... some of the pipes don't go where they should."

I asked her to explain.

"Well, the flow and return pipes for the sitting room go out through the cellar wall and come up at the end of the room."

"So what's wrong with that?"

She said it was difficult to explain but if I had five minutes she could show me.

We went down into the cellar.

The big old boiler was in the middle of the south wall and pipes ran off in several different directions to feed the water to different parts of the house. The ones that Cathy said fed the sitting room went through the end wall.

"Don't you see, this cellar is a bit bigger than the hall upstairs so you would think the pipes would go up to the rooms above not through the wall sideways."

It still wasn't much clearer to me.

"So what does that mean?"

"Either that the man who put this in was an idiot or there's another cellar the other side of this wall."

A vision of the one at Locklate loomed.

"How do we find out?"

"Well, for a start we could look to see if there's another entrance to it - perhaps a trap door in a floor somewhere or we take up some floorboards to have a look."

A quick look round in the sitting room didn't reveal anything and I didn't think this was the time to start ripping the place apart.

"Well if we do decide to convert the place then we will have to do something about it but I'll leave it for now - thanks for spotting it."

I drove her back to the farm and she shot off in her van followed by her usual cloud of dust. I wondered what she did with the time she saved driving like that?"

I gave her time to get clear and was then back up to Fannich House like a rat down a drain. It took me over two hours to find the entrance to that second cellar. It didn't occur to me at first but because the site sloped down to the Loch, the ground floor at the back of the house, which faced the Loch, was about six or seven feet higher off the ground than it was at the front. Since you went up four steps to the front door, or best part of three feet, it meant that the floor of the sitting room, at its furthest end was about eight or nine feet from the ground. Simple.Therefore, the entrance to any space under it could well be outside.

The only place I could find was a sort of coal shed which may have been the fuel store for an old kitchen range at one time. It was built under a small balcony which jutted out from the French windows.

It was, like so many other places at Fannich, stuffed with rubbish. Old deck chairs, or at least the woodworm-eaten frames (the canvas seats had long since gone), a croquet set also with woodworm, a tennis net which fell apart at a touch and a fair collection of other useless junk. All this under a blanket of filthy dust and grime.

One thing was certain. No one had moved this lot in a fair number of years. By the time *I* had moved it all I was black from head to toe!

The small door I found was only about five feet tall and very solid. It was also locked. No key on the bunch I had came close to fitting the lock. I sat for a bit and pondered.

I went to the car and got a torch and the only leaver I could find, a heavy screwdriver. This I bent in my attempt to force the door. I couldn't find any other suitable leaver in the house so I was obliged to go back to the farm to search through the sheds there. I found a heavy pinch bar which had one end shaped like a giant chisel. It couldn't have been bettered. I fairly raced back to the house and the little door.

I had imagined that all was solved but that door was made of stern stuff. I think I must have spent about twenty minutes before it gave way to my attack. When I did get in and looked at the back of the now ruined door, the reason was plain. Not only had it been locked but there were obviously modern bolts fitted both top and bottom.

If I had been expecting another wine store like the one at Locklate, I was disappointed.

This place was just filled with what at first sight looked like the accumulated junk of years. Shining my torch around, I saw that there were light fittings hanging from the ceiling and a further search revealed a switch. I tried it and somewhat to my surprise it worked.

Most of the space was taken up with those old-fashioned plywood tea chests, stacked in places three or four high. They all seemed, from their weight, to be full. The first one I tackled had part of a dinner service packed in it. The individual pieces wrapped in newspaper. Spreading some of the sheets out they were all about twenty years old and of similar dates. It seemed obvious that here were the small contents of the house which must have been packed up before the place had been let.

I stood in that cellar and was, on the one hand, glad that I had made the discovery and, on the other, dismayed by the immensity of the task that was going to face us in sorting it all out.

Not the least was the dilemma of saying nothing to anyone and thus cheating the tax man or, more honestly, getting Tim Turner back to go through it all and adding it to the valuation. The same dilemma was posed by the wine at Locklate and I had a shrewd idea that represented a larger sum of money than this long forgotten bric-a-brac.

Another thought crept into my mind as I surveyed those boxes and trunks. There had got to be another way into this place. The door had been bolted from the inside. I took a very careful look round, searching the walls and the ceiling foot by foot. Nothing.

Perhaps I was not thinking straight but eventually, it was Cathy's heating pipes that gave me the clue. There were various pipes running round the walls and branches going off at intervals up through the ceiling. I supposed to feed the radiators. Tracing the main pipes back I should find where they came through the wall from the boiler but they just vanished behind a pile of boxes and I couldn't see where they went.

I started moving those wretched crates and found that they were stacked in such a way that there was a space about five feet wide behind them. In that space was a desk and a chair. On the desk was a very serious looking computer and several boxes of computer discs.

In one corner was a step ladder which was under what was obviously a trap door to the room upstairs. I tried to lift it but either it was stuck or something very heavy was on top of it.

I retraced my way back into the main part of the cellar, out through the door I had forced and back into the house. Once you knew what you were looking for it was easy. A massive sofa stood where I reckoned that trap door must be. I pushed it out into the room and pulled back the carpet and there it was. A catch held it shut and when I pulled it I was surprised that the thing fell downwards. For some reason, I had thought that a trapdoor would pull up but this one worked the opposite way.

I still didn't understand what it all meant. Why would anyone go to all these lengths to conceal a computer? If it belonged to the Swans, and I couldn't see who else's it could be, why hadn't they taken it with them?

The memory of me awakening, on this very settee, with Marion Swan shouting at me flooded back. It seemed very likely that it was just that computer that they had tried to collect when they found me sleeping on top of the blasted thing. Slowly the light began to dawn.

I sat on that settee for some time whilst I tried to sort out what I should do.

I went back down through that trap door, and closed the door I had forced as best I could. I managed to get one of the bolts to slide home and put a couple of crates in front of it for good measure. I replaced the boxes that I had shifted so that it looked much as it had done before. I then went back up to the sitting room, closed the trap door, replaced the carpet and slid the settee back to its original position.

I had brought up with me about ten of the computer discs, taken at random from the boxes on the desk. I locked the house and went round to the storeroom where I had found the little door and replaced all the junk I had taken out, so that the door was again completely hidden.

I got into my car and drove back to the farmhouse. I remembered to replace the crowbar where I had found it, in the tractor shed. I spent the next half an hour trying to clean myself up but I would have to go back to Arisaig for a change of clothes before I would look anything like decent.

\*\*\*

I used the phone in the farmhouse to ring Anna. She had no hesitation in telling me that the time had come to involve the Police. She also told me in no uncertain terms that I would have to tell Tim about what I had found in the cellar.

"You've no alternative Robin, if you don't you're breaking the law and now you've told me I couldn't and wouldn't go along with it!" She really was quite severe.

I agreed to do what she suggested.

She went on, "I'll phone the Police in Mallaig but I expect they'll tell me to talk to Fort William and explain the situation to them. I'll give them your number and I'll ask them to call you direct.... you'll have to take it from there."

I agreed to wait until I'd heard from someone.

I think I must have dozed off for a bit because I was startled by the telephone and looking at my watch it seemed that twenty minutes had passed in a flash. It was Anna again, saying that I could expect a call from a Detective Sergeant Dunbar from Fort William as soon as she had rung off.

Her prediction was right. Only a few seconds later the phone rang again and it was the good Mr Dunbar.

He ascertained that he was speaking to, "Mr Forest.... Mr Robin Forest.... of Fannich?"

I agreed that I was he.

"I've had a Mrs Hudson on the telephone, from London. She told me that you had found several things at Fannich House that you would like us to look at."

I agreed to that as well.

"She tells me that you've found a computer concealed in a cellar under the house."

"That is true."

"And what makes you think that you should report it to us, Sir?"

I explained that, in the first instant, why should anyone hide such a commonplace item and, in the second, that the man, who probably owned it, was a convicted criminal.

"And what was he convicted of do you know Sir?"

I replied, "Yes, Sergeant, computer fraud."

"And his name?"

I told him most of what I knew about Cedric Swan's previous crime.

He thought for a bit and then said, "I think that the best thing is if we could meet you at Fannich House and look at all this. I don't think that we can do anything today.... could you meet us there tomorrow at say .... would ten o'clock be all right?"

I agreed to ten o'clock.

My next surprise was the arrival of Peter and Helen March. I had completely forgotten that I had arranged to meet them.

I got into their car and we went to look at what they thought of the possibilities of turning the place into a hotel. We spent about two hours going all over the place and in the end, they gave me their opinion.

They thought that the situation was the one huge plus. The house itself was small for a hotel and they thought that it would need at least another fifteen rooms to make it a viable proposition. I had thought more than that.

The kitchens were hopeless and would need a complete makeover. The same went for the heating and hot water system, the electrics, the sewerage system, the arrangements for car parking - in short, there wasn't much, apart from the remainder of the Estate, that made them think that the place was at all suitable.

It was a douche of very icy water but I think that's what I'd expected.

They drove me back to the farmhouse so that I could collect my car and I said that I would see them back at Arisaig. I hung about for a bit, checking that all was locked up and then set off after them.

# CHAPTER 30

It was a very silly sheep that saved my life.

I was driving along the stretch of main road, just where it goes under the old railway, when the animal jumped off the bank at the roadside. I suppose my mind was elsewhere and I was slow to react. The front of the car caught it as it made a panic dash across the road.

I braked of course but it was miles too late. In the mirror, I could see it lying in the road. Quickly, I got out of the car to see how badly it was hurt. I was sure it was dead but I couldn't leave it where it was so I dragged it to the downhill side of the road and just down the bank.

I can remember a terrific bang and a vast ball of flame. After that nothing.

Nothing, that is, until I came to. Lying on the ground below the road, with a very concerned young man who was asking me if I was all right.

I confessed that I wasn't.

My next recollection was of being lifted, on a stretcher, into an ambulance and later being prodded and poked by a young doctor and a nurse who, for some strange reason, reminded me of Matron at school.

Perhaps it was the smell of antiseptic or the bright light shining down on me. I don't really remember.

I do remember coming round again and having some bandages taken off and replaced. That hurt and I think I tried to tell them to leave me alone but for some reason, I couldn't make them understand. There was a maze of tubes and bottles and, as far as I could tell, I had no pyjamas on. That worried me quite a lot.

There was certainly Helen March with flowers and later I thought Anna came but that was impossible. She had phoned me from London and there was no way she could have come in so short a time.

I drifted in and out of consciousness, but gradually I became aware of longer periods, when I seemed to be tied to a bed with my left arm stretched out to the side. Eventually, a nurse asked me if I was awake and I managed to tell her that I wanted to get up.

A doctor came and told me I had been in an accident and that I was in a Hospital in Fort William. Then Anna - kissing my forehead and telling me that it was all going to be fine if I tried to sleep. They told me later that I had been in hospital, in the intensive care unit, for three days before I was anything like sensible. Even then, I was still far from fully aware of what was going on.

I eventually got most of the story from Anna.

My car had exploded for some reason and a man, who came along about five minutes later, had found me down the bank, burnt and with injuries to my head and to my arm.

I remembered the sheep and the ball of flame.

I think it was the fifth day when Detective Sergeant Dunbar came. He asked about the computer at Fannich House and the journey in the car. I told him about the trap door and the sheep and the flames and he went away again.

I told Anna about the computer discs in my coat pocket and she went off to find the clothes which they had cut off me. She also told me that the Police had arrested Cedric and had charged him with the attempted murder....of me. Surely impossible; Cedric was supposed to be in Montrose, in Union Place. Gradually the marbles began to fall back into their proper places and I began to grasp the story.

Dunbar came again, this time with a Detective Inspector Fraser. They told me that someone, they suspected that it was Cedric Swan, had put a bomb of some sort in the boot of my car. It had probably been attached to a mobile telephone and fired by ringing the phone. I had been extremely lucky with the sheep in that had I been in the car when the bomb went off, I would certainly have been killed. They also said that the bomb had been put next to the petrol tank and it was that that had caused the huge ball of fire.

I couldn't understand about setting off a bomb with a mobile phone but Fraser told me that anyone with expert knowledge of electronics could rig a phone to detonate such a device. The advantage was that you could set it off from virtually anywhere at any time and it would be very difficult to trace who had done it.

I asked about Swan.

It was coincidence that Sergeant Dunbar had heard about the accident over the police radio net. At first, he didn't connect it with me but when he heard my name as the only person injured, he had put two and two together and arranged for a police guard, from Mallaig, to be put on the house.

They had caught Swan actually in the house when they arrived, just an hour after the bomb should have blown me to bits. He was in the process of carrying the computer out at the time. He had some problem in explaining what he was up to and how he had known where it was hidden. The discs I had taken contained thousands of credit card numbers which they thought Swan had got by hacking into mail order firms records. As yet, they hadn't been able to unravel it all but it looked like a computer scam on a very large scale.

Inspector Fraser said, "He probably went to the house and saw your car outside, maybe he even heard you down in the cellar. It's possible that he decided to put the device in the boot of your car on the spur of the moment and then waited for you to leave, gave you time to get about halfway back to Araisaig, then set it off. Perhaps he thought he would get his computer out before anyone checked the house."

I wasn't thinking too well but one question stood out.

"Surely he wouldn't go about with a bomb just on the off-chance?"

Fraser smiled. "We thought about that as well but we think he brought it intending to burn the house down with it. There was a plastic can drum of petrol in the back of his own car which he can't explain."

He went on. "He claims it was in case he ran out of petrol! He would hardly have needed five gallons though."

It was all a bit beyond me at that stage and I was happy to take their word.

"He could have gone back to Montrose and set fire to your house from there. We would have had a hell of a job proving he had anything to do with it if we hadn't caught him trying to take the computer away."

Marion Swan was nowhere to be found. I suggested he looked for her in London. He made a note of that but said that London was a very big place.

Fraser said that he had spoken at length to Mrs Anna Hudson who claimed to be my solicitor and that they had checked with Commander Black of Lewis, Lewis, Lewis & Farr, who confirmed that she was acting as such. She had told them a great deal of the background, about Harper and his connections with the Swans.

After they had gone, Anna came and brought me fruit and flowers and the newspapers which had several pictures of my car. Hardly recognisable as anything other than a heap of blackened scrap metal. There was no mention of the Swans, only that it was thought that the petrol tank had exploded.

I was three weeks in that hospital and even though the nurses and the doctors, had been kindness itself, I was glad to leave its doors.

I just about made it, with a deal of support, to the Range Rover which Anna was driving. We had quite a problem getting me in with my arm in plaster and held out sideways on a frame. I think it was the first time I had laughed in three weeks.

We drove slowly back to the hotel at Arisaig where Anna had arranged that we would stay for a week or so, until I was a bit better mended. She had the room next door!

We took it all very gently for that week. Anna blocked any attempts I made to take an interest in the goings on of either Fannich or Locklate and she wouldn't even talk about the hundreds of other questions I wanted answers to.

They fed me and watered me till I felt like a turkey being got ready for Christmas. The one concession was that the doctors had said that the odd glass of Champagne wouldn't actually harm me. I thought it the best medicine I could get!

The only exceptions to the 'rest' regime were two visits from Dunbar and Fraser who went over virtually every event since I had first come to Britain from France. I got something of a ticking off about the attempted stabbing in London, which I hadn't reported to the police down there.

I didn't say anything about the incidents in France.

I remembered the knife which I had last seen in Tommy Black's flat and they arranged to have it collected and sent up in case it could be traced. I was very glad when Anna insisted that they went away.

Seven days later I went back to Fort William for an appointment with the surgeon who had seen to my head and arm and I managed to persuade him to put a smaller plaster on the arm. At least I could now get in the car without too much trouble. He said I was to come back again in another fortnight's time.

***

This time, Anna drove me back to Fannich. We passed the place where I had nearly been blown up, all there was to see was a new section of tarmac on the road. The fire had been so fierce that it had made the tar on the road burn. It was a sobering thought as to what would have happened if that sheep hadn't run across just when it did!

We were greeted at the Farm House by Cathy who, with her people, had just about finished redecorating most of the rooms there.

"Ach! there you are - poor wee man, you don't look too good do yer?

I did na come to see yer in that hospital.... they thought the sight o' me might cause yer to have a relapse - or the thought of my bill."

She waved at the room, "There ye're then, you'll be right comfortable now."

And as a wicked afterthought, "A right little love nest."

That earned her a rebuke from Anna, who had the decency to blush as Cathy went.

It seemed that Anna had decided that we could stay there, certainly until I was signed off by the Doctors. I queried the use of the word 'we'?

She took my hand and said, "Look, Robin, I've arranged with Tommy Black that I can take two months holiday. After that, we will see where we have got to."

A bit startled I asked, "Will it be all right.... you and I.... here alone? What....."

She interrupted, "If you're about to say, 'What will the neighbours think', firstly, we haven't got any - not close ones anyhow and secondly, to quote you, 'Bugger the neighbours'.

I reminded her about her language and we both had a fit of the giggles. Both in hospital, and in the last week, I had thought about Anna and I a great deal and I had steeled myself to take my chance when it came and now seemed as good a time as I was likely to get.

"Anna, I know that this may sound like a bit of a spring and autumn proposal but would it preserve your reputation if I asked you to marry me?"

She smiled and then to my horror said, "I certainly won't marry you just to keep my reputation intact.

If, however, you're asking if I'll marry you because you love me then that's a different matter."

I started again. "Anna, I do love you - very much. Will you marry me?"

She kissed me very gently and said, "Of course I will Robin. I was beginning to think I'd have to ask you!"

After that things got a bit confused. It's not easy embracing someone, even someone who has just agreed

393

to marry you, with one arm in plaster and with surgical dressings on your face.

Despite the drawbacks, I think the next week was the happiest I have ever known. We walked and talked. We lazed and read. Listened to music. Ate and drank. Slept and made love.

We took delivery of the little motor boat I had ordered from Mallaig. In it, we took picnics and explored the furthest and the most secret places on the Loch and along the little river. We even tried fishing with rods that we found in the big house and new lines and flies from Mallaig.

We tried to shut out the world of greed and violence, if only until the mental and physical scars had healed a bit. We tried to forget the wickedness which had so nearly denied us this happiness. We tried but we were not entirely successful. Another long session with Inspector Fraser and Sergeant Dunbar brought it all flooding back in its awful reality.

Cedric Swan had been remanded in custody. Marion was still missing but there was a warrant out for her arrest. Harper had been interviewed several times by the City Police in London and was denying everything but his other activities with his other clients' accounts were under close scrutiny and were proving to be of great interest to the Fraud Squad and The Financial Regulator.

I signed statements and gave instructions for documents to be made available from both Nick Conway and from Tommy's office.

They told me that I would have to give evidence at a trial sometime in the future and that I was to let them know if I intended going away anywhere. It was all a vivid reminder that there was a real and sometimes very nasty world outside the safe confines of Fannich.

Gradually things got back to normal. Whatever normal is.

My arm mended slowly, as is to be expected in a man of my age, and the burns healed. The doctors wanted me to have plastic surgery to get rid of the scars on my face at least but we decided against it. Anna said that she had become rather attached to my somewhat battered appearance and, if she didn't mind, then I certainly didn't. The very thought of going back to hospital had no attraction for me.

We got over the problem of Anna's work in London by installing a proper office for her in the farmhouse, equipped with the latest thing in computers and fax machines but she still had to dash south from time to time.

I found those periods painful. That dreadful loneliness flooded back as soon as she had gone.

# CHAPTER 31

It was during one of her trips south that I started on sorting out the mass of stuff in the second cellar. I borrowed a couple of chaps from Cathy for a few days and they manhandled all the boxes and chests up into the sitting room at Fannich House and I went through their contents ready for another visit from Tim Turner who was going to value it all.

Most of it was interesting but quite what we had expected to find. The smaller trappings of a well equipped, upper-middle-class household of its period; although there were some surprises. As we went through it all it became evident that a good percentage must have been in the house when Grandfather bought it.

There were eight good oil paintings by people like Sidney Percy and Adam Barland, all of which I liked. There were a bigger number of others which, although probably valuable, I didn't. There was fine china mixed with chamber pots and ornate silver alongside cooking pots. Oil lamps and stone hot water bottles, riding boots and skates - the toys of the rich alongside the tools of the less so.

Two of the surprises raised further problems.

The first was a heavy crate which contained two pairs of fine shotguns in their cases. Two rifles, presumably for stalking and a wonderful mahogany box which held a matched pair of Georgian duelling pistols by Mortimer of London, with all the cleaning tools and the moulds for making the balls. There was also a Webley revolver, with a box of ammunition. I thought, perhaps, that it had been my Father's, left over from the Great War.

I was certainly going to have to see the Police about those.

The second surprise was a leather case which held a great mass of what I supposed had been some of my grandmother's costume jewellery. Strings of beads in amber, jet and ivory. Several bracelets and pairs of earrings. All very much of the style of the early part of the century.

There was one ring. It had a large blue stone which at first sight, mainly because of its size, I thought was probably blue spinal or possibly a dark aquamarine, it was hard to tell in the poor light. I took it to the window and had a better look.

My first impression had been wrong. I knew a thing or two about such stones and I was quite sure that this was a Burmese sapphire and a good one. Also, I had a very strong feeling that I had seen that ring before. It took me some time to work it out but eventually, it came to me. It was my mother's engagement ring, I was sure of it. One of the few photographs I had of her was a studio portrait she had done in England to send to my

Father. It had never been sent but it showed the ring, together with her wedding ring on her hand, raised under her neck.

I had never thought of what had become of my mother's things when she was killed and I couldn't understand why her engagement ring might have found its way back to my paternal grandparents. By rights, I would have thought that it should have gone to her parents, that would have been logical. Could it be that they couldn't bear to have it and they had sent it on to my Father's people?

I had no compunction in tucking it into my pocket. I was keeping that one to myself.

*** 

We had everything ready for Turner when he arrived.

The total figure he arrived at was a sum far in excess of anything I had imagined. From the values he assigned to some of the things, I was glad I had kept the ring out of it! The negotiations with the District Valuers were nearing completion and he thought that he and Nick Conway would soon be in a position to get an agreement.

They were still sorting out, with Anna and a very reluctant Harper, the investments but it looked as if the final figures would be much as we had predicted. There would be enough in the pot, even after the Inland Revenue had had their cut, for the plans I had in mind.

I made a quick trip to Edinburgh on the pretext of buying some new clothes and a new motor car to replace my little sports car. While I was there, I got a jeweller to confirm my opinion that the ring I had saved was indeed a sapphire. He agreed that it was and asked me if I was thinking of selling it. I declined his very fair offer but got him to clean it properly and to provide a suitable case for it.

I met Anna that evening at the airport and later, over dinner, gave her the ring. I confessed its origins but not how I had found it.

***

The next few months were hectic.

We had a meeting in London, which Tommy chaired and we thrashed out all the details of the Estate. Some of the land in the Midlands would be sold to pay the tax liability. We were lucky there since the Government had come up with a new catchphrase, 'Brown Field Development'. A lot of what we owned certainly came well into that category.

One site, that had lain unused and certainly unloved since the sixties, was sold to a Swedish company, for a giant warehouse. A forties built shadow factory, now nearly falling down, which had been used variously as a car plant and later as a storage depot, was sold to a Japanese electronics company who were going to build a new 'facility', whatever that might mean.

I was able to repay one debt that had been troubling me for a long time.

My old friend Tony Miller, now approaching double figures in wives, was still working as hard as usual. His ever-growing company needed a site near Manchester and we were able to provide just what they were looking for. We sold it to him for, what even he thought to be, a very reasonable sum.

We made a start with the agricultural improvements at both Locklate and Fannich and the results have been solid. We got planning permission for the conversion and extension of Locklate House into a hotel and to build a golf course on the parkland. We have had long sessions with Frank Sibley, the architect that Cathy had suggested, about an annex for Fannich House and he is putting the whole scheme up for permission to go ahead. Some of the cost, he thought, would attract a government grant. Rather like robbing Peter to pay Paul, I thought.

David Dicks, a frequent visitor recently, has found a young New Zealander to take on the post as Estate Manager at Fannich. He and his girlfriend Zoe are going to 'camp out' in the main house until Anna and I can make other arrangements for a place of our own.

The blot on the horizon is Cedric Swan. His trial for attempted murder is set for next month and I don't think that any of us are looking forward to it.

The question of the credit card fraud has somehow been swept under the carpet as far as I can see. We had another visit from Inspector Fraser. He brought with him a computer wizard who tried to explain it to us. He was one of those experts who can't understand why everyone else fails to grasp what, to him, is a simple matter. He talked in that excited way often adopted by the dedicatedly dotty. We understood about a tenth of what he told us.

Swan had managed to infiltrate the computer systems of several companies who took payments by credit cards over the Internet. By using a system, related to the one he had devised, when he worked his previous fraud on the money brokers Kutners, he had managed to alter the sums involved by a very small percentage. Sums so small that virtually no one ever queried the final bill. This tiny fraction he siphoned off into various sub-accounts and then via so-called 'offshore' accounts back to himself.

Apparently, the total amounts were quite large but it represented hundreds of thousands of transactions and it would be impossible to work it all out as to who had lost what. Add to that fact that the internet industry doesn't need a scandal and you get the picture.

Fraser's 'expert' tried to impress on us all that, 'Measures were being devised to make certain that it could never happen again.' The thought crossed my mind that if you have one lot of brains working out how to stop it, you are bound to have another set of less moral brains working out how it can still go on.

Fraser also suggested that the easiest option was to see that Cedric was put away so comprehensively that he wouldn't trouble the computer industry for long enough for his skills to be well out of date by the time he did get out.

He also handed me a shotgun and a firearms certificate for the weapons I had found. The revolver had been destroyed and the duelling pistols were considered to be antiques so didn't need a certificate. I had a sneaking suspicion that they would kill someone just as effectively as any modern weapon. Add to that the fact that, if you used a charge of small shot, as opposed to a ball, it would be virtually untraceable. The Law can be unfathomable at times!

***

Anna and I decided to get married in London.

Locklate and Fannich would have been wonderful venues but neither was very convenient for guests and both were in the process of being pulled apart, before they could be put to their new uses.

It wedding itself was a small affair, I had no relatives at all and Anna, only a couple of aged Aunts. Tommy Black gave her away and Tony Miller stood as my best man. Let's face it; he had been married so often that he knew all the ropes.

Nick Conway came with his wife Miriam, Tim and his wife. The Pearsons from Locklate, Peter and Helen March. I don't think anyone was surprised when David Dicks turned up with Cathy Muir. She looked, I think the word is, majestic. We had asked Mrs Rothney but she said that she thought it was, "Rather too far for her." She did, however, arrange a party at Fannich for when we came back from our honeymoon.

We went to Venice for a few days. It was out of the season but that's why we went. We had time and space to wander and to look without that tide of humanity which, whilst supporting such places, spoils them as well. The early morning mists and the evening twilight give that wonderful city a charm and a dimension seldom appreciated except by those fortunate enough to live and work there.

We caught the overnight Pullman to Paris and spent another week wandering the Galleries and shops. Anna introduced me to one of her old haunts, a cafe in the Rue Nicotine where the food was of that near-perfect simplicity which has become a lost art in so much of the world.

One of the by-products of that contact was that we met a young man who later became the Chef at Locklate. On that basis, I felt no compunction in charging a modest percentage of our costs to 'business expenses'.

*** 

The next twelve or thirteen months were a roller coaster ride of joyfulness, excitement, some sorrow and two periods of worry and tedious engagement with the courts.

Being married to Anna brought the joyfulness in a way I hadn't any right to have expected at my time of life. We were so happy that I began to be worried by that old fear that it couldn't last. Anna, with her feet planted far more firmly on the ground than mine, tried to shake me out of it but I had been there too often in the past to ignore the feeling.

The excitement, apart from Anna, came mainly in the milestones we achieved with the developments at both Locklate and Fannich. The draft accounts for the first year of Locklate's activities under our new regime, not only gave me a deal of comfort but the evident pleasure it gave George Pearson was a reward in itself and for the huge effort everyone there had made.

The progress we had made at Fannich, where the building of the new wing of bedrooms was well on the way, under the very firm hand of Cathy Muir, gave us great hope for the whole venture.

Some of the sorrow came in the form of losing, firstly, old Angus Farr.

I did try to persuade him to take on looking after the fishing side of things at Fannich but he had more or less taken against the whole project. I suppose he had become too old for new schemes and for some reason, not too difficult to understand, thought our plans would change his world. I worried that his going would make things difficult with the other people in the little village but I needn't have worried.

Led, I think by Mrs Rothney, they all saw the benefits that the developments would bring. In particular, his son Hector was a staunch supporter and the fact that we were gradually finding work for several of the youngsters made things easier. Once the Hotel was up and running it would make a significant difference.

Perhaps the worst loss was that of Peter and Helen March.

I tried hard to get them to stay on and run the hotel when it was finished. They would have done it well, especially without the burden of having to find the capital themselves. I think Helen was in favour but Peter somehow wanted to get back down south and Helen was determined to support him. I saw no reason to undermine that; it would have resulted in a broken marriage I am sure.

We did, however, manage to ease their going by buying their hotel for a price which reflected all the work they had put into it. Anna and I thought that it would make a splendid home for ourselves and thus leave the farmhouse free for its proper role.

Peter and Helen, by a strange quirk of fate, took on the tenancy of a very decent little restaurant in Worcester where they are rapidly building a reputation for excellent food, without having the worry of the very large capital investment needed for a hotel.

# CHAPTER 32

·The two trials came as the downside of the whole affair.

Cedric Swan was tried in Fort William. The chief charge was that of attempting to murder me. Thank God he pleaded guilty. It made the whole business so much less of a worry. Nevertheless, we had to go through the rigmarole of giving evidence and thus re-living the events of the previous year.

I think he was at least a little mad. He certainly made a pathetic sight in the dock and I had the uncomfortable feeling that I was becoming sorry for him. It would have been much nearer justice if his wife and his father-in-law had been there beside him.

Of Marion, there wasn't a trace. Despite the publicity in the press and on television, which led to a number of false sightings, she seemed to have vanished off the face of the earth.

Charles Harper, on the other hand, had problems of his own. There was no hard evidence that he had anything to do with any attempt on my life, either in France, London or the one that nearly succeeded in Scotland. He was determined to let his son-in-law take the rap.

The wretched Cedric got sentenced to life.

The trial explained one thing I had failed to grasp. How had he known that I would be in the car when he exploded the bomb? An expert had given evidence that it was perfectly possible to arrange things so that the telephone call to the mobile phone secreted in the boot of the car made a connection from the car's ignition to the detonator in the bomb. Thus, it could only go off if the ignition was switched on. Thank the Lord I had left the engine running when I went back to see to that sheep.

The fact that I might have been in traffic - say passing a school bus - hadn't seemed to worry him. Placing the bomb next to the petrol tank was to make the bomb as lethal as possible and an attempt to make certain of destroying any evidence that might be gained from the fragments of the bomb itself. A trick learnt from the IRA apparently.

The second trial was in London.

The powers that be had their own questions in plenty to occupy Harper. Everything from defrauding just about everyone from sundry clients to the Inland Revenue to breaking virtually all the currency rules and regulations known to accounting. When he did finish with that basket full, the Law Society was lined up to have a go at him as well. I reckoned he deserved anything that came his way.

His trial was a massively long drawn-out affair, dependant on a paper trail that would keep the lawyers happy and well rewarded for about three months. He pleaded 'Not Guilty', somewhat predictably, and the legal eagles rubbed their hands together at the prospect. I wonder, in my more cynical moments, if there is an unwritten code amongst lawyers that, when they're in trouble with the Law themselves, they plead 'Not Guilty' in order to give their legal pals a fair run at the costs?

I had to give evidence for the best part of a day and I found it not so much trying as distasteful. Why, because of this wretched man, should I bare my financial soul to a collection of lawyers and a voyeuristic world at large?

The only moment I enjoyed was when Harper's Q.C., a young man called Long, asked me why I claimed that I had distrusted his client from the first moment I saw him?

I thought it a silly question so somewhat flippantly and foolishly I replied, "He was wearing a single-breasted suit but no waistcoat."

He was onto it like a flash. "Are you seriously asking the court to believe that was a sufficient reason for you to distrust my client?"

I was in it now and I decided to brazen it out. "In a long life as a trader where the judgement of character is all important. I have found, almost without exception, that it is best not to trust men who wear single-breasted suits without a waistcoat."

All right, I know it was at best pompous and a bit silly but I was getting very annoyed with the wretched man trying to defend the indefensible.

Out of the corner of my eye, I saw Tommy Black put his head in his hands.

I could also see Anna trying not to giggle.

Long said, "I can only suggest that you are being flippant."

Before I could think of anything the Judge, who looked to be the oldest man in the Court by a country mile, said, "Mr Long, it may interest you to know that when I was a young barrister we would have not have dared to appear in court in a single-breasted suit without a waistcoat."

Turning to me he said. "Mr Forest, was that your only reason for mistrusting the defendant?"

I decided the time had come to come clean.

"No, your Honour. It was his whole attitude. I instinctively mistrust people who patronise me, who try to blind me with mumbo-jumbo, people who treat me as a fool before they've had a chance to find out if I'm one or not."

The Judge gave what might just have been a smile and added. "Very wise.... you may continue Mr Long."

Mr Long, however, seemed to have lost the thread and pulling his gown together to hide the absence of a waistcoat said, "I have no further questions."

I didn't bother to stay in the court for the vast majority of the trial. A great deal of it was no concern of mine and I didn't wish to hear of others' misfortune at Harper's hand.

I did turn up for the end however and I was sorry when he only got ten years. He deserved a great deal longer than that. I counted myself lucky that we had come out of it as well as we had. If it hadn't been for the deal we did with him, and thus the speed with which we had got the majority out of his hands before the whole thing collapsed, it could have been a sight worse.

As it was, Anna's estimate as to what he had cost us was, in the end, on the conservative side. Never mind, I had a great deal more than I had ever imagined or deserved. The sensible thing was to put it to good use.

Anna and I made our London base in her house in Islington. I had argued against it in that I thought it up to me to provide a home for us but I was put in my place with a lecture on 'modern women'. I gave in with as much grace as I could muster and spent the money I would otherwise have spent on what we now called, rather grandly, Arisaig Sound House.

We try and spend about two weeks every two months or so there and a few days a month in an Estate cottage at Locklate which we kept for ourselves. Anna has had one of the rooms fitted out as a very up to date office and manages to do a lot of her London work from it. I have urged her to give it all up but she is adamant that she wants to do as much as she feels she can without neglecting me. Something I am glad to say she shows no sign of, to date.

I have had another room turned into a comfortable study. On one wall I have hung the picture Tommy gave me. I stuck to our 'agreement' and didn't open the parcel until I had a permanent place for it. It is an exquisite little painting by Herring, of a bull at a gate!

Locklate thrives. The agricultural and the sporting side are well in profit and benefit from the cross-links with Fannich. The Hotel and the golf course have taken buckets full of capital but they are in profit and should start to show good returns as we get the place better known. This winter we are starting on yet a further block of new rooms.

The idea of giving people the option of staying at two hotels under the same management has worked out better than we had dared hope. One specialising in formal game shooting and golf and the other in Scotland, offering salmon fishing, stalking and grouse shooting in their seasons as well as the stunning scenery. It's very popular with the Americans and oddly enough, the Germans. We have an office in Gloucester which Tim Turner oversees part-time and which runs all the property and investment side and that has provided substantial funds to replenish the coffers depleted by our capital spending.

We decided to try and repay some of the debt we owed to so many people by having a party, over a long weekend at Fannich. It also served the purpose of giving the new hotel staff there a dry run to discover any snags before the opening to the general public.

Tommy Black came, of course, complete with fishing tackle, Tim with his wife and children, the Conways, David Dicks and Cathy - we had been to their wedding about two months before!

The Pearsons from Locklate; they came with their daughter Tessa Barker, who runs the stables at Locklate, where guests can either hire a horse or stable their own. She was also taking the opportunity to look into the possibilities of doing the same thing at Fannich. A now white-headed Tony Miller came with wife number six or seven - I forget which and I suspect he had as well! He thought that both our places would be 'just the ticket' to recommend to some of his overseas clients when they came to the UK.

Anna's two Aunts came and seemed to revel in the atmosphere we were trying to create. Something nearer a country house party of fifty years ago rather than a hotel of today but with the advantages that a well run, modern hotel can provide. They regaled us with family stories of their youth. I think I then knew where Anna got her sense of fun from.

On the Saturday evening, before dinner, Anna and I stood on the sitting room balcony, looking out over the loch and the river. I think we were justly proud of what we had created; surrounded by our friends and as happy as two people have any right to be.

By Sunday lunchtime though that old worm of doubt had come back. This golden patch couldn't last. Something was going to go wrong to wreck everything we had created.

Anna, sensing my mood, did her level best to shake me out of it. She didn't succeed. She must have had a word with Tommy because he came and asked if he could have a few moments. I thought I knew what was coming and tried to put him off.

He took me by the elbow and said that he insisted. We walked down the grass slope to the edge of the water.

"Look Robin!" he started. "This doom and gloom business.... you really must shake yourself out of it. There is nothing to worry about."

He paused. "You have got a super wife, you have no money worries, you have made a cracking start to an entirely new venture and you have got as good a bunch of friends as any man could wish for. I can't see what's got you into this state?"

I looked into his face; the face of the man that I had known and trusted for the greater part of my life and I saw real concern.

"If I knew Tommy, I'd tell you, but I don't. It's that horrible feeling that things are too good, something's got to go wrong. It's like Mother, like Helen, like old Angus Findlay; every time it gets too good it crashes. Stupid, I know but I just can't shake it off, sorry!"

Tommy didn't reply for a bit and just gazed out over the loch, without turning to look at me, he went on,

"Robin, what on earth makes you think you are alone in all this?"

He went on. "Take me, if you like; I was twice in the same state. Once in the Navy .... before we got torpedoed. We were all on a high; we thought we had won the battle of the Atlantic when 'bang' we lost almost a whole ship's crew. I was devastated.

Later, when I made it to the top in Farr's, happily married and with a super son, 'bang' again, Lucy gets cancer and dies in three months."

He still didn't turn his head but I saw the moisture in the corner of his eye as he spoke.

"Live for the day, Robin, that's the best you can do, believe you me."

We both stood for a moment or two whilst we each composed our feelings. Tommy patted my shoulder and said, "Come on old chap, the others will think we have deserted them."

On the way back he said, "The only fly in your ointment is that dammed woman Marion Swan; is that what worries you?"

I admitted that she was part of it.

"Well do something about it then, don't just sit here with your mind in neutral, try and find her and see what she's up to."

I protested that the police hadn't been able to find her so why should I be able to.

"They haven't got a real motive to make the effort Robin. They've got Swan for attempting to murder you and they've got Harper for his crimes. I don't suppose they'd have much to charge the wretched woman with, even if they did catch her. Think about it."

After everyone left on the Monday morning and Anna had gone off to Fort William for something or other, I took myself off on a long walk and gave Marion Swan some serious consideration. Where would she hide? Somewhere abroad? Possibly, but that would need an identity and presumably a passport to go with it.

She would hardly travel on her own in case the immigration people were still on the alert. To get one in a different name would either mean a false one, which was only a short-term answer or a replacement birth certificate, in a different name, in order to get a real one and that wasn't that easy these days. Besides which I just couldn't see her skulking about in some corner of France or Spain. It just wasn't her style somehow.

She would have to have money. I'd no doubt that she and Cedric had salted something away somewhere and she must have to be able to get at it.

That thought was no good though. Any cache they might have could just as easily be in Tokyo as Torquay judging by the way Cedric had been shunting his ill-gotten gains about. That had been one of the very reasons the Director of Public Prosecutions hadn't gone down that route. Too difficult for even them - so what chance me?

People seldom cut themselves off from their family though. Could Marion still be in some sort of contact with father Charles? I doubted that she would bother too much about Cedric. He was going to be out of circulation for a long time and anyhow I doubted that there was, any longer, any affection between them. If she did try to keep up any contact it would most likely be with her father. After all, in his case he could well be out of jail in, say, six years or perhaps less if he could pull the ill health dodge!

It was worth considering. How could I go about finding out?

I thought about that for the rest of my walk.

# CHAPTER 33

When I got back I took myself off into my study and did a bit of telephoning. I had first thought of Nick Conway. He certainly had contacts. He had got someone he knew to find out all about Cedric's seedy past when all this first started. The trouble with Nick though was he was still in close contact with Anna and Tommy and I had a feeling that it might just be best in the long run if they were kept out of this for the time being. Then I thought of Tony Miller. Any man who had been mixed up in as many divorces as he'd been would surely know his way round the sort of people I was looking for.

I got his office and having talked my way past a secretary and a personal assistant, I found that he was still in the air on his way back from our weekend.

Would I like his 'special' mobile number? I could probably get him in the aircraft. I could picture him sitting next door to either Nick or worse, Tommy.

I declined and said I would try later.

"I can give you his car 'phone number.... you would certainly get him there?" said the ever helpful P.A. Again, knowing my luck I thought, he would probably offer Tommy a lift. I insisted I would leave it for the moment.

I did get hold of him late in the afternoon.

One of Tony Miller's faults is that he has to know everything. Ask him a straight question such as, 'Can you give me the name of a private detective who is reliable and is prepared to bend the law ever so slightly?' and he has to know why/what for/are you in trouble /what sort of trouble? I have never known anyone for such questions.

So I spun him a yarn about wanting to try to get in contact with someone in prison who I thought might be able to give me some information. Come to think of it, it was hardly a yarn. He promised to phone me back. I suggested that I would phone him back the next day.

Good old Tony was onto it like a flash. "Trying to keep it from Anna are we?"

I mumbled something in reply and he laughed.

"Look Robin, you can't fool me, I've been keeping secrets from wives forever. Okay, give me a ring tomorrow. I'll have something for you by then."

He thanked me for the weekend, asked me to thank Anna and to give her a kiss on his behalf and rang off.

The next day, I returned the call and he had been as good as his word, as always. He gave me a name, which in itself caused me to doubt his choice, Micky Trott. He then gave me a telephone number, a mobile. I asked if he had an address.

He chuckled. "Robin you're still wet behind the ears, people like Trott don't have addresses! And before you ask, they don't have offices either.

"Trott's office is usually in the front seat of a nondescript parked car, he likes to stay mobile, as it were."

Foolishly I asked, "Is he reliable?"

There was a pause. "Robin, old son. In that anyone's reliable, he is. I've used him for years and he's never let me down yet. He'll do what he's asked, charge you a lot for it and then forget it; is that what you need?"

I agreed that was just what I needed.

Tony added, "I'll give him a ring and tell him that I have given you his name, that way he'll talk to you, otherwise he wouldn't. And don't make the mistake of assuming he will work for you.... he'll listen to your problem and then decide for himself."

After the usual pleasantries we rang off, I promised to keep in touch. I put the telephone down, wondering about the exclusive Mr Trott.

At this stage I wasn't certain how I was going to play the whole thing, even assuming I could find out where Marion Swan was hiding out. I needed to make plans. I would leave Trott until I had thought a good deal more.

Three days later, Anna and I went down to London and the house in Islington. She had an accumulation of work at Farr's that needed her attention in person and I had several 'things to do', one of which was to contact the exclusive Mr Trott.

We arranged to meet, not in a car park, as I had expected but at a cafe in the Covent Garden Piazza. I must say I was surprised. Trott was perhaps, early fifties, which was older than I had expected. I had thought of someone in a flashy suit, probably with long sideburns and looking a bit seedy. He was none of these things.

You certainly wouldn't have given him a second look in the street. If you had to describe the type you would be hard pressed to define him. Bank Clerk perhaps or possibly a lower grade civil servant, an official from the local council, I just couldn't type him at all.

In fact, after our meeting, I would have found it difficult to describe him.

The only real thing that I noticed, after a close scrutiny, was that he had a large brown mole on the lobe of his left ear. Apart from that, he was about as unremarkable as you could imagine.

He got straight down to the task in hand.

"Our mutual friend Mr M told me that you had a problem and he thought I might be able to help. Care to tell me about it?"

I admit that I was not too keen to discuss the problems I had with a perfect stranger and I was starting to regret ever embarking on what, in the cold light of Covent Garden looked, at best, like a wild goose chase. Trott sensed my mood.

"Let me start then by telling you what I know of you."

He then told me in some detail about myself. My parents and their fates. My business in the Far East. My inheriting Grandfather's fortune and the subsequent problems. He told me of Harper and of his fate, of the Swans and lastly, of my recent marriage to Anna.

I was not only pretty well shocked by this tour de force, (all done without a note) but I was also rather angry. After a moment or two to think I said.

"And all this, I suppose you got from Miller?"

He smiled. "Not in the least, I admit he pointed me in the right direction but the bulk I found out for myself. Most of it is perfectly open information.... newspapers, court records, a few police statements - they're not on the record of course - Companies House.... that sort of thing. It's far easier than most people think, you know."

I told him I didn't know.

"So what do you need and why Mr F?"

I decided that I would go along with the first part of my plan and then see where that took me.

"I would like to find out which prison Charles Harper is in?"

Trott looked surprised. "You don't need me for that but if you really want to know he's being moved to an open prison in Suffolk next week. That's for free; anything from now on will cost you!"

"How on earth do you know that?" I queried.

He looked offended. "Mr F, I never disclose my sources.... you must know that."

He queried, "If I did, pretty soon I wouldn't have any, would I?"

To my own astonishment, I found myself apologising.

He grinned. "What next then?"

"Can I get a message to him?"

Trott assumed a look of weary pity. "Mr F, we're wasting your time and mine, my grandson Albert could get a message to Harper and he's only seven. What message and why, that's the questions you should be telling me about. What's the point, if you get a message to Harper  - what's he meant to do.... what are you trying to achieve? Unless you've got a plan and know what you want to do, you're wasting my time and your money."

He added, "I know you've got plenty of money - or I wouldn't be here - but I've never got enough time; so I don't waste it."

We paused whilst a waiter brought another strange frothy coffee which tasted more like cocoa than the real thing. I told him of my idea of getting a message to Harper to try and get Marion to contact me.

"Who says that he knows where she is?" he asked.

I expounded my theory that she would maintain some sort of contact with her father.

"Now, you're starting to talk sense." He commented. "Very strong, usually, the daughter-father thing, especially when the Mother is dead.... go on!"

I elaborated. "I would think that Harper has got a fair bit of money tucked away somewhere, well out of reach of the courts or, for that matter, the Inland Revenue. He'll be out of prison in, what, six years.... and Marion will want her share.... I would have thought that she is bound to be in some sort of contact with him."

Trott nodded. "So if you can contact her, what's your plan?"

422

There I was stumped. I hadn't thought much farther. "Make a deal of some sort?" I queried.

Trott looked at me and drummed the index finger of his right hand on the table.

"What sort of deal?"

He had me there, I wasn't sure. "I'm not sure.... I suppose, offer her money to leave me alone?"

He seemed as if he had lost interest in the conversation and was intent on a close study of the legs of a waitress, stretching to clear a nearby table.

So long was the silence that I said sarcastically, "Are you still with us?"

He looked back.

"Mr F, not only am I still with you but I'd think I'm about a mile in front of you."

He considered the matter a bit longer.

"In my experience, the only things that you can make any sort of deal with are, information, death, or the fear of it, money and sex. Now, no disrespect but bearing in mind you and what I already know of the lady, we can rule out the last one!

Death.... well, that could be arranged but it's dangerous and expensive; it has, however, that advantage that it is permanent.

Fear.... it's only ever a short-term answer. You keep having to remind them and even then, after a while the effect wears off." He paused to think.

I was appalled. "Do you really mean to tell me that you could arrange to have someone killed?"

"Only as a last resort Mr F. It's very difficult these days, what with all this forensic science and things. It can still be done but your only chance is to make it look like an accident or perhaps suicide but it takes a lot of very careful work.... and that costs."

He went on as if he were a salesman extolling his services.

"The real pearl is if you have got two to get rid of and you can have one killed and made to look as if it's murder, then fit the other one up to make it as certain as can be that he, or perhaps she, did it. Very neat that."

I looked at Mr Trott in a new light. Mainly one of horror.

He smiled. "It's rare Mr F; things like that don't happen these days.... well not often."

I think I had just about decided to leave when he said.

"I was just thinking.... Harper and Marion are just about the perfect case for father to marry daughter."

By this time I was so overwhelmed that I didn't quite take in what he was saying.

I said weakly, "But he can't, it isn't allowed.... it's disgusting. It's incest."

Trott came back. "Wrong, it's only incest if they have sex, otherwise it's not a proper marriage. Okay, it's not allowed but definitely not incest." He laughed. "Mr M was right about you, you know; he said to treat you gently - that you would be easily shocked and he was right. You haven't thought it through have you? I'll explain. Seriously rich father, only daughter, middle-aged, mother dead.... you with me so far?"

I nodded in wonder at this strange man.

"Inheritance tax. These days about forty per cent of everything over the price of a rabbit hutch in Surbiton.

Still with me?"

I nodded again.

"The Government, in its charity, says that if hubby leaves the money to his wife, she doesn't have to cough up the tax until she dies."

This time I nodded unbidden.

"So, daughter goes to live in Upper Patagonia say, acquires a new birth certificate and a new passport, comes back and marries daddy in some remote corner of Wales on a wet Thursday morning and.... bingo.... no tax to pay when the old man shuffles off to meet his maker or whatever."

I sat and looked at Trott with my mouth open for a full minute before thinking of the obvious question.

"People would recognise her - her friends - his friends?"

"Don't you believe it Mr F, they don't have to live together do they?"

"She could go and live, miles away; no law against that. Thousands of married couples do it every day; or she could call into California, have a nose job, change her hair and use a different accent - easy."

I tried to think of my next objection but he went on.

"Of course, in this case, there's no point."

"Why....? Why not?"

"Because we suspect that whatever old Harper has to leave will be well outside the reach of the Revenue anyhow."

That was one point that had failed to occur to me.

"No." He went on, "In this case, I suspect that she'll lay low till he comes out, then they'll both go and live in some place where the banks are a bit coy about their customers' affairs, gather their loot up, clean it up and live happily ever after."

I was still several steps behind.

"Clean it up? You mean launder it? Isn't that difficult?"

He chuckled again. "Where have you been all these years Mr F. Difficult? Not a bit of it.... my Albert could do it." He went on to remind me that Albert was only seven.

We called a halt there. The terrible Trott seemed to think that he had sat long enough in one place and he had to get 'mobile'. He said that he would 'give me a bell' if or when he had thought of a suitable plan. I declined the offer and suggested that I telephone him instead.

"Suit yourself. Twenty four hours should do it."

I asked about payment. He suggested that since he had had the word from Tony Miller, or as he put it 'the sporting Mr M' he would bill me later.

"By the way." He added, "When you see Mr M, ask him to hang onto his latest wife for a bit, he seems to forget that I've got other clients as well."

"Do you do much for him?"

He reflected for a moment. "Put it this way, I reckon he pays the rent and the rates with a little bit left over for the family holiday in Barbados as well."

In a funny sort of way, I was beginning to appreciate Mr Trott, even if I didn't like him exactly.

***

When I did phone Trott the next day he said that he had a plan which he thought would keep Marion 'in her hutch' certainly till daddy had done his time. That was the best he could come up with for the time being. He certainly wasn't prepared to talk about it over the phone and we arranged to meet, in above all places, the cocktail bar of one of the larger hotels in Mayfair.

He mystified me still further by adding, "I'll be in blue." and rang off.

I arrived for the meeting exactly on time but couldn't see Trott. I asked for a gin and tonic and settled down to wait.

After a few moments a rather smart lady, who bore a faint resemblance to Mrs Thatcher, came in, walked over to my table and sat down. I was about to ask her what she wanted when a familiar voice said, "Evening Mr F."

For a moment I just couldn't understand; all this was well outside anything I had had to deal with before and I didn't know how to handle it. In a rather more refined, low, but distinctly female voice, she said, "I'd close your mouth if I were you,..... you never know what you might catch."

I did so and then had a closer look at her. I had almost convinced myself that it was indeed Trott when I noticed there wasn't a mole on his ear.

He, or she - or whatever - saw me stare.

"Oh! the mole, I've taken it off. It's here in my bag.

Look, yesterday I was a thoroughly ordinary looking bloke but the one thing you noticed was the mole. If you had to describe me to the coppers you'd look silly saying yesterday a bloke with a mole but, today, a woman who looks a bit like Mrs T but no mole. With any luck, they'd lock you up for wasting their time."

I must confess I had to smile.

The plan was in effect simple but well thought out but it all depended on Marion being in some sort of touch with father Harper. A message would be got to Harper urging Marion to get in touch with a telephone number - the bait would be money.

Trott was quite sure if she did get in touch with what, in reality, was himself, he would be able to track her to where she was living.

"Don't you worry Mr F." I think he was about to tell me that his Albert could do it so I beat him to it. It was his turn to smile.

"We use three things: money, fear and the thought of her daddy getting fitted up in prison for some scam or other".

I could understand the money bit but was doubtful about the others.

"Fear. Well.... I'll have a chap I know go and visit her.... to deliver the first bit of money if you like. He'll explain in simple terms what'll happen if she so much as crosses your path. That should help things along. I wouldn't say he's really frightening but he's a wonderful actor and he seldom gives a poor performance.

He'll also explain that should she transgress, the Fuzz will be given her current details in very short order. We'll play up the bit about reopening the case.... new evidence.... new charges.... all that sort of thing. A story about a letter lodged in your bank should cover that.

Lastly, he'll tell her that, at the same time, daddy will be found to be involved in something really, really nasty, inside that hotel that calls itself an open prison. Something that will ensure he goes back to a regular jail for a very long time. My man can also hint that life back in a proper jail could also be made to be very unpleasant."

He, or she, sat back with the satisfied look of a conjurer producing a rabbit out of a hat.

"How does that strike you?"

I reflected that these, so called, negotiations were well outside anything I had ever been involved in. What would Tommy, dear old upright Tommy, say if ever he found out? Worse still, Anna? Was the risk worth the sort of protection it might buy? On reflection, I thought then that it might well be.

"What do you think then?

I told Trott that I thought it was a pretty disgusting scheme but I couldn't think of anything better and that we had better have a try. We talked about the details. Trott had suggested that I should pay something 'on account' and I arranged to send it to an address in Walthamstow. I did check it later and found that it was a wet fishmongers shop. Shades of Birmingham and Harper.

Trott suggested, "Nice used twenties will do fine."

I thought for the size of the advance I could have sent fifties. He looked shocked.

"Don't you know Mr F, that a good proportion of the fifties in circulation are duds, besides which a person who changes fifties gets noticed. A punter with a fist full of twenties never gets a second glance."

I hadn't known either of these things.

Those were the only two times I ever met the elusive Mr Trott and I came to regret both of them. The final 'tally' when a telephone call did come to say that 'the job was all done' was pretty steep but at the time I thought either it was money well spent or that Trott was some kind of evil genius.

I did try to find out from him where Marion was living but Trott was very close. Apart from 'a little place in North Wales' I got nothing. He assured me that the threat about Harper's future should I meet with disaster was real enough. I settled down to try and put it all behind me and enjoy the peace of mind that I thought I had bought with my hefty insurance investment.

# CHAPTER 33

The crash came just after two years after my dealings with Trott.

Harper died in prison. There was nothing dramatic about it. He had a heart attack and was found dead in the prison kitchen. It was Tommy who gave me the news. He telephoned from London. In a way, I think he was relieved that as far as he was concerned it was all over.

I remember that Anna cooked a rather special dinner that night and she produced a splendid St. Julien, from Latour. She explained that she wasn't doing it to celebrate Harper's death but to mark the end of an era in our lives. The blasted man had been, whichever way you looked at it, something of a blight over us for a long time.

I couldn't help thinking of Marion and what she might do. I had always thought that it was probably the threat to her father that might have held her in check since my 'arrangement' with Trott.

I suppose my returning black moods started to get the better of Anna's good nature after a while and she must have talked to Tommy about it.

He made a special journey to Fannich to talk to me late in the autumn. It was disguised, pretty thinly, as a visit to celebrate my birthday but I wasn't in much of a mood to be either 'cheered up' or to be 'shaken out' of my gloom.

I knew somehow that the reckoning wouldn't be long in coming.

***

Anna went to her house in London on the Tuesday. Her excuse was work but I had the distinct feeling that she was pretty well fed up with me - and I couldn't blame her.

It was a blustery, cold, showery morning on the Wednesday and I really was in something of a black mood. I hadn't been sleeping too well and I thought that a really hard day on the hills might both lift the mood and tire me out sufficiently to ensure a decent night.

I told everyone where I was going, in case of accidents. That was my first mistake.

I donned my walking gear and set off for Loch Coira. During the last summer, we had done a bit of work on the old bothy by the loch. Not exactly renovated it but we had put a roof on it and cleared it out so that we could use it as a shelter if we got caught out up there. Sometimes, we used to take a picnic and make a day of it, miles from anywhere or anyone. It was a sort of refuge for Anna and me. After all, it was where we had first been really alone together, where we had first frightened ourselves together.

I honestly don't know where Marion came from.

I was sitting, leaning back against an outcrop of rock and staring out over the water when I heard a slight scraping on some stones to my right.

I thought it was probably one of the old sheep that had got missed when they cleared the hill; you get them from time to time. They go virtually wild and get so cunning so that they stay up there till eventually their teeth go and they starve to death in the next winter.

When I heard it a second time I turned to see what it was.

It was Marion.

She was in climbing clothes like me, a small rucksack on her back. The real surprise was that she had a pistol in her hand. It was aimed straight at me.

I think I half rose but she said, "Stand up and I'll shoot you."

I sank back. I knew what was coming next.

I won't go into the detail but she told me in no uncertain terms just what she thought of me. How I had ruined her father, had Cedric put in jail, how I had ruined her life and to cap it all thought that I could buy them off with money and threats.

I was a filthy little upstart who had come along and taken what was theirs. Had them thrown out of their home, even stolen their things. All this in the foulest language I have ever heard and I've heard some.

There was no reasoning with her.

I was quite sure that she had gone over that fine edge into madness that is closer for all of us that we ever appreciate. I don't think I was in any doubt that she was going to kill me. All this was a preamble to the final act of revenge. It was all part of the enjoyment of it. I supposed that she had been rehearsing it for years; what she would tell me before she pulled the trigger!

I had taken off my rucksack and laid it on the rock beside me. There was nothing in it I could have used as a weapon anyhow but I thought that if I just sat there I was as good as dead and I may as well go down fighting as take it like a lamb.

I inched my hand to the shoulder strap by my right hand, where it was hidden by the sack itself. Just as her tirade reached a crescendo and I thought she was distracted, I heaved the thing up and flung it at her.

Perhaps it put her off, I don't really know, but she fired the pistol and I remember a massive blow to my chest, which slammed me back against the rock followed by a searing pain which literally took my breath out of my body.

Marion came closer and started to rant and rave again. On and on, over and over. She only had to come a fraction closer and that would be the end of it. One more shot and it would be finished.

The pain was so bad at that stage that I wished she would. I remember saying, even pleading, that she got it over with. In my anger and my pain, I called her just about every name I could think of or that my failing breath would allow.

In the end, that's what saved me. That and that wretched mobile phone!

We both paused to draw breath and she came to a decision.

"You think I'll bloody well kill you outright, not a bloody chance. You can lie there and bleed to death and while you're about it, you can think on all the misery you've inflicted on us. I hope it takes hours and hours. No one will ever come up here looking for you till well after you're past help.

She moved back a couple of yards, picked up my rucksack and threw it into the loch. She walked back to where I lay. For some reason, she was now well in control of herself. Gone was the ranting and raving and the swearing, she could have been a middle-class lady in her sitting room.

"I'll make just sure you can't get to that shed."

With that, she bent down and shot me through my left boot.

I just don't remember much after that. I suppose I passed out and when I did eventually come round, I was freezing cold and quite unable to move. It was dark and as still as I have ever known it. I didn't seem to feel any pain. For a few moments, I really did think that this was death.

I think what did bring me round was that I saw a shooting star, as I followed it with my eyes, in front of me the moon reflected on the water. It was the movement. It triggered something in my brain. A night in Malaya. A river, Why a river? My Father.... my father had died by a river. I wasn't going to die by a river. Gradually it all came flooding back. Harper, Fannich,

Marion, Anna, Tommy.... Tommy. A picture of Tommy surviving on a life raft in the Atlantic.

They say any form of education is never wasted. That night I gave thanks for the survival training I got all those years ago. What could I move? My right hand, my right leg. I tried my left hand, very painful. Left leg, likewise. My head still moved from side to side.

I tried exploring my pockets with my right hand. Half a slab of chocolate. I bit a piece off and it tasted like the best thing I had ever eaten. I tried to move my body but I just hadn't got the strength.

Something was digging into my left hip. I tried to move away from it but I couldn't. I tried to move it with my right hand but couldn't reach. It annoyed me so much that in the end I summoned up all my strength and lifted my behind just enough so that I could feel it with my right hand.

It was then that I realised it was my mobile phone.

I had taken it out of my pocket and laid it on the rock because it dug in my side. I must have fallen back onto it when I crashed back onto the rocks. I got it up to my face. It wasn't switched on. In a moment of panic, I thought it was broken but then remembered deciding not to even turn it on. I needed solitude.

It lit up when I pressed the switch. Then I couldn't remember anyone's number. In the end, I pressed nine, nine, nine and thank God there was an answer. I think I managed a pretty clear message to the girl at the other end.

I told her that I had been shot, twice, and had lost a lot of blood. I told her where I was, by the south end of Loch Coira - and just where that was. After I had explained as best I could she put me onto a policeman. As luck would have it, it was Detective Sergeant Dunbar.

His first words were exactly what I needed "In the wars again Mr Forest are we?"

I told him I was and please could someone come - quick.

"How bad are you?"

"Two gunshot wounds from a pistol and running short of blood."

His reassuring voice came back, "Someone's already on their way.... should be with you in about twenty minutes. Now don't die on us just yet."

He suggested that we kept the line open and I laid the phone by my side. To tell the truth I was just about all in. I think I must have dozed off for a bit but I was woken by a strange 'woof woof woof' beating noise and a voice beside me asking if I could see a helicopter. When I looked, it was lit up like a Christmas tree.

"Where is it from you?" asked the metallic voice.

"It's to my left - about two hundred yards".

It came nearer. "Another twenty." I croaked. The downward flood light nearly blinded me as I waved my working right hand.

After that, it was really all downhill.

A doctor from the mountain rescue helicopter attended to me and the crew had me on a stretcher and away to

Fort William Hospital yet again. Like the last time, I didn't really know much for the next few days but I was semi-awake most of the time. It was explained to me that I had been 'incredibly lucky'. I wasn't too sure. It sounded like 'a caring God' again.

The first shot had hit my binoculars which, being old, and made of brass had deflected the bullet away from the middle of my chest. It had bounced off a rib and come out through my side.

'Almost trivial really'.

I wished I had known that at the time.

The shot through my boot had done quite a bit of damage, mainly from the bits that had been driven into the foot but they had got them all out and repaired most of the rest. Lucky that I had been wearing clean socks, they said.

They had filled me up again with blood and with a bit of luck, all I would have to show for it would be a bit of a limp.

I only wished Marion had been there to hear the verdict.

The Specialist also explained that lots of clothes had helped. "Soaks up the blood and helps it clot" and "The frost was a blessing you know, cooled you down - very helpful."

I felt that I was almost a fraud using up their bed space. However, when I suggested that if that were the case "Please can I go home now?" They said a most definite 'no' and kept me there for three weeks.

It was largely a repeat performance of the previous time.

Anna came and after she had told me off for getting into yet another scrape, she was back to her usual loving self.

Detective Sergeant Dunbar came, notebook in hand and with the dour Inspector Fraser in tow. When I had spoken with Dunbar on the mobile that terrible evening, I had told him that it was Marion Swan who had shot me. He had sent out a warning to all the local police stations and she had been picked up early in the morning at a road block on the A86 past Spean Bridge.

She hadn't given any trouble although the pistol was still in her pocket. The only thing she had said was "I hope he rots in hell."

At that stage, she didn't know that I was still in the land of the living - just about! It was only later, when she was charged with attempted murder, that it came home to her that she had failed. At that moment, according to Dunbar, she had reverted to the ranting, screaming, tormented soul that I had seen beside Loch Coira. All this didn't help when she went on to make extravagant accusations about my threatening her father in prison.

The Inspectors opinion was that the case would probably never come to a trial in that Marion was giving all the signs of being unfit to plead. The possibility was that she might well be committed to some form of institution.

I did confess all about Trott to Anna.

Keeping those sort of secrets from someone you really do love is no basis for a happy marriage. She listened in silence, her lips in a tight line. When I had finished my tale she kissed me and then proceeded to make it abundantly clear that if I ever undertook anything like that again she would leave me in very short order. She kissed me again.

I had the distinct feeling that she meant every word.

I felt a twinge of guilt that I had left out Tony Miller's small part in the plot. Out of sheer curiosity, I did mention Trott to Tony some months later but he couldn't remember ever knowing anyone of that name. I even rang the number I still had for Trott but I got someone claiming to be 'The Hoxton Car Valeting Service'. They denied having anyone called Trott there. The lady thought I must have a wrong number. I could have sworn that I had heard that voice before, but I let it rest.

This time, leaving hospital, we got a fit of the giggles when I could barely get my leg with the metal frame, which was meant to keep my foot in the right place, into the car so that Anna could shut the door.


THE END

After a disastrous start in life, Robin Forest searches for an end to his loneliness and turns to the army as a family substitute. Posted to Malaya where his father was killed, he makes a home in what has now become Malaysia, working as a successful General Trader. On retirement, he is once more thrown into turmoil when news of a legacy brings him back to the UK. As one story bleeds into another, Robin's good fortune turns to danger. Now heir to two country estates, he reveals theft and malpractice. It becomes a cat and mouse tussle to unravel the subterfuge and bring the culprits to justice. Will Robin find the tranquillity he seeks or will the hunter become the hunted?

Books P back    £1
Fict. Adult  SI TH

780542989444

GiftAid 0000266447   14/0

ISBN 978-1-5272-3315-7

9 781527 233157

© 2018 Michael Burrans Sykes
Cover design by More Visual Ltd